THE WHITE DACOIT

Charles Wyndham, newly commissioned subaltern and descendant of the founder of Wyndham's Horse, a famous Indian cavalry regiment, is posted to command a remote outpost on the North-West Frontier. The time is 1924.

Manipulated into falling foul of the law and condemned to death for armed robbery, Charles Wyndham escapes and proceeds to live by the very crime for which he was unjustly sentenced. Berkely Mather's best novel yet – a colourful picaresque ranging from the North-West Frontier to the jungles of Deccan, and based on a real-life story.

THE
WHITE DACOIT

Berkely Mather

COLLINS
St James's Place, London
1974

Wiilliam Collins Sons & Co Ltd
London · Glasgow · Sydney · Auckland
Toronto · Johannesburg

First published in the UK September 1974
Reprinted October 1974
© Berkely Mather 1974
ISBN 0 00 221147 5
Set in Monotype Garamond
Made and Printed in Great Britain by
William Collins Sons & Co Ltd Glasgow

To Julia and Dorinda

ACKNOWLEDGEMENT

My grateful thanks are due to Major P. L. O'T. (Paddy) Quinn, formerly of the Indian Army and Indian Prison Service, for his expert advice on the criminal tribes of India and prison routine. It was, in fact, Paddy who first told me of the White Dacoit, one hot night in the Deccan some years before World War II. He was a British army officer who, bedevilled by debt, disguised himself as a Pathan and led a group of his own Indian troops in forays against Hindu money-lenders on the North-West Frontier. He was caught red-handed and sentenced to a long term of imprisonment, escaped and was caught again while living in the jungle with one of the criminal tribes, and was at one time a 'guest' of Major Quinn's. He is long dead, his name was not Wyndham nor does this story purport to be either a true chronicle or an apologia. It is a work of fiction and the characters herein are not intended to be identified with any living person. But the jungle is still there, and also the Andaman Islands, although the latter, when I visited them after the War, were no longer being used as a penal colony.

B.M.

Brede, Sussex

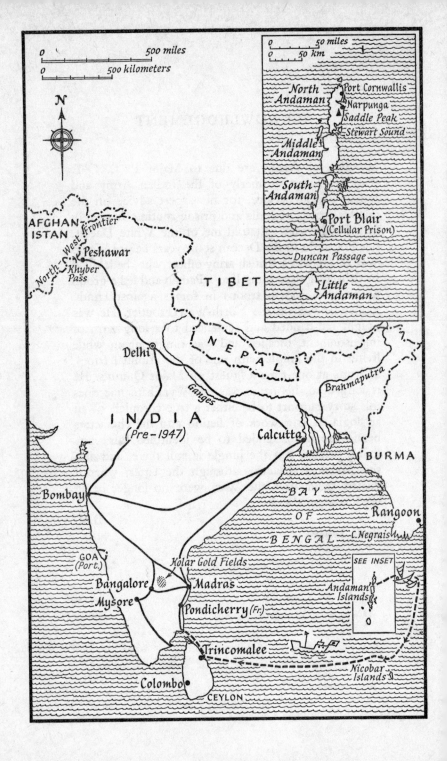

Inset map (top right):

0 ... 50 miles
0 ... 50 km

North Andaman — Port Cornwallis
Narpunga
▲ Saddle Peak
Stewart Sound

Middle Andaman

South Andaman

Port Blair
(Cellular Prison)

Duncan Passage

Little Andaman

Main map:

0 ... 500 miles
0 ... 500 kilometers

N

AFGHANISTAN

North-West Frontier

Peshawar
Khyber Pass

TIBET

Delhi

NEPAL

Ganges

Brahmaputra

INDIA
(Pre-1947)

Calcutta

BURMA

Bombay

BAY OF BENGAL

Rangoon

C. Negrais

GOA
(Port.)

Kolar Gold Fields

Bangalore

Madras

Mysore

Pondicherry (Fr.)

SEE INSET

Andaman Islands

Trincomalee

Nicobar Islands

Colombo

CEYLON

PART ONE

Chapter 1

Wyndham reined in at the top of the slope and looked down into the valley the other side. Up here the air was clear, thin and murderously hot; below there was a dust haze and he knew it would be even hotter. He could see the fort now, five miles or so ahead of him, with the village a further mile beyond it, and, to his left, across the dried-up river-bed, was the square white-walled blockhouse which he guessed would be the Afghan frontier post. The sun was directly above him, beating down pitilessly on the parched landscape and casting no shadows even in the deeply scarred nullahs which had known no water for the whole of 1924, nor would they until the brief rains of the short-lived monsoon in three months' time. He stood up in the stirrups and eased his sweat-soaked breeches away from his sore behind, regretting the loss of the English hunting saddle he had sold to Ahmed Zafar, the Afridi horse-coper, in order to pay his mess bill the previous week. Behind him he heard the dafadar halt the half-troop. He knew he should give the order to dismount, loosen girths and allow men and horses a brief respite, but that would have meant getting down and then up again himself, and he was too weary to make the effort. He gave the field signal to trot – clenched fist pumped up and down between shoulder and knee – and shook the reins on the foam-flecked neck of his big black waler, but that was not enough and he had to punch his spurs in viciously to get the tired brute out of a shambling walk. That in itself would have been sufficient to earn him a month's orderly officer duty if the adjutant had been here to see him.

But the adjutant wasn't here, thank God, nor the Old Man, nor the second-in-command, squadron commander nor any others of the eight white men who made up the King's Commissioned strength of Wyndham's Horse. The rest of the officers were Viceroy's Commissioned – jemadars, rissaldars and the lordly rissaldar-major himself, promoted from the ranks of the Pathan and Sikh troopers, or sowars. No, he, for his sins – literally – was the only officer on this jolly little outing.

'The bastards!' he spat and drove the spurs in again and increased the pace to a canter, then to a forbidden gallop, hearing the rattle and clink of steel sword-scabbards, picqueting chains and the broken-winded blowing of the Vickers gun packhorse increase in volume and tempo. The sowars were loving it. A mad sahib who let them gallop after twelve hours line-of-march at a sober walk. The Pathans were bellowing a dirty marching song – 'Zakhmi Dil' – and the Sikhs were trying to drown it with yells of 'Khalsa ki jai!'

Half a mile short of the fort he tried to rein in to a walk again and he gave the signal to march at attention, but the horses could now smell the stables with their promise of water, fodder and rest, and they were completely out of hand. He could see the open gates in the high stone wall, with the quarterguard drawn up in front of the archway, but at the last moment they slammed shut, and the half-troop finished in a wild scrimmage outside the fort instead of a Cossack halt on the parade ground inside, as Wyndham had intended. He dismounted stiffly and his orderly rode up and took over his horse. The dafadar and the other two NCOs were getting the half-troop back into some semblance of order with the flats of their drawn swords. The gates opened as he approached them on foot, and Prentice, the subaltern he was relieving, came out. He was senior to Wyndham by three years and had two pips on his epaulettes to the other's one. Normally that wouldn't have mattered away from regimental headquarters, but now the older man was tense with disapproval.

He acknowledged Wyndham's salute perfunctorily and said, 'What the hell's the matter with you? Have you gone mad?'

'You should worry,' Wyndham answered. 'You're being relieved three months early, aren't you?'

'By a bunch of raggle-taggle gipsies in a muck sweat. Surely to God you know your hot-weather line-of-march orders by now.'

'Oh, don't be a stuffed shirt,' Wyndham said. 'I've had enough of that back there.'

'Stuffed shirt be damned. You'll find it hard enough to maintain discipline up here and to keep your wretched cattle in reasonable condition without behaving like a Wild West rodeo.' Then he relented a little. 'Come and have some tea – unless you want to see your crowd into stables first.'

'I'm not that keen, cocker. Tea? Is that all you've got?'

'Bit early for a drink, isn't it?'

'Not for me it isn't. I'm shagged out and I've got a sore bum. I came up here on an issue saddle.'

'What's wrong with your own?'

'Flogged it, together with everything else I had that I could raise the wind on – including my car.'

'Bad as that, is it?'

'Don't tell me you hadn't heard.'

'A whisper.'

'It's a bloody cantata back there. Rake's Progress. There's a little conundrum running round the club: "What's the difference between Wyndham's creditors and a flock of flamingoes? No difference. They can all shove their bills up their arses." Roars of applause.'

They came through the gate and out from under the archway on the inner side. Wyndham halted and looked around. The fort was two hundred yards square, surrounded by an eighteen-foot rough stone wall with a watchtower at each corner. Stables lined two of the walls, with the troops' quarters above them – the flat roofs forming a wide firestep under the embrasured parapet. Under the other two walls were the storerooms, forage barns, farrier's shop and, as far distant from each other as the cramped geography of the place would allow, the two cookhouses – Mohammedan and Hindu. The guardroom was a small detached building on the right of the archway with, behind it, a somewhat larger one with a dispirited garden in front of it where two denim-clad defaulters were watering drooping zinnias sparingly under the eye of a lance-dafadar.

Wyndham said dully, 'Is this everything?'

'Just what you can see, thank God. If you ever had trouble you'd wish it was smaller.'

'Have you had trouble?'

'Not during my tour – but Jimmy Rankine was bottled up here for a month the year before last, and the well dried up.'

'Wasn't he relieved?'

'No. The Political Service wanted the tamasha "contained" –

so they wouldn't let a column come up until they had a pow-wow, which lasted over three weeks. Meantime the Afridis were dug in along that ridge over there, sniping anything that moved during the day and bunging fire-arrows over the wall at night. Come on, if you want a drink.' He led off to the house behind the guard-room. 'Orderly room and magazine down below – your quarters and what is termed "The Mess" topsides. Hot as hell at this time of the year – freeze the balls off a Bactrian camel in the winter.'

'Are you always as cheerful?' Wyndham asked. 'Or are you trying hard for my benefit?'

'Sorry,' Prentice answered, 'but I think it's only fair to you to tell you the worst right at the start. The Old Man sold it to me as a subaltern's paradise – wonderful riding country, and you could shoot snipe and rock partridge, and the rivers look like trout water during the rains, and you could get down to language study, and swot up for Staff College, and, of course, save money hand over fist because there's nothing to spend it on up here. Isn't that what he told *you*?'

He led the way up an outside stone staircase and into a long low room. It was furnished with a barrack table, a wooden form and two Roorkhee chairs, and through a door opening into another, smaller, room Wyndham could see a camp bed with a mosquito net suspended in untidy festoons above it. Prentice went through into the second room and came back with a bottle of whisky and two thick tumblers.

Wyndham stood and looked round again, suppressing a shudder.

'Is that what the old bastard told you?' Prentice asked again.

'No. Only about saving money, and paying my debts, or sending my papers in at the end of six months if I wasn't clear.' He watched while Prentice poured a generous slug, ignored the water chatthi he pointed to in the corner, and tossed it off neat. Prentice hesitated, then refilled his glass. Wyndham sat down gingerly, winced, and sipped his second drink more slowly. The other was looking at him closely.

'You're really not cut out for this, are you?' he said.

'Cut out for what?' Wyndham asked.

'This.' Prentice waved his hand round the room.

' "Garrison duty on the North-West Frontier of India",'

Wyndham quoted from a Sandhurst manual. ' "Soldiering in its purest and most basic form." No – you can have my share.'

'Then why in hell did you take it up?'

Wyndham sat back in his chair and closed his eyes. 'The Regiment was raised originally by my great-grandfather, old Sam Wyndham – silladar cavalry for the East India Company. Sam commanded until he died of cirrhosis of the liver, then his younger brother took over, then my grandfather, then my guv'nor, but only for a couple of months before he was killed in Mesopotamia. I was born in the Military Hospital in Risalpur – Home to a prep school at the age of eight – Wellington after that – then Sandhurst – and now this. Why did I take it up? Because nobody ever bloody well asked me if there might possibly be something else I'd prefer.'

'Then why didn't you speak up for yourself?'

'Actually I did once or twice when I was very small, and got the same sort of reaction as I'd have got if I'd been heard using filthy language in church. The Regiment! Christ, you were expected almost to genuflect as you said it. No breakfast and a thump on the ear from grandfather when you were unlucky enough to be spending the school holidays with the vicious old bastard, and you couldn't recite the battle honours – with dates – in the proper sequence.' He held out his glass. 'Give me another drink. I'll replace it. I've got a whole case in my kit.'

Prentice looked worried. 'If you insist – but I wanted to complete the handover tonight and then get going at first light.'

'What the hell is there to hand over? One fort, circa Alexander the Great, firked about a bit by Genghis Khan, propped up by John Company and run on the cheap by the Government of India since 1857. None of it missing, is there?'

'There's stores, fodder, arms and ammunition,' Prentice said coldly. 'The sheet-rolls should be checked – troop books – signal log – and surely you'll want to inspect the horses I'm leaving, if not the men.'

'Bugger 'em. In that order – first the horses, then the men. Put up all the bumph and I'll sign it – which'll make *you* fireproof.'

'It's *you* I'm thinking of.'

'I'm touched, but save your solicitude – and top this glass up.' He watched as Prentice did so. 'Thanks.' He took a letter from his pouch belt. 'Here's my chitthi. I understand that you leave me twenty-five troops and thirty nags, taking twenty-two and twenty-six respectively, which the draft I've brought up will replace. My draft is twenty-four and twenty-seven, which includes one dafadar and two lance-dafadars – but no VCO – '

'The VCO has volunteered to stay on for another tour,' Prentice said. 'You're lucky. Rissaldar Sher Mohammed Khan is the best we've got – damned good education, speaks English – '

'Another bloody babu?'

'On the contrary. He's a first-class soldier and a firm disciplinarian. I don't know what I'd have done the first few months without him.'

'What in the name of God is he volunteering for another hitch up *here* for?'

'He just says he prefers soldiering on detachment to the tamasha of regimental headquarters – but actually I think he's studying for promotion.'

'Must be catching – but what does he need to study for? He'll get to rissaldar-major in due course automatically, won't he?'

'He's got his sights cocked up a bit further than that. If this Indianization thing goes through as everybody expects, he should be a cert for a King's Commission.' Prentice rose. 'Well, I've got a few things to do. I've told the bhisti to heat some bath water for you. We've got to be a bit sparing with water, by the way. The well is down pretty low.'

Wyndham grinned. 'I won't be using much. It ruins whisky.'

Prentice turned at the door and came back. 'Look,' he said, 'God knows I don't want to lecture you, old boy, but this place could be pretty grim for anybody who got his tail down right at the start.'

'Who's got his tail down?'

'Well, you don't seem to be bursting with joie de vivre exactly, do you? What's biting you? You're a few bob in debt, so the Old Man has sent you up here a bit ahead of your turn to give you a chance to save – away from the club, the Mess and the racecourse. It happens to most of us some time or other, unless we've got a thumping big private income – and who has these days?'

'I will have – come my twenty-fourth birthday.'

'Lucky man,' said Prentice drily. 'How old are you now?'

'Twenty-two in September. I was a year late getting into Sandhurst because I failed Army Entrance the first time up.'

'So you've got nothing to worry about. Just soldier merrily on for two years and a bit and you can pack it in if you still feel the same way about things.'

'I'll feel the same way,' Wyndham said through clenched teeth. 'I hate every benighted minute of it.'

'Then quit now,' Prentice said quietly. 'Sell used cars in London or dirty postcards in Paris until you come into your money. I'm sorry if I sound priggish, but the Regiment *does* mean something to me – to most of us – and you aren't doing it much good in your present frame of mind.'

'It's not as simple as all that,' Wyndham said. 'Here, sit down for Christ's sake and pour yourself a drink. You worry me standing there on one leg.' He tipped whisky into both glasses, then, as Prentice sat reluctantly, he went on.

'I don't know why I'm telling you this, but – well – I just feel the need of a Wailing Wall at the moment. Do you want to hear it? Shut me up if it bores you.'

'Go ahead,' Prentice said, 'if it makes things easier.'

'You said "a few bob in debt". Actually I owe a total of twenty-five thousand rupees. And that's not the worst of it. The Old Man only knows of a little over eleven thousand.'

Prentice whistled in stark amazement. 'God Almighty!' he breathed. 'Here – I don't think you'd better tell me any more. If it leaked out from someone else you might blame *me* for blabbing.'

Wyndham shrugged. 'Sometimes I wish it would leak out. It would be a relief – like having a boil lanced. Painful at the moment, but the worst would be over. Then I get to thinking what I'd be losing. You see, it's this Family Trust thing. Great-grandpa, like all those other damned old rogues of mercenaries who worked for the Company, made a hell of a pile – and developed an exaggerated sense of family pride at the same time. Everything is in Trust – a life interest for each generation, the lion's share going to the eldest son, who is supposed to go into the bloody Regiment.'

'But what if he doesn't?'

'Then it goes to the one who does, if there are younger sons. As it happens, there has only been one surviving son in each of the last three generations, plus one or two girls. They're all provided for, and there's a safety clause for any generation where there are no sons – or the sons don't go into the Regiment through no fault of their own. It just accumulates then and goes on to the next gent. But the real milk in the coconut is the *penalty* clause. A bloke who gets slung out – cashiered – dismissed – guilty of criminal or ungentlemanly conduct – God help him. He doesn't get a brass razoo.'

'What if that happens *after* he has inherited?'

'His income would stop. It's *income* not capital he's getting.'

'And if he resigns?'

'I don't think great-grandpa ever thought anybody would resign from choice. There's no mention of that.'

'So in other words you've got to serve on in the Regiment until you're twenty-four – then you start drawing your income? How much will it be, if that's not too rude a question?'

'In my case something over ten thousand a year.'

'Pounds?'

Wyndham nodded, and Prentice whistled again.

'Yes, pounds. You see, we've been a singularly sparse breeding lot and the capital has built up faster than the outgoings in each generation. The poor wretched girls only got a dowry when they married, or a pittance if they didn't – in the best Victorian tradition. Oh, he was an old charmer all right.'

'So if you resign in your own good time after your twenty-fourth birthday, your ten thousand a year is safe?'

'Exactly.'

'And you think, knowing this, that the Old Man would call for your resignation before your twenty-fourth birthday – even if he knew you were that much in debt? Somehow I doubt it.'

'*I* don't doubt it. I know damn well he'd throw me out. The old sod is one of the Trustees. Every Commanding Officer is, ex officio.'

'Well, what's the position at the moment?'

'My pay is approximately four thousand rupees per annum. He thinks I owe eleven thousand – saddlemakers, tailors, bootmakers and, unfortunately, *book*makers. He has undertaken to get

16

an advance from the Trust to pay them off, but I've got to serve up here for a year, and prove to him that (a) I've incurred no further debts, and (b) that I've saved the sum of three thousand rupees. So there you have it.'

'Why in the name of God didn't you tell him the whole truth in one go – I mean about the extra debts?'

'Because my nerve failed me. If you'd been there to see how he was reacting over *eleven* thousand, you'd have understood. Twenty-five thousand would have scuppered the whole thing. He'd have called for my papers on the spot. Don't forget we're serving in the *Indian* Army, not the British, where one has the right of appeal. The Commanding Officer can crucify you here off his own bat – and no questions asked.'

'You don't have to tell *me* that,' Prentice said slowly. 'By God, I wish I could help you, old boy, but I'm as poor as a church mouse myself.'

'Oh, I haven't reached the level of scrounging from my friends yet,' Wyndham said, and tipped the last of the whisky into his glass. 'It will possibly work out. If I can stall these other sods off a couple of years more I'll be in the clear. The thing that scares me is that word might leak out that some creditors have been paid off by the Trust, and all of them might apply for similar treatment.'

'Where are they?'

'London, mostly. Several of them have sold the debts to a couple of collecting sharks. It was that year after I failed Army Entrance the first time that did it. I was at a crammer's place in town and I met a girl.'

'What sort of girl?'

'Usual sort – two eyes, two legs, two tits – what difference does it make?'

'I was wondering if you were being blackmailed or something.'

'Hell, no – nothing to blackmail me over. I was just a green youth in London for the first time and she was second from the end in the back row of the Daly's chorus. Unfortunately a distant cousin of mine in the Guards took me around a bit and happened to mention that I was the next in line for the Wyndham Family Trust – and you've no idea how news like that travels around the sharks. I was offered credit all over the place. I took her to Paris

– or perhaps I should say she took me and I merely footed the bills – and I bought her jewellery and that sort of thing. I don't need to tell *you* the form, do I? I behaved like any other adolescent just out of the egg. And she behaved like any other poor little bitch who looks across the railway tracks and sees the grass is greener the other side. Can't blame her for that.'

A trumpet was sounding the Guard and Picquet Assembly across the small parade ground.

'Are we wanted for that?' Wyndham asked.

'Not particularly,' Prentice said. 'I look in on guardmounting from time to time, but there's no need to strain anything. Have a bath, old boy, and dinner will be ready when you've finished. Don't worry. As you said yourself, things will probably work out.'

'Actually I said *possibly*.'

'Hang on to probably. I don't need to tell you that none of this will go any further as far as I'm concerned.'

'I'm sure it won't,' Wyndham said. 'Thanks for listening. It's been a relief.'

He stood at the window watching the evening activity of a cavalry unit in barracks: the horses being watered, the chaff-cutter being turned outside the forage barn, and the guards and picquets falling in under the orderly dafadar.

And then Rissaldar Sher Mohammed Khan came into view below him, walking from the guardroom, and something of the easygoing atmosphere seemed to dissipate – and sowars straightened tunics and pagris and melted round corners. Here, Wyndham decided, was where the real authority in Fort Jammadan rested – authority that depended on strength of character, pride of regiment, self-respect and a cheerful acceptance of discipline – and he felt a sudden sense of shame at his own inadequacy. This was his heritage, and here he was defaming it, whining like a spoilt child at a well-merited punishment, and boring his brother officers with his plaints. He turned away from the window and tossed the dregs of his drink on the stone floor impatiently.

'Pull yourself together, Wyndham,' he muttered, 'and start soldiering – or have the guts to get out and leave it to better men.'

Chapter 2

The woman was kneeling outside the gate and from her mouth came one long ululating howl. She was young, but with the premature obesity of habitual inactivity already upon her, and she had the pallidness of the harem under her coating of dust. But she was Hindu not Mohammedan, as Wyndham could see from the tilak mark between her eyebrows, and she was wearing a silk sari, once opulent but now bedraggled and stained. She crawled forward on her knees, and the sentry, a Pathan, barred her way with his rifle-butt. The rest of the guard were grinning and jeering from the windows of the guardroom. Wyndham couldn't understand what she was saying – it was neither Urdu nor Pushtu – although he distinguished the words for robbery and murder, which were common to both.

The sun was just rising over the hills to the east, and the howling had wakened him from the uneasy sleep he had fallen into after a long night of tossing and turning. He was trying to cut down on his intake of whisky, in the interests of conservancy rather than temperance, and he was finding it hard going. He had only been here a week and he was already half-way through his case.

He called querulously, 'What is the matter?' and the sentry snapped to attention and saluted. The woman rose to her feet and came forward in a shambling run and fell headlong before Wyndham, grasping him round the ankles and moaning incoherently. Tears were making runnels through the smudged kohl round her eyes and down over the caked dirt on her cheeks. He was conscious of the eyes of the guard on his back and he felt ridiculous, acutely aware of the brief kilted lungi he wore round his waist in lieu of pyjamas, and her upturned eyes. He tried to break free, then, as she clung tighter, he kicked out – not brutally, but harder than he intended – and his foot caught her under the chin knocking her on to her back, and she shrieked wildly. He knew overwhelming relief as the rissaldar came up behind him, already dressed in crisply starched knee-length kurta and polished riding boots, faultlessly tied pagri and gleaming buttons, buckles and spurs. He barked an order at the woman in the language she was using and it quietened her immediately. She rose to her knees and knelt before him, eyes meekly downcast, and answered his curt questions in an undertone. The rissaldar turned to Wyndham and saluted punctiliously.

'Have I the sahib's permission to speak in English? It is better that the men should not understand at this stage.' His English, though accented, was fluent and grammatical and free of babu's chi-chi. Wyndham nodded, and the rissaldar went on.

'She is the wife of the Hindu money-lender in the village, sahib. An hour ago he was taken by dacoits.'

'You mean kidnapped?'

'Yes, sahib. As you know, Mohammedans are forbidden to lend money at usury, but men must borrow before the harvest or when their daughters marry, so there is one of these jackals in every village. This one is a Bengali – a low caste buniya, but very rich – ' his lip curled under his up-brushed moustache – 'as he should be, with the whole village in debt to him, at ten per cent per month.'

'This has happened before, hasn't it?' Wyndham said. 'I read about it in the log.'

'Twice in the last eighteen months, sahib.'

'Why the hell does the fool stay here then?'

'Why does the hyena risk stealing from under the tiger's nose, sahib? Profit. If he pays his ransom he will be allowed to go free.'

'And if he doesn't?'

'A slow roasting over a charcoal fire until he changes his mind, as they always do in the end.'

'But surely that takes the profit out of it?'

'It is a matter of bundobas – arrangement. The dacoits know to a copper pice what to demand – not too much, but certainly not too little. This has been going on for centuries in the Frontier Territories.'

'So what do we do?'

'Standing Orders state that we take out a patrol and try to pick up their trail and rescue the swine – but experience tells us that they will have made their bundobas long before we come up with them, and the Hindu will be found sitting by the side of the road wailing to his gods, with the dacoits safely across in Afghanistan, where we are not allowed to follow, counting their loot.'

'Are you telling me that we do nothing, then?' Wyndham asked.

'I'm not presuming to tell you anything, sahib. It is entirely up to you – although Regulations state that we must mount a search if only for the sake of appearances. But in this case I think we might have a chance of catching them, though only a faint one. They took him just before dawn. That means that they will have to lie low until nightfall, because if they cross by day they would run the risk of being caught by the Afghan Frontier guards who would want their share of the ransom, if not all of it.'

'Pretty long shot, isn't it, Rissaldar-sahib?' Wyndham said. 'There's a hell of a lot of rough country for them to hide in.'

'A matter of kismet, sahib – luck – and perhaps a little judgement,' the rissaldar said. 'They are on foot, and hampered by a fat-bellied Bengali who wouldn't be able to move fast even with a knife tickling his rump. There are only three crossing points in twenty miles, so they would be expected to choose the nearest, which is also the safest, because it is unmanned by the Afghans. Wouldn't you go for that one, sahib?'

'Yes, I expect so.'

'Exactly. That is what Prentice-sahib did last time – and Rankine-sahib the time before – and missed them on both occasions, because they had crossed elsewhere.'

'What are you suggesting?' Wyndham asked. 'That we ambush the other two?'

'No, sahib. They will be watching from under cover and they'll know which crossing we're making for. I suggest that we act like fools who will never learn, and march out openly with a large party, and ambush the same crossing again,' the rissaldar said.

'What good will that do?'

'A slight difference this time, sahib. At nightfall we cross the Frontier and make a forced march and ambush both the other crossings on the *Afghan* side.'

'But we're not allowed to cross the Frontier,' Wyndham said, and the rissaldar looked sorrowful.

'Yes, that is a great pity,' he sighed. 'Particularly since nobody would ever know. We would drag them back this side – and look innocent. We would not be in uniform, of course.'

'I see what you mean,' Wyndham said thoughtfully, and felt the first faint stirring out of the deadly ennui he had been sunk in since his arrival. 'Rissaldar-sahib, I think you're a very great rogue. How many men do we need?'

'No more than twenty, sahib. Men who can be trusted not to talk afterwards. With your permission I will select them myself.'

'By all means,' Wyndham said. 'You know them better than I.'

They came to the crossing while it was yet broad daylight. The trail dropped from the plateau above like the slash of a knife through the cliffs which bounded it each side. The Frontier here, and for a hundred miles in both directions, was the river itself, now bone dry except for an occasional muddy pool in the black sandy bed. They halted and off-saddled and picqueted the horses half a mile downstream, then, conscious of hidden eyes watching them from the heights, they made great show of camouflaging vantage points and clearing fields of fire.

Darkness fell with the dramatic suddenness of the lowering of blinds over a window; thick impenetrable blackness unrelieved by moon and with the stars lost above the night mist. They left four men there and crept down to the picquet line and muffled the horses' hooves in empty feed bags and wrapped strips of rag round curb chains and anything else that might clink, and finally pulled Pathan khamises over their uniform shirts, and Wyndham marvelled at the speed and efficiency with which the whole thing was done under the whispered orders of the rissaldar. They set off then at a fast but noiseless walk through the soft sand, the Frontier-conditioned cavalry mounts picking their way without a stumble, as sure-footed as mountain goats, in single file, instinctively keeping the regulation interval of four feet from nose to croup.

The rissaldar led, with Wyndham behind him, and Dafadar Prem Singh, the Sikh farrier, bringing up the rear. They rode thus for a little more than an hour, then Wyndham heard the twittering call of a night bird and, warned in advance of this, he pulled up, and heard the call repeated faintly at the end of the column. The rissaldar reined back alongside him.

'We're opposite the second crossing now, sahib,' he whispered, and Wyndham forbore to ask him how he knew. 'This is the one they will use if our deception has been successful. Why would they go on another eight miles if they thought we are all waiting at the first place?'

'So we don't go on to the next one?'

'I thought, if the sahib is agreeable, that we might send Prem Singh on with four men – just in case.'

'Whatever you think best, rissaldar-sahib,' Wyndham answered. 'Where should I be? Here – or on with Prem Singh?'

'That, of course, is the sahib's choice – but I feel that it is here the tamasha will be.'

'Then it is here that I stay,' Wyndham said.

'*Achchi-bhat, sahib*,' said the Rissaldar approvingly. 'Then, if you will follow me . . .'

They moved in to the bank and waited until the dafadar and his four men had gone forward. There were twelve of them left now, Wyndham calculated, though he couldn't see them, and was conscious only of the rissaldar beside him.

'How are you so certain that one of these crossings will be used, Rissaldar-sahib?' he whispered. 'Why shouldn't they cross at some point unmarked in between?'

'If the sahib saw the terrain in daylight he would understand,' the rissaldar told him. 'The river runs through a gorge – a hundred-mile gorge – with cliffs each side dropping a sheer four or five hundred feet to the river-bed. Agile men could climb down at several points, no doubt, but not in the darkness, and hampered by a frightened Bengali. No, sahib, it will be this point or the far one. I think this one.' He chuckled softly. 'Is the sahib a betting man?'

Wyndham hesitated, and was lost. 'Er – yes – occasionally,' he said.

'A month of the sahib's pay against three of mine, which about makes it even, that it will be here.'

'Done,' said Wyndham dolefully.

'Then if the sahib would dismount I will send the horses off with half of the men. I think we will have at least an hour to wait.'

'How will you know when they get here?' Wyndham asked as he dismounted stiffly and felt his horse being taken over by an unseen hand.

'A trip-wire across the mouth of the defile,' the other told him. 'Two of the sowars are laying it now.'

Wyndham sat in the soft sand with his back against an outcropping of rock. The burning heat had gone with the sun, and the night air was striking chill now, and he was glad of the extra khamis over his khaki drill shirt. A hand came out of the darkness and he felt the rough covering of a water-bottle.

'A little something to keep out the cold, sahib?' the rissaldar said.

'What is it?' he asked.

'British Army rum.'

'I thought Mohammedans were forbidden alcohol?'

'The Sikhs stole it from the Tommies when they were laying a telephone wire near the fort.' The rissaldar chuckled. 'The Prophet forbade wine, not rum – and I never was a bigot. Drink, sahib – it's your own water-bottle which I got from your orderly, so nobody's caste will be defiled.'

'Rissaldar-sahib,' Wyndham said happily, 'as I feel now I'd drink rum out of a leper's begging bowl and to hell with the caste. But what about you?'

'After you. I am happy that the sahib is not a bigot either.'

'Cheers,' said Wyndham, and felt the raw spirit burning his throat gratefully. He handed the water-bottle back.

'Mud in your eye – without disrespect, sahib,' said the rissaldar, and drank deeply.

'Where the hell did you hear that?' Wyndham asked him, amazed.

'It was what Prentice-sahib always said when we drank rum or whisky together.'

'Prentice-sahib? But I thought he was a strict drill-and-regulation man.'

'Detached duty is different from headquarters, sahib. Back there the King's Commission and the Viceroy's have their own appointed places – and rightly so – but up here things can be relaxed a little without harming discipline. That is why I prefer to soldier here.'

24

'You want the King's Commission yourself, don't you?'

'If the Sirkar in its wisdom deems me fit in due course.'

'Where did you learn your English? It's a damn sight better than mine.'

'The sahib is most kind. Actually at Mayo College, Lahore, then at the University of the Punjab.'

'How long were you there?'

'Until I graduated.'

'As what?'

'B.A. – honours.'

'But surely you could have got a cadetship at Dehra Dun, or even Sandhurst, on the strength of that?'

'A matter of money, sahib. My father suffered severe financial losses about that time, and I did not wish to be a burden upon him. Oh, I could have got any number of clerical jobs, but I had no fancy to be a babu, so I enlisted in the ranks, and have not regretted it. Promotion came fast, and not through influence. I think I have earned it.'

'You bloody well have,' said Wyndham with feeling. 'Here, pass us the bottle and we'll drink to that. Cheers – sorry – mud in your eye.'

'Mud in your eye, sahib,' said the rissaldar, and chuckled softly again.

And then stones rattled sharply in a mess tin at the end of the trip wire.

Wyndham felt his wrist gripped and squeezed.

'Here they are,' whispered the rissaldar. 'Ahead of time. No shooting, sahib, if we can help it.'

They stood up and waited. Wyndham felt a constriction in his throat and realized it was not only excitement. He was experiencing the inevitable nervousness that is never absent from impending action. The rissaldar waited tensely, then gave the cry of a night bird again and they heard it repeated softly in the distance, then four electric torches stabbed the darkness together and they saw a tight group of half-a-dozen masked men gazing transfixedly at them in a circle of light.

'Stand still or we'll kill you,' called the rissaldar.

Their hands went up, and the sowars moved in silently and a fat man crawled from under an enveloping blanket and bayed to the whole pantheon of Hindu gods that he was a poor man being despitefully used. The rissaldar went forward and cuffed him into silence while the sowars joyfully stripped the others of everything of value that they carried and then drove them off into the darkness.

'So that is it, sahib,' the rissaldar said with quiet satisfaction. 'This usurer is a very happy man.'

'But what about the prisoners?' Wyndham asked. 'Surely we take them back?'

'As the sahib wishes, of course, but I wouldn't advise it. If it were earlier it would be a different matter, but it will be light soon and we'll be in full view of the Afghan Frontier posts – on *their* side of the line – moving slowly with prisoners on foot.'

'So what do we do?' Wyndham asked.

'I suggest we mount, putting this bag of guts on a spare horse, and get back quickly into our own territory. That way there will be no trouble with the Political Department. It is the usual procedure when there is any risk.'

'I'll leave it to you then.' Wyndham shrugged uncertainly.

'Thank you, sahib. That will be better.'

'At the same time I don't like the idea of these devils getting away with it . . .'

'They can be shot if the sahib prefers it.'

'In cold blood?' Wyndham said, horrified. 'Good God no.'

'Then let them go in peace. They have gained nothing but sore feet, and having been recognized by our men now they will never risk a raid across *this* part of the Frontier again. Let us mount, sahib, and be on our way rejoicing. Allah looks kindly upon the compassionate.'

They came back to the fort as day was breaking, and Wyndham slept the sleep of the just and woke feeling lighter-hearted than he had for months.

Chapter 3

The rissaldar tapped on the open door, and Wyndham, at ease in a Roorkhee chair, called cheerily, 'Come in, Rissaldar-sahib. Sit down.' He pointed to the other chair and indicated the bottle of whisky on the table in one gesture. 'Help yourself.'

'The sahib is most kind,' the other murmured, and poured himself a modest peg.

'Mud in your eye,' Wyndham said, and topped up his own glass. 'I owe you a month's pay, but I'm afraid you'll have to wait until I go down to Risalpur next week, unless a cheque is any good to you.'

'It is nothing. Let it wait the sahib's convenience. Is the Colonel-sahib pleased with us?'

Wyndham shrugged. 'You know the Colonel-sahib better than I. Have you ever known him to be pleased about anything? I reported by telephone this morning and got a rollicking off him for not capturing the dacoits.'

'Exactly, sahib.' The rissaldar nodded. 'But you would have incurred his even deeper displeasure if you had told him that you let them go rather than risk trouble with our own Political people. Crossing the Frontier is a serious offence.'

'I hope the men won't gossip,' Wyndham said uneasily.

'They won't gossip, sahib,' the rissaldar said quietly. 'They are very happy.' He took a canvas bag from under the skirt of his tunic and placed it on the table. 'And Setal Dass, the money-lender, is very happy also. This comes with his thanks and compliments.'

'What the devil is it?' Wyndham asked.

'Perhaps the sahib would examine it.'

Wyndham untied the thong round the neck of the bag and looked inside. He tipped the contents on to the table, and his jaw dropped and his eyebrows shot up in amazement as gold coins clinked on the bare wood. He looked at the rissaldar, who was watching him closely.

'Gold mohurs, sahib. Two hundred and fifty of them,' he said.

'But – but – I don't understand . . .'

'A coin no longer in circulation. They date back to the East India Company days when they were worth fifteen rupees each. Now any money-changer or shroff in the bazaar will gladly give thirty for them – and up to fifty if you bargain with them.'

'God Almighty!' shouted Wyndham. 'I can't accept this. You know I can't. Take it back to him.'

'But it is dasturi, sahib,' the rissaldar told him softly. 'That means the *custom*. Every officer who has ever commanded here has taken his just reward.'

'I don't believe you.'

'I'm not a liar, sahib.'

'You're asking me to believe that officers – *British* officers – take bribes for doing their duty?'

The rissaldar shook his head. 'A bribe, sahib, is money given for an illicit purpose. This is a *gift* – a gift given in gratitude.'

'One I'm not prepared to accept, Rissaldar-sahib. Take it back to him, and tell him that if he ever again offers me a gift – present – baksheesh – call it what the hell you like – I'll put a horsewhip round his black arse.'

The rissaldar smiled. 'If you did that, sahib, he would think he was not offering you enough – which actually he is not – and he might even double it to keep your goodwill.'

Wyndham's hand was shaking as he poured himself another drink.

'Rissaldar-sahib,' he said, 'you're an educated man. You hope sometime to gain the King's Commission. You know our code. Why did you bring this to me? Why didn't you stuff it down his damned throat when he offered it?'

'With respect, sahib,' the rissaldar said, 'I've already told you why. Because it is the custom.' He leaned forward earnestly. 'Listen, sahib – please listen to me. These swine bleed my people white. The law allows them to. It not only allows them, it *protects* them – and they grow rich and fat at the expense of poor devils who scratch a living from the hardest earth in Asia. A man borrows a hundred rupees and puts his thumbprint on the hundi, the bond. He is actually given ninety, which means that the first month's interest of ten per cent is paid. Thereafter he pays ten rupees on the first day of every month – a hundred and twenty rupees in the year – *but the original hundred is still owing.* And so it goes on for years . . .'

'You've said yourself that it is the law,' Wyndham said. 'All right: alter that law. It is your country.'

'But you – the British – rule it. I'm sorry, sahib – it's not your fault, nor mine. We're soldiers, not lawyers – but this way, the way of dasturi, a little justice is done – and what is more important, it is *seen* to be done.'

'How could my taking a bribe be justice?'

'Because every sowar in this small garrison whose pay is a bare twenty rupees a month is today a little richer – as also am I – I'm being quite frank with the sahib. We are all peasants – farmers – ourselves, you know. My father was better off than most, admittedly, but he was ruined by one of these bastards. He borrowed money to educate me – a lot of money by his standards – and eventually he was sold up – and he hanged himself for the shame of it.'

'I'm – I'm sorry, Rissaldar-sahib,' Wyndham said, 'but I still can't accept this.'

The rissaldar rose and scooped the coins back into the bag.

'Very well, sahib,' he said quietly. 'I shall return it to him – and I shall collect back from the sowars the fifty rupees each they have received. They will not understand – nor will they be happy about it . . .'

'I don't give a damn what *they* get from him,' Wyndham muttered, 'as long as I don't know about it officially. That goes for you too.'

'All accept their share – or none. That is our protection, sahib.'

Wyndham was sweating. He balled his fist and pounded softly on the table.

'What protection would I ever have in the future if that bloody Hindu knew I had taken this?'

'No more nor less than every other officer who has commanded this post has had – since the days of your father, and your father's father, and *his* father. The protection of dasturi, sahib. Break that dasturi and you break the protection also, because then the men will think that you or I, or both, are keeping it all – and there *will* be gossip and bad feeling, and next time a damned money-lender is taken you will not see them work as they did last night. He will be taken over the border, and he either pays exactly double what he pays us or he dies under torture. It's as simple as that, sahib. Dasturi.' He saluted, turned and marched stiffly to the door.

'Wait,' said Wyndham. The other turned. 'All right. Leave it. I'll think about it.'

The rissaldar put the bag on the table and went out. Wyndham reached for the bottle again.

He went down to Risalpur on the normal monthly duty visit the following week and sold the coins without haggling, for seven thousand rupees, which was sufficient to wipe out his overdraft and put him over a thousand in the blue for the first time in nearly two years. He made privy arrangements then with the supply sergeant to send him up a case of scotch at regular intervals, and returned to the fort in a happy and contented frame of mind.

And two months later the money-lender from Safrabad, a village at the far end of his sector, was abducted. They rescued him in much the same manner as the former one, but once again they had to cross the Frontier to do it, so the dacoits had to be allowed to 'escape'. The rissaldar handled the sale of his mohurs this time, which put him a further eight thousand five hundred rupees in credit. This he sent back to England by bank draft to the more clamorous of his creditors. But the outcome was not quite so happy as far as his Commanding Officer was concerned, and he had an uncomfortable session at headquarters.

'Rescuing fat-backsided Hindu money-lenders butters nobody's parsnips,' Lieutenant-Colonel Mortimer-Caulk told him acidly. 'Catching dacoits and seeing them hanged, or even shooting 'em on the hoof *does*. It's training and the use of a little intelligence that does it, young feller. Don't let the next lot slip through your fingers or I'll be down on you like a ton of bricks.'

He went back to the fort somewhat crestfallen and the rissaldar smiled wisely. 'The sahib is too honest,' he said. 'Honesty is like the chlorine we put in the drinking water. A little of it purifies – too much rots the liver.'

'What do you mean?' Wyndham asked him glumly.

'You shouldn't report the incidents where we do not catch the dacoits. None of the other officers did.'

'You mean . . . ?' Wyndham gaped at him. 'Well, I'll be damned.

So he didn't report negative sorties thereafter – and there were two of them in the next six months, the money-lender being rescued on each occasion.

Then came the third. The rissaldar came to his quarters at sunset. 'It is not a money-lender this time, sahib,' he said. 'It is not even a Hindu. It is Iqbal Khan, a rich zamindar the other side of Muzlafabad. He was abducted by a band of Orakzai Pathans last night.'

'That's a long way from the actual border,' said Wyndham, studying the map on his wall. 'With luck we ought to be able to bag a couple this time.'

'As Allah wills,' said the rissaldar. 'We will be ready to march in an hour, if the sahib pleases. I have reason to believe that they are holding him in the high ground above the Dhondi Pass.'

Wyndham did not ask him how he knew. He had learned by this time that there were channels of information, 'grapevines', that would never be disclosed to a white man. He just accepted it. He was at peace now. He had paid off all his creditors in England, and the Trust had settled his debts out here. In a few more months he would meet the Colonel's eye and show him his bank book with a possible twenty or thirty rupees over the three thousand he had been under orders to save from his meagre pay. He grinned to himself. Holy mackerel, he had spent nearly that on scotch in the last twelve months. He had the whisky tolerance of an Assam tea-planter, with the Gurkhas and Parsees reputed to be the sub-continent's most yeomen tipplers, although lately he had been making a genuine effort to cut his intake down.

They marched steadily for three hours. He was getting used to it now, and had developed the night-sight of a Pathan. There were twenty of them, as usual – half Mohammedan and half Sikh, as the rissaldar was always careful to arrange in order to avoid intertribal jealousy. They found the zamindar just where the rissaldar had thought, at the top of a dried-up nullah, spread-eagled between four tentpegs. He was of tougher fibre than the average Hindu money-lender and had evidently held out for a long time, but he was still alive, moaning softly, and there was a sickening smell of burnt flesh on the night air. He revived as the rissaldar cut him loose and he shrieked exultantly that he hadn't told the bastards where he kept his money. Then Wyndham heard a rustling in the sparse shrub that dotted the hillside below them, and he switched on his powerful torch and caught the figure of a man full in the beam. He emptied his pistol at him and the man ran, staggered, then dropped. The rissaldar was shouting, 'No shooting, sahib! – No shooting!'

Wyndham slid down the hillside, reloading as he went. The man was still twitching. He covered him with the pistol and stirred him with his foot and told him to get up. The rissaldar dropped down beside him.

'I told you not to shoot,' he said angrily, and Wyndham turned and looked at him in amazement.

'*You* told *me*?' he said. 'Who do you think you are addressing, Rissaldar-sahib? You are forgetting yourself.'

The rissaldar didn't answer. He bent over the recumbent figure and shone his torch into his face. He was wearing a kullah, the pointed felt cap of the Orakzais over which they wind their loose black turbans, and the tail of the turban itself was tied across his face maskwise. The rissaldar jerked the cloth away and Wyndham saw the whites of the man's upturned eyes and realized that he was dead.

The rissaldar said quietly, 'I don't think this is the time for you and me to quarrel. We are in trouble.' And with a sense of complete unreality Wyndham saw that the dead man was Dafadar Prem Singh, the farrier, who had not been detailed for duty with this column. He stared in unbelief, then turned to the rissaldar.

'But . . . I . . . I don't understand,' he stammered.

'Don't you, sahib?' the other said, and the servility had gone from his voice. 'You mean to say that you really didn't know that half the troop act as dacoits while the others are the rescuers? Oh, come, sahib – you're not as innocent as all that.'

'You *bastard*!' Wyndham shouted and struck out wildly. 'I'll have you hanged for this.'

The rissaldar brushed the blow aside. 'You'll have *me* hanged?' he said. '*You* shot him – not I. I think you'd better pull yourself together, sahib, and start considering your position.'

'My position is that of your superior officer,' Wyndham said. 'Consider yourself under arrest.'

'Don't talk like a fool,' the rissaldar told him contemptuously.

'You've had the better part of thirty thousand rupees from me over the last year. How are you going to explain *that* at my court martial?'

'Prove it,' Wyndham said, but without conviction.

'I'll tell you the name of every shroff in the bazaar to whom you have sold gold mohurs – and the dates – if necessary.'

'It won't be necessary,' Wyndham said hollowly. 'I shall make a full statement on our return to the fort. I shall be in trouble, of course, for accepting illicit gratuities – but I'm prepared to face up to that. You'll be in greater trouble.'

The rissaldar laughed shortly. 'I doubt it. Now suppose we're sensible for a moment. If you keep your head the whole thing can be covered.'

'How can this fellow's death be covered?' Wyndham spat. 'Talk sense.'

'Quite simply. He died like a hero, charging the dacoits without a thought for his own safety. His widow will even get a pension.'

'The men will talk. It will leak out . . .'

'It won't. Every single man in the detachment has, at some time or other, played the part of a dacoit.' The rissaldar paused, then added slowly, 'with the exception of yourself. That has worried them rather. Some of them have been muttering and wondering when *you* were going to take your turn. I think it might be a good idea if you led the next raid, sahib. We'd all feel safer.'

'I won't,' Wyndham raged. 'I won't! I won't!'

The rissaldar took a sudden step forward and wrenched the pistol from Wyndham's nerveless hand. 'Then in that case *you* die a hero's death also, trying to save poor Prem Singh. And every man here will tell the same story. A great pity. You would have been finishing your tour of duty at the fort next month, wouldn't you? Still, it will be a very fine funeral – on a gun carriage, with the massed regimental trumpeters sounding Retreat and the Last Post, and the name of Wyndham will be emblazoned once more on the Roll of Honour.' He raised the pistol. 'You have until I count ten to make up your mind, sahib.'

But Wyndham didn't need the ten. Eyes closed and face twitching, he nodded at five, and the rissaldar chuckled. 'I knew the sahib would make the wise decision,' he said softly. He passed over the water-bottle. 'Mud in your eye, sahib.' Wyndham drank deeply – then, and when they returned to the fort as dawn was breaking.

He emerged scarified from his next interview at headquarters. 'God Almighty, boy,' the colonel shouted. 'You've been up there nearly a year and you haven't seen hide or hair of one of these blackguards, and now you've lost a damned good farrier. Pull your bloody socks up. I'm keeping you there until you've got a couple of entries in the game book. Good Lord! The Tochi Scouts catch or kill an average of two a month.'

The rissaldar was pleased. 'It will save the trouble of initiating yet another young officer into the business before I myself finish my tour up here,' he said. 'Be of good cheer, sahib – I'll send a patrol across the Frontier one night to bring back a couple of corpses to please the Exalted One.'

'I'll have nothing to do with murder,' Wyndham quavered.

'A pity the sahib hadn't made that resolution before Prem Singh was shot,' the rissaldar said softly. 'There is a rumour afoot that he had been demanding a bigger share and the sahib took strong measures to correct this.'

'You know perfectly well that's not true,' Wyndham said, aghast.

'I know, sahib, but these are simple men – and they are troubled. The sahib will lead the next raid, just to reassure them.'

'I won't! I won't! I won't!' Wyndham began again, then finished brokenly, 'When . . . ?'

They left the fort at nightfall and rode north-east along the goat-track that ran parallel with the almost dry Narwhal River – the rissaldar leading, followed by Wyndham, then Dafadar Ishaq Hussain, the big Trans-Frontier Afridi, and twelve sowars, a smaller party than usual. They halted after an hour, dismounted and changed into Pathan clothing, with their turban-tails draped across their faces so that only their eyes showed through four narrow slits. Wyndham's were blue, and it worried him.

'There's nothing to be nervous about, sahib,' the rissaldar assured him. 'Many Pathans have blue eyes – and your skin, such as can be seen, is as sun-darkened as that of any of us. It's just your voice you must be careful of. You're fluent enough now in

34

Urdu and Pushtu – but you still have a sahib's accent. Speak at little as need be, and then in an undertone.'

'I'm not going to say a word – to anybody,' Wyndham mumbled.

'You may have to. You are in command – pukkha command, not just the appearance. I shall have gone off to join the rescuers before we reach the village,' the rissaldar said impatiently. 'Come on, sahib. Pull yourself together. You're not a woman.'

'I'm not going to torture anybody,' Wyndham said flatly.

'Leave that to Ishaq Hussain. It probably won't be necessary, anyhow. This fat pig has had a visit from us before. He'll squeal and tell his women to dig up his money-bags as soon as you burst in through the door. We'll give you an hour before arriving at a stretched gallop – so be well down the trail by that time, because on this occasion we are going to fire some shots to give it realism, and we don't want any more regrettable incidents, do we?'

The village was as silent as the grave when they entered it on foot shortly after midnight. It was just a collection of a dozen or so mud and rough stone huts, with a small whitewashed mosque in the centre and, on the outskirts, a larger house surrounded by a high stone wall that was broken only by an iron-studded teak-wood gate. Without a word, one of the sowars placed himself flat against the wall, facing it, then a second ran noiselessly forward and leapt on to his shoulders as lightly and effortlessly as a circus gymnast, and then a third went up and placed a sheep-skin over the broken glass that was embedded in the cement on the parapet. He climbed over, and dropped down the other side. A dog started to bark furiously, then stopped suddenly and whined, and Wyndham guessed that the sheepskin was smeared with cheetah fat, the merest scent of which will terrify the fiercest watchdog.

The dafadar nudged him and they moved silently along to the gate and heard the muffled clink of chains being unfastened the other side. The gate creaked open and they passed through. They were in a courtyard and Wyndham could hear the snuffling of cattle somewhere in the darkness, and then a man's voice started to sing, high-pitched and dirgelike, and he jumped.

The dafadar whispered, 'It's all right, sahib. The fool of a watchman sings to keep himself company.' He placed his hand on Wyndham's arm reassuringly, and added, 'The sahib needn't tremble. There is no danger.' And it had the effect, at one and the same time, of steadying and infuriating him. He struck the hand away and swore at the other man and heard him utter an apology.

The quarter moon came up over the rim of the surrounding hills, and Wyndham could now see the house ahead of them. It was the usual type of rich man's residence in these parts, where wealth called for more than ordinary security, square and ugly, with the ground-level given over to stables and cattle byres, and the only entrance twelve feet up with a ladder suspended from a hook beside it and a few narrow slit windows piercing the otherwise unbroken face of the wall. The chowkidar, an old and skinny man, was seated on the ground at the corner of the building, and Wyndham heard him break off in mid-song and yelp in terror, then on a hissed command, commence singing again shakily as a sowar held the edge of a knife to his throat. Again the silent gymnast went into action and the man who had climbed the wall went up and lowered the suspended ladder, and as it came down all further need for secrecy was ended. Two sowars went up with axes and attacked the door thunderously. It splintered in a matter of seconds, and they went in with levelled rifles. The dafadar stood aside with exaggerated politeness, and Wyndham climbed the ladder with his knees trembling. Someone was shining a torch round the large single room, and then others pushed past him and lit a large brass oil-lamp that hung from the roof by a chain. There were three men here, alike in their loose muslin shirts and dhotis, shaven-headed except for minuscule pigtails, their well-fed sleekness in marked contrast to the lean Hillmen who surrounded them. They knelt on their sleeping mats in the last stages of terror – an old man and two younger ones.

'Father swine and two fat piglets,' the dafadar muttered. 'Hold the point of your knife to the old one's gullet, sahib, and listen to him squeal.' Then, as Wyndham shook his head, he went forward and did it himself. 'Where's your money, you old bastard?' he demanded in Pushtu, pushing the knife in and breaking the skin. Blood trickled down and stained the white muslin, and the three of them shrieked in unison. Behind him Wyndham heard other shrieks, and turning, he saw three women being pulled out from behind a curtain which hung across one corner of the room. One of the sowars was holding his Pathan khamis up and exposing his genitals and the shrieks grew in volume. Wyndham turned away, fighting down a wave of nausea. The old man was babbling in Hindi that he had no money in the house and that there were women in the village better-looking and younger than his wife and two daughters-in-law. The dafadar pushed the point of the knife in a little further and two of the others were dragging one of the sons towards the open hearth in the middle of the room where a dull fire was smouldering. They spun him round and planted his rump in the embers and held him there a long half-minute before kicking him to one side to make room for the old man, but it was not necessary. He was moaning, 'Under the fire – under the fire.' The hearth was a solid slab of granite and the uninjured son was already levering it up with a crowbar. There was a recess some four feet by two in the stone floor beneath it, and in it were two steel chests. The old man was weeping as he took a bunch of keys from under his shirt and unlocked them. The nausea had now overcome Wyndham, and he was retching and heaving through the door into the darkness outside. He was conscious of the dafadar behind him.

'It will be necessary for the sahib to check what we have found,' he said. 'It is the rissaldar-sahib's order – to avoid disputes later.'

'Get away from me, you bastard,' Wyndham snarled, and the dafadar shrugged and smiled. 'Drink some whisky-pani, sahib,' he advised. 'They tell me it is good for the guts – if one *has* guts.'

They left within fifteen minutes of entering, the dafadar kicking and cuffing a couple of the younger sowars who wanted to dally awhile with the women, after setting fire to a forage barn and driving the cattle out on to the hillside for the sheer wanton unnecessary hell of it, and the rissaldar overtook them an hour later down the trail with the 'rescuers'. He was delighted with the size of the booty: a thousand gold mohurs and two thousand silver rupees, with a miscellaneous selection of crude but valuable jewellery, worth perhaps another two or three thousand. But he was disappointed with Wyndham's showing.

'You'll have to do it again, sahib,' he chided. 'The men are murmuring – and it was a very foolish thing to call **an** Afridia bastard. All of them are – and sensitive about it.'

Wyndham stayed **drunk for three** days, and didn't report this one to headquarters.

Chapter 4

He was less nervous this time. This was the last, because the Colonel had notified him officially that he could take his overdue leave in a week's time, handing over to his successor, Peter Renfrew, and then rejoining his squadron at headquarters. He wondered whether Renfrew, a subaltern on probation from a British unit, would be initiated into dacoity before the rissaldar, who must now be a wealthy man by local standards, was posted away from the fort. He hoped not. Renfrew was amiable and rather stupid, and he talked too much. He also wondered how much truth there was in the rissaldar's claim that every officer who had ever commanded up here had indulged in 'dasturi'. He was beginning to doubt it, and there had been occasions, usually after a few drinks in the Mess on his visits to headquarters, when the temptation to take Prentice into his confidence and question him had been well-nigh overwhelming – but he had fought it down. The less said the better. His debts were now paid and he had 'saved' the amount the Colonel had ordered. In a year's time he would come into his inheritance, and he would then shake the dust of this place, and the Army, from his feet, and it would all merge, he hoped, into a completely unreal dream.

This was a longer ride than usual. The village was a good fifteen miles away and was right on the Frontier.

'No shooting this time, sahib,' the rissaldar had impressed upon him. 'Not even into the air. The Afghan customs post is a bare mile away and we don't wish to alert them. If he disgorges anything worthwhile – say, not less than three thousand rupees – there need be no rescue. Just come away and rendezvous with us two miles down the trail. No money – then bring him with you and we'll let Ishaq Hussain deal with him for ransom. Allah go with you, sahib.'

It took them a full five hours to reach their objective, and he was almost asleep in the saddle when the dafadar reined back alongside him.

'We leave our horses here,' the Afridi growled, 'and I shall go in with three of the men. You wait with the others until I send word back, then come forward, posting four men as horse-holders.' And he glided away into the darkness. There had been no pretence of politeness – not even a 'sahib', and Wyndham could detect the cold hatred in the other's voice. He hadn't wanted to bring him, but the rissaldar had brushed his objections aside. 'He's the most experienced man, next to myself,' he had said. 'You'll have no trouble with him. Ishaq Hussain likes money too much to let personal grudges interfere with his operations.'

It was the easiest yet. The village was quiet, and the money-lender's house was less fortress-like than most, and when Wynd-ham arrived he was already sitting snuffling on the floor with his moneybags in front of him.

'A little under two thousand,' Ishaq Hussain muttered. 'He must have more somewhere. I'll sit the swine on his fire until he remembers where it is.'

'No,' Wyndham said sharply. 'Just take this and let us go.'

'The rissaldar said three thousand,' the other insisted.

'I don't give a damn what the rissaldar said,' Wyndham answered. 'Do as you're told.'

'Very brave, eh? – You must have drunk much whisky-pani while you waited out there,' the Afridi sneered. 'I take my orders from a *man*, not a puling boy with the stomach of a woman.' He snapped an order at the sowars and they grabbed the Hindu and carried him bodily to the cooking fire in the corner of the room. He screamed and struggled and then suddenly other men were bursting in from outside – Hillmen like their own people, but all wearing the long grey mazri shirt of the Tochi Scouts, and armed to the teeth with Lee Enfield rifles and wicked Khyber knives. Someone kicked the lamp over and blazing oil licked across the dry rushes on the stone floor, and Wyndham had just enough wit to dive through a narrow glassless window behind him. He avoided the gate leading out of the courtyard and sprang for the surrounding wall, cutting his hands to the bone on the jagged chevaux-de-frise on top. He dropped down the other side and felt his ankle buckle sickeningly under him. He hobbled desperately along the village street right into the arms of a patrol, and went down under a rain of thudding rifle butts.

A bucket of water over his head and an ungentle boot in his ribs brought him round. It was broad daylight and he was lying on his back in what had undoubtedly been a recently occupied cow-byre, because he was plastered with filth, and a swarm of flies rose and then settled again as he stirred. A voice said in Pushtu, 'Put your wrists together in front of you, budmash,' and a hard hand swiped him across the face as he was still trying to collect his wits. A lean Scout NCO was squatting in front of him dangling a pair of heavy, old-fashioned handcuffs. Wyndham shook his head and croaked, 'I am a British officer. Call your company commander,' and the Pathan gaped at him unbelievingly and then rose and hurried away. He came back with another man, dressed identically in loose pantaloons, mazri shirt and untidy Hill pagri, without badges of rank or any other mark to distinguish him from the first – but Wyndham recognized him as someone he had frequently seen in vastly different style in the Risalpur Club.

'Wyndham, isn't it?' he said in English, standing looking down at him. He was tall, rangy and aquiline – burnt to the shade of an old riding-boot.

Wyndham mustered a wry grin. 'That's right,' he acknowledged. 'You're Philip Coates, aren't you? Sorry for the box-up. I was fancy-dressing with some of my chaps in an attempt to grab a crowd of hairies who we had reason to believe were going to knock the local money-lender off.'

'Yes – so I heard,' said Coates drily. 'You don't have to say anything at this juncture – in fact I'd strongly advise you not to, because I'm supposed to write down anything you say, and it can be repeated in Court.'

A cold hand was clutching at Wyndham's vitals, but he made an attempt to bluff further. 'You ought to have been a copper,' he said. 'You did that very realistically.'

'I *am* a copper, of a certain sort, as you very well know,' Coates told him. 'And my advice stands. Shut up until you've got a lawyer at your elbow. You're under arrest for armed dacoity, Wyndham. Handcuff him!' he added to the NCO.

'What the hell do you think you're doing?' Wyndham screamed, but the other walked out of the shed without answering, and the Pathan said, 'I do not know what this madness is, but you heard my sahib's order. Wrists together.'

41

They took him down to the Scout fort that night and an assistant surgeon came up from Miranshah and strapped up his damaged ankle. Coates was the only British officer on the post and he was coldly polite but not altogether unkindly. He allowed Wyndham to bath in his quarters and even lent him clean clothes before locking him in the guardroom, but he would answer no questions.

The first shock had passed now, leaving him frightened but wary, like a wounded animal that retires into the thickets knowing, perhaps, that logically it is finished, but refusing to give way to panic. From listening to his guards talking outside the cell-block he was able to piece together a picture of what had happened. There had been a fight and some of the sowars had been killed – the number varying from six to ten – and three had been wounded and taken prisoner, while the rest had managed to make good their escape across the Frontier, but try as he would he could not ascertain the fate of the rissaldar and Ishaq Hussain.

The adjutant came up from Risalpur on the second day to tell him formally that a Summary of Evidence was to be taken and that he had the option of nominating a defending officer or retaining civil counsel. He pondered long over this. A lawyer would be safer than an untrained officer, but would cost money. He had money now, but that fact in itself might be damning as the prosecution would undoubtedly know that he had been in difficulties when he was first posted to the fort.

'What would you advise?' he asked at last, and the adjutant told him stiffly that it was not his job to advise as he would be taking the Summary. Coates, not so closely concerned with regimental honour, was more helpful.

'Plump for a lawyer,' he said. 'There's an Irishman who practises at the Punjab bar, name of O'Farrell. He's expensive, but you're going to need all the help you can muster.'

'Help?' Wyndham said glumly. 'I'm going to need a bloody miracle. How do I get hold of him?'

'You'll go before your CO for arraignment tomorrow. Tell *him*.' He did, and the colonel, looking bleakly at a spot six inches above Wyndham's head as he stood before him between two brother subalterns with drawn swords, remanded him in close arrest.

O'Farrell came up from Lahore a few days later, a short, red-haired, red-faced man who moved in a finely atomized aura of Irish whiskey.

'I have one question to ask you,' he began.

'I'm guilty,' Wyndham said, looking at the floor, 'but . . .'

'That wasn't the question,' O'Farrell told him sharply. 'Fortunately I didn't catch your answer anyway. What I do want to know is, have you got ten thousand rupees, or certain prospects of being able to raise that amount? – because that's what it's going to cost you.'

'You'll get your money,' Wyndham assured him.

'Good – but don't be opening your gob again unless I tell you.' He rose and went to the open door, where an embarrassed Prentice sat on guard. 'Will you please be moving out of earshot while I talk to my client. He won't be running away.' Then, when Prentice had hastily dragged his chair up the corridor, he came back. 'This is the form,' he said. 'You are charged with four counts of dacoity, which as you no doubt know is their word for armed robbery. That's a holding charge only. They may add to it, reduce it, or amend it, according to what the Summary brings out. Dacoity is a felony under the Indian Penal Code, carrying a penalty upon conviction of anything up to life imprisonment. Normally this would be tried in a civil court, but since this area is under military jurisdiction you will go before a court martial. You understand all this?' Wyndham moistened his dry lips and nodded, and O'Farrell went on, 'A Summary of Evidence is a preliminary to all General Courts Martial. Witnesses are summoned and they make their statements in your presence with, of course, me beside you. The statements are on oath and you, or I on your behalf, may question them at the end of it. Everything is taken down in writing and is signed both by the deponent and you. You yourself may make a statement at this stage should you wish to do so. I'll be deciding upon that when the time comes. All this evidence is then submitted to the general officer commanding, who reads it, always assuming that the old gentleman *can* read, and decides whether or not to convene a court martial. If he does, you'll be judged by a bench consisting of a full colonel, a lieutenant-colonel, a major, a captain and a subaltern, with a Deputy Judge Advocate General to advise them on points of law.

He's a civilian lawyer like meself and he stops things getting to the monkey-house stage. Normally your own adjutant conducts the prosecution, but since you're defended by me in this case, they'll be appointing an officer with legal qualifications from the Army Legal Department. I know 'em all and can make mincemeat of the bloody lot – except one.'

'Who is he?' Wyndham asked.

'Never you mind. I'll be sacrificing a goat to Vetal, the god of criminals, that we don't get him.' He took a sheet of paper from his briefcase. 'I have to be notified in advance of the witnesses they are calling. Here they are.' He read, 'Setal Dass, money-lender. Know anything about him?'

'I seem to have heard the name,' Wyndham said, 'but I've certainly never met him.'

'Roop Chand – also a shark. Anything known?'

'Certainly not by me.'

'Abdul Faqira, zamindar?'

'Yes – we rescued him from the dacoits.'

'Two wounded sowars now in hospital – Haidar Khan and Bhim Singh. The grapevine tells me that the Frontier Constabulary have been working on them to turn King's Evidence. I hope not. A sick wog properly handled will swear his mother's life away.'

'My rissaldar, Sher Mohammed Khan, and Dafadar Ishaq Hussain . . . ?' Wyndham asked anxiously.

'The rissaldar is dead and the other feller is among those who made it across the Frontier. No, the ones I've just read out are the only people you need worry about. I'm supposed to submit a list of defence witnesses, by the way. . . '

Wyndham shook his head hopelessly. 'There's nobody I can think of.'

'I have had an anonymous letter from a gent who says that if I'll undertake to pay him five thousand rupees – to be left under a flat stone on the Bannu road – he'll produce six unimpeachable witnesses to supply you with an alibi for any of the relevant dates.' O'Farrell grinned. 'Let's hope it won't come to that.' He replaced the list in the briefcase and took out a flat flask. 'I don't think your military pal can see you from up the corridor, so take a good pull at that. You look as if you could do with it.' Wyndham drank gratefully and the Irishman said, 'Cheer up – I've handled less promising ones than this, though God knows not much less. I'll see you at the Summary.'

'But – I mean – don't you want my version of it?' Wyndham asked.

'Christ no,' the other said. 'You'd be prejudicing yourself. I'm an honest man. I only defend the innocent.' He winked and went.

Wyndham alternated between fits of wholly unwarranted, almost manic optimism and correspondingly deep periods of gloom during the taking of the Summary. Every word had carefully to be taken down in longhand by the adjutant, who spoke fluent Pushtu, Urdu and Hindi, but who in accordance with military usage had to pretend he didn't, so the proceedings were all in English – third hand in some cases – through a board of interpreter-babus who seemed far more anxious to say what the prosecution wanted to hear than to do justice to the accused. The depression came on those occasions when he heard evidence that could have been turned to his advantage ending up in cold official language in the record that didn't help him at all.

But then, when O'Farrell rose at the end of the testimony and started, with deceptive mildness, to cross-examine and often to demolish the witness, his spirits would rise accordingly. There were many more witnesses now – the list that was originally presented to O'Farrell swelled with new names each day. The identity parades were the worst part of it, when he had to stand in the open, by day and after dark, in the clothes in which he had been captured, with groups of Hillmen similarly clad, while villagers filed past and peered into their faces. Sometimes they passed him by and fingered somebody else, and he knew heart-stopping relief, but far oftener the finger was for him and his bowels would turn to water.

'Don't be worrying about it,' O'Farrell used to say on these occasions. 'I'll make mincemeat of 'em. Sure you look like a wog in those clothes, but these buggers can pick a European by smell – and I'll prove it to the satisfaction of the court. Anyhow, we're not disputing that you were there, on several occasions, but you had a reason for it – an excellent reason. Now come on, once again, what was that reason?'

'I went out with my rissaldar, in disguise,' Wyndham would recite. 'Our object was to gain intelligence of the dacoits and to study their methods. We kept it as dark as possible, naturally, because had the sowars known about it they would inevitably have gossiped in the bazaar, and the whole thing would have been wrecked.'

'Of course. That's our story and we're sticking to it, come hell or high water. Isn't that what you said immediately you came round after your foul mistreatment by those Tochi Scout hairies? Sure it was.'

Wyndham could never decide whether O'Farrell believed him or not. He almost hoped that he didn't. If the Irishman was carefully constructing a defence out of a tissue of lies it would possibly be better if he knew the worst right from the start. Several times he tried to unburden himself, but O'Farrell invariably shut him up.

'I'm a lawyer, not a priest,' he used to say. 'Hold your tongue, or you'll be prejudicing yourself. You had a reason for being there. What was it now? Let's be hearing it again.' And Wyndham would go through the recital once more.

The nights were hell, particularly those on which O'Farrell was unable to slip him the heavy silver flask. The medical officer gave him some sleeping pills, grinding them up in water and watching while he drank the draught, to avoid the risk of his hoarding them into a lethal dose, but they seemed only to have the reverse effect and to keep him in wide-eyed, sweat-soaked wakefulness. It was then that the idea of escape would recur to him. The officer-escort, relieved every two hours, used to doze in a Roorkhee chair in the corridor. Renfrew did more than doze. He used to snore. Out past him on tiptoes – his ankle was better now. Over the wall by the angle of the stables, drop down to the river, grab a couple of mussaks, the inflated bullock skins they used to ferry sheep on, and float with the current for ten miles or so to where the Frontier was a bare three miles away – and then steal across.

And what then? But he never took it beyond this point, because he knew the futility of it. No money, unarmed, clad in the shirt and slacks which was all they had left him – No, it was useless even to think of it. Besides, if he deserted he would be treated as one who had been Dishonourably Discharged – and that was the end of any faint hope he still had of inheriting. On the other hand, if he were acquitted there was still a chance. He'd always be regarded with suspicion by his brother officers – and that bastard the colonel would hate his guts more than ever – but that could even be an advantage. They'd all want him out of the Regiment in double-quick time – he'd probably get leave until his twenty-fourth birthday, and then the Trustees would only be too happy to let him take the cash, and let the credit go. He could hear them – a gaggle of three Commanding Officers, past and present, with the quorum made up by other cavalry colonels if Wyndhams were thin on the ground, a brace of snuff-dry lawyers and for some reason, known only to the old reprobate who had founded the line, the Bishop of Nairn – gathered in the committee-room of the Cavalry Club in London, he hoped after an excellent luncheon: 'Yes – pity – you get the odd man out in the best of families. Regiment better without the feller. Let him inherit and send his papers in and trust that he'll drink himself to death in a year or two.'

It was this hope that sustained him through those long weeks. This and the possibility that the GOC would not consider the evidence sufficiently conclusive to convene a court martial, and would decide to avoid more adverse publicity and deal with the matter himself. The most the general could do without a court martial would be to reprimand him for 'unseemly and injudicious conduct' and privately advise him to resign his commission – advice he was not bound to accept, certainly not on the spot, and once again he could go on until he inherited.

But this second hope was shattered after two weeks of creeping, twitching suspense. O'Farrell came to see him unusually early one morning, and Wyndham could sense his unease immediately. He sat down, avoiding Wyndham's eye, and busied himself with a file of papers in his briefcase.

'Er – um – Let me see now,' he began awkwardly. 'Oh, yes – knew there was something I had to take up with you. Yes – the matter of my fee.'

'I told you you'd get your money,' Wyndham grated.

'Oh, sure, sure – I know that, but I was wondering how it was to be paid.'

47

'By cheque – naturally.'

'You've got that much?'

Wyndham fought down his anger. 'I'd hardly give my own lawyer a rubber cheque. Of course I've got it.'

'You couldn't be giving me the cheque now, I suppose? Sorry to seem mercenary, but it's Bar Council's regulations out here. Fees must be paid before the case comes up in court.'

'Do we know that it *is* coming up?'

'It'll be coming up all right. The old gentleman signed the convening order last night,' O'Farrell said.

'What are the charges?' Wyndham's voice shook slightly.

'I don't know that yet. The adjutant will be reading it to you and giving us a copy later this morning.' He cleared his throat again. 'Er – the cheque . . . ?'

Wyndham's English cheque-book had been left with other private papers when they searched his room. His Indian account held only the three thousand rupees he had 'saved', but he had nearly a thousand pounds in London. He opened a tin uniform case and took the book and made out the cheque. O'Farrell put it in his wallet with an apologetic smile, clapped him on the shoulder and told him to keep a stiff upper lip, and left.

The adjutant read the convening order out to him later that morning. Second Lieutenant Charles Wilberforce Wyndham had been charged with armed dacoity and the murder of 'a person subject to Indian Military Law, namely 524893 Farrier-Dafadar Prem Singh, on the twenty-seventh day of July nineteen-twenty-four.'

Chapter 5

His orderly was helping him into the full dress uniform of Wyndham's Horse, said to have been designed jointly by the Founder and the French madam of a Bombay bordello in 1822. High-necked, knee-length kurta of silver-braid-encrusted royal blue Pachmina cloth, tightly encircled by a foot-wide crimson and gold cummerbund, with a high turban to match, white buckskin breeches and black riding-boots, with silver spurs and chain-mail epaulettes. Everything, in fact, that he would have worn on Viceroy's Review – except his sword. That, he knew, would already be resting on the green cloth-covered Court Martial table, to be returned to him in the case of an acquittal, or broken on the farrier's anvil otherwise. They had moved him now from close arrest in the comparative comfort of his own quarters to custody in the rigorously guarded cell block.

O'Farrell, in shabby black gown and dusty wig, was reassuring him for the fiftieth time in the last ten days. 'Of course it's a capital charge,' he was saying. 'A killing, however unintentional, in the commission of another crime *has* to be called murder – but don't be letting it worry you. It strengthens our case. If you had been there purely to rob these people you wouldn't be shooting one of your own men, now would you? Of course you wouldn't. You were there to protect them, for God's sake. An Officer of His Majesty George the Fifth, King-Emperor, doing his duty. You fired at some dacoits in the dark, didn't you? Of course you did. *Some dacoits who had already shot your farrier.* Don't forget that – because that explains why you reported him, quite truthfully, as being killed by the other side. Are you listening to me?'

White-faced and shaking, Wyndham nodded.

'Good – well, hold fast to that and try and compose yourself. It's first impressions that count. You haven't got a jury here, you know – just five officers, who are jury *and* judge – and none of 'em wanting to send you down, for the good name of the Service.

So give 'em a chance. When you march in there with your escort in ten minutes' time let 'em see an upright young officer, brave but not brass-faced, secure in the knowledge of his own innocence and the inherent fairness of his peers. And not a word out of you – understand? Not a damned cheep until I put you up meself at the end of the defence case – and then answer my questions – shortly, concisely, clearly and, above all, truthfully. They'll mostly be calling for a straight yes or no. If I'm holding the front of my gown with both hands, like this, it's a no I'm after. If I'm twiddling with a pencil or shuffling some papers, it's yes.'

And then Rankine, his escort, had arrived, dressed as was Wyndham himself, but with the addition of pouchbelt and sword, and there reality ceased and became a kaleidoscope of impressions. A quick, jingling march from the guardroom to the regimental gymnasium, the only room in barracks big enough to hold the court and the public – a public which had gathered from as far as the Punjab, with even, so Rankine told him, reporters and foreign correspondents of the London Press up from Bombay, Calcutta and Delhi. The quarterguard in full dress, with ceremonial lances thudding from the Rest to the Order, and somewhere a trumpet sounding the 'Still', and a resultant silence broken only by the chirping of mynah birds in the stunted trees that surrounded the parade ground, and their own footsteps in the dust. A sea of faces that turned towards them as they entered – predominantly brown, with a sprinkling of black, and the first two rows of the public enclosure solidly white. A long table with five men seated the other side: a colonel in Staff red, a lieutenant-colonel in the rifle green of the Gurkhas, a major from the Punjabis and a captain of the Dogra Regiment, and finally, as brilliantly attired as himself, a subaltern from Probyn's Horse, British, but with the earlong bobbed hair of that regiment showing below his turban. And behind them, like a crow among peacocks, the deputy judge advocate general in wig and black gown like O'Farrell, who was sitting at the Defence table to the left of the Court facing the prosecutor, a fat little captain of the Army Legal Service. The colonel was bowing courteously in acknowledgement of their salutes as they halted by the two chairs for Accused and Escort, five paces in front of the table, and introducing himself and the other members of the Court; a string of ranks, names and regiments which meant nothing to Wyndham, followed by the ritual question, 'Have you any objection to being tried by General Court Martial by any or all of us?' A voice he didn't realize for a moment was his own, answered 'Not at all, sir.' Then he wondered if he should have left the reply to O'Farrell.

They were all standing now, and helmets and turbans were being removed by Christians as a Bible was passed from hand to hand during the swearing in of the Court '. . . Do solemnly swear that I will well and truly do justice according to Indian Military Law . . .', then a slight contretemps as the official short-hand reporter declined to be sworn on Bible, Koran or Vedas, he being a Kashmiri Jew, and a consequent half-day delay until a scroll was brought over by a rabbi from the Nowshera syna-gogue. And so the whole first morning went by in a dragging routine of formalities, and Wyndham's nervousness was replaced at first by impatience and a feeling of frustration, then by a deadly ennui. Twice Rankine's elbow had to jerk him into wakefulness in order to give an answer to the Court.

But in the afternoon things were different as each of the three military witnesses squirmed and prevaricated under the decep-tively gentle probing of the fat captain.

'. . . Yes, I knew that what we were doing was wrong – but I was frightened . . .'

'Frightened of whom?'

'Of . . . of the rissaldar . . . and . . .'

'And? (softly) Come, sowar, you have nothing to be frightened of now. This Court is your father and your mother – here to protect you. Who else were you frightened of?'

'The sahib.'

'Which sahib?' And again the finger would be pointed at him. 'Did this sahib ever threaten you?'

'Never – but the rissaldar told us of him, and his terrible anger – and we saw him shoot the farrier.'

'Do you know *why* he shot the farrier?' And then O'Farrell would purse his lips reprovingly and murmur an objection which the Judge Advocate on each occasion sustained, but not before the damning answer had been given: 'Because the farrier was keeping back some of the money.'

'May it please the Court, I submit that even if it were true that the accused shot the deceased – which we do not for one moment accept – the witness could not possibly know what was in the accused's mind at the time. I ask that the question and answer be expunged.'

O'Farrell came to see him in the cells that night, and Wyndham sensed real danger for the first time.

'Forget those fuzzy-wuzzies,' the lawyer said. 'You refused one of them leave to go home and get married, and another feller was promoted over the head of the second one, and you reprimanded the third for being scruffy on parade – anything at all. I can put that over, never fear. What is worrying me though is two bank managers that little fat bastard is calling tomorrow – one from Ferozepore and t'other from here. The grapevine tells me it's about largish sums of money remitted Home. Now listen to me, listen very carefully. I don't want any admissions that might tend to incriminate you, understand? But I do want to know if you can give me a feasible answer to what I know damned well you're going to be asked. Where'd you get it? Can you tell me that? And for God's sake don't be saying you won it at the races unless you can prove you were *at* the races on certain days – and what you betted on – and how much.'

'I . . . I . . . can't . . .' Wyndham mouthed.

O'Farrell rose. 'Then have I your permission to confer with my learned and gallant friend with a view to our pleading Guilty to dacoity in return for their dropping the murder charge?' And Wyndham, past speech, nodded.

O'Farrell came again next morning, hollowly cheerful, and said, 'They won't wear that one, but not to worry. We'll get over it – and I won't be putting you on oath when your time comes, so they can't cross-examine you. Now, chin up. You were looking like McGinty's goat with the bellyache all day yesterday.'

It ended in the late afternoon of the third day – abruptly and anti-climactically – with the fat captain shrugging and saying with an almost apologetic smile, 'And that, may it please the Court, is the case for the Prosecution,' and sitting down.

O'Farrell was on his feet making a perfervid oration, but Wyndham hardly heard it. He was watching the Court, and they were avoiding his eye as the junior Member scribbled on a piece of paper and the Court orderly passed it to the president, and then the major and the lieutenant-colonel were in whispered colloquy and the captain was writing furiously on the record and the president was waiting for it impatiently. They didn't even retire. There was a scrape of chairs as they rose and a sharp intake of breath from the public gallery. Rankine grasped his elbow and helped him to rise.

'The verdict is that the accused stands Guilty of all charges, and the sentence is that he shall be cashiered and handed over to the civil power, there to suffer death by hanging in the manner prescribed by Law. Verdict and sentence are subject to confirmation. I pronounce this General Court Martial dissolved.'

He stumbled on the way back to the cells, and Rankine and O'Farrell had to support him, then blind rage came to his aid and he threw their hands off and screamed incoherent filth – at Rankine, at the lawyer, the Court, the Regiment and the Army – before collapsing in a shuddering, twitching heap. The station medical officer gave him an injection and they managed to get him out of uniform and into civilian clothes, and then two nervous Eurasian police sergeants took him down to Peshawur on the mail truck and lodged him in the condemned cell at Central Jail.

He lay in a merciful coma for three days but rallied sufficiently on the fourth to be able to understand the brigade major when he read the promulgation of sentence, in which the GOC had commuted the death penalty to imprisonment for life. At first it didn't register, even when the two warders who had been on constant watch in the cell congratulated him and later moved him from its comparative privacy to the more open long-term wing, then he knew overwhelming relief that bordered on exaltation. O'Farrell came to see him that night.

'Let me explain the position to you,' the lawyer said. 'You're an embarrassment to them here. Any European in an Indian jail is, particularly one up here on the Frontier. They'll probably get the medical authorities to certify that you're not physically up to a long period of confinement in a black man's country, and they'll be shipping you home.'

'Thank God for that,' Wyndham said fervently.

'I wouldn't be too certain meself.' O'Farrell pinched his lower lip. 'You're by way of being a bit of a celebrity now, you know.

The papers will be on to it when you arrive in Tilbury. Then, when they release you, there'll be another hoo-ha.'

'That's too far ahead to worry me at the moment,' Wyndham said gloomily.

'That's just the point. Life sentence in England nowadays is from twelve to twenty years, making due allowance for good behaviour. Here, as I just said, you'll be an embarrassment, so they'd be opening the gates for you – very, very quietly, to avoid political trouble and charges of favouring a sahib – in, say, five to seven years. You go to another country, change your name, and the thing's forgotten, even if you returned to England later. You'll be still a young man and you could make a fresh start. I'd think about it if I were you.'

'But would I have any option in the matter, one way or the other?'

'In your particular case, yes. They can't send you to England, or any other country, against your will, because you're a statutory native of India, having been born here.'

Wyndham laughed drily. 'They could hang me, but they have to ask my permission before shipping me out. How bloody funny.'

'The law seems very funny at times – especially to a layman. But that's how it stands.'

'So the question is, which would be the more bearable? Cracking rocks in Dartmoor for twenty years, among other white men – or dibbling rice and weaving sisal with niggers for seven out here?'

'You're being too pessimistic in both cases. They wouldn't be putting an educated man on cracking rocks, even in Dartmoor. They wouldn't send you to Dartmoor anyhow. Maidstone is for overseas prisoners, and you'd be a trusty in no time – in the office or the library or somewhere. The same thing applies here – more so in fact. A sahib is still a sahib, even the wrong side of the wall.' He rose and held out his hand. 'Good luck, me boy. I'm sorry it wasn't an acquittal, but it could have been worse, now couldn't it?'

'I trust my cheque was met without trouble,' Wyndham said just a little sourly.

'It was indeed,' O'Farrell answered unblushingly. 'You must

have a nice little nest egg put by. They say you got away with at least a lakh and a half of rupees.'

'They're liars – whoever "they" are.' Wyndham said, and O'Farrell winked and tapped the side of his nose with his forefinger.

'Sure, sure,' he agreed. 'But if you decide to do your time out here and you ever want to get your hands on a bit of it, drop me a postcard and tell me you're worried about your Aunt Agatha, and I'll apply for a visitor's permit.'

'What good would money do me inside?' Wyndham asked.

'You'd be surprised. Just wait until you get to know a few of the ropes. You've got my address.' He winked again and went.

'He's not staying in Peshawar,' the Inspector-General of Prisons for the North-West Frontier Province said firmly. 'He'll corrupt the subordinate staff and unsettle the native prisoners. Get him out of it.'

'Certainly, sir,' his harassed deputy said. 'But where to?'

'The United Kingdom naturally.'

'He's standing by his statutory Indian nationality.'

'All right – the Punjab, United Provinces, Bombay Presidency – anywhere you like – but not here.'

'We've tried them all – and Madras and Bengal. They won't have him.'

'So that just leaves the Andamans,' the IG said, and the deputy blinked. 'It's for lifers and long-term convicts, isn't it?'

'But surely not for Europeans, sir?'

'Show me that in the book of words.'

'Well . . . er . . . I know it's not down anywhere, but I've not heard of one ever being sent there . . .'

'Equal treatment for all races, creeds and colours. That's what the militant politicians out here and the starry-eyed ones at Home are always yelling for, aren't they?'

The deputy looked troubled. 'There'll be an awful howl in the English papers, sir. Talk of Devil's Island and all that sort of thing . . .'

'Nonsense. Devil's Island is French and punitive, the Andamans are British and reformative – or so they tell us.'

'But a convict sent to the Andamans is not supposed to come

back. At the end of his term he is given a grant of land and marries locally or sends for his woman from India . . .'

'I'm fully aware of that,' the IG said coldly. 'I'm also aware of the fact that this fellow is a lifer who has chosen, for some reason best known to himself, to be regarded as an Indian native. All right – who am I to gainsay him? He's let his side down, dragged the honour of a splendid regiment in the mud and . . . and . . . and he's a bloody nuisance. Apply for a transfer there, and if it bounces get through to New Delhi on the telephone and I'll talk to old Teddy Forsythe. He was a Wyndham Horser himself once, so the further we post this blackguard the better he'll like it.'

'A white man in the Andamans?' a shocked Under-Secretary to the Executive Council was saying in New Delhi. 'Surely not.'

'Nothing against it, sir,' his personal assistant assured him. 'And it would certainly please old Gandhi to have a sahib de profundis.'

'*Ex*-sahib – but even so I'm not having him paraded in fetters and legirons to make a Hindu holiday.'

'Actually, they have a greater measure of freedom there than in a provincial prison on the mainland – and only violent types and chronic escapers are fettered.'

'Been reading it up, have you?'

'Yes, sir – and I must say that if I had to make the melancholy choice I'd rather be there than anywhere in India itself. Then again the whole wretched thing is far more likely to die a natural death there. Convicts seldom come back from the Andamans, whereas there are releases every day from the ordinary prisons – and jailbirds are likely to talk to newspapers and we get another crop of highly apocryphal legends about the White Dacoit.'

'Should have hanged the fellow while they had the chance,' the Under-Secretary said resentfully. 'Or he should have had the decency to shoot himself. Hm – all right – I'll sign it, but I'm not altogether happy about it. And listen, Galvin, I want him moved there secretly. If it leaks out beforehand we'll have the Press, photographers and the whole damned rabble sniffing around.'

'With respect, sir,' said the other, 'if we attempt any sort of cover-up it *will* leak. I would say that the safest way would be to send him with a chalan in the ordinary course of events.'

'What's a chalan?'

'A draft of convicts. They assemble from all over India at Alipore Jail, Calcutta, and then go by steamer to Port Blair, three times a year. The next lot are due out in a couple of weeks' time.'

'But damn it all, he'll stand out like a white pigeon in a flock of crows, won't he?' the Under-Secretary said.

'He passed as a dacoit without difficulty, sir. He's naturally a swarthy type and on top of that he's as sunburnt as any Pathan.'

'Poor devil.' The Under-Secretary repressed a slight shudder and drew the big buff form towards him.

'But can we keep it dark once he's there?'

'I don't see any difficulty in that. They all serve the first year in the Cellular Jail under rigid conditions, then they're posted to logging camps throughout the whole archipelago – really isolated, some of them. The staff of the Penal Colony are bound by the provisions of the Official Secrets Act, and, of course, the convicts' mail is censored. In a year he will be forgotten, which after all is no doubt what the chap himself would wish, sir.'

'Out of sight out of mind, in other words.'

'Exactly, sir. Not the first time it's happened in that family. There was a Major Wyndham in 1880 who eloped with a corporal's wife in Razmak and was never heard of again. . . .'

The superintendent said, 'Inspector Howlett and Sergeant Lawson will take the prisoner by car from Peshawar Cantonment to Rawalpindi on the night of the 27th. They will travel on the 28th to Calcutta, per the Frontier Mail, on which a second-class compartment has been reserved. From Howrah Station, Calcutta, they will be conveyed by closed van to Alipore Jail where they will hand over the prisoner on Form PL.272, returning to this station with due expedition thereafter. The prisoner will be kept strictly incommunicado throughout the journey and is to be given to understand that he is in transit to the Central Prison, Madras. This will be their only briefing, and no further orders will be committed to writing. Section 27 (B) of the Official Secrets Act, India, 1909, Amended 1921, will apply. Acknowledge all clear, verbally.'

Chapter 6

They steamed into Howrah late on a wet monsoon night, and the inspector said, 'Well, this is it, sir . . . er . . . Wyndham.'

'But this is Calcutta, not Madras.'

'I think you'll be staying here for a couple of days before moving on – but it's as far as us two go.'

The journey had not been unpleasant. The policemen had bought a crate of Solan beer in Rawalpindi and had packed the bottles round a maund of ice in a metal container under the electric fan, then, after giving him the novation of 'you play the game with us and we'll play the game with you', had unlocked his handcuffs. They even allowed him to stretch his legs on the platform at intervening stops, but, after seeing people he knew travelling in the first-class section of the same train, he retreated to the compartment and laid low thereafter. Both policemen were ex-British Army NCOs, formal and uncomfortable at first, but still possessed of that indefinable soldiers' freemasonry that transcends rank and stretches to include even the outcasts among them when Authority is absent. There was compassion there, but it was not apparent. Rankine and Prentice had come to see him before he left, and their visit had been an unalloyed agony of tongue-tied embarrassment to all three, so much so that he had exercised his option of not seeing any more visitors, even when the colonel and the chaplain called.

They walked along the platform, three Englishmen in travel-crumpled civilian clothes, and Wyndham, his topee pulled down over his eyes, was thankful for the wretchedly dim lighting of the place as they went through the barrier and battled against the solid press of bodies that meet all trains at all hours in India. He found himself separated from his escort and knew something approaching panic because they represented the only stable element in his rapidly changing world, then for one wild moment he thought of escape, but a hand grasped his arm from behind and he heard a relieved mutter, 'Jesus, I thought my job and

pension had gone for a crap then. This way, sir . . . er . . . Wyndham. Railway police office. Won't be long now.'

They struggled through the crowd into the police office and
Wyndham realized that he had been expected, because the
cramped, dusty, smelly place was packed with Bengali constables
who stared at him owlishly. An Indian inspector came out from
an inner office and chattered angrily in English, 'What is this,
man? No handcuffs, no russi? There are regulations here –
regulations the same for Indian prisoners and European.'

'No skin off your black arse,' said Howlett. 'You haven't
signed for him yet. Where's the bloody gharry we're supposed to
have meeting us?'

'Outside in station yard, but I am warning you – serious breach
of regulations bring bad consequence. Rules for escorting of
prisoners call for . . .'

'Bollocks,' said Howlett. 'Show us the gharry. Come on,
Wyndham. Sorry about this, but all bloody Bengalis are bastards.'
He gestured to the sergeant and then joined them together with
handcuffs. 'This pig's orphan will only be putting in a squawk at
the gate when we get to Alipore, and I'll be on a fizzer when I get
back.'

They went out again through the crowd and into the driving
rain and climbed into a black maria that stank of unwashed bodies
and urine, and sat in a row on a narrow wooden seat, and there
was a thunderous clanking as two constables bolted the double
doors from the outside.

'God Almighty,' breathed Howlett. 'Our mob wouldn't cart
pigs in this.' He produced cigarettes, lit three and passed one each
to Wyndham and the sergeant, and they sat in uncomfortable
silence as the van crawled across the pontoon bridge spanning
the Hooghli and turned right past the Armenian Ghat. Wyndham
watched the play of lights through the high steel-meshed windows
as they bumped over the uneven road, and tried to make his
mind a blank. He'd found this increasingly easy over the last
months. When things appeared too overwhelming he would
retreat within himself and stay there, like an animal in hiding,
until something, often something quite trivial, made life momentarily more bearable – sunlight on the hills above Risalpur as he
walked on exercise round the prison yard the day after he had

been reprieved, Pathan children laughing on the road outside, a coolie in the fields gazing blankly at the passing train suddenly grinning and answering Sergeant Lawson's lewd gesture through the window with an even lewder one. But now there was nothing – no relief. Even his cigarette was hot and acrid and, although he did not recognize it then, he was suffering the added agony of sudden withdrawal from alcohol.

They were crossing the Maidan now, and Howlett, to break the oppressive silence that was weighing on all three of them, said, 'Ever been in this dump before, sir?' and didn't correct it self-consciously to 'Wyndham'.

'Calcutta? Yes – once, to play polo last year,' he answered.

'Bit different this time,' said the sergeant, a man of blunter sensibilities than Howlett. 'I was stationed here in 'nineteen with the Worcesters. Got a bloody big dose in Kariah Road.'

'That accounts for it,' said Howlett. 'They say you go balmy after a couple of years with the sort you get down here.' And they were still bickering acrimoniously when the van turned into the drive that led up to the prison.

They climbed down into the covered runway between the outer and inner gates, and chains were rattling and bolts grating and he stood blinking in the light that reflected back blindingly off the whitewashed walls. Howlett unlocked him from the sergeant and muttered, 'This is where we leave you. Keep your chin up and your nose clean and it will soon be over – and then it'll be Blighty, Home and Beauty. I'd slip you a few annas and some smokes, but these bastards would have it off you and you'd be chalking up your first black mark. Good luck, sir.' And Lawson gave him a thumbs-up sign and winked – and they vanished into a doorway. A small black warder in an ill-fitting uniform was prodding him with a rattan cane and saying, '*Chalo, tum – jaldi! jaldi! jaldi!*' and he was hustled by two others into another door.

An Eurasian assistant surgeon and a couple of minor officials looked at him curiously as he stood in the middle of a small bare office, still in his auto-induced limbo of unreality, and someone was telling him, first in Hindi then in English, to undress, and the small black man was prodding him again and yelling at him to hurry. The assistant surgeon checked them with upraised hand

and said quietly, 'Undress, please. I am sorry, but it is regulations. I will be as quick as possible,' and this small courtesy had the effect of bringing him back to the present, and he found himself blinking back tears. He was thumped and tapped, and the cold circle of the stethoscope explored his chest and back, his teeth were counted and his eyelids turned back and he was being subjected to the squalidness of the 'rigorous bodily search' and he could hear the assistant surgeon's muttered findings being repeated as they were written down, '. . . well-nourished, free from lice and apparent infection . . . unusual body marks nil less small mole two inches seven o'clock right nipple and tattoo mark left forearm, dragon two inches by three-quarters inch . . .', this last the result of a bet he had lost to Rankine.

Then it was over and they had given him some clothes in place of his own, which he saw being checked, listed and stuffed into a numbered canvas bag. There were only two garments in the bundle the warder dropped in front of him, and it wasn't until he had hastily pulled them over his nakedness that he realized that they were the usual convict dress that he had seen on Indian prisoners but had never remotely associated with himself – ungainly blue denim shorts and a smocklike shirt of the same material, with a red diamond-shaped patch bearing a white-stencilled number let into the chest and back. Then somebody else gave him a roughly-woven straw hat and a pair of loose sandals, a blue durri sleeping-mat, a small coarse towel and a round brass pot, but his nerveless fingers couldn't retain them and they fell to the floor.

'So the burra sahib, the great one, the white lord wants a servant – a bearer and a coolie to carry his asbab to his palace, does he?' the small black man almost whispered in Hindi. 'Oh, my friend, what a lot we have to learn, and what a mountain of grief lies before us until we *do* learn it. Pick up those things that a kindly Government, who is father and mother to us all, has given you.'

But once again the mechanism of dissociation had come into function, and he just stood gazing blankly ahead of him, until in the end it was the assistant surgeon who led him gently across the wide prison yard and into a cell in the Transit Section. He put his hand in his pocket and handed Wyndham a small brown pill.

'Here, swallow this,' he said. 'You'll feel even worse in the morning, but at least it will get you through this first night. Cheer up, man. It won't be as bad as this the other end and in a year you will get your own clothes back, and live like a rajah.'

He gagged and retched on the pill but eventually it slipped down, and almost immediately he felt it taking effect and there was a violent drumming in his ears and soft black clouds were enveloping him. The assistant surgeon lowered him on to the durri and then turned back to the grated doorway.

'Make this poor devil's load one whit the heavier, o small brother to the monkeys, and the superintendent sahib learns who sells rations and allows access to the women's wing for two copper pice a time,' he said to the black man.

A white man was standing the other side of the grating looking down at him, and someone in the background was parroting in Hindi, '*Khara ho jao!* Stand up, prisoner, when the great one speaks to you.'

'Get these bloody people out of it,' the white man said in English. 'I want to see him alone.'

There were retreating footsteps and the white man said, 'Wyndham – pull yourself together and listen to me. Here – take this.' He passed a lighted cigarette through the bars. Wyndham took it mechanically and drew on it gratefully, then slowly got the other man into focus. He saw a thin brown face and a clipped military moustache under the brim of a felt pork-pie hat.

'I'm the superintendent – and there's not a damned thing I can do for you outside the strict letter of the Jail Manual. You understand?' Wyndham nodded dully and the other went on, 'You asked for it, you know. If you hadn't invoked this stupid Indian Statutory Native thing you'd have gone into the European Wing of the Allahabad Jail and you'd have been half-way home to England by this time. But you're here now and you've just got to make the best of it. *There's no special provision for a European serving a life term* – not here, anyway – but I understand things will be different the other end. If you can stick it out for the next two or three days the worst will be over, but if you don't think you can you'd better say so now, and I'll get the medical people to move you into hospital, but that will only be prolonging things because you'll miss the chalan and you'll be here in Alipore for the next three months until the December draft. So what's it to be? Hospital, or bite on the bullet?'

'I'll stay,' mumbled Wyndham.

'I think you're wise,' the other said. 'You've hit the bottom of the shaft here. From now on things can only improve, as long as you don't lose your grip. Hang on to that – it's the philosophy of most of the customers who pass through this place. The sensible ones. Give me that cigarette butt, please, or you'll be earning a bad mark. Good luck.'

And somehow he did manage to hang on until the third morning, when the clanging of a bell in the Transit Wing woke him long before dawn. Doors and gratings were being thrown back and warders were yelling in Hindi, 'Up! Up! Princes of Light, Favoured of Allah, Chosen of Rama. Over the Black Water, where unspeakable delights await you: food fit for kings, sahibs' whiskee-soda, and lovely fat whores like only unto the houris of Paradise. Stir yourselves, pig-begotten sons of noseless mothers!'

The Transit Wing had been a strictly khamosh (silent) area up to now, and Wyndham had hitherto heard only the subsonic hum inseparable from all prisons, and the constant hawking, spitting and coughing which is as much part of life in India as breathing. But now khamosh was shattered with a vengeance and a thousand convicts were yelling in seemingly as many different languages – screaming abuse, cursing, singing and beating on the walls with their brass lotas, and the warders seemed to be taking it all in good part – kidding, jeering and laughing.

They were herded out into the yard under floodlights arranged along the parapet of the surrounding walls, and Wyndham saw a continuous line of Armed Constabulary elbow to elbow in khaki uniforms topped with red and blue glengarry caps, incongruous above dark Bengali faces, with bayonets fixed on Lee Enfield rifles. Then they were counted and checked, recounted and checked again, finally arrangee in groups of twenty, two by two in double file, and from somewhere chains were being dragged and laid on the ground between the pairs – chains that put Wyndham in mind of a charm bracelet he had once bought a girl in London, with miniature thimbles, keys and lucky black cats on it, but on this one the charms were heavy and very rusty handcuffs. They were fastened to it – right wrist, left wrist, according to which side of the chain they happened to be standing. He was unlucky in that it was his right wrist that was fettered.

A white officer snapped an order and the Constabulary moved smartly into position each side of the fifty groups, and the big gates swung open and they moved forward and out into Belvedere Road. The yelling had now ceased and someone at the head of the column had started a long, high, tremulous dirge that had a sort of beat to it that automatically their feet kept time to – slower than military marching tempo and without its lilt. The song was being taken up along the column in a patois of several languages which Wyndham couldn't at first understand except for the last two lines of each stanza – '*Kala Pani, Kala Pani, hamlog até hain*' which he translated as 'Black Water, Black Water, Here we people come.' He wondered dully what this meant. He had heard the term several times this morning. Kala Pani was the generic name in most Indian languages for the ocean, so he assumed that it was a reference to Madras, which was on the coast.

It was getting light now and, in spite of himself, Wyndham started to check their route. The Maidan was ahead of them, with the grey bulk of Fort William overshadowing the Hooghli, and further on was Government House, where the polo team had been guests. He remembered the governor's matronly wife who had clucked kindly over the younger members of the party, and he grinned wanly as he pictured Her Excellency's face in the unlikely event of her looking out through the stately portals of the place as the column passed, and recognizing him, and for the first time he was thankful for his hideous palmetto hat which flopped down over his face in a ragged veil.

But the head of the column swung left before the Maidan, and they skirted the racecourse and crossed Diamond Harbour Road, and ahead of them Wyndham saw lights reflecting off the stippled surface of the river, and above the morning mist, the masts and funnels of ships. The road was crowded with coolies making their way to the docks at Kidderpore, and squads of police were clearing a way for the column with their steel-shod lathis. Two drunken British sailors, returning to their ship tight-packed in a

one-man rickshaw, were bellowing 'Yes, We Have No Bananas
. . .', and one of them threw a cigarette over the heads of the
escort. It landed among Wyndham's group and caused a riot as
the convicts fought and clawed for it. Wyndham, his wrist nearly
dislocated, was dragged sideways on the chain and he went down
under a rain of threshing feet. He struggled upright through the
press of sweating bodies only to receive a whistling thump across
the shoulders from a lathi, which sent him down again. His
partner on the chain hauled him to his feet and snarled in Urdu,
'On the ground you'll die, fool, when the boys get excited.
Haven't you learned that yet?' And to add to his misery he found
that he had lost one of his sandals.

They turned off the Dock Road at last and halted on a long
ramshackle wooden wharf to which a battered, rust-streaked
cargo steamer was moored. Wyndham made out the name *Ramuri*
on her high fo'c'slehead. The escort NCOs were shouting, 'Sit
down all of you, and shut up' and he sank down thankfully but
awkwardly, European fashion with his legs stretched out in front
of him, instead of on his haunches as the others were doing. His
chainmate glanced at him curiously and noticed his one bare foot.

'Lost a chapli, have you?' he said. 'Fourteen days' rigorous
punishment when the bastards find that out. What are you? A
fool – or just an amateur?' Wyndham looked away without
answering, and the other shook the chain between them per-
emptorily. 'I speak to you, son of an owl. Lost your tongue, or
are you another of these Southern soors who doesn't understand
decent Urdu?'

'Neither one nor the other,' Wyndham said wearily. 'Just one
who desires a little peace.'

There was a long moment of silence, then the other said
quietly, 'Munshi's Urdu – *officer-sahib's* Urdu – and sitting like a
babu in an office. Salaam, brother. I have heard of you. I come
from the Punjab border and served for a time in the Frontier
Force. I know my way about. Stay close to me.'

'Have I any other option?' Wyndham asked sourly.

'You mean the chain? That is only for the march down. They
unlock us on the ship.'

'How do you know?'

'My second journey to the Kala Pani. There was a killing – just a friendly affair in the family, but the new commissioner sahib called it murder, the fool, and I was sent over the water. My officer sahibs made a great outcry because I am a brave man, holder of the Indian Distinguished Service Medal won in the Great War, so I was paroled.'

'Why are you coming back?' Wyndham asked, and the other chuckled.

'A bhai-bundi – a tribal brother, you understand? – made free of my two wives in my absence. One I could have overlooked, but the second was a pearl of great beauty, the bitch, and had cost me five oxen and a camel – so it became an affair of honour, naturally, and again they called it murder. Kismet – here I am once more, this time for life. Still, there are worse places than the Kala Pani, sahib.'

'Don't call me "sahib",' Wyndham told him.

'You are right. There are many here – politicals mostly – who do not like the sahib-log. What shall I call you then? Um, let me see. Sirdar? – yes, that can mean anything from wise man to soldier.' He turned and regarded Wyndham closely. 'As tall as I – six feet – and like me, with the mark of the drill square upon you even as you stumbled in these damned sandals over the paving stones; sun-blackened and with dark hair, but the eyes are blue – still, so are those of many Pathans and Baluchis. You'll pass among these animals without rousing too much curiosity – until you speak the sahib's bhat – very pukkha and British haw-haw. Do you know any other languages?'

'Pushtu and a little Hindi.'

'Good. Mix them all up a little, and sometimes put in a sahib's "shit", "bloody" and "bastard", then you will sound like a soldier and not many will take liberties. If they do, say, once again in the sahib's tongue, "Fuck off", which is understood by all, and push hard in the face with the flat of the palm – which is also understood by all.'

'Thank you, my friend,' Wyndham said, then they were called back on to their feet and the head of the column started up the gangway.

The thin drizzling rain of the dying monsoon was falling, and their scanty clothing was soaked by the time Wyndham and the big Punjabi reached the deck. A warder unlocked them and

66

another checked their numbers against a list, and Armed Constabulary sepoys, who seemed to be more cordially detested by the convicts than the regular police, hastened their passage along to the gaping, grating-covered hatches on the foredeck with darting bayonet points. Two white-clad ship's officers leaned on the rail watching them, and Wyndham heard one of them say, 'Jesus! These buggers stink worse every trip. It'll be a relief to be back on the pilgrim run.'

The Punjabi elbowed him aside as he was about to step over the coaming and on to the ladder that led down into the bowels of the hold. 'After me, bhai,' he said, and winked.

Down they went into the gloom and the stench of bodies and cattle-dip disinfectant, then, near the bottom, the Punjabi, who was now four men ahead of Wyndham, slipped and brought others down with him into a flailing mass of arms and legs, and for some minutes there was near panic as men screamed and cursed. He felt his arm gripped and he was drawn aside and there was a fat chuckle in his ear.

'Here's a chapli for the left foot,' the Punjabi whispered. 'Now let us claim two places near the bars where we can breathe, while these stupid bastards are still rubbing their bruises and wailing.'

Above them a ship's bell started to clang and it brought silence for a moment. Looking up he could see white-topped uniform caps against the sky and someone was bellowing in English through a megaphone. 'Right, munshis, translate the usual bullshit to them. The trip takes four days. Only one ration issue a day, so they'd better watch their grub. Good behaviour – play the game with us and we'll play the game with them. Any arsing about and they'll get the steam hoses turned on 'em – and a bloody good paddywhacking when we get to the Andamans. Use the latrine buckets and not the deck. Carry on, Mr Thompson, please.'

Chapter 7

The shock was still upon him after they had dropped the eighty miles down the Hooghli from Calcutta to the open sea. 'Madras,' he kept repeating. 'They said they were sending me to Madras.'

'I do not know Madras,' the Punjabi shrugged, 'but I am told it is full of dirty little black Indian Christians who sell their mothers and sisters to any with four copper paisa to spare. The Andamans are not bad, Sirdar. Believe me – I have been there.'

'But – but prisoners never come back,' Wyndham faltered.

'*I* came back.'

'You were a special case.'

'Allah the Compassionate! Aren't *you*? I've never heard of a sahib being there before – not as a prisoner I mean. You won't stay for long, I'll wager. Here – eat some of these chapattis and some jaggri. Soon this accursed ship will start to dance like a Hindu temple whore and all these animals will be sick, and you won't want to eat. Come on, Sirdar – we're soldiers, you and I'.

'What is your name?'

'I'm Mirza, son of Sadaq, but here I prefer to be called Jawan.'

'But "Jawan" just means "soldier",' Wyndham said.

'Exactly. That is the way of Indian prisons. Try to be known by your number or a nickname. That way your own name stays clean until you come out again. Not that it matters in my case. I have killed twice, so I am there until I die.'

'It doesn't seem to worry you.'

'Why should it? What is written is written, and worrying won't *un*write it. No, I'm not worrying, Sirdar. I shall do my year in the Cellular Jail and then come out and get my old job back as ganger to a logging crew. The Government pays seven rupees a month to outside workers, and if you keep the idle bastards under you hard at it, the Timber Company will give you another twenty-three. That is more than I was ever paid in the army.'

'But your family, your friends, your home?' Wyndham said. 'Don't you want to see them again?'

Jawan chuckled. 'No more than they want to see me. I left with rifle bullets pinging round my arse after my last tamasha. The man I killed came from a strong branch of the tribe. My old father, with tears running down into his white beard, begged me in the name of the Prophet to take myself off and never come back. In truth, I'm not at all certain that it was not he who told the police where they might find me. He has five other sons, all of whom work hard and do as they are told.'

'But to spend the rest of one's life as a prisoner – doesn't it *mean* anything to you?'

'Yes, it means that I wasn't hanged, and for that I am thankful – as you should be, Sirdar, if I am not being offensive.' He stretched and flexed his muscles. 'I told you, the Andamans are not bad – as long as one remembers that one is a man among rats and maintains one's pride. Soon I shall have a platoon of these same rats working for me, and I'll have a small hut with a vegetable plot in front of it, with a patch of tobacco – and a woman or two to care for my comfort.'

'Are there women convicts there?'

'Not convicts. There are the locals – small and ugly as monkeys and as like to knife you as not as the fancy takes them, but even they are better than nothing. No, the proper bundabas is to have one's own sent out from India, which a lifer can do after four years' good behaviour. Then, of course, there are the daughters, and in some cases the widows, of other long-term prisoners – if one can save enough for the dowry. Have you left a woman behind you, Sirdar?'

'None that matters.'

'You are not legally married?'

'No.'

'That is good. One can only import one's pukkha wife, and can only get married out here if one is officially shown as single in India. In the case of a sahib, who I understand is only allowed one wife at a time, it could make for difficulties. But don't worry. We'll be coming out of the Cellular Prison at the same time, and I'll arrange something unofficially for you.'

'What about children?' Wyndham asked.

'They are born free,' Jawan said. 'When they come of age they can leave the islands if they wish, though not many do. There are government schools there and the intelligent ones get good jobs with the prison administration or the Timber Company, or go into business, or become fishermen or farmers, or open shops. There are always opportunities for the hooshiarwala – the clever man. Some have become very rich. Cheer up, Sirdar. I am a humble man from the Upper Punjab and I do not wish to presume – but I *am* a man, as are you, and I think if we care to throw in our lot together that there can be much for us over the Kala Pani.'

They ran into a violent monsoon hurricane the first night and for twenty-four hours they weltered in a pitch-black hell filled with the moaning and screaming of terrified men. A narrow shelf ran round their portion of the hold, some three feet above the deck, and Jawan swept it clean of bodies as one would sweep flies from a table, and dragged Wyndham up on to it, then secured both of them to projections with turbans he had snatched from Sikhs in the darkness, and there they rode it out, at least clear of the sludge of vomit and the contents of overturned latrine buckets that slopped ankle-deep and overflowed the bilges.

The crew unbattened the hatches when the storm had blown itself out, and allowed them up on deck in squads and mercifully turned the salt-water hoses on them. Wyndham, lying more dead than alive in the scuppers, heard someone say in English. 'Is this the white man?' and felt a foot stirring his ribs. He opened his eyes and nodded feebly, and the stirrer, a ship's officer, said, 'I don't give a damn what the bloody warders say – let the poor bastard stay up on deck until we get in tomorrow.' He saw Jawan being hustled off with the others towards the hatch, and he managed to croak, 'That chap saved my life down below. Can you let him stay up here – *please*?' The officer nodded curtly and Jawan crawled back gratefully, and later, when it was dark, someone dropped some fresh fruit and white bread beside them, without a word – and then some cigarettes and matches.

'You see what I mean, Sirdar,' chuckled Jawan, whose recuperative powers exceeded Wyndham's. 'There are always opportunities for the hooshiarwala. We at least stayed above the shit and pig-swill down below – and now we feast like rajahs.'

The rattle and splash of the anchor woke him, and he rose and leaned on the rail and studied the shore. They were in a long harbour that was enclosed by two curving spits of land with lighthouses winking alternately at their seaward extremities, and ahead of them was a cluster of lights that were paling in the early dawn. A soft breeze was blowing from the shore, bringing the damp smell of recent rain on hot soil, and above the lights of the town he could make out the crests of low hills against the sky. Jawan ranged up beside him.

'Port Blair, Sirdar,' he said softly. 'There, to the right where the other lights are, is the Cellular Prison. You will see it when the sun comes up – very nice and white, like the Taj Mahal. We, you and I and maybe a few others – the murderers and therefore men to be feared and respected – will be in the dangerous wing, away from these thieves and rapers of their sisters. Stay close together when they handcuff us to the chain, and with luck we will have cells on the same landing.'

Then the ship's officer came up and said, 'Right, you blokes had better get down below again. We've squared the guards on board, but the ones from the shore might get a bit raspy if they find you loose on deck.'

'Thank you,' said Wyndham simply as they moved away.

'Don't mention it,' said the other, and added awkwardly, 'Best of luck. It's not too bad here, from what they tell me.'

It was light when they came up again and the hills were achingly green against the blue of the sky, the town a cluster of low dun-coloured buildings and, dominating the low land between it and the sea, was the prison, stark and white behind high walls. There were launches and tenders alongside now, and a double line of sepoy warders made a corridor to the gangway leading down the ship's side. They filed through, Wyndham close on Jawan's heels, and an Anglo-Indian officer in a white uniform checked their numbers on a long list and called out, 'Two more "D's". Put 'em on Number 5 chain,' and he found himself once more yoked with Jawan.

They chugged the few hundred yards to the jetty below the prison, herded together on a flat lighter, and the other prisoners, subdued and frightened until now, started falteringly to sing again, '*Kala Pani, Kala Pani, hamlog até hain,*' drumming to the rhythm with their feet on the hot iron deck. They scrambled

71

ashore, and sepoys were shouting, '*Panch namba pahla! – panch namba pahla!*' and Jawan laughed happily and said, 'That means Number 5. What did I tell you? Nine of us, and we go ahead of the rabble.'

They marched up the slope and went in under the archway while 'the rabble' were still being counted and checked on the jetty. The short passage between the outer and inner gates was arched and vaulted, and the walls were covered with a fresco of polished chains and antique fetters and long, inch-thick canes. Jawan jerked his head towards the canes as they passed. 'To warm the backs and arses of the stupid and unwary, Sirdar,' he said. 'One of the best jobs in the prison, flogging. Always given to two Pathans or Punjabis, one of whom must be left-handed so they can work together. Eight annas and double rations for each job. *You're* not left-handed by any chance, are you? No? Pity. We might have done well as a team.'

They halted in the blinding sun and Wyndham looked up at the main bulk of the prison. Eight radiating spokes, he saw, with a central tower as the hub – three-storeyed, with lines of small barred windows on one side and vertical bars on the other. He felt a sharp dig in the small of his back, and a voice snarled behind him, 'Look to your front, owl,' and for a moment red rage almost choked him and he spun round, but Jawan with a quick twist of the chain between them pulled him up short. 'Easy, Sirdar, easy,' he muttered out of the side of his mouth. 'Plenty of time to deal with that Bengali bastard when you know your way around. I'll have the black son of a whore eating out of our hands inside a week – you see.'

A table and chair had been set out in a patch of shade, and another officer in a white uniform came out of the main building, attended by two Indian warders, and sat down.

Jawan whispered. 'Big man – next to the burra sahib super-intendent himself. Sergeant in British Army before he came here.'

They filed up before him singly and Wyndham found himself looking into a face that was brick-red from the sun rather than brown, pink round the jowls from a recent shave, with pale blue eyes like pack-ice, and a clipped ginger moustache. His white helmet with the red pagri of the Prisons Department sat squarely on his head like a guardsman's bearskin, and his tunic with the gleaming silver buttons, although showing the incipient damp patches round the collar and under the arms of the heavy sweater was, as yet, still fresh-laundered and starched. The man looked at him directly but expressionlessly and Wyndham felt his own eyes shifting and dropping like those of a menial being taken to task. He wanted desperately to return the stare, but he was too conscious of his straggly month-old beard and stinking clothes.

The man said quietly, 'Can you read?' then, 'I'm not being funny. That's a question I must ask everybody. If the answer's yes, you get a copy of *Gaol Regulations* in your cell in your mother tongue, which means you get to know your way around quicker and save yourself a lot of trouble.' He made a tick on the list in front of him and answered his own question. 'Yes – English. You'll be in chowki here for a year, Wyndham, which may be cut down by the superintendent to a shorter period if he thinks you are really trying. There's no special treatment for Europeans – get that absolutely straight. You'll have to work like the rest – and work very hard. Your Andaman number is E oblique B, seven, three, five, two. Until they get to know your name, or nickname, the warders – that's the havildars, naiks and sepoys, who are mostly Bengalis and Garwhalis and don't speak English – will generally address you by the last three figures of your number, in your case "teen, panch, do". Remember that. The superintendent will be seeing you some time within the next two days. I, incidentally, am the chief gaoler – that's the second-in-command – and my name is Mr Meakin. And now, finally, I have to ask you if you have any questions, requests or complaints – and once again I am not being funny.'

'None,' said Wyndham.

'Sir or sahib,' said Mr Meakin. 'Please yourself which, but don't forget in future, or you'll find yourself on report. That goes for every officer here, including the jemadars and subedars – Indians, like you had in the Army. And you take your hat off and hold it in front of you with both hands when you're being spoken to. You'll find it all in the Book.'

'No complaints, sir,' Wyndham said, removing his hat. 'But I would like a bath.'

'You'll be getting the lot – shave, haircut and a delousing –

73

before kit issue. Right – hat on, pace to the rear, and rejoin your squad smartly.'

Wyndham went back to his place thinking of his first interview with the regimental sergeant-major at Sandhurst – 'I call you "sir", you call me "sir", but by Christ *you* better mean it – sir.' And he was actually grinning for the first time in months.

Jawan muttered warningly, 'Don't laugh, Sirdar. That bastard can see right through the back of a man's head,' and then went forward as his transit number was called.

They bathed then, long lines of men in G-strings, for Indians, even in prison, are surprisingly old-maidish about complete nudity, wading waist-deep through troughs of sea-water like cattle-dips that reeked of raw carbolic, scrubbing themselves with handsful of sand and ashes that made their bug-bites and septic sores sting unbearably but which helped to wash away the memories of the hell of the last five days. Then they were shaved by convict barbers wielding shears and blunt razors – heads, faces and pubic hair – anywhere that could nurture lice – and dry-fumigated, medically inspected by a team of Anglo-Indian assistant surgeons, and documented and fingerprinted once again, and finally, at the blacksmith's forge, their 'chakas' were fitted to their necks on chains and riveted into place – discs of mild steel bearing stamped letters and figures that told the initiated the number, category and sentence of the wearer. Their filthy transit garments were collected and others issued in lieu, and Wyndham found himself in possession of two coarse white smocks with red diamonds on front and back on which his number was stencilled while he waited, and a pair of shorts and one of slacks with broad red stripes let into the side seams, sisal-soled sandals, two G-strings and a somewhat better made straw hat than his transit one, a towel, two scratchy blankets and a coarse grey khaddah sheet, a bolster, a linen bag and a collection of zinc and earthenware vessels, a bundle of twigs like a miniature witch's broom, and throughout the protracted business of collecting them and giving 'daskat' thumbprints on the receipt vouchers, Jawan was at his elbow explaining the use of each.

'One set of clothes for work, Sirdar, and one kept clean in the cell to wear at night after the bath. They realize here that we men of importance like to keep ourselves clean – not like these misbegotten offscourings from the mainland prisons. The pots – one for food, the other for water, and twice a week even tea. The big clay chatthi with the lid – that is a kunda for what may be necessary in the night, and for one small bidi cigarette, an Untouchable will empty and clean it for you each morning. The twigs? Chew the ends into fibres and use them to clean your teeth, with a little salt . . .'

And then at last it was over and the nine khatarnakwalas (dangerous men) were led into one of the spokes on the southern side, and up three flights of clanging iron stairs, with the jubilant Jawan muttering behind him, 'The top landing – excellent, Sirdar, excellent. There we get the sea breezes at night, and you can see over the wall to where the women do their washing at the dhobi ghat . . .'

The cell was larger than he expected, and clinically clean and airy – twelve feet or so deep and a little more than half that across. There was a small window and a ventilator in the rear wall, while the front one and the door were formed entirely by bars, as was the opposite wall of the landing which looked out into the open. The sepoy warder clanged the door to on him and went on with the others, and Wyndham heard Jawan chortling happily. 'I am here, Sirdar – right next door. I felt this was a lucky day. Kismet. But now to work. Arrange things as I tell you, then we will get a good mark from the ghee-gutted fool of a havildar when he comes round at the same time as the food. Your bed, the cement platform in the corner – harder than a Delhi whore's heart, but you soon get used to it, two blankets folded on top – finger-tip to elbow-length just like the army, khaddar on top of that – same size, towel on top of that again, clean clothes out of sight under the blankets, food and water bowls on top of the lot, upside down. Tomorrow I will show you how to shine them with sand and ashes. Kunda in the right-hand corner as you stand with your back to the bars. Ha! Do it all like that – two cells properly turned out for inspection without our having to be shown – and Havildar Purandari will be blinded by wonderment.'

'Do I have to call this one "sir" or "sahib"?' Wyndham asked.

'No, he would think you were making a mock of him. Just "Havildar-ji", but you stand to attention when he speaks to you. He's not a bad little rat as warders go – rejected for the Army because of flat feet – but he likes to imagine he's a hell of a bahaduri.'

There was an approaching rattle of pans and degshies on the lower landings, and the subsonic hum, never completely stilled in a prison, rose to a crescendo as pots were rattled against bars, and hungry men howled like animals at feeding time in a zoo. Then a short, stout man in smart khaki, with the intricately wound turban of the Maharatti, was rapping on the bars of his door with a heavy babul baton. Wyndham stood to attention, looking to his front at his own height rather than directly at the other, as seemed to be the prison custom.

'Shabash (well done),' said the havildar, looking past him at the correctly arranged kit. 'A soldier, eh? I understand and respect soldiers. I am an educated man, speaking some English – "you playing games with me, I am playing games with you", isn't it? Have they given you a name yet?' he went on in Hindi.

'Wyn . . .' began Wyndham, but Jawan called out from the next cell.

'All men are calling him "Sirdar", Havildar-ji.'

'Oh, and who is talking to you, bloody Jawan?' the havildar asked. 'Not liking it outside, eh? Got to come back to the old Kala Pani. Who did you kill this time?'

'Some miserable little sod who said all prison officers were bastards, who never slipped a soldier an occasional cigarette, even soldiers who kept their cells like palaces, and worked like ten men and earned their havildars much shabash from the super-intendent sahib,' Jawan answered unhesitatingly. 'I tried to tell him that there was such a one here – a prince among prison officers who . . .'

'Fill their bowls – and that fool's mouth,' grinned the havildar to the orderlies behind him, and winked at Wyndham and passed on.

He found he had a large bowl of dal or split peas and curried vegetables, and he recognized the savoury smell of the sesame oil in which they had been cooked, and four great chappatis, and in the second bowl was a pint of lukewarm over-sugared tea.

'How many chapattis, Sirdar?' called Jawan.

'Four.'

76

'And the dal-bhat? Up to the top, or two fingers below the rim?'

'Up to the top.'

'Double rations – and the little bastard dropped me two cigarettes and a match. We'll smoke them later, after lights out, but be careful to mask the glow from the open bars. Ha – ai-ee! What did I tell you? Not such a bad place, is it? And the old jadoo magic still works.'

Wyndham, full-fed, leaned on the bars and looked out. The sun was sinking over the hills behind the prison, and the sea was casting the crimson reflection back and bathing the white walls in a glow of pink.

He felt almost at peace.

Chapter 8

'Lieutenant-Colonel P. J. R. McClintock, MRCS, LRCP (Lond.), LSA (Dublin), Indian Medical Service, Superintendent Andaman Islands Dependency Penal Establishment,' the highly polished brass plate at the entrance to the Central Administration Block stated. 'Barracuda' the convicts called him, which is a large and fierce fish found in those waters, more dreaded than the shark or giant manta ray. It is also an Urdu pun. 'Bara' means great, and 'Khuda' God. The implication was a little unfair on both counts. He was neither large nor fierce and, to quote him in his more mordant moments, 'If I could walk on the waves and turn water into potable liquors, I wouldn't be stuck on an island in the Bay of Bengal with three thousand wicked bastards. I'd be chief production manager for Guinness's, back in Dublin.' Which didn't mean that he disliked his job or wasn't very good at it. He had no strong feelings one way or the other. Actually he was a frustrated gynaecologist, who, after several years' service as regimental medical officer on almost entirely male-populated stations on the Frontier, had applied for transfer to the Civil List of the IMS in the hope of a hospital posting to one of the garrison towns in Lower India, where the sexes were rather more evenly balanced. Unfortunately he chose a time when the Central Government was implementing a somewhat idealistic policy of reformation rather than retribution, and appointing doctors to the formerly purely disciplinary office of superintendent at the larger prisons. It was a forward-looking and laudably humane measure, but the fact remained that it was still the Meakins who ran the day-to-day routine of the system. McClintock was facing his chief gaoler now.

'With all due respect, sir,' Meakin was saying.

'Which means that you are about to come out with something peculiarly offensive,' smiled the superintendent. 'Sit down, George. You worry me standing there like a drum-major. What have you got against the feller – other than that he's an ex-officer?'

'Again with respect, sir,' said Meakin, sitting and removing his helmet. 'It wouldn't make any difference to me if he was an ex-Prime Minister, bishop or towel-boy in a joyhouse. As far as I'm concerned he's a second stage prisoner who's been here exactly six months.'

'How has he behaved in that six months?'

'Clean sheet – like eighty-five-point-five per cent of the rest of the chalan he came with. The eighty-five-point-five who aren't being suggested for parole six months ahead of their time.'

'What is the purpose of this first twelve months in chowki, George?'

'To straighten 'em out, knock some discipline into 'em, and to impress on them that they'll come back here at the double if they kick over the traces when they go out on parole . . .'

'Quite. You're talking in percentages. We're agreed, I take it, that over ninety per cent of the people here are illiterate. Right?'

'Yes, sir . . .'

'Which means that they can't read the Book, so it has to be fed to them line by line – and it's a bloody big Book. It takes time. This fellow *can* read. David Nehemiah, the school instructor, tells me he is word perfect. Second point – discipline.' He counted on his fingers. 'English public school – which can be considerably more uncomfortable and certainly just as rigidly run as this damned place – I've had some. Then Sandhurst – not exactly a bed of roses, I'm told. Then three years in a cavalry regiment on the Frontier. I think it can be assumed that he knows the meaning of discipline . . .'

'Didn't seem to do him much good though, did it?'

'Ever scrump apples from an orchard when you were a boy, George?'

'Yes – and I've done a bit of poaching in my time, too, but I never roasted nobody over a slow fire, nor shot a gamekeeper. Jesus, sir, you're not reckoning this bloke as just a jolly laughing boy having a bit of a lark, are you? He's no different from the rest of the dacoits and goondahs out there. He's a vicious young bastard – a murderer – and he's let his colour down . . .'

'*Ah!* Now we're coming to the real point of it. *That's* what you've got against him, isn't it? He's let the Sahib-log down . . .'

Meakin grimaced like a man drinking vinegar. 'The Sahib-log

means the gentry – the nobs – people like yourself. Me? If I wasn't in the army or this Service I'd probably be a bricklayer's labourer or on the dole. The Sahib-log doesn't mean a monkey's wang to me, sir. Order does, proper running and pukkha drill does, and blokes doing what they're told does, because it's in the Book. That's all. I don't give a damn whether they're black, white, brindle or khaki. To me they're all cons, and that man is just another of 'em – one that talks posh, and who would treat me like a bit of crap if he wasn't scared rigid of me, but otherwise no different from the rest.'

'You give yourself away with every word, George,' McClintock said. 'You've got a grudge against him – not because you think he's from the other side of the railroad tracks, but because he's *crossed* those tracks – the wrong way – and it offends your God-given, Aldershot-blessed sense of order. So it's thumbs down on my little experiment in early rehabilitation, is it?'

'You're the boss, sir. If you want to turn him loose ahead of his turn, who am I to argue?' Meakin shrugged.

'Don't get miffish with *me*, George,' McClintock said sharply. 'You know perfectly well that I don't fly in your face in matters of administration. Only policy. All right – no parole yet, but I see no objection to making him a convict overseer at the moment. Do you?'

'I'd rather have that big Punjabi they call Jawan. He knows the ropes – been here before.'

'Doesn't seem to have done *him* much good either,' grinned McClintock.

'They look at things different from us, sir. He went back to his village and found some coon had been screwing his woman. He had no option but to knock him off – or be branded lily-livered.'

'Second killing,' McClintock said. 'He was lucky not to have been hanged.'

'Bloody good regimental association pulling for him,' grunted Meakin, rising and putting his helmet on. 'Very good, sir. Sirdar teen, panch, do, for CO. I'll put it in orders.'

'Put them both up,' McClintock said.

'Sorry, sir, there's only one vacancy.'

'Oh, for Christ's sake stop throwing the Book at me, Mr Meakin,' McClintock snapped. 'I said put them both up.'

'Jawan sath, ath, char, for CO also, sir,' said Meakin expressionlessly. 'Very good, sir.' He saluted, stamped, turned and marched stiffly to the door.

'You will wear a pukkha sahib's topee, and I a blue Punjabi turban instead of these cursed camel's dinners, and both of us will have leather belts, and proper army chaplis and we carry babul truncheons that will fell an elephant, properly used,' Jawan said happily. 'And we get wheaten chapattis instead of jowari, and meat twice a week and tea every day, and we go outside in charge of work parties, and our cell doors remain unlocked from reveille to sundown for us to come and go at will. And we have a whistle on a chain just like the warders, and all men tremble at our coming, and the sepoys show us proper respect because they have to rely upon us to report any budmasheri (villainy) we hear about among the lower orders. And we get *five rupees* in prison paper money each month to spend at the canteen, and as many bidis as we can smoke. Oh, Sirdar, didn't I tell you there was much for us here if we threw in our lot together?'

'What about these bloody chains round our necks?' Wyndham asked. 'Do we lose those?'

'Regretfully, no, Sirdar – not until we gain full parole – but we have shirts that button to the neck instead of smocks, so they are hidden. Wah! Wah! Ajib! Allah looks kindly upon me, and the God the mission padre talks about seems to be looking after you, also.'

Wyndham had been called from the sisal baling shed that morning, where he had worked a full eight hours every day since arrival, clad only in a G-string, plastered with the dust that mixed with sweat and penetrated every crevice in the body, and scarified by the saw-edged fibres. Double armful from the heaps that were brought in bullock carts by outside working parties and dumped behind them – raised shoulder high – head high – pause – balance – bring down on the spikes of the endless belt that clacked and rumbled the length of the shed – step back – turn – another armful – shoulder high – head high – pause – bring down on the spikes – to the rhythm of '*Kala Pani, Kala Pani, hamlog até hain.*'

He was strong – stronger than the majority of the chronically malnourished who worked there, but he hadn't their knack of detaching himself in a yogalike trance and working unfeelingly, almost unconsciously, until the whistle blew every fifty-five minutes and they turned to the water chatthis that stood in a row outside the shed – red for Hindus, green for Muslims, yellow for Buddhists, and white-daubed for the Untouchables and Christians – to drink until their bellies distended, before the whistle blew once more at the end of the all too short five minutes' break, and the rhythm took up again – '*Kala Pani, Kala Pani, hamlog até hain*' – and sometimes he would be overcome with the heat, noise and dust and would crumple at the knees. But always Jawan was there at his side to haul him back to his feet and into the rhythm again, because to fall out was 'dhargabazi' which meant fraudulent malingering unless real sickness was confirmed at the hospital – and dhargabazi could earn another four hours' work after the rest of the shift had returned to their cells.

Meakin, the eternal old soldier, had said, 'I've been watching you, Sirdar – watching you very closely. You've done all right – took it like a man, with no lead-swinging, so I put a word in for you with the superintendent and he agreed with me, and you're to be a CO – that's Convict Overseer not bloody Commanding Officer – you and your mucking-in chum Jawan. Piece of cake it is – if you keep your nose clean – get me? Your nose clean and your ears and eyes open. Any little thing you pick up that you think I ought to know about, you tell me quietly after morning orders – *me*, not the jemadars or subedars. OK? You play the game with me, I play the game with you, and before long I'll be putting you up for full parole. Dismiss.'

'Thank you, sir,' Wyndham murmured, bowed, and took the regulation pace to the rear.

'Everything to gain – everything to lose,' Jawan had told him as they sat in the open passageway outside their unlocked cells that night, smoking openly and polishing their new belts and chaplis with spit and beeswax stolen from the saddler's shop. 'Here your education begins, because we don't want to lose *anything*. First thing – never trust a Sikh, a Sindhi or a Bengali. Secondly – learn to recognize the criminal tribesmen, the Vetalpujawalas – they that are born to crime and who sacrifice to their god with stolen gold and human blood at the first full moon after Dushera, the

Hindu festival which falls after the break of the monsoon. Learn also about the Rumalwalas – the adepts of Thuggee, who strangle with a silk scarf when they rob. There are not many of the latter here, though, because they are generally hanged in India when they are caught. I know only of two – I will point them out to you. One is a warder.'

'And they can't be trusted either, I take it?' Wyndham said.

'On the contrary, once *they* trust *you* they'll go to the gallows mute before betraying you.'

'How do you know when they trust you?'

'A grip of the hand – thus – like the sahibs' freemasons give each other. Do it again, Sirdar. No, not quite – *thus*. That's better – and again. Good. And from a distance, a sign like this – watch carefully. It must be done quickly, so that none but the initiated may notice and recognize it – so – hand wiping the sweat from one's face thus – thumb thus. No, *thus*. That's better. Again – and again. Good. And the answer – thus – flicking the snot from the nose like an ignorant and uncouth man. That's right. Now, again – and again – and again. Perfect.'

'But when do you give these signs – and why?' Wyndham asked.

'The answer to both is, when you need help, Sirdar,' Jawan said. 'That can be at any time – here inside the prison, or outside when parole comes. Up till today you've been a babe in a steel and concrete womb; now you go into the world again. Let me give an example. When I was a CO here last time I saw a Sikh trip a sepoy warder in the saw mill. I managed to grab the warder, but not before both his legs had been completely severed by the circular saw. He died later. I chased the Sikh and felled him with my baton, and dragged him before the havildar. He was tried and later hanged on the gallows here in the yard, and before the trap was sprung he called out in a loud voice, "Sikhs – bring vengeance upon Jawan." There was a howl from all the long-haired whiskery swine who were craning their necks from their locked cells of "We will be revenged." I was on duty on the gallows, and I gave a rude gesture to them with my baton as the bastard dropped and his neck snapped. I was very brave, because that morning I had been told that I was not only coming up for full parole, but that I was to be repatriated to India – and freed.'

He lit another bidi from the butt of the previous one and then went on, 'I was not feeling quite so brave a month later when I was given a railway ticket on Howrah Station in Calcutta and told to get back to the Punjab and to keep out of trouble in future. I am a Muslim, and as such I am not supposed to drink strong liquor, but I am not a bigot and I had developed a taste for it in the army, so I had had three or four large Bengali rums, and I went to sleep at the end of a long third-class railway carriage. When I fell asleep there was the usual crowd of women, children, Hindus and Muslims that one finds on any train, but when I awoke they all seemed to have got off at stations the train had stopped at, and in their places were about fifty Sikhs, and I was unarmed and alone, and they were looking at me – just looking – and my belly turned over. I wondered why they had not already cut my throat – then I saw the reason. There were three railway policemen escorting a chained criminal at the other end of the carriage, and they could not risk it. But then we came to another station, and the police party got off. I tried to get off also, but my way was barred. Nothing was said – I was just held back, and I knew that when the train was running again I would be rushed, and dealt with, and dropped out into the night . . .'

'But how could they have known who you were and what you had done?' Wyndham asked. 'That had happened here in the Andamans – now you were in India.'

Jawan smiled. 'I shall teach you much, Sirdar, but don't ask for the impossible. How does news travel in India – across the Kala Pani and over the high mountains – quicker, sometimes, than the telegraph itself? I do not know. They that use the secret means probably do not know, either – but news *does* travel. My grandfather said that in the Great Mutiny in 1857, before there even *was* a telegraph in India, they knew in Simla of the massacre in Cawnpore eight hundred miles away an hour after it had occurred. Ask the swallows and the cranes how they know when to fly south from the snows across the Hindu Kush, and north again when they have gone. Have you ever seen camels before an earthquake? No? I have – hours before it happened. They will burst their kneeling pegs and stand upright, facing the direction from which it will come, and they will sway from side to side and their bellies will rumble, and somehow the other animals will

84

understand, and the panic will spread. But as I was saying, Sirdar – there I was with death staring me in the face – death under the kirpans of filthy Sikhs. I was up against an open window but unseen hands were holding me from behind, so I had no chance of jumping. I was ready, Allah forgive me, even to call upon the police had I seen any, but there were none about. Then I saw this man in the forefront of the crowd on the platform – a man like any other – a low-caste Hindu in dirty peasant's clothes. He was not wearing his turban on his head. It was across his shoulders, and he was holding the ends of it thus, in both hands, at shoulder-height – like a man who dries his back with a towel. It is a common enough stance – many men do it without thought when their heads get hot in the summer – but it also happens to be the seeking sign of the Thugs, the Rumalwalas, when they also have a nim twig, the stick we clean our teeth with, in the left side of their mouths, and they are rolling it idly with their tongues – thus. This man was doing that, and I caught his eye – '

'You mean that he instinctively knew you were in danger and had come to help?' Wyndham said incredulously. 'No, Jawan, I cannot believe that. You have spoilt a good story.'

Jawan laughed shortly. 'No, I don't mean that at all. This fellow was no doubt a messenger sent to meet somebody on the train who he did not know by sight – railway stations are natural contact points for these people. It was some business of their own, but I gave him the "come to my aid, I am in danger" sign – the wiping of sweat from the face that I have just shown you – and I glanced meaningly at the Sikhs who were clustered around and behind me. He acknowledged by clearing his nostrils brutishly and moved on a few paces, and that faint hope died because I thought he was not going to help me. The station-master's whistle sounded and the train started to move, and then it jerked to a stop as the brakes were jammed on, and railway officials and police were running up and down cursing and yelling to see who had applied the emergency stop switch – you know, Sirdar – the red handle above each door on the train with the notice in many languages, "For Emergency Only – Penalty for Improper Use Fifty Rupees". This seemingly stupid peasant farmer had jumped through an open door, pulled the switch down and just dis-appeared into the crowd – as I did, with the greatest alacrity, in the confusion. I provided myself with a good knife and took care not to find myself alone among Sikhs thereafter.'

'But there are many Sikhs here,' Wyndham said. 'Aren't you still in danger?'

'There are many of the Brotherhood here also,' chuckled Jawan, 'and I am known to be a bahari – that is one who, while not of the criminal caste or even race himself, has been initiated and is therefore under their protection. No, Sirdar, I am in no danger here.'

'But why were you initiated in the first place?'

'Because I am a sensible man, as I hope you will be also. As a CO one is in the position of being able to do many little unconsidered favours without great inconvenience to oneself. You know what the police and prison sahibs say – "You play the game with me and I'll play the game with you"?' He shrugged. 'So – you play the game with the Brothers. The only difference is that the Brothers keep their side of the bargain – *always* – as long as you keep yours. But Allah the Compassionate help you if you ever betray them.'

'So,' smiled Wyndham, 'I go round doing small favours for the Brothers like a missionary sahib . . . ?'

'No, Sirdar, you never volunteer *anything* – *ever*. That is the surest way to arouse their suspicion and mistrust. You must remember that these people are like the jungle animals. They trust nobody – nobody, that is, but another full Brother, or a bahari,' Jawan told him earnestly. 'And you must never let them suspect that you know even the few simple signs I have shown you – not until you are initiated and they show you themselves.'

'But why should they initiate *me*?'

'Leave it to me. I shall let it be known, very carefully and discreetly, that you are a man of goodwill. Very fair, very honest – a pukkha sahib . . .'

'Anything but that,' Wyndham said. 'The sahibs have cast me out.'

'You can cast a tiger out of the jungle and put him in a cage, but the stripes remain. I said these people trusted nobody but another bhai-bundi. That is right, but they have a certain respect, if not liking, for a sahib. They will watch you with curiosity at first, then with interest. Then one day an opportunity will occur, and you render one of them some slight service . . .'

'But you said I must not make the first move?'

'You mustn't – but if something happens and your response is the natural reaction of a man of goodwill, that is different. In my case one of my timber getters fell into the river while wearing bar fetters, and I went in after him and saved him from drowning, at some slight risk to myself. I did not know then that he was a Brother, and I made the effort simply because he was the best worker in my gang. But that was enough. They studied me, and in time, quite a long time, an approach was made. We wait for just such another opportunity, Sirdar. It will come.'

The lock-up bell was sounding and on the lower landings gates were clanging and locks grating. They went back into their respective cells, and that night Wyndham slept in sybaritic luxury on a two-inch thick sisal mattress for the first time.

He was fast learning the philosophy of the prisoner: of taking that which each day brought, enjoying that which was good, and closing his mind to all else – including the future.

Chapter 9

And the ensuing weeks brought much that was good. Tea twice a day – the first in the early morning as the sun rose over the rim of the ocean – strong tea, hot and thickened with coarse brown sugar and goats' milk, and spiced with red pepper in the Andamani fashion, from the big zinc cans placed outside the cookhouses to which the COs were allowed recourse after the early duty warders had taken theirs, and usually there were wheaten chapattis to go with it, and often fruit left over from the assistant surgeons' mess – mangoes, small red bananas, sweet limes and even, on occasion, a slice of melon or pineapple. It was taken leisurely and luxuriously, this unofficial largesse that did not count against their daily ration, savoured by the privileged as they leaned against the walls, babul batons dangling from their wrists, as the lesser breeds without the law filed past with lowered heads and averted eyes to ginna-hazir – the counting parade.

It was good to sit on a high stool under a palm tree and watch his squad squatting in front of their rows of concrete-imbedded spikes, husking and splitting coconuts, then spreading the halved shells, white faces uppermost, in hundred-yard squares. Five squares per shift was his norm, Kariappa, the azadi (free) foreman from the coconut oil and copra company had told him, with a bonus of a hundred bidis or ten English cigarettes for each quarter square above that. It was good thereafter to smoke English cigarettes exclusively, at no more cost than an occasional walk along the rows, with a word of encouragement here, a frown there and, the final sanction, a sharp rap with the baton across the shoulders of laggards. It was good to sit in the shade behind the warders at the two main meals of the day and eat one's fill, and to be allowed to swim off the beach under the prison wall at the end of each shift, to have one's laundry done by another convict for one cigarette per week, to buy a toothbrush and paste, soap and Kiwi boot-polish at the canteen. It was good to be addressed respectfully as Sirdar-ji by his squad, and to receive their salaams.

It was good to be shaved every day by the barber, instead of once a week as hitherto. And it was good, and immeasurably wise, to trade his surplus cigarettes and food for bidis and the coarse brown sugar they called jaggri to reward the pace-makers in his squad and thus increase their output and his own resultant bonus.

'Shabash, Sirdar,' Jawan chuckled approvingly. 'You are learning fast. Never milk the buffalo and make it pull the plough at the same time. The last fool in charge of the coconut squad just used to thrash them, so they sulked and the output dropped to four squares a day, which was why Kariappa had him stripped of his belt and baton and posted to the lime pits.'

'But Kariappa is a civilian. How could he do that?' Wyndham asked, and Jawan smiled and tapped the side of his nose with his forefinger.

'Don't try to learn it all at once, Sirdar. *He* works on bonus from his company too – so when output drops he is unhappy. He doesn't like to be unhappy – so he becomes paymaster to the babus in Administration. They have means of bringing things about. Keep on the right side of him *and* of your squad. But don't over-reward them. That is worse than giving no baksheesh at all.'

And so he learned, and prospered like the green bay tree and, being neither Hindu nor Muslim, he was able to keep clear of the ever-constant danger of underground prison politics. He even earned the approval of Mr Meakin, who watched him one day as he walked through the squatting rows like a firm but not sadistic galley slavemaster.

'That's right,' grunted the chief gaoler. 'Keep 'em at it. A busy con is a happy con. But keep your ears and eyes open at the same time, you know. Remember what I told you – any little thing you think I ought to know . . .' and he tapped himself on the nose as Jawan invariably did when he was indicating that a nod is as good as a wink to a blind horse. It worried Wyndham vaguely, and he took it up with Jawan that evening as they sat and smoked on the landing.

'All part of the system, Sirdar,' the Punjabi told him. 'A good CO *is*, in fact, the ears and eyes of the Great Ones above us. If one doesn't scavenge some jackal meat and lay it before them from time to time one soon loses favour, and the belt and baton go to somebody else.'

Wyndham felt a cold hand at the pit of his stomach. 'Was the bastard giving me a warning?' he asked anxiously.

Again the nose was tapped with the forefinger. 'Say a *hint* at this stage, Sirdar – and don't worry about it. I have already given the matter some thought, and shortly I hope to net two mynahs at the one throw.'

It came a week later. Even Wyndham, unattuned as he was as yet to the subtle undercurrents of the huge prison, realized that something was astir among the convicts as he sipped his tea and watched them march to ginna-hazir that morning. It put him in mind of the one tiger shoot he had been invited to in the Central Provinces in his first year with the Regiment, when he had sat all night in a machan, the platform slung between the branches of a tree, bored, cramped and unhopeful, listening to the bleating of the goat tethered as bait twenty yards away in the thickets. The jungle was wakening just before the sun rose, and birds were twittering and a troop of monkeys quarrelled in a nearby nim tree. Then suddenly there was silence – utter and complete – as if the whole world was holding its breath. It lasted a full dragging minute that seemed an age – a silence that was stifling and oppressive, almost tangible. Then it had passed, and all was normal again – birdsong, the chattering of the monkeys and the rustling of the undergrowth as a sounder of wild pig made its way back from a waterhole. Only the bleating of the goat was missing. Wyndham had seen nothing, heard nothing, but he knew before he climbed down at full light and saw the uprooted stake, severed tethering rope and drag marks in the scrub, that the tiger had been.

They were not marched to work that morning, but were kept standing for an hour while the shadows cast by the climbing sun shortened. Then a jemadar beckoned to four men at the end of the long front rank and led them off to a shed near the arched gateway. They went in and came out again some minutes later, carrying stout timber beams, and there was a catch of breath from the parade that was something between a sob and a sigh as they slotted them into holes in the ground and formed a monstrous inverted triangle. Then Mr Meakin came out, in full white uniform instead of the informal khaki shirt and shorts he normally wore until superintendent's orders at midmorning. He stood and looked at them for some minutes, his eyes running along the rows of downcast faces, and the silence was broken only by the shuffling of feet and the COs in serrefile behind the rear rank, snarling, 'Stand still – look to your front' – and the sharp thud of batons on the shoulders of those within reach. Then, as Mr Meakin held up his hand, even that was stilled. He pointed to the triangle with his leather-covered, lead-weighted cane and said in his ungrammatical but quite understandable Hindi, '*That* is not for the man who did this thing. For him there is something else. *That* is for the men who know, and do not speak. Back to your cells – and bread and water until *I* know.'

Then they were marching back across the parade ground, and Wyndham was poking and thumping with his baton as officiously as the rest of the COs, and yelling, 'Move! Move! You sons of pigs', feeling Mr Meakin's eyes boring into his back, and cursing the topee he wore which marked him among the turbans and Muslim kullahs of the other COs. He found himself beside Jawan, who winked and once more touched the side of his nose.

'A thousand bidis and some sweetmeats stolen from the canteen last night,' he muttered. 'See me outside when your crows are locked up.'

The COs were not returned to their cells. They hung about miserably and singly, afraid to be suspected of conferring together, and the warders closed their ranks and avoided them, and their own havildar, Purandari, normally an inveterate scrounger of cigarettes from the affluent Wyndham, checked him sharply when he saw him smoking behind the bath-house.

Jawan, strangely cheerful, joined him and said, 'Cheer up, Sirdar, there is nothing to worry about. The thief will be discovered before the bara sahib's orders. He is a miserable little Madrassi Harijan called Bundu, and he will have a hundred bidis and a handful of sweetmeats wrapped in a palm-leaf and hidden in the latrine where he works.'

'How do you know?' Wyndham demanded. 'And *if* you know, why the hell haven't you reported it, instead of making us all go through this tamasha?'

'Sirdar, Sirdar, Sirdar,' said Jawan reproachfully. 'When will you learn never to ask questions of that sort? It's bad prison manners.'

'What will happen to him?'

'Does it matter? He would, in the ordinary way, be sentenced to thirty strokes, penal diet for a month, and an extra year here in chowki.'

'Poor little bastard,' Wyndham said, and Jawan snorted impatiently.

'That's something else you'll have to learn. Never feel sorrow for anybody – not even yourself. It's wasted in this case, anyway, because he will only get the strokes. You will save him from the rest.'

'*I?*' said the startled Wyndham.

'You. You will go to Meakin sahib tonight and tell him that the thief is Mudiar Singh in the corn-grinding shed. They were below their task of sixty pounds per man yesterday so were kept back for an extra four hours, which gave him the opportunity of slipping away and breaking in through the back window of the canteen after dark.'

'But he'll ask me how I know!' shouted Wyndham.

'He won't. *He* knows his prison manners even if you don't. If he did, though, you would merely say that you got it from an informer, and he'd take it no further. Believe me, Sirdar – I know what I'm talking about.'

'All right then, but why can't I go to him now, and save this fellow from a flogging?'

'Because Meakin sahib knows, none better, that nobody is likely to talk before a flogging in case they somehow get involved themselves. After a flogging it's different. That's when somebody is more likely to say, "Ho! Ho! Ho! Poor bloody Bundu, and it wasn't him after all. It was that crafty son of a whore Mudiar Singh, and he's got the loot hidden behind the flour bins in the grinding shed. I'm going to have some of it when this has died down, or a little bird is going to chirp in the subedar's ear." Remember that, by the way – the flour bins in the grinding shed – and don't forget to tell him.'

'But *is* it there?'

'Naturally – or why do you think I'd be telling you?' Jawan shook his head sorrowfully. 'Sirdar, sometimes I feel you're shaping well. and I'm helping to make a man of the world out of you – a real hooshiarwala. Then I find you acting and thinking like a sahib again – "Why this? Why that? How do you know? Don't let them flog poor Bundu."' He spat. '*That* to poor Bundu. It's *his* black arse that will be getting it – not yours or mine. That's all that matters.'

He was small and simian, and he crept from the punishment cells and stood shivering and blinking in the blinding sunlight, and the havildar bellowed, 'Forward, filth, to the triangle. What are you waiting for?'

'Grab him and run him up,' said Meakin angrily. 'And why isn't he fettered?'

'Harijan Untouchable, sahib,' said the havildar timidly, but made no movement forward.

'Then detail a couple of Isdis to do it. Do I have to teach you your bloody job?'

A Goan and a Madrassi, both Christian and with therefore no caste to be defiled, came forward from the ranks and took him by the wrists and led him to the triangle. An Anglo-Indian assistant surgeon in a white coat glanced at him perfunctorily and made a token pass over his ribby torso with a stethoscope and called 'Fit for punishment', and his smock was pulled over his head and his shorts down to his ankles. Straps went round his wrists and two ropes were hauled taut over pulleys at each end of the triangle, until he was standing arms spread, on tiptoes. Then a canvas collar was placed over his neck and another one round his kidneys. The two floggers, a massive Ludhiana Sikh and a sinewy Pathan, stripped to the waist and took up their positions, holding the six-feet long oiled and flexible canes and spinning them in swishing arabesques.

'The left-handed Pathan is not bad,' muttered Jawan from the side of his mouth. 'He was here in my time. But that Khalsa-ki-jai bastard is useless. Three swipes and he's blowing like a foundered tonga pony.'

'Lay on,' called Mr Meakin, and as the first stroke whistled through the air and ended in a dull thump, the subadar started to count, 'Ek – do – teen – char – panch – chay – ' and a thin continuous bubbling cry was coming from the Harijan.

93

Wyndham, his eyes closed tight and his stomach heaving, was trying to block out all sound, but Jawan's authoritative commentary was coming through.

'Not bad, not bad at all for a little Madrassi monkey. That squealing is only his breath being held and let out through his teeth – it's supposed to help. He hasn't really yelped yet though. Ah, now he has – sixth stroke – it's usually the third that tickles them up – sat, ath, nau, das – only twenty to go. Ah, fainted – I bet the Sikh is glad of the rest. That stinking stuff in the bottle is going under his nose now – nearly takes the top of your head off. All right – he's with us again – giara, barra, tera, chaudra, pundra – half-way mark. By the Prophet he's taking it well . . .'

'Tisra' (thirty) counted the subadar, and somebody threw a bucket of water over the mangled thing on the rack, and it ran red into the white sand. The medical orderly handed a rectangle of lint to the Goan who placed it over shoulders, back and buttocks, then tied it in position with tapes round neck and waist, and they lowered him from the triangle and carried him off, face downward, on a stretcher.

Mr Meakin pinched his lower lip and nodded wisely. 'Mudiar Singh, eh?' he said. 'Yes – I was pretty certain it wasn't that lousy little sweeper. He wouldn't have the guts. Framed him to throw us off the scent, the crafty sods.' He pressed a bell on his desk, and a jemadar came in and saluted. 'Crash search of the corn-grinding sheds,' Mr Meakin ordered. 'With particular attention to the flour bins. If you find anything, lift Mudiar Singh. Chalo – jaldi.' He winked at Wyndham and grinned. 'Let's see how good your stoolie is. If it's a true bill you give him twenty bidis – no more, no less. If it isn't, you put your baton across his arse – twenty swipes – no more, no less.'

Jawan leaned back against the landing bars and sighed contentedly. 'Everybody happy,' he murmured. 'Meakin sahib because you are learning the ways of this place and are becoming a good CO and he will get the credit for it, Bundu because he comes out of hospital and gets three months' remission, and the superintendent sahib has put him on double rations for two weeks, the warders because all is harmony again, and I am *very* happy because no man is ever flogged by one of his own race or caste, so I replace that Sikh at the triangle tomorrow, and Mudiar Singh will think he has been through his own grinding mill when I've finished with him, and I'll be eight annas the richer, with an extra bowl of mutton pilau in my belly. Ai-ee! Justice is a wondrous thing.'

'Wondrous,' said Wyndham drily. 'What have you got against Mudiar Singh that you should have gone to all this trouble?'

'Nothing at all – except his race and creed, and his long hair and whiskers, and the sight and sound and smell of him. Apart from those small points, I love him like a brother. But you sound ill-pleased, Sirdar. *You* should be happiest of all. You have established yourself in the good graces of the Great Ones – *and* the Brotherhood.'

'How do they come into it?' Wyndham asked. 'And for Christ's sake don't tap your nose again and tell me not to ask questions.'

Jawan chuckled joyously. 'You shouldn't – but it is a *good* question, and I shall answer it, or how else will you appreciate my cleverness? Bundu, as you know, drives the Chariot of Paradise – the tank on wheels that is drawn by a pair of oxen and takes the shit from the latrines to the disposal tips – and as such he is permitted to go in and out of the prison without let or hindrance. The guard at the gate just hold their noses and wave him on, and none would dream of searching him or his cart. A very useful messenger indeed. The Brotherhood, who have much traffic with the outside – stolen stores one way and drugs and tobacco the other – would be lost without him. He is therefore under their protection – a bahari – as you are now, since you have helped him.'

'How can the things he carries be used again, since he is supposed to defile all he touches?'

'Simple, Sirdar. A Brahmin priest, who for a small consideration mutters a prayer, waves a hand and sprinkles a little urine *said* to be that of a sacred cow, and all is pure again.'

'But where do they get *him* from?' Wyndham asked.

'G Wing,' Jawan grunted. 'There are thirty-seven of the bastards there – all together, like bugs in an Untouchable's blanket.' He grinned. 'You're learning more here in a year,

95

Sirdar, than they'd have taught you in a lifetime in the army. Yes, you're the Protected of the Brotherhood now – but don't be careless – and never, *never, never* turn your back on a Sikh.'

Chapter 10

Mr Meakin said, 'We'll have to move Wyndham out of it, sir.'

'But you were all against his being paroled early,' the superintendent said.

'I don't mean paroled. To one of the camps.'

'Why?'

'The Sikhs are after him – and if there's anything I dislike it's a murder inside the walls.'

'I don't particularly like them *out*side the walls either.'

'Nor me, but outside they're an act of God – like typhoons, earthquakes and being struck by lightning – and they can hardly blame *us* for it. Inside it's different: Courts of Inquiry, CID over from Calcutta, the bara sahibs breathing down our necks and asking why we didn't know about it in advance. Well, you've had some of it, haven't you, sir?'

'I have indeed,' the superintendent said, 'but I'm in wholehearted disagreement with turning a man out to fend for himself just to save a little administrative bother.'

'He'll be all right as long as there's no Khalsas on the camp. Say Narpunga for instance.'

'Why are they after him?'

'You remember the bidis and sweetmeats whipped from the canteen last month?'

The superintendent winced. 'Two floggings for it – one undeserved.'

'I wouldn't go as far as that. The sweeper *did* have some of the stuff, but the point is that the real bloke, Mudiar Singh, was caught as a result of something Wyndham told me – and they know it.'

'*How* do they know?' the superintendent asked, and Mr Meakin looked pained.

'I couldn't answer that with any degree of certainty, sir,' he said primly, 'but my snout – er – informant – assures me that they *do* know, and they've had a panchnama – that's a meeting of the five senior whiskeries and . . .'

'I'm perfectly aware of what a panchnama is, Mr Meakin,' Colonel McClintock said coldly. 'You might inquire into the circumstances under which they were able to hold it without somebody knowing about it at the time. Anything over three convicts gathered together in association is a breach of the Consorting Regulation, is it not?'

'I'm in process of doing that at the moment, sir,' said Mr Meakin, reddening slightly. 'Anyhow, they're laying for Wyndham and I strongly advise his removal from the Cellular Jail. I'd like to make an entry in the Diary to that effect.'

'By all means – but there's no need for a paper umbrella . . .'

Mr Meakin took a deep breath. 'I'm not in the habit of putting up paper umbrellas, but I have reason to believe that this is serious . . .' he began, and the colonel halted him with upraised eyebrows.

'I'm sure it is – if you tell me so. What I was about to say when you interrupted me was I would advise against an entry in the Diary until after the move. I don't altogether trust the office babus.'

'Who does?' growled Mr Meakin. 'Sorry, sir. See what you mean . . .'

'When is the next boat for Narpunga?'

'Tuesday week.'

'Do you think Wyndham ought to go into Close Confinement in the meantime?'

'I don't think so, sir. That would only be advertising it. I'll put him on his guard, and I'll detail a couple of other COs to keep an eye on him.'

'Yes, do that, George,' the colonel said, easing the tension. He rose and went to a big wall map and studied the coloured pins that were clustered in various parts of the attenuated two-hundred mile strip that formed the archipelago: North Andaman, Middle Andaman, South Andaman and, a droplet far to the south, separated by a twenty-six-mile strait from the main group, Little Andaman. Strings led from the pins to a closely typed legend in the margin. 'Narpunga,' he read, putting his finger on a spot midway down the east coast of North Andaman. 'Assistant

Gaoler Philimore in charge – Probationary Assistant Gaoler Richards 2 i/c. How is he getting on, by the way?'

'All right I believe, sir,' Mr Meakin answered. 'Of course I don't see him all that often. He seems to be rubbing along quite well with Philimore, who isn't the easiest of men. It's that wife of his.'

'I didn't know Richards was married.'

'He isn't. I meant Philimore's wife.'

'What's wrong with her?'

Mr Meakin wrinkled his nose. 'A shocker. He got mixed up with her when he was on leave in Madras three or four years ago. Pretty enough – bit darkish – I should say a straight fifty-fifty – you know, Tamil on her mother's side, Seaforth Highlander on her father's. He should never of married her.'

'But he's Anglo-Indian himself, surely?'

'Yes – but respectable. There's a difference, you know. His old man was a senior guard on the BB and CI Railway, whereas she was an absconder from a Catholic orphanage. She was working in Madam Duval's when he met her – had been for a whole year – age seventeen.'

'We're gossiping, George. I don't think you'd better tell me any more.'

'You did ask, sir – and I take it nothing goes outside this office.'

'You know perfectly well it doesn't,' the colonel said. 'Um – I wonder if it would be altogether wise to send Wyndham there, in that case?'

'Good God, sir!' Mr Meakin exploded. 'No officer's wife under *my* command would be having it off with a *convict* – no matter what she was before she married into the Service . . .'

'It's not what *she* was I was thinking of. It's what *he* was – and is. European, ex-officer, exceptionally good-looking in spite of the knocking around he's had . . .'

'Whatever he was, he's a *convict* now, sir,' Mr Meakin rumbled. 'Anyhow, it's hardly likely they'd come into contact. The married quarters are two miles from the camp, and the sepoys' lines are in between – and I can't see Philimore letting her hang round the work parties. He's a martinet. He can be a fair sod too when he likes – sorry, sir.'

'Well, what about Richards? He's a bachelor you say?'

Mr Meakin smiled. 'No danger there, sir, or I wouldn't have recommended him being posted when Mr Whybrow was here, before your time. Nicely brought up lad from Bangalore – got an education – St Joseph's, Naini Tal. Bit religious. I don't think he'd know what to do with one if he saw it, if you'll pardon the manner of speaking.'

'All right, George, I'll leave it to you,' the colonel said, and nodded in polite dismissal.

'Narpunga,' Jawan said thoughtfully. 'There they cut great logs and float them down the coast to the saw-mills on Ish-Stewart Sound. It is not the best of camps, but certainly not the worst.'

'Damn them,' Wyndham said gloomily. 'Moving me when I was getting nicely settled in.'

'Very wise – with all these Sikhs here.'

'I can look after myself.'

Jawan shook his head. 'Not yet. Oh, I am not insulting your manhood. It is just that you are still thinking like a sahib. You've got to think – and act – like *them*, or me, or the rest of those animals out there – and you haven't been here long enough for that.'

'I'll miss you,' Wyndham said, and Jawan shook his head again.

'That is one of the things you must learn, Sirdar. Never miss anybody – or anything. Take the best out of each day as it comes, and be content with that. We'll meet again, never fear – back here in Port Blair after we are paroled.'

'But why aren't they moving you also? You were the chalah-kiwala (crafty one) who arranged the whole thing.'

Jawan tapped the side of his nose and winked. 'Because this time I was *very* chalahki. Nobody has connected me with it. I did it this way purposely, so that Meakin sahib – *and* the Brothers – would think that you were the clever one, a man to be reckoned with. Didn't I tell you that beforehand? "Two mynahs under the same net". Don't worry, Sirdar – just carry on as you have done here, only use your club a little more, because Narpunga is one of the places where the timber company pay extra for good output – in money, not just cigarettes. See that the foreman pays you in cash, not in promises to save it for you until you go on parole.'

'Is one allowed to have cash?'

'Officially no. You need a good hiding-place. You probably haven't learned where convicts normally keep their money, so I advise you to use a hollow piece of bamboo about four inches long, plugged with clay at each end and with a sliver of camphorwood inside to keep out the white ants. Bury it well away from the camp, and for the sake of Allah never let anybody see you visiting it. You'll be all right, Sirdar. Just be careful of Philimore sahib.'

'Who is he?'

'The gaoler in charge. A hard man.'

'English?'

'Partly – perhaps one should say mostly. You sahibs have a word for it when you speak of fair Anglo-Indians – "just a little coffee in the milk". He has a wife. In her case there is a lot of coffee in the milk. She is more dangerous than a queen cobra.'

'In what way?'

'A bitch who is always on heat. Meakin sahib won't have her back here in Port Blair because of the trouble she has caused in the married quarters, and it has held up her husband's promotion.'

'How the hell could you possibly know that?' Wyndham asked, amused.

'Damn fool questions again,' growled Jawan. 'I *know* – that's all. The whole prison knows. There was a young Maharatti wrestler once – good-looking lad, as randy as a stopped-up billy goat. Philimore suspected something, rightly or wrongly, and the boy was accused of a murderous assault on a sepoy warder, with half-a-dozen expert liars as witnesses. He got sixty lashes, which is exactly double the maximum allowed, although only thirty went down in the punishment book, and then a month in standing handcuffs and bar-fetters – again double the maximum – on restricted penal diet. It is said that she saw him from the verandah of her bungalow when he was crawling back to camp at the end of it, and she laughed and made a whore's gesture to him with her middle finger – thus – and Philimore saw it, and the boy went through the whole thing again, and that settled his hash for him, and he died shortly afterwards. There was no other gaoler or assistant surgeon there in those days. There is now, and he wouldn't dare do it again. But even so, take no chances. If she looks your way, drop your eyes and hurry past.'

'The way I feel at the moment,' grinned Wyndham, 'I'd almost be inclined to take the risk.'

'*Don't,*' Jawan said emphatically. 'Have one of the local women in the bushes if you must – for a few bidis or a piece of canteen soap. *Their* husbands only use poisoned arrows if they catch you at it. Don't laugh, Sirdar. I am in deadly earnest.'

Whistles were shrilling, and above them, from the central tower, the alarm bell started to clang. Wyndham, half dozing on his stool behind the coconut squad, saw Jawan coming backwards round the corner of the grinding shed, wearing a red cloak over the grey CO's shirt, thrusting, parrying and swinging with his baton, then close upon him, knee-to-knee, came the Sikh, Mudiar Singh, slashing two-handed with a foot-long sugar-cane knife. Then he saw that the cloak was blood, and the big Punjabi, weak from the loss of it, had gone down on his knees, still fighting. Wyndham ran forward, picking up his stool and holding it as a shield. He thrust it at the Sikh and felt the knife go into the wood and stick for the vital second he needed to bring his baton up, over and down. Mudiar Singh staggered back, and Wyndham struck again, this time back-handed, like a tennis stroke, across the face and below the protection of the closely wound turban, and then sepoy warders were around them, jabbering, yelling and clubbing, and somewhere Mr Meakin was shouting in the background, and the Sikh was being dragged away in a shuffling run, and other convicts were slinking out of sight to avoid being named as witnesses. It was over in less than a minute.

Wyndham dropped to his knees beside Jawan and raised his head, and the big man grimaced ruefully under his red mask.

'The bastard knew who it was all right,' he muttered. 'Remember my advice, Sirdar. Never turn your back on a Sikh or a Sindhi. Watch them – watch them all the time – in here and outside – because you're on their list too.' And his head fell forward.

Mr Meakin, standing over them, said, 'He's damn right. It's solitary for you, my lad, and no grub that hasn't been examined by the assistant surgeons. Bloody pity – you'd have been away tomorrow. Now you'll have to stay until after the trial. Right –

stand up, and pull yourself together. This is the nick, not a young ladies' seminary. The wogs are looking at you.'

Wyndham, blinking back tears, walked to the Solitary Confinement Wing in front of a jemadar and between two warders.

Purandari grinned through the bars at him and said, 'We're moving you up on to the next landing the other side, where you'll get a good view of it tomorrow morning.'

'I don't want to see it,' Wyndham said.

'Oh, bara sahib's talk, eh? You'll go where you're taken. You should be grateful after four weeks in this hole. Don't want to see it? That's a poor compliment to old Jawan. I bet he'll be looking up from hell laughing his head off.'

But he did watch that evening as squads of convicts – none of them Sikhs – brought out the numbered beams from the shed by the main gate, and slotted them deftly together until they formed a platform over a six-foot square pit which was covered by concrete slabs when not in use. Then planks were laid upon it, and two stout uprights and a crossbeam were raised, and under it was a trap and a complicated system of bolts controlled by a lever, which caused Mr Meakin a good deal of worry and irritated swearing as they tested it with a large bag of sand on the end of a rope. But at last, as darkness fell, it was arranged to everybody's satisfaction, and it was left under a sepoy guard, who sat on it, smoking bidis and dangling their legs over the edge.

Wyndham woke to the tolling of a bell next morning and stood up and looked down through the bars. The prison yard, the scene of the bustle of ginna-hazir on all other mornings at this time, was strangely quiet and deserted except for a hollow square of sepoys standing at ease round the gallows, and a shrivelled little man in shabby European clothes and a khaki topee who was fiddling with the trap mechanism again. Mr Meakin, in full uniform, came out and shouted in English, 'Leave it alone, for Christ's sake, Pereira. The bloody thing was working all right last night.'

'Dew make wood swell, sir,' answered the little man. 'Trap sticking small bit.'

'I'll "small bit" you – by five rupees – if it sticks with him on it,' grunted Mr Meakin.

Then a barred gate, out of Wyndham's vision, clanged back, and the sepoys snapped to attention under Mr Meakin's 'Party – party – 'HUN!', and they came into sight below him: first a Sikh in flamboyant robes, carrying an unsheathed sword, followed by another with the Granth Sahib, the Sikh bible, balanced on a cushion, then Mudiar Singh in a neatly wound, dazzlingly white turban in place of the drab blue of the prison issue, his hands tied behind him, supported by two COs and followed by the superintendent and a small group of warders. They mounted the steps and the little man fussily arranged the condemned man's feet on a white diamond-shaped patch in the middle of the trap, and then bound his ankles together with a webbing strap. He stood up then and took a white canvas bag from under his jacket, and rose on tiptoes to place it over Mudiar Singh's head.

'Not over his turban, you bloody fool,' Mr Meakin snapped. 'He's a Sikh. Do you want a riot?'

'Regulations, sir . . .' quavered the little man.

'Bugger the regulations,' said Mr Meakin. 'Do as you're told. Never hanged a Sikh before? Come on – the rope – quick. He's going to keel over in a minute. Stand clear you others. Right!'

The little man threw his weight on the lever and the trap crashed open and Mudiar Singh dropped from view. The taut rope jerked once or twice, then spun slowly, then was still, and both Sikh priests called, 'Long live the Sikhs.'

'I could think of something a bit more appropriate than *that*,' Mr Meakin said wryly, and wiped his face. 'God – I hate these things. Why the hell do we have to have them before breakfast?'

The superintendent was walking away rapidly towards the Administration Block, and the little man was kneeling on the edge of the trap looking anxiously down into the pit. An assistant surgeon went forward and climbed down a ladder behind the scaffold, a stethoscope round his neck, to reappear a few minutes later and give a thumbs-up signal to Mr Meakin.

'No complaints?' said Mr Meakin. 'Good.' Then his eyes widened in horror as the little man, relieved at the successful culmination of his task, lit a cigarette. 'Smoking over a dead Sikh?' he said indignantly. 'Don't you know it's against their religion? Put that bloody thing out.'

Wyndham marched down to the jetty with twelve replacement convicts and escort of six sepoy warders under a havildar. He had been out only once before – to the courthouse in Port Blair for the trial. The ugly little Prisons Department coaster, the *Luxmidama*, was already alongside, her tall thin funnel belching smoke from the cheap coal that was supplemented with residue from the coconut oil mills. He was the only CO, and as such he was not handcuffed to the chain with the others, and he still retained his badges of office – the topee, shirt, belt and baton. Mr Meakin, standing in the shade of the wheelhouse, beckoned him to one side as they came up the gangway.

'All right, Sirdar,' he said. 'Keep your nose clean up there and you'll have nothing to worry about between now and parole. There's no Khalsas in Narpunga. Play the game with Mr Philimore and he'll play the game with you – blah, blah, blah. Only he's inclined to play it a bit rough at times if you get on the wrong side of him – *no* bloody blah, blah, blah.' He leaned forward and dropped his voice. 'You'll be a long way away from me, but I can still help you quite a lot down here – a *hell* of a lot – particularly round about Parole Board time – with recommendations and such, and what jobs are going and that sort of thing. Get my meaning?'

'Yes, sir,' said Wyndham. 'Thank you very much.'

'Good. Well now, you're a man of intelligence – good education and all that. You can use your loaf and reckon out how many beans make five. Any little thing you see or hear up there that you think I might be interested in, you keep buttoned up' – he tapped himself on the lips – 'tight as a trout's arse until this steamer comes in the next time. Then you wait a suitable opportunity and you slip the griff to the serang. That's the coon you can see behind me in the wheelhouse now. Got him? Good.'

'Do I write it down, sir?' Wyndham asked.

'Jesus Christ no – that would be asking for it if you or him was ever dived on suddenly for a spot search. Everybody is liable, you know – civilian employees as well as prisoners. No, you just give him a whisper in Hindi – like say "Three hundred and fifty sal logs went down the coast last week – three hundred were entered in the book" or "Prison labour helping to build the new drying sheds for the fish canning company – one hundred men a day shown on the pukkha departmental debit voucher and credited to Government, twenty-five paid for in cash at half rates, the difference being split between their foreman and certain other interested parties." That sort of thing.'

'Would I be in a position to gather information like that, sir?' Wyndham looked worried.

'Are you really as innocent as all that, Sirdar?' Mr Meakin asked. 'Or are you bullshitting me? Of course you'll be in a position to. You heard things down here, didn't you? It'll be even easier up there. Just keep your ears and eyes open, that's all. But when you're passing anything on, see you're passing it *all* on. Don't go keeping any of it back or twisting it – like "Mudiar Singh broke into the canteen, and framed the sweeper" when all the time it's "Jawan broke into the canteen and framed Mudiar Singh and made a red herring out of the sweeper." If I'd known it all, Jawan would have been given the tip not to be a naughty boy – no more than that, the sweeper wouldn't have got his arse tanned, Mudiar Singh would still be grinding corn in the mills, and you wouldn't have been responsible for the untimely demise of your half-section. Watch it, Sirdar. Things can be so easy for you in the next few months, or on the other hand they can fold up and come down on you like a brick craphouse. *I'll* be watching *you*. Dismiss.' He nodded curtly, turned and went down the gangway.

Wyndham leaned on the rail and watched the town slip from view behind the headland, leaving just the huge white prison dominating the landscape like some crouching, waiting, albino monster, until that too had dropped out of sight below the horizon. On the well-deck the convicts and sepoys were chaffering with the crew of free men and parolees for bidis and Burma cheroots against the pipes, cigarette holders and other bric-à-brac they carved from bamboo roots and scraps of bone. They had been searched before leaving the prison and their sleeping mats and blankets had been unrolled for inspection, but obviously not too rigorously because the hatch had become a miniature bazaar and there was a holiday mood upon them that was in marked contrast to that of their arrival some months earlier. They carried two days' prison rations per man, of jowari chapattis, rice, vegetables and spices, and it was being collected up in big brass pots and cooked communally in the ship's galley, together with fresh fish and fruit bought from the crew, and soon all of them were eating happily together without thought of creed or caste.

The serang, a Chittagong lascar, invited Wyndham and the havildar to share his evening meal, a Lucullan spread of Japanese canned food – crab, herrings in tomato sauce and ochrous peaches, which Wyndham would willingly have traded for a plateful of the savoury mess he could smell down on the well-deck.

Afterwards he sat and watched the dark coastline on the port side, that was relieved only occasionally by the flash of a lighthouse on a promontory or the sparse pinpoints of a fishing village. The sea was like a millpond, and a soft breeze was coming off the shore, and someone down on the well-deck was strumming a sitar, and the convicts were singing in a high-pitched but muted monotone – for once not the eternal *Kala Pani*, but a Bengali love song about dark eyes, alabaster skin and parted lips.

He started to ponder over Mr Meakin's last words. How much *did* the old devil know in advance about the real undercurrents of the prison? Was it worthwhile spying for him? Spying on whom? Then he put it away from him. It had been a good day. That was all that mattered.

He flicked his cigarette butt over the rail and watched it curve like a firefly in the breeze and die in the wake of the ship. Then he stretched out on his dhurri and went to sleep. To hell with tomorrow.

Chapter 11

The shore came steeply down to the water's edge, and it was clothed densely with coconut palms and casuarina, with, at intervals, deep scars through the bush that marked the path of the logs as they slid down into the lagoon from the ropeway that ran along the crestline. There was no beach here, only a tumble of pink, white and umber coral rocks where the vegetation ended and along which the surf was making a line of white foam. A curving breakwater, part natural coral, part concrete, ran from the shore out to a reef which was just becoming visible above the dropping tide. The rising sun was dead astern of them as they steamed slowly into the small harbour and nosed up to a concrete wharf where a knot of convicts waited to take their lines. Above the wharf, on a ledge in the steep foreshore, Wyndham could see a cluster of ugly wood and corrugated iron bungalows – half a dozen or so, with a larger one surmounted by a cross on higher ground above them. A path ran obliquely from the wharf to this small village, and two men in khaki shirts and shorts and topees were walking down it. One, with the assistant surgeon's habitual badge of office, a stethoscope, round his neck, was a dark Anglo-Indian. He stopped as they came on to the wharf, and instinctively sought a patch of shade by a small hut, although the sun was not yet hot. The other came on to the edge of the wharf and looked up at the ship, full into Wyndham's face. Wyndham saw a tall, spare man with pallidly fair skin drawn tightly over high cheekbones, small indeterminately coloured eyes that were completely expressionless as they held his, and a mouth that was fixed in a faint permanent grin by the puckered scars of a badly treated hare-lip. Wyndham straightened and stepped back from the rail. The man slowly raised his hand and beckoned, Indian fashion, which is with the back of the hand towards the one who is being called, fingers pointed downward and jerked quickly, and Wyndham hurried along to the break in the rail where the prisoners were setting a gangplank in position. He jumped the small gap to the wharf and came up to the man and saluted. The other looked at him – a long slow stare that started at his feet and went up to his face.

He said, 'Wyndham . . .' and as Wyndham answered 'Yes, sir,' he went on, 'I'm telling you – not asking you. Shut your mouth until I give you permission to speak. You're not in the army – not any more – so I don't want any of your saluting. Convicts salaam their officers here. Understand?'

'Yes, sir,' said Wyndham again.

'Good. Well understand something else. You're posted here as a CO, but that doesn't mean that I have to keep you as one. You drop that belt and baton and start working for a living the moment I'm dissatisfied with you. There's no silver spoons here, my lad, just because you're a European. And in future you hold your topee in front of you with both hands when you come before me, or you'll find yourself wearing a straw hat again – bloody quick. Now get your party ashore and fallen in for rigorous search and FFI. *Move!*'

Wyndham checked his salute in time, and converted it to a salaam – head bent and the back of the wrist to the centre of the forehead – turned, and went on board again, passing the serang as he came out of the wheelhouse with a mailbag. The Chittagongi muttered, 'The men have dropped all that they shouldn't have, Sirdar. One of the crew will leave it under the logs behind the wharf shed tonight, as is the custom. Be careful of that half-sahib Philimore and pray for the day someone runs amok and chops the son of a whore.'

Then came the squalid routine of the rigorous search, naked in a line on the wharf, clothes spread on the ground in front of them, bending forward at the waist as a rubber-covered finger probed their bodies. Wyndham, his flesh creeping, had to submit with the rest, and he wondered dully if he would also be hand-cuffed to the chain for the march to the camp, but he was spared this and he walked with the havildar at the rear of the column.

They went up the road past the bungalows, and a woman came out on a verandah and watched them. Wyndham saw her out of the corner of his eye and was careful not to turn his head. The havildar giggled as they rounded the next bend, and made a circle of his forefinger and thumb and pushed the middle finger of the other hand through it.

As they came to the log road that ran parallel with the ropeway at the top of the coastal rise, a battered Model T Ford pick-up overtook them and passed in a shower of dust, with Philimore at the wheel. Ahead of them, masked until now by the false crest of the nearer hills, a great mountain soared, twin-peaked and densely jungle-clad.

'Zin Pahar – Saddle Mountain,' the havildar told him. 'Evil spirits and people like monkeys, who eat human flesh, live there. They used to come down to the camps at night just before the monsoon, and they would lay in the jungle and make clicking noises with their tongues, and it has been known for prisoners to climb through the wires in the hope of having a woman – and getting chopped and finishing up in a cooking-pot instead. Now all except COs are fettered at night.'

They marched for nearly an hour. Below them the coast was opening out into a dazzlingly white sandy beach, backed by a screen of palms and jacaranda trees in a riot of blossom, but its beauty was marred by the stark frame of a long, low, palmetto-roofed shed that was enclosed by a high barbed wire fence.

'The barracks,' the havildar told him. 'Used now only by the logging crews. There are two others further along the coast towards Port Cornwallis, where they are building a place for drying fish. That is a good job, Sirdar, if you can get it. The CO just lies in the shade on the beach until the boats come in, then he checks the number of tubs and sees that not too much fish is stolen and smuggled back into camp. We people do not mind, provided we get a bit of it, but Philimore sahib will give thirty lashes for as much as a finger-length tiddler found on a prisoner. You have to be careful.'

They halted in front of the barracks, and looked longingly at the creaming surf a bare fifty yards away, because the sun was directly overhead now and the heat was beating down in almost tangible waves. Philimore came out of a small detached hut and called over his houlder, 'Get the bastards allotted to squads and working right away, Mr Richards.'

Another man came out and said, 'What about medical inspection?'

'They've all had a finger up their arses, and Tegetmeier has signed the chit. That's good enough for me,' Philimore said. 'I'm going on to Cornwallis. I'll look in on the way back this evening. Carry on.' He climbed into the Ford and drove down a corduroy runway to the hard sand by the water's edge and turned north up the coast.

The other man came across to the squad and greeted the havildar in Hindi and shook hands, then he moved along the line to Wyndham. He was younger than Philimore – perhaps about Wyndham's own age – but shorter and slighter; dark, but with the olive darkness of the Mediterranean rather than Asia; straight-featured and with clear brown eyes. Anywhere but in India he would have passed as an Italian or a Frenchman of the Midi. A good face, Wyndham decided – grave, composed, but with a latent good humour clearly evident. He said, 'Wyndham?' and then when the other, standing to attention and looking to his front, did not answer, he went on, 'My name is Richards.' And again he put his hand out. Wyndham, surprised, hesitated, then took it. 'Yes, Wyndham, sir,' he said.

'This is not a bad place,' Richards said. 'The work is hard, of course. There is an output figure to be maintained, and if possible improved upon, but it's not a backbreaker.' He looked along the handcuffed line and grinned as he caught their side glances at the surf. 'They're hoping for a swim. It's not permitted during working hours, but I'm going into the office for exactly thirty minutes. You and the havildar explain to them that if they're not back here and fallen in when I come out again it will spoil it for another occasion.' He turned abruptly on his heel and went inside.

The havildar unlocked them, and, yelling like children granted an unexpected treat, twelve G-stringed convicts raced for the surf. Wyndham followed more slowly and moved up the beach a little and waded out through the breakers until he was shoulder-deep in water, then swam out towards the reef, looking down through the unbelievably clear depths to the multi-hued coral and waving green weeds below. He became aware of somebody swimming behind him, and, turning, he saw the havildar.

'Richards sahib very good man,' he said, surprisingly in English. 'Philimore sahib pukkha bastard.'

'You better not tell *me* that,' said Wyndham, 'or you'll be losing your bloody stripes.'

'That's all right, Sirdar. You good man too.'

'Where did you learn English?'

'Me Madrassi. All Madrassi talking very good English. Listen, Sirdar – good place for talk this. Back there too many people listen. Lot of prisoners talk English but don't say. This very good camp for *that* . . .' He lifted one hand from the water and rubbed his forefinger and thumb together. 'Make it plenty money. Soon you go to parole – then you need it.'

'*How* do I make it?'

'Soon I tell you all things – but you keep chup-chup.' He tapped himself on the lips with the same expressive forefinger. 'In evenings after work finish, Richards sahib always let men go swimming. You come this side same like now. When I got something to tell you, I come too. You want cigarettes, you want whisky, you want English paper, books, you want *woman* – all right – I make pukkha bundobas. But all the time you keep . . .' He tapped his lips again. 'You don't tell Richards sahib. He good man, but he still prison officer. He go tell Philimore sahib – then plenty trouble – woop-woop-woop on arse with bloody big stick, confee, standing handcuff, solitary cell – everything. You remember, Sirdar. Now we get men back on parade.' He turned and swam for the shore, and Wyndham followed thoughtfully.

The next few days passed quickly as he learned the complicated and, at times, meaningless routine of the place. They were organized in a 'Circle', with headquarters under Philimore at the little port where they had landed, Narpunga, two miles to the south. There, also, was the hospital, in the charge of Tegetmeier, the Dutch-Tamil assistant surgeon, and the chowki, or closed prison, for the punishment of local wrongdoers whose offences were not considered sufficiently grave for return to Port Blair, and the post and telegraph office and a general store owned by a parolee. Fifteen miles to the north was Port Cornwallis, a small town in its own, civilian right – with the offices of the timber and fish canning companies, a Government meteorological station and a small shore establishment for the Royal Indian Marine armed survey vessel, *Indira*. Richards's domain was the 'Sub-Circle', here at Dakki, with three squads of fifty convicts each, when at full strength. Each squad had its own camp: 'A' just above them, on the ropeway, 'B' engaged on forestry clearance work two miles inland, on the slopes of Saddle Mountain, and 'C', recently split into two smaller squads, 'C/1', helping to build an extension to the fish canning plant, and 'C/2', all fishermen from the Madras coast before their imprisonment, now forming the nucleus of a new inshore trawling fleet. There was a havildar, a naik and six sepoys with each squad, and one or two COs as available. In addition to this there was, here at headquarters, a small detachment consisting of Richards himself, the Madrassi havildar, Subramanian, a babu, a medical orderly and half-a-dozen sepoys. Richards moved constantly round the camps by motor-cycle and pony, and lived in a small bungalow that was little more than a hut, up on the ropeway, roughly equidistant from all parts of his command. All camps were connected to headquarters by a field telephone which seldom functioned because the Andamanese used to steal the wire, so communication was normally by runner or, in case of emergency, a red flare fired from a Very pistol.

'We work a ten-hour day, six days a week,' Richards explained. 'Unless the output falls back. Then it's increased to twelve, or even more if Mr Philimore says so, and the rest day is suspended. Warders and you chaps only get a rest day every other week, I'm afraid, because of guard and stand-by duties. The men have as much freedom as conditions warrant. On their rest days they fish and swim, and trustworthy people are allowed to go a mile from the camps to gather fruit. I use those damned handcuffs as little as possible, but for some reason I could never understand they must always be on the chain when travelling between camps – and, of course, they are all fettered at night, but that's for their own protection, to stop them wandering.'

'Do any ever attempt to escape?' Wyndham asked.

Richards shook his head. 'None in my time. Where could they go? The nearest land is a hundred and twenty miles away. Cape Negrais in Burma. India is the better part of a thousand – to the north and the west.'

'The fishermen? Couldn't they steal a boat?'

'Maybe – but they couldn't navigate out of sight of land. The great majority of them haven't the faintest idea where they are. This, to them, is just the Kala Pani – overseas – a long way from home.' He smiled. 'You weren't thinking of it yourself, were you?'

'Not me,' Wyndham assured him. 'I'm too near parole.'

'Good – I'd hate to lose you. I want to keep you here at head-quarters.'

'Thank you,' Wyndham said simply.

'Not at all. It will make things much easier for me. The office babu is useless – and I don't trust Subramanian.'

'Any particular reason?'

'Prejudice. I don't trust any Indian Christian. A man who would change his religion for a bowl of rice hasn't much principle in my opinion.'

Wyndham's rest day fell on his second Friday there – the Muslim sabbath – which meant that roughly a third of the labour force were off work. Richards came into the office early in the morning. 'I'm going up the reef in my boat,' he said, 'fossicking for seashells. You can come if you like. I usually take Subramanian, but he won't be off until Sunday.'

The boat was the usual Andamanese canoe, hollowed from a twenty-foot log, shaped and smoothed with nothing more than the small native obsidian adze to an almost unbelievable precision, and balanced by a light outrigger. A group of convicts carried it down over the sand and pushed it out beyond the line of the surf. Wyndham climbed in with some trepidation, but found it to be remarkably stable under skilled handling – and Richards *was* skilled. He hoisted the triangular sail that was woven, silk-smooth, from janewa grass, and set between V-shaped spars from the centre thwart, and she came round into the wind, lifted and sped through a gap in the reef. Wyndham had done a lot of sailing off the Cornish coast in a long series of otherwise deadly dull school holidays at his grandfather's gloomy manor near Polperro, but it had never been as exhilarating as this. He wanted to sing and shout. Richards, sitting balanced on the after outrigger spar with the steering paddle, caught his eye and smiled. He didn't smile often, but when he did his whole face was transformed. 'Wonderful, isn't it?' he said. 'It's the only time I really enjoy here – these few hours I manage to snatch away from that bloody camp.'

'You don't like the job?' Wyndham asked.

114

'It's a job.' Richards shrugged. 'And one shouldn't quarrel with one's bread and butter. They're hard enough to come by. Things haven't been easy for us Anglo-Indians since the war.' And Wyndham was surprised, because it was seldom an Anglo-Indian referred to himself as such. Even the really dark ones were inclined to talk about 'Home' and 'the Old Country' and hint at a childhood spent in London.

They sailed some five miles up the coast, running before the wind, parallel with the reef, then suddenly Richards changed course in an abrupt ninety-degree turn in towards the coast. They were balanced on the crest of a big creaming roller and they screamed in through a gap in the reef that allowed a bare foot each side of the hull and the outrigger, and the impetus kept up as they crossed the lagoon, standing directly for a line of high cliffs that dropped sheer into the water, for here the beach had ended again. Wyndham looked apprehensively at Richards, but he was intent on his steering, holding the course right up to the last possible moment before twisting the blade of the paddle and bringing the canoe up all standing in the deep shadow of an overhanging rock. Then, without a second's pause, he twisted again and shot forward round a pink needle of coral that rose higher than the mast above the surface and hid the entrance to a cave. They sailed into this, and Richards leaned forward unhurriedly and slipped the shrouds from wooden cleats each side of the narrow hull, and the twin masts dropped in a smother of sail. They drifted on slowly under their dying momentum, then grounded gently on a narrow white sand beach, and Wyndham started to breathe again.

Richards looked at him and laughed. 'I should have warned you,' he said, 'but I only decided to turn in here at the last moment. I discovered this place by the merest accident when I was hunting for morchi shells – and I've never brought anybody here before.'

Wyndham looked about him and gasped. They were in a grotto that soared upwards like the vaulted nave of a cathedral until the roof was lost in darkness, but down here at water level the light, though suffused to a soft greenish blue, was quite adequate. It ran back no more than some fifty yards before ending in a sheer wall, and it was perhaps half that in width. The entrance through which they had come was just wide enough to take the boat with only inches to spare.

'What do you think of it?' Richards asked.

'Unbelievable,' Wyndham answered. 'But do you mean to say that nobody knows of it but you?'

'As far as I know. There's only this one way in, and you can use it for less than half an hour, dead at half-tide as it is now. If the water's higher the outrigger would foul the sides, because the entrance narrows towards the top. If it's lower you'd ground on what I call the doorstep.'

'So you've got to be careful about getting out in time?'

'Yes. I was once stuck here for twelve hours. I could have swum out, of course, but that would have meant leaving the boat.'

'No danger of being swamped?'

'None at all. This beach gets covered, but the ledge above it remains clear. There's even a fresh water supply here. It trickles down the wall and forms a pool on the ledge.' He pushed off from the beach with a paddle. 'We'd better get out now before we're trapped again.'

They came out into the tiny backwater formed by the coral finger, and Richards reached out and held on to the projection. 'Take a look round to make sure the coast is clear,' he said. 'I'm always scared of a couple of locals being about, fishing in the lagoon. I'd hate this place to be discovered.'

'Aren't you taking a risk, showing it to me?'

'I don't think so. Actually I have an ulterior motive.'

'What?' Wyndham stood up and looked round the lagoon, and gave a thumbs-up sign.

'Morchi shells.'

'What are morchi shells?'

Richards felt under a thwart and brought out something that shone translucently in the sunshine – a conical shell some four inches in diameter at the base and convoluting along its six-inch length to a delicate point. It was a deep blue that merged into pink at its narrower end, while the inside was a purple that changed to mauve as Richards turned it slowly towards the light. 'That,' he said, handing it to Wyndham. 'Beautiful, isn't it? That one is broken, as you can see, which makes it valueless. I get five rupees for good specimens from a dealer in Calcutta.' He pushed out into open water, and Wyndham helped him to raise the mast again.

'I see,' he said. 'But what is the ulterior motive?'

'That cave is a good place for them, but you need to be there at low water. I found six the day I was trapped. I'd like to go again, but it would mean having to leave the boat outside unless I was prepared to be stuck there for another twelve hours – and that's too much of a risk.'

'I see. So?'

'Well, I thought if you'd care to come out with me on future occasions you could drop me and I'd swim in, and you could go off and fish for an hour or so, and then pick me up later. Of course I'd split the proceeds with you of anything I found in there, and hold it until your parole, if you'd care to trust me.'

'Good God,' said Wyndham. 'Do you realize what a day like this means to me? I'll do that willingly – for nothing.'

'No, it would have to be a proper business deal,' Richards said. 'Good – then I'd better show you how to handle this thing. Have you ever done any sailing before?'

'Quite a lot. Dip-sail lugger mostly – on the Cornish coast.'

'Yes, of course,' said Richards slowly. 'Trevorrow Hall is near Polperro, isn't it? Right on the coast.'

'What the hell do you know about Trevorrow Hall?' Wyndham asked, startled.

'The family seat, surely,' Richards answered. 'We happen to be second cousins.'

Chapter 12

Richards said, 'Samuel Wyndham, the founder of the Regiment. Two sons, John – who would have been your grandfather, I think, and Malcolm . . .'

'Who put up a black and got slung – like me,' said Wyndham. 'He was *my* grandfather.'

'Good God. But your name – Richards – ?'

'He had two daughters. One of them, Emily, was my mother. She married my father, Ivor Richards.'

'Well, I'll be damned. I knew I had a grand-uncle Malcolm, of course, and that he'd come some sort of a cropper out here, but I never heard any of the details. His name was always taboo in the family. Did you know him?'

'Only as a kid. He died in 1907. I was born in 1900.'

'Where did all this happen?'

'In Bangalore – that's in Southern India, you know, near Mysore. Grandpa had changed his name to Hesketh, but everybody knew who he was, although it was never talked about. He joined the Mysore police and rose to be inspector. He never went back Home.'

'Just as well he kicked the bucket before *my* little lot,' said Wyndham wryly. 'You don't happen to know what *his* particular peccadillo was, do you?'

'He was supposed to have fallen in love with a beautiful Afghan princess and run off with her.'

'Would that have been your grandmother?'

Richards smiled. 'Grandma was a very nice old lady from Meerut. She was nanny to the presidency magistrate's children when old Malcolm met her. There was a little colour there, but not much. The princess story was just to cover something not quite so romantic. Money and drink, I believe.'

'Too much of one and not enough of the other?'

'So I heard. Great-grandfather apparently believed in keeping his sons on a tight rein.'

Wyndham laughed shortly. 'A family tradition that has been handed down ever since. You're talking to an expert. Well, Cousin Richards . . .'

'My Christian name is Paul. Yours, of course, are Charles Wilberforce . . .'

'You're not suggesting that we use them, are you?'

'Why not . . . when we're away from camp? Blood's thicker than water.' He leaned forward without self-consciousness and held out his hand. 'Anything I can do to make things easier, I'll do gladly.'

'That's damned good of you, old boy,' Wyndham said, shaking hands. 'But you don't want to go running into trouble.'

'I'm not a fool, and I certainly wouldn't break regulations openly, but there's a lot of needless brutality going on here. Philimore is a bad man, which is a pity. The majority of gaolers that I have worked with are as hard as hell, they've got to be, but they're fair, and they don't make prisoners' lives a misery just for the sake of it. This fellow is a sadist – and he's got it in for you particularly.'

'Why? I haven't done anything to the bastard.'

'It's a natural reaction with a certain type of Anglo-Indian when they come into contact with the genuine Home product.'

'Home product be damned,' Wyndham said. 'I was born in Risalpur.'

'It makes no difference. There's no colour in you – so as far as Philimore is concerned that makes you one of Them. He's one of Us.'

'Aren't you both making too much of this? What the hell does it matter?'

'It doesn't matter to me – not now I'm older and have a bit more sense. I know there was a touch in my grandmother, and considerably more than a touch in my father, and I accept it, and it doesn't worry me, but with the Philimores of this country it's a constant canker eating into them. He calls you the "pukkha-fucker sahib" and swears you're looking down on us.'

'I didn't know a convict could look down on *anybody*,' Wyndham said. 'The bloody man's mad.'

'There are times when I'm sure he is.'

Wyndham grinned. 'He's got a bit of a handful with that wife of his, according to latrine gossip.'

'I'm sorry for the poor devil,' Richards said. 'That's someone *he* can look down on – other than convicts – ordinary convicts, who he doesn't regard as human anyway. He certainly gives her a hell of a life. She'll take a knife to him one of these days.'

'Which mightn't be such a bad thing from what you say.'

Richards shook his head decisively. 'If you kill anybody in this colony – anybody at all, let alone a prison officer or a warder – no matter what the provocation – you hang. That goes for convicts, parolees or ordinary civilians. It's got to be. There are over seven thousand prisoners here – a high proportion of them murderers already serving life sentences. Nobody could be allowed to get away with it – not even a woman. Philimore isn't worth *anybody's* neck.'

'I see what you mean,' said Wyndham. 'Well, now – look here, Paul, I've enjoyed today more than I thought I could ever enjoy anything again – and you've mentioned further trips . . .'

'If you want to come.'

'Of course I want to come. But is it wise? If Philimore gets to hear of it he's going to take it out on both of us.'

'I don't think that would make much difference. Regulations state that we must always take a warder or a CO with us when we go out fishing. I shall continue to take Subramanian occasionally, when I'm not going after shells.'

'I wonder,' said Wyndham.

'Wonder what?'

'How much you people really know about the undercurrents of this place.'

'Oh, we all have our grapevines . . .'

'What about Subramanian?'

'Well, what about him?'

'He got into my ribs the day I arrived and hinted that there are ways of making money here, and that he'd put me wise to them – but that on no account was I to tell you.'

Paul laughed. 'As a matter of fact he warned me about *you*. He said that you were Meakin's man.'

'He could have been right. Meakin had a word in my ear before I left and told me I could do myself a bit of good if I watched points up here – short delivery of logs, and cooking the labour chalans, and that sort of thing. I was to send him the tip via the serang on the steamer. But how the hell would Subramanian know that?'

'How do any of them know about anything? That's the grapevine. A lot of what one hears is true, a lot is inspired guesswork, and still more sheer lies, either for their own ends, or because of the Indian habit of telling you what they think you want to hear. You listen to everything, then sort it out for yourself.'

'Is there anything you'd like me to pass on to you if I hear it?'

'If you really think it's important enough – but don't go out of your way. I don't want to sound too virtuous, but I try to keep clear of prison politics as much as possible. I'd advise you to do the same. Keep your nose clean, as they say here, until parole time. You haven't long to go now.'

They caught fish off the reef and landed on the beach and cooked it in the native fashion – wrapped in wild banana leaves and buried in hot ashes – and feasted royally on it, with white bread from the bakery at Narpunga and tinned butter – the first that Wyndham had tasted for nearly a year – and bottled beer and fresh fruit – and the day sped by all too quickly, one of the happiest Wyndham had ever known.

They sailed back as the sun dipped behind Saddle Mountain, with Wyndham steering and handling the simple but sensitive rig under Paul's instruction – back to the world of chains and fetters and ginna-hazars – and Philimore.

He was standing at the water's edge as they ran into the beach, and he greeted Paul with a curt nod, ignoring Wyndham. 'Got any fish to spare?' he asked.

'There's a couple of nice beckti there,' Paul told him.

'Good. Tell this fellow to put them in the truck.'

The indirect order was more offensive than if it had been addressed straight to him. Wyndham picked up the fish and started to cross the sand towards the Ford. 'Come here, you,' Philimore called after him sharply. Wyndham turned and came back, and Philimore went on in Hindi, so that the convicts who were lifting the canoe from the water could understand, 'Didn't I tell you about removing your topee and salaaming when a sahib spoke to you?'

'I am sorry, sir,' Wyndham said. 'I did not realize that you had spoken to me.'

'Well, keep your ears open and salaam now.' The voice was low, sibilant and dripping with malice. Wyndham, a fish in each hand, hesitated uncertainly, then laid one down in front of him in order to comply.

'Not in the sand, you bloody fool!' roared Philimore, and started forward. He poked Wyndham violently in the chest with his cane, causing him to drop the other fish. A red film seemed to descend before Wyndham's eyes and he was conscious only of the contorted face in front of him. He took a lumbering step forward through the sand, his fists clenched, then Paul was between them, and in that split second sanity returned.

'Pick up those fish and take them to the truck,' he said sharply. 'And for Christ's sake try not to be so damned clumsy.'

Wyndham salaamed, retrieved the fish and turned and walked away across the beach.

'So you saved your pal's bacon, eh?' sneered Philimore. 'A pity you hadn't let him swing at me. Thirty of the best across his aristocratic arse would have done that bastard the world of good.'

'There'd have been a hearing,' said Paul, 'and I'd have had to testify that I'd seen you strike him first – without provocation and not in self-defence.'

'You'd have liked that, wouldn't you?' Philimore said.

'Don't try and pick a quarrel with *me*, Philimore,' Paul said quietly.

'Mister Philimore to you.'

'Mister Philimore my bloody arse. There's only you and me here at the moment, and I've got something to tell you . . .'

'And I'll be having something to tell *you* – in front of the superintendent.'

'You won't,' Paul answered succinctly. 'I've got too much on you – and you know it. Regulations cut both ways and to my knowledge you've broken every one in the Book. Well, you're not breaking them on *my* patch, that's all.'

'I want that fellow returned to Narpunga – where I can keep my eye on him,' Philimore said. 'I think he's having too many favours shown to him up here. Bad for discipline.'

'I can't argue with that, of course, but I want the order in writing, together with any charges you have against me for preferential treatment.'

Philimore smiled, and the puckered scars at the corners of his mouth contracted, baring his two incisors and the irregular yellowing teeth between them. 'No charges, mera bhai,' he said. 'I'm too old a cock for that. You'll get the order all right – and a note with it saying you've done a damn good job with him, but that word has reached me that he's starting a racket up here, and he's been trying to suborn the warders, and that I don't think you've had quite enough experience yet to deal with it.'

'What a bastard you are, Philimore,' Paul said. 'You'd break a good CO – and God knows they're hard enough to come by – just to wreak your spite on him, for no reason at all except that he happens to be white and you're a half-chat.'

'What the hell are *you*?' screamed Philimore.

'I'm one too, but it doesn't twist my guts like it does yours. I come from a decent self-respecting family . . .'

'With a twenty-five rupee a month education from the fucking priests, you mealy-mouthed son of a bitch . . .' Philimore began, and Paul hit him – a sharp jab in the solar plexus that travelled no more than six inches but which had the other back on his heels retching and gasping.

'One of whom taught me that,' Paul said. 'What are you going to do about it – *mera bhai*? Not a witness in sight – and that poke won't leave a mark. Do you want to finish it properly – here and now?'

'No, no – not now,' gasped Philimore. 'There's plenty of time. Yes – plenty of time. By Jesus, Richards, you'll pay for that. Oh, my God – you'll *pay*.'

He walked away through the gathering darkness to the truck, swung the starting handle, backed, turned, and drove off. Paul watched the receding path of light as it picked out the palm trunks on the slope and then turned on to the ropeway, then he made his way slowly through the sand to the office. Wyndham, taking the fettering keys from the wallboard, turned as he entered. Paul smiled tautly.

'Don't say "I told you so",' he said.

'I wasn't going to. This hasn't made it too bad for *you*, has it?' Wyndham asked.

'No worse than it was before. It's a bit more out in the open that's all.'

'You thumped him, didn't you?'

'Only a token thump. I was scared stiff that you were going to. Don't, for God's sake, ever let yourself be provoked into that. It would be a certain flogging and your parole put back a year.'

'I'll watch it. But what will it mean for you?'

'Nothing – not directly. It would be his word against mine. I don't think those other prisoners saw it – and if they did they'd back me. I'm afraid he's going to take you into Narpunga though – unless I can think of some way to stop it.'

'Don't try. Between us we'd probably only make matters worse. I'll keep my nose clean no matter what the swine does to me. With luck it will only be for another three months until my parole comes up – but you've got your career to think of.'

'Some bloody career,' said Paul bitterly.

'A wise man doesn't fight with his bread and butter. You said so yourself,' Wyndham reminded him. 'I'm the last bloke on earth entitled to preach, Paul, but for your type of man there's more in this job than just padlocking convicts on to a chain and working them into the ground. I've learnt a lot since I've been here. Given a chance and reasonably decent treatment and many of them make good when they come out of chowki, don't they?'

'Given a chance, granted. But what chance have they – have any of us – against a sod like Philimore?'

'But all the staff aren't Philimores. I can honestly say that he's the only out-and-outer that I've met here who makes things harder than they need be.'

'One Philimore can undo the work of ten others who might possibly see a reformative aim in the system,' said Paul gloomily.

'I don't believe that.'

'Don't you? Well, listen to me. I just said that if any other of those prisoners had seen me strike Philimore and had been called as witnesses, they'd have backed me. That's true – but only to a point. If they thought that I was likely to bite the dust, and Philimore would still be in the saddle, they'd swear my life away. You can't blame the poor devils. That's life as they see it. The first law of survival. Back the stronger, and to hell with the weaker

– even if the weaker is trying to do something for you. That's Hind ki ukl' – Indian common sense.'

'You've got your tail down,' said Wyndham. 'And I'm talking like Samuel Smiles's Self Help. Cheer up. Even if I've got to go in there, I've still got a shot in my locker if the going gets too tough.'

'What?'

'Like I said – Meakin wants me to fossick out any dirt I can find up here and send it down to him by the serang. If I send enough of the pukkha khubber, somebody's likely to come up for a look round, which will mean that Philimore will have too much on his plate to bother about making *my* life a misery.'

Paul smiled faintly. 'You're already thinking like these people here,' he said. 'Hind ki ukl'. Be careful. You need a *very* long spoon when you're supping with Philimore's kind of devil. He's an ignorant swine, but he's as chahlaki as a bazaar buniya – and that sort of thing can bounce back on you. No, Charles, if you've got to go, then just screw up every ounce of resolution that's in you and take anything he cares to dish out. "Yes sir, no sir, three bags full sir" – hat off, look straight to your front, and a bara salaam when he dismisses you. That's pretty horrible advice, but it's the best I can give you. You've just got to hang on for three months, and not give him the shadow of an excuse to run you for anything.'

'I will,' said Wyndham, then on an impulse he put his hand on the other's shoulder. 'Whatever happens – thanks for today. Thanks for everything. I can't even begin to tell you what it has meant to me.'

'We're Family,' said Paul simply. 'That's more Hind ki ukl'. The Family sticks together.'

He went back the following morning, walking the two miles through the dust along the ropeway, handcuffed to Subramanian.

'I'm sorry about this, Sirdar,' said the Madrassi, 'but it's regulations when travelling between camps. Philimore is showing you the kala chihra – the black face – enmity, but don't worry. You keep your belt and baton – for the moment, anyhow.'

'How do you know that?' Wyndham asked, unconvinced.

'The office babu has gone sick, and he has nobody else down

there who reads and writes enough English to keep the accounts. You're safe until the thieving bastard comes out of hospital – then you can always slip something into his curry that will send him back again. I recommend enough ground croton seed to cover an eight-anna piece. That is tasteless, and it will make him shit more in a day than the maharajah's elephant in a month.' He winked. 'It could be very profitable once you know the run of things. I can help you a lot. But don't trust Philimore's cook. He's dishonest.'

Philimore kept him standing in the sun outside the wharf office for an hour before calling him in, but then he was surprisingly casual and matter-of-fact – as if the events of the previous day had never occurred – or if they had, he'd forgotten them. His whole manner, if not cordial, was not entirely uncivil. It was that, Wyndham was quick to realize, of a man who had a job to do – a conscientious man who was far too sensible to let personal rancour interfere with the carrying out of that job.

'The bloody babu filed into hospital this morning,' he said. 'I could do the useless swine's job in one hour a day, but I haven't got that hour. Too damn busy on more important work. I can spare you the rest of today to take you through things, then you'll just have to pick up the routine as you go along. You man the telephone when I'm not here, and take down any messages that come through. What is it they call you? Sirdar, isn't it?'

'Yes, sir.'

'Good. Right-ho, Sirdar, let's see how you shape. Nice cushy job if you run things properly. You play the game with me, I'll play the game with you. Fall out and get some grub at the bawachikhana and be back in half an hour. OK – salute if it comes more natural, and forget the salaam.'

Slightly dazed, Wyndham came out in the sunlight, and the world seemed a brighter place. The creeping dread that had been on him since the previous evening was now lifted, and he felt that he wanted to sing, shout and turn handsprings. Sumbramanian, scrounging tea and chapattis at the bawachikhana before his walk back to the camp, sensed the change immediately and chuckled fatly.

'What I tell you, eh?' he said, lapsing into his pidgin English with a quick side glance at the cook. 'You all right here. This son of a bitch got plenty fiddles going. Babu got to be in with them or Mister God-all-bloody-Mighty Philimore up shit creek, because he don't write proper nice like babu or pukkha sahib. He born in a whorehouse and don't go to school like Richards sahib or you. You just keep chup-chup and learn all things, then I come in here when God-all-bloody-Mighty up in Port Cornwallis at night banging McDonald Memsahib, and tell you all things.'

'Who's McDonald Memsahib?' Wyndham asked.

'Very nice memsahib – very rich – nearly white. McDonald Sahib own hotel and big store there, but he go die. Now she got lot. This bastard want to marry her, but he got that one topside.' He pointed over his shoulder to the bungalow on the hill.

'How do you know all this?' Wyndham asked without particular interest.

'Bloody monkey tell me – what you think? Sirdar-ji, you don't ask question like that in this place. You just listen – learn all thing – keep in here.' He tapped himself on the head, then converted the movement into a lewd gesture, winked and went off.

Wyndham walked slowly back to the wharf office.

Chapter 13

Wyndham looked up as Paul came through the door into the office, rose, put on his topee and saluted.

'It's all right,' Paul grinned. 'The coast is clear. I saw him go past to Cornwallis an hour ago. How are things?'

'Unbelievably smooth,' Wyndham said. 'He was quite civil when I arrived, and the ice has been melting further ever since. He's been positively cordial the last few days. I'm expecting to wake up and find it all a dream.'

'So I heard over the grapevine. I take it you're proving useful.'

'Evidently. There's nothing to strain one's intellect in the job. The ledgers are simple enough. He pencils in the entries lightly and I ink them in afterwards.'

'Normal procedure,' Paul said. 'If he's ever caught on the fiddle he could say that the books were cooked in his absence. How do you reconcile them with the chalans and vouchers that come in with the logs?'

'I don't have to, thank God. They've been cooked at the other end – all except the ones from your office. All I know is that a bloody sight more timber goes down to the mills than is accounted for, but I'm keeping my nose well out of that.'

'Wise man. What else do you do?'

'Put his reports and drafts into reasonable English, and one-finger them out on the typewriter afterwards, man the telephone and tell whoever wants him that he's out inspecting the labour, when I know damned well that he's over seeing his lady friend in Cornwallis . . .'

'Oh, you know about that, do you?'

'No more than everybody else on the station. I'm grateful to her for keeping him occupied. For the rest, I lock up our eight prisoners at night, and let them out in the morning.'

'You've got no warders here at all?'

'The naik has been evacuated to Port Blair, sick, one's on

leave, and the other is in the chowki himself for drunk and disorderly.'

'My God – so he *does* need you,' said Paul. 'Good thing, if it means decent treatment for you, but don't let it blind you to the fact that he hates your guts. Don't trust him an inch.'

'I'm not likely to, but at the same time I can't help being thankful that things have worked out this way.' Wyndham rifled through some letters on the desk. 'Incidentally, I've got some news for you. Your leave is sanctioned – twenty-eight days' annual furlough plus twenty-eight accumulated from last year.' He handed the other a form. 'It arrived on the steamer the day before yesterday.'

'And that bastard hadn't the decency to let me know,' said Paul. 'Actually that is what I came down to find out.'

'I tried to phone you,' Wyndham said, 'but the line to your place is down again.'

'To take effect from fifteenth of next month,' Paul read. 'Assistant Gaoler Reddi to relieve me. He's the first of the new Indianization intake in our grade. Not a bad chap.'

'Where will you be going?' Wyndham asked.

'Bangalore – and with a bit of luck I won't be coming back.'

'Well, I hope you have the bit of luck,' said Wyndham, but he couldn't keep the dismay from showing in his face.

'It's a job I applied for on leaving school – Railway,' Paul explained. 'The Permanent Way Inspectorate on the MSM – that's the Madras and Southern Maharatta – but things were pretty quiet at the time. Now it's come up again, and I had a letter last mail. They'll give me an interview at the end of next month. My God, I hope it comes off. I want to get married.'

'Can't you marry out here?'

'Who'd bring a wife to this?' Paul asked. 'Certainly not me. No – this would be a career. My old man was on the railways . . .' He sensed the other's dejection. 'Of course, I mightn't get it – and in any case you'll be on the point of parole in three months' time and . . .'

Wyndham laughed. 'Was I looking sour? Take no notice. The best of British luck to you, cocker.'

'It's Anglo-Banglo luck I need at the moment. This is only an

Intermediate Grade appointment – not one that you have to have an engineering degree from Home for.'

'Stop harping on that, for Christ's sake,' Wyndham said. 'Home is where you hang your hat – not a paradise over the ocean for the breeding of pukkha sahibs. Degree my arse. I bet your old man could tell you more in a week about the running of an Indian railway than any Cambridge professor could in three years.'

'Maybe – but there are times I wish . . .' He broke off. 'I'd better be going. That lousy khansama saw me arrive, and he'll be timing me so he can tell his boss. If Philimore says anything, tell him I came in to see what was wrong with the phone. I'll see you before I go, of course. Look after yourself.' He winked and gave a thumbs-up sign and went quickly.

Wyndham busied himself with the simple routine of the evening, collecting his flock of eight prisoners – four working desultorily on shoring up the wharf piles, the cook and his helper from the bawarchikhana, and two sweepers – and locking them up in the small chowki. Philimore's khansama, a cringing little Goanese, should also have been locked up, but he was, contrary to regulations, allowed his freedom for his master's convenience. He was sitting on the hill-side below the bungalow as Wyndham marched the squad past. Like Subramanian, he took pride in his command of English.

'Oh-ee! Mister Sirdar sahib,' he cackled. 'Lock dam' buggers up. Verree bad mans.'

'Sod off, you little bastard,' Wyndham said out of the side of his mouth, 'or I'll put you with them,' and the other rolled on the ground, howling with shrill merriment. 'Oh, Mister Sirdar sahib – you verree funnee man,' he called after them. 'Give me one bottle brandee baksheesh and I cook you plentee dinners – pukkha English Blightee dinners, when sahib go Cornwallis side to make choot with number two memsahib.'

There wasn't much that went on here that wasn't common property, Wyndham thought wryly, as he took the chowki keys to Philimore's bungalow. They were kept in an allegedly secret hiding-place under a loose floorboard in the living-room – another flagrant breach of regulations.

The woman was there when he arrived, standing in the shadows at the back of the room. He had seen her before, but only fleetingly in the distance. She came forward and held her hand out for the keys. Wyndham hesitated, touching the brim of his topee with his baton in salute.

'Mr Philimore showed me where he wanted them kept, madam,' he said.

'What difference?' she shrugged. 'Whole station knows that. One day Meakin will come up here in the commissioner's motor-boat when he's away in Cornwallis, and catch him. All right, put them there yourself.' Her voice was flat and toneless, and the accent heavily chi-chi. Wyndham passed her and lifted the reed matting and the board underneath and dropped the keys into the space below. He rose and turned back to the door, conscious of her eyes upon him. This was the first woman he had been this close to in over a year, and he felt as gauche and ill at ease as a pimply adolescent.

She said, 'You're the pukkha Blighty sahib they talk about, no?'

'Someone's made a mistake,' he said gruffly. 'I'm not a sahib.'

'Oh yes, you're a sahib all right. You think I don't know?' She giggled. 'I know plenty of sahibs – officer sahibs, sergeant sahibs. My father was very big man at Home. We had a big house with plenty of servants – *European* servants. You know Northampton?'

'Not very well, I'm afraid,' he said. From the corner of his eye he saw the khansama pass the front of the bungalow on his way round to the cookhouse at the rear, and his skin prickled. 'Look – if you'll excuse me . . .' he mumbled, and she laughed gratingly.

'What are you frightened of, pukkha sahib? I only say "how d'you do" and you run like hell.' She mimicked him. 'Look – if you'll excuse me . . .'

She came forward fully into the evening light, and he saw her plainly for the first time. She was pretty in an overblown way, like a short-lived tropical bloom at its prime, but her cheap make-up was wrongly applied – stark white powder giving her dark olive skin a slate-grey patina – and she reeked of sandalwood oil and phul-nana.

'Would you like a drink?' she asked, and when he shook his head she went on, her voice rising angrily, 'Goddam! What the

hell's the matter with you, man? I only want to talk to somebody.
There's nobody here in this bloody station can talk English proper.
I'm losing my tongue. You think I'm going to bite you or some-
thing?'

Wyndham said, 'I'd like to talk very much, but I've got my
position to think of – not to mention yours. If I were caught
round here I'd be in serious trouble – and things wouldn't be
too easy for you, would they?'

'A lot *he'd* care,' she spat. 'He's over in Cornwallis with another
woman. He's there every night.'

'He'd care all right if he heard that there'd been a prisoner
here talking to his wife and drinking his whisky.'

'Who's going to tell him?'

'That khansama of yours for one. He's watching us now from
the cookhouse.'

'Oh, *him*?' she said contemptuously. 'I'd have the skin off his
black arse if he told lies about me. You don't have to worry about
Furtado.'

'All the same it would be better if he wasn't around,' he said,
and winked conspiratorialy. 'Some other time, eh?'

She giggled again. 'I think you're very bad man, pukkha sahib.
All right – some other time.' She returned his wink.

He made his way down the hill to the office in a cold sweat,
determined to devise some other means of returning the keys in
future. But it was not easy. He tried to give them to the khansama
next time Philimore was away, and the Goan recoiled as if he'd
been stung.

'Not me, Mister Sirdar sahib,' he squealed. 'That woman tell
Philimore sahib I have keys, even for one minute, I catch bloody
hell – so do you. Why you not take them yourself?'

'Too busy,' Wyndham said lamely.

'Too busy for *that*?' He made the familiar sign with his forefinger and thumb. 'You all right there. She like plenty jig-a-jig.'

'Well, give it to her and leave me alone,' Wyndham said
wearily.

'She only like big man – young man,' the Goan said regretfully.
'You all right there, I tell you. You come up there night-time I
cook you very good dinner. Only give me one bottle brandee
baksheesh.'

'Where the hell am *I* going to get a bottle of brandy from,' Wyndham asked irritably, and the Goan guffawed.

'You don't know that yet?' he asked incredulously. 'Same place Philimore get it and babu *used* to get it. Medical store.'

'I haven't got the keys.'

'No bloody fear you don't have keys. Doctor Tegetmeier should have keys, but he – what sahibs call it?' He lifted an imaginary glass to his mouth. 'Can't have one drink – have too many – get drunk whole month . . .'

'Alcoholic?' said Wyndham, interested.

'That right – so he say to Philimore, "You keep keys for Chri'sake – and I keep job." Oh, I can tell you plenty things about this place.'

'Well, go and tell 'em to somebody else,' Wyndham said. 'I'm busy. Piss off.'

But he knew it was only a matter of time. Philimore, safe in the knowledge that in Wyndham he had a pearl of price he could leave in competent charge of things, was spending four or five nights a week away from the station.

'I told you, didn't I?' he said one afternoon before setting off in the Ford. 'I said when you came here – "You play the game with me, I'll play the game with you," I said. Well, here you are – you've got the best bloody job on the Island. I thought you were one of these toffee-nosed bastards when you arrived, so I roughed you up a bit – but you're a good bloke, Sirdar.' He took a key from his pocket. 'Hop up to the medical store and get a couple of bottles of brandy. You'll find five left in a case on the shelf facing you.'

The medical store was a small room at the end of the hospital verandah. There were no patients at the time, and the place was silent and deserted, as Tegetmeier had gone down to Port Blair on the last steamer to a conference called by the superintendent, but the orderly, a parolee, was in the medical inspection hut at the gate to the compound, and he winked knowingly and made a drinking motion with hand to mouth as Wyndham came out with the bottles discreetly hidden in a piece of palmetto. 'Little foxes make games while tiger is away, eh, Sirdar?' he said, and Wyndham answered with his customary non-rancorous formula of profanity.

Philimore was sitting at his desk in the office when he got back, with a ledger that Wyndham had not seen before in front of him. 'Got 'em? Good,' he said. 'Keep one here for me. The other's for yourself, but for Christ's sake don't flash it around. Give us the key back.'

Wyndham stared at him in open-mouthed amazement, and Philimore chuckled and tapped the side of his nose. 'Like I said – you've got a bloody good job here.' He turned the ledger round towards the other. 'Three signatures – here, here, and here – and the dates alongside 'em. Try the signatures on this piece of paper first. Simple enough – old Tegetmeier writes like a bloody crow with inky feet.'

Wyndham took a deep breath, but he didn't hesitate. He studied the preceding signatures in the receipts column and embarked on his first attempt at forgery. Philimore studied it critically. 'Um – not bad,' he said. 'Better than the babu. But have another shot – not so heavy on the downstrokes. That's better Now in the book. Fine – lovely, lovely. The dates – good.'

'Three bottles in a fortnight, sir,' ventured Wyndham. 'Won't anybody question that?'

'Hell, no. Standard treatment for snake-bite. Actually the doc gives 'em the local native spirit – just as good – and I help him out by drinking the pukkha stuff for him. If he got too much of an accumulation he'd go on a bender.' He laughed. 'Freddy Philimore, little friend to all the world, that's me.' He rose and went to the door, with the ledger under his arm. 'OK, Sirdar, me old cock, hold the fort and don't lose any of the customers. See you in the morning.'

Wyndham stood in the doorway and watched the Ford disappear over the rise, then turned back and looked at the two bottles on the desk. He had not tasted spirits of any sort since the surreptitious pegs O'Farrell used to slip him at their conferences before the trial, and the need for it that had been constantly upon him in those days had become quiescent, but now the old familiar dryness at the back of the throat was here again and his thirst was becoming clamorous and demanding. He put one bottle under some papers at the back of a drawer in the filing cabinet, and took the other into the lean-to shed behind the office, where he slept. He sat on his charpoy with the bottle in both hands, resting on his knees, savouring the anticipation that was enhanced rather than otherwise by his subconscious fear.

'One – one *only*, you bloody fool,' he whispered to himself. 'Get drunk now and act the fool and you could ruin everything.'

He stumbled round the shed vainly searching for his forbidden pointed knife to prise the cork out, his need becoming more insistent by the moment, cursing and almost weeping, then he found a nail and he dug it out clumsily in pieces, and slopped a full four fingers into his pannikin, the bottle rattling on the rim. He gulped it down in one, and felt the fire of it grip him by the throat, then spread warmly in his stomach and throughout his whole body.

He lay back on the charpoy with his eyes closed, relaxed and, for the moment, content, then his hand went out to the bottle again. He allowed himself a bare inch in the bottom of the pannikin this time, and he sipped it the merest droplet at a time, savouring it on his tongue, then he resolutely rammed a twist of paper into the neck of the bottle in place of the fragmented cork, and hid it behind the charpoy.

There was a spring in his step as he marched the prisoners to the chowki a little later, and he joked lewdly with them in high good humour as he ushered them into the compound, asking them in Hindi if they'd like him to lock a few women in also – and one of the sweepers winked and said, 'Yes – Feelimo' memsahib. That one would have us all on our backs by morning – and still be begging for more,' and there was a howl of glee from the others, and somebody called out after him as he came down the hill, 'If you want some help up there, send for me, Sirdar sahib.' That sobered him quickly, and he fought down the half-formed thought that had come to him earlier of going up to the bungalow after dark.

The woman was on the verandah as he passed, but he pretended not to see her and continued on his way to the little harbour. For something to do and to put the thought of the bottle behind the charpoy out of his mind for the hour or two that still remained before he normally went to bed, he got some tackle from the office and fished with some small success but little interest until darkness fell.

He was pleading and reasoning with himself as he entered his shed. 'One, Wyndham – just one. Don't be a fool. Yes, yes, yes – I know. You could take a whole bottle and still get on parade once, but what happened today? One Parsee peg and you were as drunk as David's sow – cracking jokes with those soor ka bachas and laying yourself open to their innuendos, starting dangerous gossip among them – *bloody* dangerous – and for two pins you'd have been up there rogering that half-chat strumpet – and you'd have been caught on the job, as sure as God made little apples. Hang on – just hang on for not quite two months now, and you'll be on parole, with this bloody thing off your neck, and there'll be a chance to start thinking about picking up the pieces again. Yes, just one, Wyndham – just one.' And he was still reasoning as he poured out the third, but he did stop then and put the slightly less than half-full bottle away behind the charpoy.

Somebody was shaking him violently in the darkness and babbling in a mixture of Hindi and pidgin English. He sat up muzzily and felt the top of his head almost lift off.

The Goan was saying, 'Please, please Mister Sirdar sahib – wake up – WAKE UP!'

'What the hell's the matter?' he mumbled.

'Philimore sahib – he have bloody big smash up in motor-car . . .'

'Where?'

'Little way down road. He coming back from Cornwallis. He crawl to bungalow – but I think he go die. No doctor. What to do?'

'Have you called the medical orderly?' Wyndham asked, swinging his legs off the charpoy.

'He not there, bloody bastard. Every night he go off to drink at fishing village . . .'

'What about the memsahib?'

'She no good. Silly bitch see blood – yell head off and lock herself in bedroom – won't come out . . .'

Wyndham stood up and groped for his trousers.

'The damned phone is still out,' he said. 'Listen – I'll go up there. You go down the ropeway, jaldi, jaldi malum? Call Richards sahib – tell him. Say we want doctor from Cornwallis . . .'

'Yes, Mister Sirdar sahib. I go quick. Bloody good job you here, eh?'

Wyndham came out into the hot, still darkness, then turned back and felt for the bottle behind the charpoy. He pulled out the plug and raised it to his mouth, then checked himself and rammed the plug back and put the bottle carefully in the front of his shirt in order to free his hands for the climb up the low cliff that would save the five extra minutes it would have taken by the road. He heard the Goan's hurrying footsteps receding.

The bungalow was in darkness. He came up the steps and called, 'Mr Philimore, sir – are you there?'

There was no answer. He stepped inside the living-room and his feet came up against something soft and yielding. He bent and felt it and his hand came away wet. He fumbled in his trouser-pocket for a box of matches, struck one and stooped again – and saw the woman.

She was lying on her back with her knees drawn up and her hands were clutching at her belly. Her cotton frock was ripped down the front, revealing her torn underclothing, and she looked as if she had been dipped into a bath of red paint. The match burnt his fingers, and he fumbled for another with nerveless fingers, then he was caught full in the beam of an electric torch, and Philimore said, 'I'd have liked to see you hang, you fucking bastard, but this will save trouble all round.'

The blast of the gun deafened him and he felt as if a clumsily thrown brick had hit him on the shoulder. He went back against the door, and through it, and rolled across the verandah, then off it on to the sloping hillside and over the low cliff. A patch of kika thorn broke his fall, then another, then he was in the gutter at the side of the road. The beam of the torch stabbed downwards towards him and the gun blasted again twice and he heard the bullets phut into the gravel in front of him, but he was now pressing back hard against the cliff face, safe for the moment. The light was joggling along the cliff top as Philimore ran round the long way, and Wyndham, guided purely by animal instinct to escape, ran blindly across the road, down the slope the other side and on to the wharf. He paused for a brief second to catch his breath, then continued his shambling run along the wharf and on to the reef at the end of it. Behind him the light was coming obliquely down the sloping road, and he saw it playing over the piles of timber by the office.

He slipped into the water and started to swim north, parallel to the line of surf at the bottom of the cliffs.

Chapter 14

The tide was making, and he was dimly aware of it carrying him along the reef, so he lay on his back and floated. He was not conscious of any pain in his shoulder, but it was numb and he was unable to use his left arm. He tried to bring the events of the last fevered half-hour into focus, but his mental cogs were not meshing, and illogically, the only thing he could remember with any clarity was pushing the bottle of brandy into the front of his shirt. He could have done with that now, but he had dropped it somewhere. Faintly over the water the sound of a furiously driven motor came to him, and for a moment he thought it was Philimore's outboard-driven canoe, and he felt an upsurge of panic, but then he saw headlights moving fast along the ropeway. Philimore on his way to rouse Richards, he concluded – and the effort of that small deduction started his thought processes working again.

Philimore had tried to kill him. Why? Because he had suddenly come on the scene and jumped to the immediate conclusion that he, Wyndham, had killed the woman? Possibly – but then, his words – 'I'd have liked to see you hang, you fucking bastard, but this will save trouble all round.' Those were hardly the words of a man acting on the impulse of blind, uncontrollable rage. They had been cold, deliberate and dripping with malice. And besides, he had been waiting there in the dark for him. The Goanese – and his lies about the accident? Had *he* killed the woman and then cleverly framed him? Could be, although he and his race, while crafty, were seldom violent. What would be his object? Jealousy? Hardly. He couldn't picture the dried up little monkey of a man as a Lothario. She, poor little bitch, could have done better than that. So what was left? An elaborate plot of Philimore's contriving? It fitted. Motive? The comfortably placed widow in Port Cornwallis that he wanted to marry, obviously. Yes, that fitted all right – and he, Wyndham, poor bloody stupid Wyndham, fitted also, perfectly. The degree of freedom Philimore had allowed him – far exceeding that of Richards. The complete run of the station while the lord and master was away. He could easily have had a havildar and a couple of warders sent down from one of the camps. That's what he should have done. The trusted CO could have remained in charge of the office, but he should, according to regulations, have been confined at night. But here he was locking the others up and then, on the specific orders of Philimore, taking the keys up to his bungalow – the opportunity for dalliance tailor-made for him. And then the liquor, the final touch, to make him pot-valiant and randy. And it almost had. He'd been on the point of going up there, hadn't he? It was only a last-minute shred of fear-inspired caution that had held him back. But Philimore had the answer to that prepared in advance. If Wyndham's libido failed to supply the motive power to get him to the bungalow, the story of the accident was ready. That would have involved Philimore taking the Goan into the plot, but there was little risk in that. As Richards had said, any one of them would swear his own mother's life away for a trivial advantage. Furtado would have everything to gain by co-operating and a pretty bleak outlook if he didn't.

He saw the lights of the truck stop, then go out, and he calculated that this would be a halt at Paul's hut on the ropeway. A guess that was confirmed by another pinpoint of light coming up as a Petromax lamp was lit. He watched it for some minutes, then the headlights gleamed again and moved on fast. Then the faint staccato popping of a motor-cycle came to him, and a single light moved back in the opposite direction. That told its own tale, he decided. Philimore was going on to Port Cornwallis to report to the police post there and no doubt communicate with Port Blair from the wireless station, while Paul went back to take charge at Narpunga. It couldn't be the other way round because he remembered Philimore's oft-repeated boast that he was the only man on the island who was sufficiently versed in the vagaries of the ancient Ford to drive it.

The current was sweeping him along faster now as it was forced into the narrowing gut between the reef and the beach, and the distance between him and the light in the hut, which had been left burning, was decreasing perceptibly. For the first time he started to wonder dully what his next move would be. Where was he going? What was he going to do? And he hadn't any of the answers, less one, he decided miserably. To turn at right angles to his present course and swim out to sea, and to keep swimming until he tired and sank. That, of course, would be the ultimate, and only sensible, solution. But that would mean that Philimore, the bastard, would get clean away with it. Two people safely dead so that he could be mine host of a tenth-rate pub. The very thought of it brought a sour taste to the back of his throat. But there was no alternative – other than going tamely back to the shore and giving himself up. Fetters again, the trial, listening hopelessly to expert perjury, and then that ghastly scaffold in the yard of the Cellular Jail. But would he get that far? Wouldn't Philimore, if he came face to face with him, gun him down out of hand? He remembered the pedantic officialese of the passage in the Book covering attempted escape '. . . justifiable use of firearms while in hot pursuit of an absconding felon who fails to stand and surrender when ordered.'

He thought briefly about the possibility of stealing a canoe, but he put it away from him as hopeless. Something just short of a hundred and fifty miles to the nearest point of the mainland – Burma – without food, water or a compass. He'd never make it – and if he did, what would he do when he got there? No money, naked except for his convict's necklace, and, again to quote the Book, the knowledge of the standing reward of five thousand rupees to anybody who detained an escaper and handed him over to the police, or half that to 'such person lodging information that should eventually lead to the apprehension of said absconder or escapee.' And, conversely, the penalties for aiding a fugitive '. . . not exceeding five years' rigorous imprisonment.' No – that was out.

His shoulder was still not paining, but he could feel himself weakening and he knew he had lost a lot of blood. He gazed longingly at the dark line of the hills behind the beach. He was almost abreast of the light now, and it was shining like a welcoming beacon. Oh, God – if he could only talk to somebody – to ask for one word of guidance. He had no right to involve Paul in this, but at least he wouldn't be shot on the spot if he gave himself up to him. He'd have a trial, and that which he'd say at it would ensure that Philimore wouldn't be having it all his own way thereafter. He'd at least have the satisfaction of making it uncomfortable for the son of a bitch, whatever his own fate might be. And finally, he would be able to give the nearest approach he had to a friend in the whole bloody, lousy, cock-eyed cesspit of a world, the true facts of the case. It was this last point that decided him. He turned towards the beach and swam slowly in.

The camp was dark and silent. The warders slept in a hut at the end of the barbed wire compound, and one was supposed to make a circuit of the fence every half-hour, but Wyndham knew that this was honoured in the breach more than the observance, so he risked walking up the corduroy track rather than leave fresh footprints across the sand. He knew what he was going to do now, and it brought him some marginal ease of mind. He would lie up in the jungle behind the hut until Paul returned, and then surrender to him – and he'd do whatever the other advised. He'd have to be careful. The prisoners were unlocked at dawn, Paul's orderly among them. He'd come up to the hut and make chhota hazri (early breakfast), then, after performing a few simple domestic chores round the place, he'd go back to the camp for his own meal. That would be the time to come in – provided, of course, Paul had returned from Narpunga by then. He climbed the slope and walked wearily, almost somnambulistically, along the ropeway. Out of the tepid sea his shoulder was beginning to hurt. The hut was padlocked but the small lean-to cookhouse behind it was doorless and he was able to slake his by now intolerable thirst from the water chatthi. He crossed the small clearing behind the hut and sank into a patch of undergrowth just as the sound of a motor came to him.

There were two of them – the Ford and a police patrol truck, and they swept up and stopped in front of the hut, and Wyndham's heart almost stopped with them, but then he heard Philimore call out over the noise of the still running engines, 'Richards won't be back yet. I told him to stay there until we arrived,' and someone grunted an acknowledgement and added querulously, 'Tell that bloody fool of a constable to keep those dogs quiet in the back of the truck, will you. They must have smelt a jackal or some damned thing,' and Wyndham could hear snarls and whines and the rattle of chains as dogs tried to leap down on to the track. Then the two vehicles jerked forward and went on their way. He had heard of the police dogs from Port Cornwallis and, in fact, had once seen them when they were brought down to track a prisoner who had run amok and vanished into the jungle – a brace of rather dolorous beasts of uncertain breed that were credited by the convicts with almost supernatural powers.

He fell into a feverish sleep immediately, waking again with every nerve stretched to screaming tautness in what seemed only a few brief minutes. The sky was lightening along the eastern horizon, so he pulled himself painfully to his feet, only to feel his knees buckle under him. The orderly would be here soon, so he would have to go further back into the jungle and wait until he had gone again, but then he realized that the sound that had awakened him was that of the approaching motor-cycle. He waited in the shelter of the undergrowth, steadying himself against the trunk of a palm tree, and Paul rode in, blipped the engine and then switched off. Wyndham staggered forward and fell flat on his face. Paul jacked the machine up and went over to the other without a word and tried to raise him by the shoulders, felt him wince and grasped him round the chest.

Wyndham gasped, 'I've got – to tell you – what happened . . .'

'You're wounded, aren't you?' Paul said. 'I'd better have a look at that first.'

'I – don't want to – drag you – into anything . . .'

'Shut up – until I get you inside. Come on – lean on me . . .'

'Your orderly . . . ?'

'Never mind about him. This way.' He held Wyndham upright with one arm as he unlocked the door, then lowered him down into a cane chair and pulled his damp and bloodstained shirt over his head. Barely conscious, Wyndham felt the sting of antiseptic, then the comfort of lint held in place by firm bandaging. Paul said, 'Sniff this,' and held a bottle of ammonia under his nose. His head jerked back and he gasped and spluttered but his senses cleared momentarily.

'All right – what *did* happen?' Paul asked grimly.

'Philimore had gone to Cornwallis,' Wyndham said faintly but clearly. 'I was asleep. Furtado, the khansama, woke me and said Philimore had had a crash in the truck down the track and had crawled to the bungalow badly hurt. I sent him down here to get you, and I went up to the bungalow. It was in darkness. I went in and fell over the woman – struck a match – she was obviously dead – blood everywhere. Then a torch shone on me and Philimore said, "I'd like to see you hang, but this way'll save trouble" – or something like that – then he fired. It got me in the shoulder. I ran – rolled down the slope – he fired a couple of times more. I made it to the water – dived in – swum along the reef. Came here to give myself up – but I wanted to tell you – my side of it – before that bastard takes me over . . .'

'*Their* story is that Furtado was awakened by a woman scream-ing,' Paul told him. 'He looked into the bungalow and saw Mrs Philimore fighting you off. He didn't know what to do. He was frightened to go to her assistance himself. Then he saw the lights of the truck in the distance, so he ran down the track to meet it and warned Philimore. He came in and tried to overpower you, but you were fighting drunk and waving a blood-stained knife. You attacked him, and he had no option but to draw his service revolver and let you have it – purposely in a non-vital spot, he says . . .'

'Like hell. He tried to kill me. He just happens to be a rotten shot, that's all,' Wyndham said wearily. 'All right – you've got the two versions. You take your choice which you believe.'

'I have,' Paul said simply. 'I believe yours.'

Wyndham felt absurdly like weeping. He swallowed hard and said, 'Thanks – but you're under no obligation to . . .'

'I know that – but I also know Philimore. The whole thing fits . . .'

'You mean the bint in Cornwallis?' Wyndham said. 'Yes, I'd worked that out for myself.'

'She was the last brick in the wall. He hated his wife anyhow. Felt she'd held his promotion up – and he was probably right . . .' He paused and took a deep breath. 'But, by God, he's got the case against you packed tight, I'm afraid. Furtado is word perfect. You've been up at the bungalow two or three times, and she's had to chase you off. She threatened to report you to her husband.'

'Then why the hell didn't she?'

'Afraid that she'd be blamed for encouraging you, according to Furtado – her only confidant. She's had a bit of trouble that way before, and Philimore nearly took the hide off her,' Paul said.

'Then they've got a knife which Furtado has identified as belonging to you. Forbidden pattern, pointed . . .'

'Everybody has them. I bought mine from a warder for twenty cigarettes – and missed it this afternoon . . .'

'And brandy. There was an empty bottle rolling around on the floor . . .'

'Probably the one I took up there.'

'Where did you get it from?'

'*He* gave it to me. He sent me up in the afternoon to get two bottles from the medical store. He told me to keep one for him in the office, and that I could have the other myself.'

'Again I believe you – but you must admit that it's a pretty unlikely story.'

'Looking back on it, yes,' Wyndham said ruefully. 'But at the time I was too delighted to get it to start questioning motives. I knew I was proving useful to the swine and I thought he was just keeping everything sweet. Incidentally he got me to forge Tegetmeier's signature for them in the ledger.'

'I know that. The police were very interested in the brandy angle. They found a crudely made duplicate key to the medical store when they searched your shed. They checked and found that you'd removed two bottles yesterday afternoon and one a few days before, and cooked the book. And other stuff is missing – powdered milk and chlorodine and sulpha guenodon – all saleable to the locals.'

Wyndham gestured hopelessly. 'Well, that's it, then. I can make a statement, but as you said, it all sounds pretty unlikely even in my own ears. I'm glad *you* believe me though – or say you do.'

'I do,' Paul said firmly. 'But it's no use our blinding ourselves to the fact that you're in a clamp, Charles. The first thing is to get you away from here. The police truck will be going backwards and forwards along the ropeway . . .'

'Get me away *where*?' Wyndham asked impatiently. 'If you try you're going to land in the cart yourself. Don't be a damned fool.'

'If you *don't* get away, you're going to hang,' Paul said quietly. 'I can see one chance – a slim one, but still a chance.'

'What?'

'The boat.'

'What boat?'

'My boat – properly provisioned – and I can give you a compass and a chart of the Burma coast . . .'

'Which implicates you immediately . . .'

'Not of necessity. I don't discover it's missing for three or four days, by which time you should be there. It's only a hundred and thirty miles approximately to the nearest point – Cape Negrais, at the mouth of the Irrawaddy – and at this time of the year you'll have the wind and current dead behind you.'

'But surely there'd be a sea search?' Wyndham was fighting down a wild surge of hope.

'Not unless a boat is missing. That will be checked right along the coast this morning. No missing boats – right, you've gone inland . . .'

'But how will you cover the fact that yours is missing?'

'It's there today,' Paul said. 'Tomorrow and the next day, and the next, I'll be out with a squad of warders beating the jungle for you. They can hardly blame me for not realizing it's been pinched if I only get back after dark each day.'

'Oh, God,' said Wyndham, catching his breath. Do you really think there's a chance – without getting you into trouble, I mean?'

Paul nodded gravely. 'A chance,' he said. 'But as I said, it's a pretty slim one.'

'I don't care how slim it is, as long as I don't have to sit here like a lame duck, waiting to be taken.' Wyndham seemed to be inwardly praying.

'There should be nothing too difficult about the actual crossing,' Paul said. 'Providing you don't run into a monsoon storm. All you've got to do is to keep going dead north-east, and you must hit land. That cockleshell will make five knots before the wind. Six miles or thereabouts an hour – theoretically you should cover a hundred and forty-four miles in twenty-four hours. Double that – call it forty-eight hours if you like – and you're still not being too optimistic. But we can talk about all that later. The thing now is to get you under cover.'

'But where?'

'The best place I can think of is the cave where I took you before.'

'But that would involve getting the boat out . . . ?' Wyndham began, but Paul shook his head.

'No – it's only a short walk from here across the headland. We went the long way round by boat. Can you swim under water?'

'Reasonably well.'

Paul rose and picked up a woven straw bag. 'I'll get some grub,' he said. 'I keep a bit of tinned stuff here. There's drinking water already there.'

'But isn't there a chance of running into your orderly?' Wyndham asked nervously. 'It's almost light.'

'They all stay locked up while a search is on,' Paul told him. He started to rummage in a cupboard. 'Let's see. Yes – here's some beans, bully beef, sardines, biscuits. Mustn't forget a can opener. Yes, here we are – and a knife. Do you read much, Charles?'

'When I get the chance. Why?'

'I can give you the choice of the *Bible, Indian Prison Regulations* and *Pickwick Papers*.'

'I know *Regulations* by heart,' Wyndham said. 'Meakin gave me a copy in my cell. Better make it *Pickwick Papers*. God gave me up as a bad job a long time ago.'

'I'm not a religious man,' Paul said. 'But I don't think He ever gives anybody up completely – not while they keep trying. Right, wait here while I see if there are any lights coming from either way.' He went out, and returned a few minutes later. 'All clear,' he said. 'We cross the road into the scrub the other side. Keep right on my heels and try not to rustle the bushes too much. It will take us about half an hour to get to the point above the entrance, then there's a stiffish climb down. Do you feel up to it?'

'I feel up to anything,' Wyndham said. 'But I can't help being a bit worried about you. What if someone comes looking for you while you're away?'

Paul slapped his holstered revolver. 'Keen and efficient young officer,' he said. 'I've been out searching the cliff tops. Don't you worry about *me*, Charles.'

They pushed through the dense scrub, parallel to the ropeway, with the sea on their right. Wyndham's earlier weakness had passed, but Paul paused for him to rest several times.

'I'm all right now,' Wyndham protested.

'You're not,' Paul said. 'You've lost a hell of a lot of blood. Fortunately the bullet seems to have gone right through without hitting a bone, but you mustn't take any chances with it. I'll bring fresh dressings when I come next – oh, and a file, and you can pass some of your time getting rid of that necklace of yours.'

'I'd be lost without it,' Wyndham said wryly.

'You'll be lost *with* it if you're picked up over there,' Paul said tersely. 'Come on – let's get moving.'

They came to the top of the cliff as the sun rose like an orange tennis ball above the horizon, and Paul swung over the edge and climbed down a few feet.

'Right,' he called softly. 'Over you come. Don't look down, and don't worry about your feet. I'll guide those. You just concentrate on handholds. How's your left one?'

'It's all right,' Wyndham muttered through clenched teeth, but he was suffering the agonies of the damned by the time they got to the bottom.

The tide was half-way on the ebb, and he could see the top of the pink finger of coral a hundred yards or so along the foot of the cliff. Paul stripped and left his clothes, belt and revolver under a rock, and lowered himself into deep water. Wyndham followed him, and found the chill refreshing.

It was quite a short swim under water – then they were in the cave.

Chapter 15

There was no sound but the muted sigh of the swell that rose and fell in the cave in synchronism with the surf outside, but the ever-present sixth sense of the hunted jerked him into wakefulness. It must have been full daylight but the tide was covering the entrance and in here there was only a soft green dimness. He rolled to the edge of the shelf in the wall to which he had retreated as the little beach below had become submerged – and he saw them immediately. Two heads like those of black seals.

They trod water in the middle of the cave for some minutes, their small hard eyes searching the walls, then one of them spoke to the other in a soft, clicking, sibilant chatter, and they upended like feeding ducks, kicked, and swam back through the entrance, their dark bodies shadowy against the light for a moment – then they were gone.

He lay, weak and trembling with the shock, wondering whether this was a chance visit or part of the search. They were Andaman-ese – the small aboriginal native, less than five feet, like the African pygmy. They were wrongly reputed to be cannibals by the convicts, and they were rarely seen near the settlements, but Wyndham had heard that a few were employed by the police, and their reputation as trackers transcended that of the dogs. He waited with his eyes fixed on the light patch below the surface that was the entrance, expecting to see others flash down in a dive and turn and come up towards him. Then, when they didn't, he told himself that they hadn't seen him. Then again, as the dragging minutes passed, he was convinced that they had, and that the whole pack was waiting outside for the tide to fall, like terriers by a rat hole.

The level of the water dropped – lower – lower – until there was a streak of undiffused light at the top of the entrance, and outside sounds were once more coming to him: the surf on the reef, wind in the undergrowth on the cliff face, and the cries of sea birds. Hour after hour he waited, until the 'doorstep', as Paul had called it, was again awash, not daring to leave the ledge in case they returned and caught him like a fly clinging to the wall, or on the beach below. Then as daylight was fading, he ventured down and swam to the entrance and peered out.

The lagoon was silent and deserted, and he came out into the warm evening air thankfully, because inside it was dank and chill and he was cramped from his long vigil on the rocky ledge, and his shoulder was throbbing painfully. He had no watch but he judged it to be about six o'clock. This time yesterday he was locking up the prisoners – half drunk. He would have sold his soul for a drink now. He stretched out on a sloping rock until the tide turned and started to rise again, then he reluctantly slid into the water and went back. It was pitch dark inside now and he completely lost all sense of direction and kept coming up against the rock face instead of grounding on the beach, then something cold and slimy below the surface brushed against his legs, and he screamed and thrashed wildly until he realized that he was in a patch of long-fronded seaweed. He pulled himself together and swam round the wall until his feet felt the sand again. Shaking like a leaf he climbed the fifteen feet to the ledge and drank from the tiny fresh water pool, then lay on his back staring up into the darkness. He was exhausted and his whole being was craving for more sleep, but he kept imagining small black figures swimming silently under water and creeping up on him, and the cave, so short a time ago a friendly place of refuge, was now one of creeping, paralysing terror, so he remained in shivering wakefulness.

Wyndham was not a physical coward, but he was weak and feverish from his wound, and the events of the last twenty-four hours had frightened and disoriented him. Fortunately he realized this, and his mind went back to some half-forgotten lecture at Sandhurst: '. . . there will be times when you'll be frightened – deadly frightened. Those times will be mostly when you're on your own. With your men there to watch, you will instinctively behave properly. Alone, you should keep your mind fully occupied – *positively* occupied. Praying and reciting poetry are both negative . . .' So he began to marshal the problems that would face him on the passage. Water? How much would he need, and how would he carry it? Plugged coconuts? That's what the locals used, he'd heard somewhere. Hell of a job to fill them from this pool. He'd need a funnel. Wonder if Paul had one? But how the devil would he get enough of them down here to him? Drop 'em over the edge? Heads below! Stand clear! He started to hum the silly words of a Cockney ditty,

> 'There stands a luvverly row er cokernuts,
> There stands a luvverly row er Balls,
> There stands me wife – the darlin' of me life,
> Singin' roll er bowl, a penny er roll er bowl.'

Then he was shouting it, howling the refrain until the echoes reverberated round the unseen vaulted roof – and he went on to others – the bawdy songs he had heard British troops singing on the march, the whole long and dirty repertoire, until he came to,

> 'A workman working at Woolwich Dock,
> Came home one morn at five o'clock
> And found his pal was chock-a-block
> In his wife in the pride of the morning . . .'

and he stopped in mid-bellow as the ghastly appositeness of the doggerel came home to him. But it had served as a safety valve, and sanity had returned when, perhaps an hour or so later, he heard Paul calling softly in the darkness.

'OK,' he answered. 'I'm here – on the ledge.' He felt for the watertight tin the other had given him and struck a match, and Paul swam across and hauled himself on to the rock.

He said, 'I was scared when I saw the Cornwallis police launch anchored off here this afternoon.'

'*You* were scared?' Wyndham said with feeling. 'They sent a couple of Andamanese divers in. Fortunately the beach was covered, and I was up here.'

'I should have warned you about that, but it never occurred to me that anybody else would know of this place. Don't risk going on to the beach again when it is uncovered. They've got eyes like hawks even in the half darkness, and they might spot your footprints.'

'Do you think they'll come again?'

'You never know, although at the moment everybody's inclined to think you've gone inland. At least, that's one theory.

Philimore is positive that you've drowned. You left a blood trail right along the wharf to the water's edge. How is your shoulder?'

'A bit stiff, but not too painful. Suppose I had drowned, what would have happened to my carcass?'

'You'd have floated out until the turn of the tide, and then the current would pretty certainly have washed you up into the swamp to the south of Narpunga – unless, of course, the sharks and barracuda had got you,' Paul told him. 'They've got some prisoners watching down there. Double rations and five hundred bidis for the first one to spot you, dead or alive.'

'I'm an important bloke,' Wyndham said.

'*And* dangerous. The police and prison staff have been told to take no chances. Shoot on sight and ask questions afterwards.'

'They haven't questioned Philimore's story?'

'I don't think so. Furtado has corroborated everything he has said, and the orderly has told how he saw you taking some brandy from the medical store in the afternoon, and, finally, the prisoners have sworn you were drunk when you locked them up.'

Wyndham sighed. 'The devil of it is that they're right – or almost. I did take the brandy, although the orderly couldn't have known what it was then, because I had it in a bag – but it shows that he'd been put up to it. I wasn't actually drunk when I locked up, though I'd had two or three stiff snorts from the bottle Philimore said I could have.' He turned suddenly to Paul in the darkness. 'Look – my story is pretty thin, and I couldn't blame you for not believing it. You don't have to, you know – although I swear it's the truth.'

'I've never doubted it for a moment,' Paul said quietly. 'In fact, since seeing and hearing Philimore I'm more convinced than ever. The whole thing is too pat – too logical – too absolutely *right*. If he had any real intelligence, instead of sheer low cunning, he'd slip up in a detail here and there – and correct himself afterwards. That will come later though, because he's going to be in trouble for all sorts of irregularities – busted regulations, dereliction of duty – everything – when the departmental inquiry is held. He'll probably be fired, or at least asked to resign, for that.'

'He should worry,' Wyndham said gloomily. 'He'll marry his bint and live the life of Reilly thereafter – and losing his job for being an idle and corrupt bastard still doesn't clear me of murder.'

'I'm afraid not. You've been tried and condemned already as far as the Authorities are concerned.' Paul leaned forward. 'Help me pull this up. I've brought some stuff in a waterproof bag. Dump it all out beside you. I want to take the bag back with me.'

Something caught in Wyndham's throat. 'Christ, you're taking some risks,' he said. 'And *why*? Why should you do all this for *me*?'

'I told you. Family.'

'And what a bloody family. Do you know their history – from old Great-grandfather Sam downwards?'

'Pretty well. My mother was very proud of her descent. Look – when you land you should make for the Siamese border – it's barely a hundred miles due east from the coast, south of Rangoon. There's no extradition treaty between them and India. I've put a map in with this stuff I've brought tonight – not very good – it's just a sheet torn out of an atlas but it will help. And there's two hundred rupees wrapped in a piece of oiled silk. I'm afraid it's all I have here . . .'

'I'm not taking it ' said Wyndham firmly.

'Don't be a damned fool,' Paul snapped. 'You wouldn't stand a chance without money. You'll have to buy some clothes for a start – nothing of mine would fit you – and food, and something to get along with until you find your feet.'

Wyndham didn't answer. Again he felt a catch in his throat.

Paul went on, 'Bangkok is a big port. Native craft as well as steamers. They run to Java – that's Dutch, and Timor, and even to the Northern Australian coast. Christ, man, you've got the whole of the Far East ahead of you. I almost wish I was coming with you.'

'Don't *you* be a damned fool,' Wyndham mumbled.

'I must get back,' Paul said, rising. 'You'll have to stick it out here for another twenty-four hours, I'm afraid. I'll be taking a patrol inland tomorrow, and won't be back until sundown, but then I'll bring the boat round and you can be off.'

'No,' Wyndham begged. 'I've changed my mind. I'm sorry I've let you go to all this trouble for nothing . . .'

'Then what the hell *are* you going to do?' Paul asked angrily.

'Work my way up the coast. If I can pinch a boat and do things off my own bat, I'll do it . . .'

'You won't, you bloody fool. You wouldn't have a chance.'

'It's your boat that worries me. If I'm taken in it you'll be implicated.'

'If you're taken in it then it will be assumed that you've stolen it.'

'But all this stuff of yours. That will connect you with it.'

'Anything that is likely to arouse suspicion must be dumped before they come up with you – that will be the compass, map, money and a bit of tinned stuff – oh, and a couple of files to work on that necklace. You must keep everything in the bag ready to drop over the side in one piece.'

'But the other stuff?' Wyndham insisted. 'The food . . . ?'

'Fruit that could have been pinched from anywhere – and two two-gallon water containers from one of the fishing boats. I've got it all worked out.'

'But the boat itself? You keep it on the beach – and it takes four men to lift it.'

'I've got that worked out, too. I had it put in the water yesterday, because it was drying out and warping. It's often done.' He chuckled. 'You know, I've rather enjoyed it all. It's been like playing chess. Thinking of all possible moves and counter-moves in advance. Charles – we're going to do it. *We are going to do it*. Up the Wyndhams. Good night.' He slipped silently into the water and Wyndham heard him call softly before going through the entrance.

'Thank God there's no moon,' Wyndham said.

'There is,' Paul told him, 'but it's behind that big cloudbank to the south. I'm afraid that's a sign of wind.'

'Just what I want, as long as it's in the right direction.'

'Yes – but you can have too much of a good thing. Know anything about sea-anchors?'

'A bit. It blows on the Cornish coast too, you know.'

'All right then – if it gets too much, stream that rope with the net of coconuts on the end. As long as they're nose on to it, these things will ride out anything.'

'You said last night that you almost wished you were coming with me,' Wyndham said.

'And I wasn't pulling your leg.'

'And I'm not pulling yours when I say "so do I". God, old boy – I hope I'm not letting you in for anything.'

'We've had all that out. You won't let me in for anything as long as you keep your head. Remember the address?'

'Paul Richards, number seventy-two Palighat, Frazer Town, Bangalore, Mysore, South India,' Wyndham recited.

'Disguise the handwriting, of course, and sign it "John Moody". My father will forward it if I'm not there. Just say that you're interested in buying some morchi shells and have I any for sale? If you think it's safe for me to write back, give a real post office number, underlined. If it's not, make one up and don't underline it. Remember all that?'

'I think so.'

'Good. Well, I'll take you out to the gap in the reef, and swim back . . .'

'You will not!' Wyndham said emphatically.

'Don't let's argue again,' Paul said shortly. 'I know the gap. You don't.'

They paddled across the mirror-smooth lagoon. Behind them Wyndham could hear the palms stirring in the rising wind, and he knew a lift of heart as he felt it on his right cheek. Just in the correct direction.

'Don't raise your sail until you're a mile or so out,' Paul cautioned. 'If the moon came out somebody might spot it from the lighthouse at Cornwallis. The survey sloop won't worry you. It's round taking soundings the other side of the island.'

'What about the police launch?'

'Down to the south in Stewart Sound – combing the mangroves. It's not coming back until tomorrow afternoon – by which time you ought to be nearly there. Don't forget to dump your prison shirt and slacks before you get in. There's a piece of rock up in front to sink them.'

'You think of everything, don't you?' Wyndham smiled.

'I've tried to. There's a hunk of cotton cloth under the thwart. Tear it in two and use one bit for a loin cloth and one for a turban. Just what the well-dressed Tamil is wearing. I believe there are lots of them working in the rice paddies, so you wouldn't be conspicuous at a distance, but for God's sake get rid of that necklace. You'll really have to work with the files.'

'I'll watch it.' He repeated the address again. 'Paul Richards, number seventy-two Palighat, Frazer Town, Bangalore, Mysore, South India, Mr John Moody wants to know if you've got any morchi shells for sale. Underline a post office box number if it's safe to answer – don't if it's not.'

'Good. Hang on – here's the gap. Don't paddle. Leave it to me.' They shot through between combers and Paul said, 'Keep the light at Cornwallis half-left, then get on to course with the compass – north-east all the way. You'll do it, Charles – you will – you will – *you will*.' And then he went over the side, and Wyndham heard him swimming fast towards the reef – and the catch was back in his throat.

He paddled steadily for what seemed an hour or more, the lighthouse dropping astern rapidly, then, not without difficulty because the wind was steadily rising, he got the twin masts up, and the grass sail set and drawing. He uncovered the old but serviceable army prismatic compass that hung round his neck on a thong, and glanced at the pre-set luminous guide point. North-sixty-East. He was heading too far south. He twisted the steering paddle and bore a little to port. Forty-five. That was it. Dead on.

Then the fear and despondency of the cave slipped from his shoulders and once again he was singing – but this time there was no note of hysteria in it.

Chapter 16

The Cornwallis light was now only an intermittent flash on the western horizon, and the loom of Saddle Mountain was lost in the night sky. He picked up the Pole star and kept it well to the left of the pointed prow of the canoe, and was thus relieved of the necessity of having to check frequently with the small compass. He had no difficulty in keeping a straight course, but he had to retain a constant pressure on the steering paddle. Twice he tried to run before the wind while filing at the chain round his neck, but each time he nearly broached to, and the outrigger lifted frighteningly, so he gave up the attempt and decided to wait for more favourable conditions.

The sea, glass smooth when he started, was now coming up in long rollers from the south, and the wind was whipping the crests from them in a stinging spindrift that soaked him to the skin. It was not unpleasant at first as both the wind and water were warm, but after a time the coarse wet material of his shirt started to anneal with the dressing on his shoulder into a soggy lump, so he pulled the shirt over his head and was about to throw it away, but changed his mind and stuffed it under a thwart when he realized that he would need some protection against the blazing sun next day.

Steering was becoming more difficult now, because his course lay obliquely across the line of the rollers, which meant that he was constantly climbing up to the broken crests and sliding down into the intervening valleys like a crab – and in the valleys he was blanketed from the wind and the canoe had a decided tendency to yaw. But overall he was still making headway, and he was, as yet, reluctant to lose time by heaving to and putting her nose into the weather.

But the storm was increasing in force, and the wind was gusting and changing erratically in direction, giving him a violent corkscrew motion, and the twin masts were bending like canes, so eventually he had to lower them and try and stow the sail one-handed, while still holding the light craft against broaching to with the steering paddle which, now that the way was taken off her, was becoming heavier and less effective. He managed, after a fashion, and felt for the long grass rope in the bottom of the canoe, and bent it on to the net of a dozen coconuts that Paul had stowed in the nose, then he paid it out over the stern, and felt the strain lessen almost immediately as the bow swung up into the wind. The weather was now streaming past him, and he sat hunched in the stern facing the wind and the spray that had become a solid particulate cloud that whipped and stung his bare torso like flying gravel. But at least he was relieved of the galley-slave toil with the steering paddle. He had a burning thirst, but the water cans were under the tumbled sail and he could not risk endangering his precarious balance by rummaging for them.

He was not frightened. This was something physical and understandable that he could draw satisfaction from in fighting; something that helped to restore his confidence and self-respect. He was running, certainly, but with a purpose now – using once more the wits and initiative that had become stultified in the past year. He'd beat these bastards yet, he exulted. That he'd made a holy hash of things up there on the Frontier, he freely admitted to himself – but he hadn't deserved all they'd dished out to him since. A cashiering and even a few years' imprisonment he'd have accepted as fair. He hadn't meant to kill one of his own men, for God's sake! But a death sentence – none the less nerve-shattering because it hadn't been carried out, then a lifetime in this place. How many long-term men in a thousand ever went back to the mainland? Seventy-four, he'd seen in some statistics or other in the office – and none of them murderers. And here they were trying to stick another crime on him! One he hadn't committed, but for which he'd take that ghastly walk for absolute, rock-bottom, dead certain if they caught up with him. Well, they wouldn't. He'd reach Burma or drown – cheating them either way. Mr Pereira wasn't collecting five rupees on *him*. And having reached Burma, he'd go on. Like Paul said, Bangkok – wangle a berth as a sailor. They probably wouldn't be too pernickety about papers on a foreign ship – stow away if necessary. The vital thing was to get away from here – the 'here' that had already become a 'there', he reflected with satisfaction.

He soared to the top of the next overtaking crest and in a momentary rift in the flying spray he thought he saw a light far away to starboard. Then he was plunging into the next valley. He strained his eyes as he came up again, and this time he was certain. Not one light, but at least three, irregularly spaced in a line in the far distance, and he yelled triumphantly as he thought for a moment that he was already in sight of the Burmese coast – but then he sobered. He could not have been more than nine or ten hours under way – the last couple of them hove to. Seven hours at five knots while running before the wind – say forty miles or thereabouts with perhaps two or three more gained by general drift since he lowered the sail. No – he hadn't even reached the half-way mark yet. No good getting over-optimistic. He wasn't doing so badly, nonetheless. They were ships, of course. He'd have to be careful when daylight came. He wouldn't want some mistakenly kind skipper to scoop him up as a shipwrecked mariner, only to decant him into the arms of the police at the next port. This bloody *necklace*! He should have done something about it earlier. He'd start again with the file as soon as the wind dropped.

Then the outrigger, unsupported in thin air as the main hull balanced on the crest of a roller, snapped cleanly off – right through both connecting spars – and the canoe spun like a floating log jumped upon by an unhandy lumberjack.

He went down fast, enveloped in the sodden grass sail, and such was the absolute totality of the catastrophe that he didn't even feel resentment. Just acceptance. This was it. Well, he'd said Burma or drown, hadn't he? Balls to the lot of them. At least he wouldn't hang. Then the instinctive will for survival asserted itself, and he kicked and struggled and broke surface, to find himself alongside the overturned hull, entangled in the trailing rope, and he grabbed at it wildly and hung on.

And he was still hanging on when the wind dropped at dawn and the sun came up into the now cloudless sky, unconscious and almost drained of blood, because the wound in his shoulder had opened and the sea around the waterlogged hull was stained pink. He was unaware of the hands that pulled him over the low bulwarks, or of the faces that were gathered in a circle around him, looking down on him as he lay on the iron deck, stark naked except for a steel necklace and an old service prismatic compass on a thong round his neck.

Someone was pillowing his head and squeezing water into his mouth from a sponge gripped in a hand that smelt of fish. There was a face behind the hand, but it was an immeasurable distance away and he couldn't get it into focus – nor was he particularly interested. He was interested only in the water, and they, he, or whoever it was, wouldn't give him enough. His dehydrated system was shrieking for buckets, cascades, streams, oceans of it, but they just tantalized him with the sponge – hour after hour, in trickling, stinking droplets. He tried to grab the hand, struggling feebly and whimpering petulantly like an infant teased with a feeding bottle, and the effort forced him softly but inexorably back into oblivion.

Then later there *was* a feeding bottle – an improvised affair that he recognized as a cracked teapot with a rag teat in the spout, and he was conscious of the taste of watered-down canned milk. He was fond of it normally, and he eked out for days the can a month he allowed himself from the canteen. But now it was making him sick. All he wanted was water – and for his shoulder to stop hurting – and to be done with the stink of fish.

When he came to again he was in fact being given more water in a porcelain cup with flowers painted on it that rattled against his teeth, and this time he saw the face – flat, yellow and impassive – and he was conscious of a vibration below him, and the distant rumble of engines, and beyond the man who was giving him the water he made out the rail of a ship, and the wake was creaming past. He was lying on a straw mat under a tattered canvas awning, and there was some washing strung on a line between a winch and a ventilator to one side of it.

He was still incapable of coherent thought, but he was aware of being taken somewhere he didn't want to go to. He was even conscious, by some instinct akin to that of migrating birds, of travelling in the wrong direction towards something that was repellent to him – something that must be avoided at all costs – and in the temporary absence of the fishy dispenser of water he tried to crawl to the rail and to climb through. They moved him into a small airless cabin then and locked him in, and that brought the past back to him in all its horror. He was a prisoner again, and the knowledge plunged him into depths from which he had neither the strength nor the will to rise.

But the flat-faced one was there the whole time, feeding him, coaxing him, renewing the dressing on his shoulder, chiding him gently in a language that was totally unknown to him but the import of which was unmistakable.

And so, in spite of himself, after what seemed aeons, but which was actually little more than a week, his strength started to return, and they carried him back on to the open deck where the fresh sea breeze dispelled the claustrophobia of the cabin, and with partial recovery came full comprehension.

He was on a trawler – that was self-evident. Her name was on a paint-blistered board on the side of her rusty wheelhouse in block letters and what he assumed were Japanese characters. The *Tegato Maru* and her port of registry, Hakodate. There were two other ships – one somewhat larger, and the other a twin of this one – battered, rusty, but workmanlike. They sailed like a duck with two ducklings, in line astern normally, but sometimes, when a hail came from the larger one, the two smaller craft would fan out to port and starboard of the mother ship, and they would pass lines from one to the other, and the winches would rattle as the nets and seine boards went over the stern, and they would steam slowly ahead for an hour or two before bringing them inboard again – and the decks would be a heaving mass of glittering silver and red and yellow guts as they cleaned the fish and stowed them below in the ice-rooms, or laid them out to dry in the sun in salt under nets to keep the gulls off. He remembered snatches of conversation between Philimore and people from the fish canning company about the 'stinking, dirty, bloody, thieving Jap bastards' who were trawling the Bay of Bengal bare – and one occasion when the RIM survey sloop had arrested two of them inside the three-mile limit. They were, however, allowed to re-bunker and take on water in the Andamans, and he had often seen them at anchor from his cell window at Port Blair. It must have been the lights of these three he had seen before he was wrecked, he decided – hove to in the storm.

They were heading south now, slowly and with many stops for trawling, logging no more net gain than a possible twenty or

thirty miles a day. Far to the west he could make out the faint
outline of Saddle Mountain. He wondered dully if they already
knew about him over there, then decided that they didn't because
this vessel, and as far as he could see, the others, were not equipped
with wireless. No, these Japanese were in no hurry. He was quite
safe aboard her. They'd hand him over when they went into port
in the ordinary way – and claim the reward. Quite a nice little
bonus – five thousand rupees. They'd have to haul an awful lot
of fish for that. That they knew what he was, he had no doubts
whatsoever. Some of them, if not all, would have been ashore in
the Andamans and seen the necklaces before. Oh, yes – they had
a pearl of price in him, and they knew it. That's why they were
taking such good care of him – feeding him three or four times
a day, on unfamiliar but not unpalatable food. Fish, cooked and
raw, a sort of seaweed, rice and canned milk and fruit, small
wheaten cakes that he felt were specially baked for him by the
little grinning cook, who used to come out of his galley and
grasp his own right wrist with the finger and thumb of the other
hand, then point to himself and go through the motions of
running, and finally dissolve into peals of laughter. Was he
trying to tell him that he, also, was a convict on the run? He'd
made a better fist of things if that were so, Wyndham reflected
sourly.

He never quite made out how many of them there were.
Perhaps twenty or more. They all looked alike, and none of them
spoke English or any other language that he knew, but they were
all friendly, and the man who had first taken it as his especial
task to feed him water was particularly so. If Wyndham ate, he
was delighted. If he turned away from the food he was genuinely
cast down. Wyndham decided to give both him and the cook a
hundred rupees each before he was taken ashore, because he had
fastened the little oiled silk roll that Paul had given him to the
strap of the compass that still hung round his neck with the
chain and disc. They were an honest crowd, at all events. He
alternated between gratitude to them for what they had done for
him, to hatred for what they were about to do.

The days dragged by. They were still standing south. Saddle
Mountain had dropped below the horizon now, and one night
Wyndham saw the flash of a lighthouse far to the west. Long

beam – three shorts – another long – then two shorts – a pause – then the routine was repeated. That was Port Blair. He remembered how the light used to flash through the bars of his cell. So they were not calling there? Not right away, anyhow. Maybe they would at the end of this sweep – unless, of course, they went straight back to Japan when their fish holds were full. He wondered what sort of chance he would have there. Hakodate? He seemed to remember from some atlas or other that that was up on one of the northern islands of Japan.

With the dawning of this new glimmer of hope he started to take an interest in the things around him. The course? He wandered up to the wheelhouse and the man at the helm was delighted to show him the simple workings of the place – the engine-room telegraph that was marked plainly in English, 'Stop – Half Ahead – Slow – Finished with Engines' etc., and bore the trademark of a famous Glasgow firm – and the compass, that was notated N, E, S and W with the half-cardinals and numbers between also understandable. There was a chart pinned out on a table – British Admiralty, again in English, but overprinted in Japanese characters. There was a tiny flag on a pin stuck into it, which he took to be today's noon position, and from it he guessed that the large island they had passed to port some hours previously must have been Little Andaman – detached to the south of the main group by some twenty-six miles of open water.

That put the Nicobars straight ahead of them. He wondered if they were likely to stop there, and whether it would benefit him in any way if they did – but he decided that it wouldn't. The Nicobars, islands similar to the Andamans, although not any longer a penal colony, were under the same administration. He smiled his thanks at the helmsman and left, not wanting to show too great an interest in the chart at this stage. But he went back frequently in the days that followed, and saw that the course had now bent to the west. Were they going to circle completely round, he wondered, and eventually go back to the Andamans?

He offered in dumb show to take a trick at the wheel. The captain, distinguishable from the rest of the crew only by the wreck of a white-topped cap that he wore on his cropped head night and day, seemed a little doubtful at first, but allowed him to take the wheel for a short time under his own guidance, then, when he showed his competence, they were delighted to let him do it regularly, even providing him with a stool, a luxury not permitted the others. He was able to puzzle things out for himself after that. He noticed that they never fished in really deep water, but always where it was shoaling, and the areas where they had shot their nets were neatly marked on the chart in pencilled circles. There was a line of them extending right down the Burma coast, then more round the Andamans, and more again the last few days near the Nicobars.

But now they were in deep water, and would be for the next five hundred miles if they kept on their present course – all the way to the coast of Ceylon, which lay dead ahead. And hold it they did, steaming steadily in the wake of the mother ship until, on the fourth night after dropping Great Nicobar astern, Wyndham saw a lighthouse flashing far over their bows. Trincomalee, he learned from the chart – a major British naval station. Was this the answer? Were they going to stand right in and then make a signal to the shore? And would he find himself taken off by a naval patrol and then shipped off back to Port Blair in chains once more? But what was their reason in bringing him this far, only to hand him over, when, if that had been their intention, they would only have had to make a slight diversion to have accomplished the same end days ago?

They never let him steer at night, indicating by signs that he was not yet fit, and needed to sleep. But sleep wouldn't come that night, and he sat miserably watching the light coming nearer. Then, as the man at the wheel struck midnight, the captain, sleeping on the hatch in a quilted kimono and his never-doffed cap, rose, stretched, yawned and cocked an eye forward, then called an order which Wyndham heard acknowledged through the open windows of the wheelhouse. He felt the course change, hard to starboard, and saw the light slide round until it was dead on their port beam – and they were standing due north. The captain took up an Aldis lamp and blipped it several times, and it was answered twice far in the distance, because the three ships always widened their interval and sailed in line abreast at night.

So whatever else they intended to do, they weren't handing him over to the navy. Almost sick with relief he dropped into a deep exhausted sleep.

The coast was a thin blue line on the western horizon when he woke at dawn, and the sea, deep blue for the last few days, was pale and clear. They were still steering north – moving at no more than quarter speed in line astern – then after the cook had brought out the pots of steaming, jasmine-scented tea and rice cakes that was their breakfast, the mother ship's siren sounded wheezily on the still air, and they turned to starboard and went out to their position on the right flank, while their twin raced fussily to port.

He went up to the wheelhouse, but the captain, standing beside the man at the wheel and watching the course closely, smiled and shook his head. Quite sensibly he wasn't trusting his ship in shallow coastal waters to an amateur. Wyndham smiled his understanding back and glanced at the chart, but it told him nothing, as the little flag was still at yesterday's noon position. The captain, sensing his interest, stepped across and put his finger on Point Pedro, which is the northern-most tip of Ceylon, and then drew it up across Palk Strait to the Indian coast.

So that was it, he decided. A round-the-coast tour of the Bay of Bengal, fishing the shallows, with a side trip to the Andamans and the Nicobars, allowing nothing to divert them from their predetermined programme – like ants – or Japanese. But eventually they would have to put into port – the dictates of fuel, water and provisions would make that necessary – and every port practically right round the whole perimeter was British, or British controlled, from Ceylon in the west to the extreme south-east corner and the tiny sliver that was Siam. And after that came Malaya, and Singapore on the Straits of Malacca, also British. Yes, they had a wide choice. Anywhere would do – as soon as their holds were full, and there was no need for expensive diversions and loss of fishing time.

But it cut both ways. Once let them get within swimming distance of the shore – *any* shore that wasn't the Andamans – and he would be off. But he'd have to get rid of this necklace first. He must steal a file and start work under cover of darkness tonight. Cut through one link, but leave the thing in position, tying the two ends together with a piece of string. Many of the crew habitually wore sweat-rags round their necks to wipe off their faces from time to time. He'd have to get one, and use it as a cover. At all costs he mustn't let them see that he'd managed to get rid of it. That would rouse their suspicions immediately, and he'd probably find himself back under lock and key.

The siren sounded from the mother ship again, and two of the crew dropped over the side into a small boat and ferried the line across that carried the head of the net. That was something that might stand him in good stead. He had noticed that when they were in the fishing grounds they never bothered to hoist the boat inboard at night, but just left it moored under the stern.

They trawled all that day, shooting the nets and hauling in again at hourly intervals, and Wyndham gave a hand with the gutting, clumsily at first, but more expertly when some of the others good-naturedly showed him the knack of doing it with one slash of the razor-sharp knife without taking a finger off with it. He worked with them all day, but he still had time to look for a file, and he found one without difficulty in the engineer's cubby-hole abaft of the funnel.

They came up alongside the mother ship in the evening, and there was a long colloquy through megaphones from bridge to bridge, then, as darkness fell, the three trawlers anchored in line, spaced out at half-mile intervals. They were close inshore now, probably no more than two miles off the low-lying coast – coast not unlike that of the Andamans – sandy beach ending abruptly in dense palm and mangrove jungle, but lacking the dramatic backdrop of the hills. It appeared to be totally deserted, and no lights showed other than the flash from a lighthouse far to the south – Cape Calimere, Wyndham learned from the chart. That was why they were risking anchoring so close inshore, because they had obviously been poaching all day, well inside the three-mile limit. Madras a bare two hundred miles to the north, he reflected, as he sat right up on the fo'c'sle head, shielded from view by the winch, filing hour after hour on a link in the necklace. Madras, a big port for deep sea vessels, and also native craft – and short of there Nagapattinam and Cuddalore and, he noted with particular interest, Pondicherry, French, and entirely independent of British India – all fairly large ports according to the chart.

He gazed longingly at the dark line of the shore. Yes – this would be the place to make a break for it, but he realized the limitations his sickness had put upon him. Two miles – and no doubt some of it at least against the tide? No – he'd never make it. The boat? No again, he'd abandoned his half-formed intention of stealing it, for sound pragmatic reasons. If he just disappeared there would be a chance that the captain would not report the incident officially, but if he repaid the undoubted kindness of these people by stealing a valuable piece of their equipment, one could hardly blame them if they reacted angrily and gave the police at the first port they put into the fullest details.

No – first things first, he decided. Get rid of this damned thing round his neck and wait for a slightly better opportunity than the present one. Just a bit closer inshore one night. All other things being equal, he felt he could cope with a swim of one mile, even in his present weakened condition.

He was still filing when dawn broke – his right hand, holding the file, red raw and bleeding from contact with the rough beard he had grown since he last shaved weeks before, and his wounded shoulder aching intolerably from the strain of holding the chain with his left hand. And suddenly he was aware of the cook standing behind him with his breakfast of tea and rice cakes. The little man stared at him, then put the bamboo tray down on the deck softly and laid his finger across his lips, then turned and went swiftly and silently along the deck. To call the captain, Wyndham thought wearily, and he looked at the distant shore, trying to whip up his resolution to the point of diving over the side and risking everything in one last desperate effort.

But the cook was back in a matter of minutes with an implement that looked like an elongated pair of garden shears with short strong blades and handles over two feet long. Again signing for silence, he slipped one blade between the chain and his neck, and, squinting sideways, Wyndham saw that the fulcrum of the blades was reinforced by a powerful ratchet, and he recognized the thing as a pair of bolt-cutters. The cook strained, the muscles in his skinny but powerful arms standing out like cords, then there was a sharp click, and the necklace clinked on to the deck in front of him. The cook dived on it and picked it up with finger and thumb, holding his nose with the other hand to register distaste, then, before Wyndham could stop him, he whirled it round his head and threw it over the side. Wyndham stared after it in dismay, but the little man was grinning and capering with delight, and going through his handcuff pantomime. Wyndham pointed to the captain, who was sleeping in his accustomed place on the hatch, then to his own neck, and shook his head in disapproval. The other picked up his meaning immediately and shrugged, his whole attitude betokening complete unconcern, but he did at least give him the sweat rag from round his own neck, and when Wyndham unrolled the oiled silk package of ten rupee notes from the compass strap and held them out as an offering, he refused them indignantly, winked, slapped him on the back and carried on waking the crew.

There was much signalling between the three ships after that, then they weighed anchor and crept further inshore, anchoring again later, a bare half-mile from the beach, at a spot where a section of reef broke the force of the surf and made an area of comparatively smooth water. Then they swayed the huge wooden tub that they used to fill, Japanese style, with near-boiling water each night for bathing, into the small boat, and two of them paddled ashore. Wyndham saw boats setting out from the other trawlers also, and guessed their purpose. They were obviously topping up their tanks – economically from some river, rather than pay heavy watering charges in port. He looked wistfully at the beach. If only they had come in here at night. He could see the two men from each ship shuttling back and forward between the beached boats and the palm trees, where there was obviously a well, weighed down by twin buckets swung from poles across their shoulders. It was heavy work, and when they returned they looked exhausted. They brought the water inboard by suction pump, then the captain detailed two different men for the next trip, and Wyndham saw his opportunity. He volunteered in dumb show to go along, and the captain nodded his agreement, then stepped back into the wheelhouse and handed him a cloth bundle – and shook hands. Wyndham looked at the bundle, then at the captain, but he had turned away, apparently no longer interested. He started to unroll the bundle, but the cook came forward and gave him another, smaller one, and another man slipped a packet of cigarettes into his hand, and yet another a sharp gutting knife,

and other small gifts were being pressed upon him with con-
spiratorial winks, and his hand was being shaken. Then he was
in the boat with the other two and he was seeing the receding
ship through a blur as they paddled shoreward.

Chapter 17

He sat in the shade of a palm tree and opened his bundles. They had given him a shirt and trousers, unmistakably Japanese in design and appearance, but clean and serviceable, a pair of sandals, a sash, a knife, a ball of cold boiled rice and some dried fish, cigarettes, matches, a porcelain cup with Fujiyama and cherry blossom in garish reds and blues on it – and inside it, five Straits dollars and some Siamese coins. Yes, they knew what he was all right – and they were giving him a chance. He wondered if they were aware of the price on his head, and if it would have made any difference if they had been, and he marvelled afresh, and felt humbled by the kindness of simple men.

The trawlers had gone now, creeping slowly north close in to the shore, with one distant wheezing blast from the *Tegato Maru* that he knew was a farewell salute before she disappeared round a headland.

And so, once more he was free, and probably in a better position here than he would have been had he succeeded in making it to Burma. Granted India was the country he had offended against, and logically would be the one most likely to be hunting him, but on the other hand it was the country he knew best – better even than England. Here he could merge into the background – pass as an Anglo-Indian if necessary, or even perhaps as a sailor temporarily 'on the beach' as he understood the term was for a man who had got drunk in port and missed his ship. His thoughts kept coming back to that – a port – ships. That was what he wanted. But there was much he had to do first. He had only seen himself briefly in a tiny bit of scratched, fly-speckled mirror once or twice on the trawler, but it had been enough to show him that he was wild and unkempt, with a beard, and he badly needed a haircut, and he would have to get hold of some clothes rather more Western in appearance than these. He would be conspicuous dressed as he was now, and therein lay danger.

He started to walk north along the hard sand at the edge of the surf. The Coromandel Coast, he had heard this called – an area as desolate as any in the whole sub-continent – just sea and sand and endless palms and mangroves, but it certainly suited his purpose now. He had a long walk ahead of him – two hundred miles, to Madras or proportionately less to one of the nearer ports, but that was not worrying him unduly at the moment. It was just sufficient to be free and to feel the absence of the necklace. He had no worries about food, even after that which he was carrying was finished. He had learned a lot in the Andamans. There was wild fruit for the picking in the jungle – coconuts, bananas, mangoes and papayas – and there was an abundance of shellfish on out-croppings of rocks along the shore, and there was bound to be *some* sort of human habitation here, however sparse, and he had money. A fortune! Two hundred rupees – not to mention this last largesse from the Japanese. No, he was not worried – not worried about anything, except for a slight but persistently nagging concern for Paul. Had he managed completely to escape suspicion? Where would he be now? Wyndham had lost track of time, but he reckoned that he had been at large rather more than six weeks. Paul would no doubt be in Bangalore at the moment – either half-way through his leave or already established in his railway job. That would be the very first thing he would do when he reached civilization again. Send him a letter – 'John Moody wants to buy some morchi shells.' He'd stare when he saw the Indian postmark, Wyndham chuckled. He wondered if it would be safe for them to meet – perhaps in Madras, which was not far from Bangalore. He wanted to, because he felt he had never adequately thanked the other. He had taken such a lot for granted – and not only from Paul. Old Jawan. How in hell would he have got through those first months – that ghastly voyage from Calcutta, those periods of suicidal depression – had it not been for that earthy, cheerful presence? Then the Superintendent in Calcutta, and that decent assistant surgeon. There *were* good men, even in Indian prisons, on both sides of the bars – *and* outside. Why should these Japs have helped him at, whether they knew it or not, such a loss to themselves?

He found himself praying. Just a chance, just one more chance, O God.

He walked until the sun went down, then he came to a shallow
fresh water stream that crossed the beach, and he traced it back
into the jungle until he found a clear pool, and he drank and
bathed and ate sparingly, and smoked a rank Japanese cigarette,
then moved out into the open again to where the steady onshore
breeze kept the mosquitoes away, and he slept soundly until the
dawn chorus of mynahs and small green parrots in the nim trees
woke him. He searched for fruit unsuccessfully, then allowed
himself a mouthful of rice and leathery, odoriferous salt fish
before pushing on again. He calculated that, with care, the food
he was carrying would give him one small meal a day for the next
four or five. Two hundred miles to Madras, assuming that the
intervening towns were unpromising – that would take him ten
days. Twenty miles a day was a despised infantry march, he
reckoned. He could keep that up indefinitely now that his
strength was really returning, but he would have to get some
solid food somewhere. And he did, almost miraculously on the
third day. The beach ended abruptly in a mangrove swamp
through which a brown and sluggish stream meandered to the
sea, and in it were the rotting stakes of a long-abandoned fish
trap – a jagged, gap-toothed palisade of bamboo pushed into the
muddy bottom at the optimum point where full tide started to
push the fresh water back, and there were several fish in it. He
spent an anxious but enjoyable hour repairing some of the wider
breaches, then waited while the tide ebbed, and finally one fish
was stranded – a deceptively lethargic two-foot beauty that led
him a dance through the shallows, wriggling from his grasp each
time he dived on it, until he managed to stun it with a rock. He
bore it in triumph back into the fringe of the jungle and cooked
it as he had with Paul, wrapped in leaves and buried in hot ashes.
He feasted to bursting point and then slept right through the
night, cutting down drastically on his self-imposed twenty miles,
but waking stronger and more refreshed than he had felt for a
long time.

He saw his first signs of life on the fifth day, just as he finished
his last few grains of rancid rice. It was a fisherman in a small
canoe, paddling parallel to the shore outside the line of the surf.
Wyndham waved to him, but the other, a small and very black
man, either did not see him or just ignored him. But he knew

that there would be a village somewhere in the vicinity, so he was prepared for it when he came round the next headland.

It was a collection of a dozen tumbledown thatched huts with a few canoes drawn up on to the beach in front of it. Children were playing in the sand, and women were dibbling rice shoots into a flooded paddi at the edge of the jungle. He had almost reached the huts before the first child saw him, and his arrival drew much the same reaction as that of a hawk over a chicken run. There was a long shrill shriek of sheer terror, and women and children were running wildly either towards the huts or the jungle. Wyndham came forward, making namasté, which is a sign of greeting and an intimation of good intent – palms together in an attitude of prayer, and head bowed.

An old man came out of one of the nearer huts and quavered something in a language that Wyndham didn't understand, so he stood grinning imbecilically and, he hoped, ingratiatingly, and made eating signs. He tried a salutation in Hindi which clearly meant nothing to them, so he tried again in Urdu with equally negative results, then finally, in desperation he fell back on the jail patois, and thought he saw a slight gleam of comprehension in the old man's myopic eyes. Either that or his mime did get him some food, however – a cold mess of rice, fish and raw chilis that had him gasping and gulping water from a gourd after the first mouthful.

The old man sat on the ground between Wyndham and the huts, regarding him nervously, and he could hear the women and children twittering softly in the background. He finished his meal and belched loudly in polite appreciation of a full belly, and the old man bowed his acknowledgement, but made no further response, which in Wyndham's experience was unusual. The law of hospitality is sacred throughout India, irrespective of creed or caste. Once one has eaten a man's food one is a friend, and remains such during the remainder of one's stay within the territory of the host. But quite obviously that was not the case here. They really wanted him to go, so rather sadly, because he was longing desperately for human contact, he rose and made namasté again and offered the old man a few cigarettes, which he refused quite courteously, but equally firmly. No, they just didn't want him here. He salaamed, and started on his way again along

173

the beach, without making the cardinal mistake of offering payment in money. Then the man in the canoe arrived, shooting a breaker right up on to the sand, and behind him Wyndham saw other canoes, half a dozen or more, coming in from the open sea through a gap in the reef. So he stood and waited.

They beached the canoes in a line, and the women and children, emboldened by the arrival of their menfolk, streamed out of the huts to gather up the catch, and Wyndham could see the old man delivering his news, and it was obviously losing nothing in the telling, because the others advanced on him, and each of them was carrying a heavy hardwood paddle. He cursed himself for not taking the hint earlier and leaving, but there was nothing for it now but to play it off the cuff and hope for the best, so he grinned and namastéd, lit a cigarette nonchalantly, and offered the rest of the packet around, and to his overwhelming relief they were accepted – and one of them thanked him in Hindi. They were small and black, almost simian, with negroid features but straight hair – not unlike the few Adamanaese he had seen in the islands. Dravidians, he realized – the original inhabitants of the entire subcontinent, driven down into the jungles of the extreme south by successive invasions of Mongols, Persians and Aryans, who took over the richer and more fertile lands to the north and remained there, until taken over themselves in turn by Portuguese, Dutch, French and finally the British. These were the unconsidered dross of three thousand years of war and spoliation, once with a civilization and culture older than that of the Chinese, now degenerated to a standard that was almost sub-human. The Outcasts, the Untouchables. Wyndham had heard of them, of course, but had never come into contact with them before. Few people had because they seldom came out of the jungle. He didn't altogether blame them. They hadn't much to thank the outside world for.

He struck matches and moved among them, lighting their cigarettes. They were dressed, or perhaps undressed, in the irreducible minimum of G-string and, in the case of the women, a short khaddar loincloth, with the exception of the man who had spoken Hindi, who wore the tattered remains of a pair of khaki trousers. Wyndham had prepared a story in advance for any such encounter as this. It was highly improbable and unconvincing,

but the best he could manage under the circumstances, and he told
it to the trousered one now. He had been wrecked a hundred
miles down the coast and was walking to Madras. He could see
the plain disbelief in the other's eyes, but he ploughed on
regardlessly.

'The sahib is fortunate,' the man said drily when Wyndham
had finished, rather lamely. 'As fortunate as I, when I came
among these people.'

'You are not of them?' Wyndham asked.

'Of the monkey people?' the other said indignantly. 'Do I look
like them?' and Wyndham noticed then for the first time that he
was, perhaps, a shade lighter and somewhat taller than the rest
of them. 'No,' he went on. 'I am a Madrassi – Klistian, like the
sahib.' He crossed himself in proof of it – but backwards, touching
his navel first, then his forehead, then the right shoulder, and
finally his heart – and Wyndham remembered Jawan demonstrat-
ing just this during their tutorials on the landing outside the cells.
He wiped sweat from his brow in the 'come to my aid' sign, and
the trousered one grinned broadly.

'I thought so,' he said. 'Where from, Brother? The Kala Pani?'

Wyndham felt a surge of panic. If this man, the first he had
spoken to in India, had guessed correctly immediately, what
chance did he now have?

'No,' he said, too loudly. 'Don't be a fool. No man comes back
from there. It was the prison in Colombo.'

The trousered one looked contrite. 'Of course,' he said. 'As
my Brother says, I am a fool. What help do you need, my Brother?'

'Clothes,' Wyndham told him. 'Trousers such as you wear, a
shirt, shoes, socks, a topee. Sahib's clothes. Do you understand?'

'I understand, my Brother . . .'

'And I shall also require a razor, scissors, soap, a towel . . .'

The trousered one looked doubtful. 'All that would cost
money,' he said.

'How much money?'

'It is difficult to say. I have not been into a decent bazaar for
over two years. Perhaps thirty rupees – maybe more – even
forty . . .'

'I have fifty,' Wyndham told him, and the other beamed.

'No difficulty then, but it will take time. There is no place nearer than Nagapattinam where such things could be bought.'

'Could you go there?'

'Me? I can go anywhere except Pondicherry. I was in that damned French prison for five years – for something I didn't do . . .'

'Naturally,' Wyndham said solemnly, and the other giggled appreciatively. 'What is your name?'

'Somari, my Brother. What is yours?'

'Call me . . .' began Wyndham, and stopped. This was something he hadn't thought of. 'Sirdar' was certainly not advisable.

'I shall call you "Mallah" (sailor) since you had the misfortune to be shipwrecked here,' Somari grinned.

'Yes, that will do,' said Wyndham. 'All right, Somari. How long will it take you?'

'To reach Nagapattinam by canoe, one day. One day there, another back. Three days,' Somari answered promptly. 'I shall start in the morning.'

'I shall come with you, and wait outside the town,' Wyndham said.

'If you wish, but it would not be wise. A police launch moves up and down this coast. If we were stopped and questioned . . .' Somari shrugged.

'So I wait here?'

'You will be quite safe with these people. All are Brothers.'

'I am not. I am only a bahari.'

'As I am – but it is the same thing. We are all under protection. Right, come, Mallah sahib. They will give you a hut where you can rest.'

He lay awake most of the night debating on the wisdom of what he was doing. What guarantee had he that this little brute wouldn't sell him to the police? His prison-sharpened instincts had smelled out Wyndham for what he was immediately. 'Kala Pani' – the 'Black Water' – their name for the Andamans – and the Andamans only. He would certainly know of the standing reward of five thousand rupees. A fortune – enough to set him up for life. Yet, Jawan had assured him that the Brotherhood would never betray one of their own kind, no matter what the inducement. But Somari, on his own admission, was not one of them – any more than Wyndham himself was. They were both baharis – outsiders, on sufferance at best. He had been an absolute fool. He would stop the little man in the morning and get his fifty rupees back, and go his own way, but that way would have to be changed now. Not up the coast to Madras as he had intended. The police would only have to lie up under cover at the edge of the jungle and wait for him to pass along the beach. No, he'd have to change his whole plan. Go inland, cross right over to the other coast, and make for Bombay – or better still, Goa, not such a big port, but two hundred miles or so nearer, if he remembered his geography aright – and, of course, it was Portuguese.

Yes, perhaps that would be better in any case. But he was still making a virtue of necessity. The fact remained that he had made a bad tactical error in enlisting the help of this fellow – enlisting the help of *anybody*. He was on his own. He would be on his own for the rest of his life. He must get used to that – and accept it.

He rose at dawn and went through the tiny village in search of Somari, but the little black men just shrugged and stared at him blankly as he asked for him in dumb show. Then one, rather more communicative than the others, mimed a man paddling a canoe and pointed up the coast. So the little bastard hadn't wasted any time, Wyndham thought grimly.

Well, *he'd* better not waste any, either. He'd wait until the men had gone out fishing, and then he'd be off. Up the coast until he was out of sight, then he'd take the first turning to the west that looked in any way promising – a river flowing out of the jungle would be the best, it would make some sort of path, and his water problems would be solved. But what about food? The sea was a better provider than the jungle, in his experience. But beggars couldn't be choosers. He must try and steal something from here – rice, and something to cook it in. There were brass pots and things lying around. Damn and blast it! If only he had followed his instincts yesterday and taken food and gone on without delay.

But either they didn't go out fishing every day, or they were taking a holiday, because they just lay around and watched the women working, and he felt they were watching him also – covertly, slyly.

He ranged round the camp idly, like a man with nothing to do but kill time. There was a quantity of rice spread out to dry on grass mats at the edge of the camp – just where the jungle came down to meet the sand. If only he could get at that without being seen, he could make a bag out of his shirt and carry five or six pounds with him. That would keep him going for days with care. Darkness, that's what he wanted. He'd have to possess his soul in patience until nightfall, then start out when they were all sleeping.

They fed him twice during the day and he ate like a starving man each time – ate until he nearly sickened himself, storing food in his belly as a camel stores water at an oasis. They served his food on a big flat clam shell, nearly eighteen inches in diameter, with water in a half-coconut shell – neither of any use for cooking, but he stole a brass pot from beside the rice paddi, and smuggled it into his hut.

He was in a ferment by sundown. Had Somari been speaking the truth when he said the nearest town was Nagapattinam – a day's journey up the coast? If that were so, he would have reached there by now. A police launch? Was that true also? If it was, it would be down here in a fraction of the time the outward journey in the canoe had taken, so he could expect them momentarily. He lay in the darkness of his hut, biting his nails and sweating, listening for the beat of an engine. Then, when he could stand it no longer, he burrowed through the reed wall at the back and eased his way out. They all seemed to be asleep, and there was no sound from any of the other huts apart from the occasional whimper of a child.

He stole through the shadows to where the rice gleamed palely in the starlight, and took his shirt off and tried awkwardly to turn it into a practicable bag, but the smooth grains trickled out of a dozen gaps and he nearly wept with futile rage and frustration, then he thought of his voluminous Japanese trousers, and he made a better fist of things by knotting the bottoms of each leg and turning them into twin bags which he was able to sling round his neck.

He set out then along the fringe of the jungle – not north, as they would expect him to go, but back the way he had come. The sand was dry and powdery here, and his footprints wouldn't show. He had passed a river a couple of hours before reaching this village, he remembered. It was shallow but wide, and the jungle was thinner because the ground was rocky. That was the place. He'd turn due west and keep going along its course until daylight, then lie up and watch his own track for signs of pursuit.

Then a little dancing shadow appeared before him, and there were more each side and behind him, and they were chattering softly but urgently as they closed in on him. He swung the rice bags at the nearest of them and tugged the gutting knife from his waistband and got his back to the trunk of a palm tree and faced them, holding the knife, Pathan style, point upward and stiffly out at arms' length. They backed off, but still kept him encircled in a tight cordon, and, now that his eyes had become accustomed to the darkness, he could see that they were all armed with something – either heavy paddles or fish spears. There were at least twelve of them – the whole damned male population of the place. The little bastards had obviously been watching him all the time, waiting for him to make a break. Obviously Somari had guessed that he might have a change of heart when he had had time to think things over, and had warned them. They were not letting five thousand rupees slip through their fingers. Well, so much for the Brotherhood. Like everything else he'd ever heard in prison – bullshit.

His eyes ranged round the dark, motionless figures like those of some vicious animal brought to bay. Could he break the cordon and make a dash for it? Well, he could but try.

'Right, you little sods' he muttered, and lunged forward with the knife – and a hardwood paddle landed neatly across his skull, and he fell face downward into the sand.

Chapter 18

Someone with a voice like a rusty file sharpening a saw was singing 'Abide with Me' when Wyndham came to. He opened his eyes, then closed them quickly again and said petulantly, 'Shut that ghastly row up, for God's sake.'

'Not liking hymn, sahib?' Somari asked in English.

'Not liking bloody noise,' Wyndham grunted. He opened his eyes again. He was back in the hut, lying on a sleeping mat, and the Madrassi was sitting in the doorway carefully polishing a brown shoe. Wyndham shook his head tentatively and winced. It ached excruciatingly, and when he raised his hand it came into contact with a bandage. He tried painfully to marshal his thoughts, but the effort was too much.

'What are you doing here?' he demanded.

'Cleaning shoes, sahib,' Somari told him. 'Very nice shoes – size eight, like sahib said. No good for walking on beach, though.'

'Where did you learn English?'

'Oh, plenty place. 'Oly, 'oly, 'oly Mission school – then work in British soldier barracks long time – Cor fuggin 'ell – then get job in – '

'Why didn't you tell me you spoke it?'

'I got good manners, sahib. Sahib speak Hindi – I speak Hindi. Sahib speak English – I speak English. Sahib speak French – I speak French – '

'*French?*'

'Bonjour, M'sieur le gardien, comment ça va? Got to say that to bloody screws every morning in Pondicherry jail, or get kick up the ass toute suite.' Somari breathed on the shoe and rubbed it lovingly with a scrap of cloth. 'Like silver rupee on black woman's belly,' he said with satisfaction.

'Why are these people keeping me here against my will?' Wyndham asked.

'I tell them that. I say, "Sahib go too far from village, you stop him – or I put 'oly, 'oly, 'oly evil eye on you." That scare the shit out of 'em. Sahib want a drink? I nick bottle of Solan rum in bazaar. Good stuff.'

'*No*,' Wyndham said decisively. 'What right have *you* to try and keep me here?'

'Sahib seen neck?' Somari asked. He picked up a small cheap shaving mirror from a bundle beside him and brought it across to Wyndham and gently raised him, and he saw below the line of his straggly beard the livid white pattern of the chain and disc that had been shielded from the sun for over a year.

'Only one place they put chain on prisoner's neck,' Somari said quietly. 'That Kala Pani. Cop seeing that, you get picked up toute suite.'

'I see,' said Wyndham slowly, and added, 'Thanks.'

'That's all right, sahib,' Somari said cheerfully. 'I know that sahib maybe think that Somari go pinch my fifty chips – maybe go tell cops. I bugger off, quick. Can't blame sahib for that. Only nach'ral. Cor fuggin 'ell.'

'But you *didn't* pinch the fifty chips.'

'No. I get all things. Very nice shirt, pants, socks, shoes, size seven topee, razor, comb, boot polish, soap, toothpaste, pyjamas, nice suitcase – ' Somari was picking up the items in turn and exhibiting them proudly.

'That lot must have cost more than fifty rupees,' Wyndham said, astonished.

'Oh, some I buy, some I knock off. Spend twenty-eight rupees nine annas. Got change here.'

'Cor fuggin 'ell,' said Wyndham in tones of deepest wonder. 'You never came into contact with a gent named Jeeves in your travels, by any chance did you?'

'Yes, corporal in Royal Fusiliers, big ginger feller. Sahib know him?'

'I was thinking of another one,' Wyndham said, and started to laugh. He laughed until he was weak and shaken, and Somari looked worried.

'Sahib better sit in sun some days until neck get browned off pukkha same like rest,' he said. 'And I cut hair very nice and you have shave – '

'You can cut hair too, can you?'

'Yes, one time barber in barracks; one time cook; one time

Mess Waiter. Klistian religion very nice religion. One man can do all things, not bugger up caste like Hindus: eat beef, eat pork, drink rum, smoke cig'rettes, have any sort of woman – all same just like sahibs. Oh, very high class.'

He examined his neck constantly in the mirror in the ensuing days, watching the melanin in his skin redistribute itself evenly over the chain pattern and the lower part of his face that had been bearded for so many weeks. Somari was no idle boaster. He trimmed his hair to a conventional Western length and, after a series of consultations, they decided to leave him a fairly heavy moustache. These two things alone, he felt, altered his appearance considerably. In the regiment he had been clean-shaven, but wore his hair at the exaggerated length affected by all Indian cavalry. In prison he had been close-cropped and, except for Sunday when they had their weekly shave, he usually had a dark stubble.

He was eating regularly and fully, with an easy conscience, because, poor though these people were, they had an abundance of fish and rice, while there was fruit in the jungle for the picking. He swam and took long walks up and down the beach, and hauled on nets and helped to carry canoes to and from the water – and his strength came back to him apace. He talked to Somari about Madras, and the possibility of getting on a ship there, but the Madrassi was not hopeful.

'No good, sahib,' he said positively. 'All sailors got little blue book. No book – no job. Any sailor get pissed, stay ashore, get picked up by police and put on next ship that comes in – DBS.'

'What's that?'

'Distressed British Seaman. Police don't like European on the bum in Indian port.'

'How do you know all this?'

'Meet plenty in jail.'

'Which jail?'

'All jails. I been in five – Calcutta, Chittagong, Travancore, Coimbatore and Vizagapattam.'

'And Pondicherry.'

'I don't count Pondicherry. That not a jail. That pukkha bloody hell.'

'What about Madras?'

'I don't go to jail there. Keep name clean always in home town. Man got to live *somewhere* without bloody cop always picking up.'

'What have you been in for mostly?' Wyndham asked, which was a measure of their intimacy now, because the question was a grave breach of prison etiquette.

'Oh, pinching,' said Somari airily. 'Nice pinching – I never do dacoity.' Dacoity was armed robbery.

'Where did you become a bahari?'

'Coimbatore – long time ago. One of these poor little buggers get bad kicking from other men. I look after him. We come out together. I broke and little bit sick with fever. He take me back to village – like this one, but not by the sea. Right back in jungle near Bangalore – '

'You know Bangalore?'

'I know. Very nice place – but I don't like jungle.' He shuddered.

'Why not?'

'Big trees – bush – Move away from path get lost. Nobody ever go there – nobody but these little buggers. They like – what you call 'em – chimgadar – fly at night – ?'

'Bats?'

'That's right. You don't see 'em – hear 'em – but they there all the time. I stay there one year – learn plenty – but I still don't like.'

They had many such conversations, with Wyndham questioning and probing – but Somari never questioned in return. Thief, guttersnipe, the little man had a natural courtesy that made Wyndham feel a clumsy, ill-mannered lout at times. He had kindness too, as Wyndham realized when he saw him distributing boiled sweets to the children after his return from Nagapattinam – pinched, he was careful to explain – not bought foolishly with the sahib's money.

'How did you come to this place?' Wyndham asked him once.

'Run away from jail in Pondicherry. I still got two years to do,' Somari explained. 'Can't go north to Madras because they think that is where I will go, so all bloody gendarmes go up that way. I come south instead – come to this place after ten days. Pretty hungry. Stay here.'

'Will you stay here for ever?' Wyndham asked, and a look of horror came over the other's face.

'Jesus Christ, no!' he said emphatically. 'I come to Madras with the sahib.'

Wyndham shook his head gently. 'No good, Somari,' he said. 'I should have told you before. I'm wanted for murder. Every policeman in India will be looking for me. If I'm arrested you're bound to be taken in also. Then they'll find out about you, and you'll be punished for helping me – and almost certainly sent back to Pondicherry.'

'The police don't find you if you're with me,' Somari said positively. 'Not in Madras.' He held out his hand, palm upwards. 'I know it like that. I take you to places you'll be safe like here. Get some money – then you can go on. Money very good thing – take you anywhere.'

'Where would we get money from?' Wyndham asked, and Somari tapped the side of his nose and grinned.

'But you keep your name clean in Madras,' Wyndham said.

'Oh, I don't go *pinching* in Madras,' Somari said. 'Plenty other places for that.'

'You'd be better off on your own,' Wyndham told him. 'I'd only be a hindrance. Anyhow, why should you want to help *me*?'

'We friends,' Somari said simply. 'Besides, *I* want the *sahib's* help.'

'How could *I* help you?'

'The jungle,' Somari said earnestly. 'Like I told you, sahib – jungle frighten the shit out of me – '

'But you don't have to go into the jungle to get to Madras. You just keep to the beach. It's like this the whole way.'

'Sahib forget Pondicherry. Fifty miles of French coast – more bloody gendarmes than coconuts,' Somari said. 'Have to go inland there – maybe a hundred miles round. No good for me – no good for sahib, either. They pick you up – no papers – hand over to British India police.'

'Yes, you're right,' said Wyndham thoughtfully. 'All right, Somari, it's a deal. We go together – but only as far as Madras. I'll give you half the money I've got – '

'Don't want sahib's money,' Somari said firmly. 'Get off this bloody beach, I get plenty.'

'Pinching again?'

'Well, a little bit. Man can't get it any other way, he *gotta* pinch,' Somari grinned.

'How about *trying* the other way? Get a good job – save – maybe get married – settle down?'

'Cor fuggin 'ell,' said Somari with feeling. 'Been married plenty times. No fuggin good.'

'You haven't met the right girl,' Wyndham smiled.

'*All* the right girl,' Somari said with assurance, 'until you get 'em in bed. Then wake up in morning and find they wake up first – and go pinch your money and bugger off.'

They set out ten days later. Wyndham wanted to make the head-man a small present of money, but Somari turned it down flatly.

'They don't want paying,' he said. 'Got plenty food here.'

'Not paying for *food*,' Wyndham explained. 'A *present*.'

'Baksheesh? You only got paper money. That no good to them.'

'I've got some coins as well,' Wyndham said.

'Give 'em that and all the women run like bloody hell into jungle.'

'Why?'

'Men make hole in coins – and hole in wife's nose and hang 'em on wire. Wife no like.'

'But I must give them *something*,' Wyndham insisted.

Somari sighed and delved into the suitcase and produced a small, cheap alarm clock.

'Give him this,' he said resignedly. 'I knock it off in bazaar.'

'But what the hell would he do with an alarm clock?'

'Christ knows – hang it round neck – stick it up ass – anything but tell time with it. Nice people these, but same like monkeys. Come on, sahib – we better be going.'

Wyndham turned several times and waved as they walked along the beach, but the line of immobile little figures made no response.

'They very sad,' Somari explained.

'How do you know?' Wyndham asked, remembering their complete lack of expression.

'Nice people. Police don't come here – but if they did, could put their asses in fire, beat with bamboo, do anything – but they don't talk about us. Like I said – monkeys.'

'Don't call them monkeys,' Wyndham snapped angrily.

'Oh, I don't mean *any* monkeys,' Somari said, quite unabashed. 'I mean *three* monkeys. See damn-all, hear damn-all, say fuggin nothing.'

Wyndham wanted to carry the quite heavy suitcase, but Somari wouldn't hear of it. He balanced it on his head and strode out in a mile-eating half-trot that Wyndham had his work cut out to match. The other's lack of a presentable wardrobe worried him.

'Why didn't you buy some clothes for yourself in Naga-pattinam?' he asked.

'What? And bugger them up in jungle?' Somari said indignantly. 'I'm not bloody fool, sahib. Get 'em all other end. Madras clothes – very lovely.'

He, Wyndham, was still wearing those that the Japanese had given him, the new ones meticulously folded in the suitcase.

They marched all that day, resting only for an hour when the sun was at its height, and, as the swift tropical twilight closed in, Somari, who seemed to know the unchanging coastline as well as he boasted he knew the back alleys of Madras, said they were five miles short of Nagapattinam.

'How do you know?' Wyndham asked him.

'Smell it,' answered Somari succinctly. 'Best going now, sahib, we go into jungle – have food – rest three-four hours – then pass town in night.'

'No police on the beach, like Pondicherry?'

'Only few in town, maybe one or two round harbour,' Somari said. 'Lazy buggers go to sleep most times.'

The moon had risen by the time they set out again, and it worried Wyndham, particularly when they rounded a high headland and he saw the town laid out before them. A lighthouse was flashing at the end of a long breakwater and he could see the area of the place. It looked the size of a small city, with straight, seemingly brightly lighted streets. But Somari kept unconcernedly on.

'That damned suitcase,' said Wyndham. 'Any policeman we run into is bound to ask questions – and take us in if he's not satisfied.'

'We don't run into any, sahib.'

'I wonder,' Wyndham said nervously. 'Don't you think it would be better to go round – inland?'

'Through jungle? Take one day – two days. Ten bloody town same like, this side of Madras. Go round them all, it take a month. Don't worry, sahib. I know. I been here before – only Pondicherry bad place.'

And he was right – almost, Wyndham decided. The lights, so concentrated when viewed from the height of the headland, were more spaced out as they got closer, and the small houses round the harbour that reminded him somehow of a holiday he had spent in Holland just after the war, were for the most part dark and shuttered. He remembered then, from some long-forgotten geography lesson, that this had been the principal Dutch settlement on the Coromandel coast in the days before Clive.

A dog was barking somewhere, and in the distance a man was singing in a high shrill monotone, but otherwise there was not a sound above the lapping of small waves on the outer side of the breakwater. Dhows and Malayan prahus were moored alongside the quay, their curving spars etched against the night sky, and there was a heady smell of spice on the air. Further out he could see the anchor lights of three or four steamers in the roadstead. He looked at them longingly. Here was the way to real freedom if he could only make it. Somari seemed to guess his thoughts.

'No good, sahib,' he said. 'Got to have tikkut. No tikkut – no job. We get some money – *buy* bloody tikkut then.'

They had almost reached the northern arm of the breakwater where the lighted area ended when the police came upon them.

There were three of them – a havildar and two constables – and one of them had a flashlight and the full beam caught them.

'Run, sahib,' Somari gasped. 'You right – me left – '

Wyndham heard the yell, 'Halt, you people!' as he ran blindly over the edge of the quay. He landed in mud ten feet below, and felt himself sinking, but the breath was knocked out of him and he could not struggle, which was probably all that saved him. He lay still as the level of the stinking ooze came up to his chin, and then higher, until he could feel it trickling into his open mouth. He saw three heads silhouetted against the sky as they looked down on him, then the beam of the torch swept slowly along the mud – reached him – and went on – and he could hear them arguing in Hindi.

'There were two of them. I tell you I saw two –'

'One carried a bundle – '

'He ran the other way – '

'Fool – you *would* see them – just as we are coming off duty – '

'Silence, you! One fell over the edge here – '

'Well, he's not here now – or the bastard has drowned in the mud – '

'That will save everybody trouble. Thieving Tamils. Let's look for the other.'

'What the hell's the use? He'll be a mile away by now. If you'd only had your wits about you – '

And then they had gone, and Wyndham heard the dying clatter of their nailed chaplis on the cobbles. Only then did he move – one last desperate effort to reach the wall in front of him – an effort which made him sink faster. His thrashing arms missed the stones by inches – then he felt a rope touch his face, and he grabbed it. It was the bight of a mooring warp from a dhow that was beached behind him – the loom of whose flaring bows had saved him, because it put him in deep shadow down here. He heaved with all his strength, and emerged to waist height, then rested, his chest feeling as if it would burst. Inch by inch he worked his way through the slime until he was up against the rough planking of the dhow, and he was able to reach up to the break of her low freeboard, and finally pull himself clear.

There was a gangplank from the bow to the quay and he dragged himself across it, dripping liquid mud like a man crawling out of a barrel of molasses.

So this was it, he thought miserably. One minute poised in full flight – the next, right back to square one, like the snakes and ladders he used to play as a small boy. Why had he allowed that stupid, cocky, feckless little bastard to over-ride him? How the hell could any ill-assorted pair like themselves expect to get through even a lightly policed town such as this at midnight? He'd probably been caught by now – and he had everything with him in that bloody suitcase. Clothes, money – the lot. Well, the hell with him. Serve him damned well right. He'd probably go up before the magistrate and be charged with theft. And if they checked his fingerprints properly he'd be identified as an habitual criminal. And after serving whatever they handed out to him, he'd be extradited to Pondicherry. He said, 'Serve him right,' again, savagely – but his heart was not in it. He felt the same sense of loss as when Jawan had been killed. He seemed to have an affinity with criminals. Only natural, he reflected bitterly. Wasn't he one himself?

He crossed the quay as quickly as his tired legs would allow him, into the shadow of the buildings the other side. What should he do now? Was it any use looking for the silly little devil, he wondered?

Then a throaty chuckle right at his elbow nearly caused his heart to stop.

'Very clever to jump into shit like that, sahib,' Somari said. 'But we better find some water – quick. You stink like an Untouchable's billy-goat.'

Chapter 19

They put a good five miles behind them before stopping, then Wyndham thankfully dragged his stinking clothes off and plunged into the surf.

'Was it really shit?' he asked Somari anxiously, as they scrubbed at the clothes with handfuls of sand. 'I thought it was just bad-smelling mud.'

'Oh, it shit all right,' the other assured him cheerfully. 'All Arab dhows empty latrine buckets there. Very good thing.'

'What the hell do you mean by that?' Wyndham demanded wrathfully.

'Coppers know you are there all the time, but they are Hindus, so they don't pull you out – or they lose caste. Don't look for me, either. Just get the hell out of it quick. Cost one thousand rupees to Brahmins to get caste back if they lose it.' He laughed joyously. 'Oh, bloody fine thing to be Klistian. 'Oly, 'oly, 'oly – bugger the Hindus and Muslims.'

Wyndham took firm charge at the next small town they passed, making a wide detour inland with Somari moaning dismally every extra step of the way. He was a town sparrow to the core, and his hatred of the jungle was a very real thing.

'Coppers in this place don't come out at night, sahib,' he wailed. 'I *know*.'

'Yes, you knew in Nagapattinam too, didn't you?' Wyndham said grimly.

'Oh, they just coming off duty there. I hear them. That different.'

'We'd still have been pinched if I hadn't landed up to my neck in the you-know-what.'

'That very funny,' Somari giggled.

'You say that once again and I'll kick your black arse for you,' Wyndham swore.

'Oh, ho, ho – sahib very funny too – but bloody long walk through jungle isn't.'

'All right, you go straight through the town. I'll go round

and meet you the other side. But I'm carrying the suitcase.'

'No – I come, sahib,' Somari said dolefully.

'Good. It will be practice for Pondicherry – unless you want to walk through there too.'

'Oh, my God – Jesus Mary, no. Walk ten thousand miles to miss that place.'

'What's so different about it? Jail's jail wherever you are.'

'Indian jail, hard work but food not bad – keep nose clean, no beatings. "You play game with me, I play game with you." French jail, work all day half night – food very small – plenty chubbiduster with big stick – screw saying, "You play game with me or I se rompre le cou, salaud – break your bloody neck, you bastard." Oh, no good, sahib.'

'And you say there are a lot of policemen there?'

'Every bugger who don't work in brothel is a gendarme or a screw. No other jobs there. In jungle they have little stone houses all round border with one sous-officier and six soldier. All time watch. Machine-gun – bup-bup-bup.'

'Is the border marked?'

'Yes, like I say – with little stone houses and machine gun.'

'But that would be *inside* French territory – '

'Inside, outside, every bloody side. They don't care where they shoot. No people on British side – only jungle with plenty sher and chita – '

'Tiger and panther? I don't believe you. Not this far south.'

'Sahib – I tell you I see them when I'm working on chain gang. Going gr-grr-grr all time – '

'Good. Well, if we see any, you make a noise like that and they'll push off.'

'Sahib bloody funny man,' Somari said with gloomy irony.

They were feeding more regularly now, on food bought from fishermen – ordinary people, not Dravidians, who were not averse to a little bargaining, which Somari would carry out while Wyndham waited some distance off in the trees.

And so, at last, they came near to Pondicherry, with Somari's fear growing as the distance decreased. But he was surprisingly well-informed about the area.

'They don't have miles there, sahib,' he told Wyndham. 'Only keelo-meet. Eighteen keelo-meet from north to south along coast road.'

'How do you know that?'

'I build the bloody thing – me and some other men.'

'What about the other way – east to west?'

'Got big road that way too, from harbour to border – twenty-five keelo-meet.'

'About ten by fifteen miles,' mused Wyndham, and made a rough calculation of the perimeter. 'Fifteen and fifteen plus ten – that's forty. But we've got to stay well away from the actual border. Add another five miles to each of the three sides – fifteen – call it twenty. Sixty miles overall. Three days' march on the beach, Somari – but maybe double that if the going is rough this way.'

'I tell you that now. *Bloody* rough,' Somari gloomed. 'Jesus, Mary, Joseph.'

'You can slip in one to St Christopher, too,' Wyndham grinned. 'He'll probably listen to a good Catholic.'

'Only Catholic in Madras and Chittagong. Seventh Day Adventist in this place.'

'Why?'

'Catholic have to 'oly, 'oly, 'oly at seven o'clock on Sunday morning in French jail, but SDA come round at ten and bring buns from American mission. Very nice.'

They turned off the beach at a point that Somari estimated to be about three miles short of the border. Wyndham was glad to do so, because the endless vista of white sand with the sea on the right and the green palms to the left, mile after mile, had been getting on his nerves for the last few days. There was a path of sorts at first which he thought might lead to a village, but it ended abruptly at a small stone temple, old and overgrown with liana, but with an image of Siva, bearded and holding a stone lingam and freshly daubed with vermilion and indigo, on an altar inside the crumbling entrance arch. There were offerings of fruit, flowers and saffron-dyed rice in front of it, together with the three products of the sacred cow in brass dishes – milk, dung and urine. Somari laughed uproariously and expounded some highly libellous theology.

'Silly bugger Hindus,' he explained. 'Plenty of these places in jungle. Women don't get babies, very bad, so husband send 'em to temple to put flowers, coconut, cowshit in front of god – pay plenty rupees to Brahmin priest – women stay all night and make 'oly, 'oly, 'oly. Nine months after – get baby.'

'Always?' Wyndham asked.

'You bet – if priest not too shagged out.' He clenched his right fist and held his arm aloft and slapped himself on the biceps. 'Bloody good job, Brahmin priest. Plenty choot – and get paid for it.'

Now there was no path and the trees met overhead and blotted out the sky, and Wyndham thanked his lucky stars that he still had the old service compass round his neck on its thong. They kept going steadily but painfully slowly due west, with Somari getting more despondent by the hour. Wyndham, breaking trail through the matted undergrowth, was worried. Theoretically they were moving parallel to the border, about three miles to the south of it – but that was only assuming the French territory to be a regular rectangle. Almost certainly it would not be, and, if it curved and jinked, they might easily pass between two of Somari's 'little stone houses' and find themselves over the line.

The little man was flagging but he steadfastly clung to the suitcase until Wyndham took it from him by force. And to add to their misery they had a water problem, because they hadn't seen a stream or a pool since leaving the beach.

'How far we come, sahib?' he asked forlornly after they had been travelling for what Wyndham judged to be seven or eight hours.

'Oh, quite a way,' Wyndham lied cheerfully. 'We'll camp when we come to water. Tomorrow we'll be more than half way – ' And then they heard a bugle, heart-stoppingly close, higher in pitch than those of the British, and sounding a call unknown to Wyndham. It was answered far behind them, then again, seemingly to their left, which, again theoretically, should without doubt have been British territory – and a fourth time to their right, until the whole jungle was echoing with it.

'Oh, Jesus!' Somari moaned. 'Les poilus – that's what they call their bloody soldiers. All round us. They know we here – '

'Shut up,' Wyndham muttered, and looked up into the overhead screen of foliage. 'Come on – climb.'

They were under a banyan tree, its enormous trunk lost among the aerial roots that dropped from its lower branches to the ground. He boosted Somari up before him, then passed him the suitcase, and they climbed like monkeys, right through the green ceiling into the evening light. There was open ground to their right through which a path ran back parallel to the route they had been following, and Wyndham realized sheepishly that they had been within a hundred yards of it, probably for some hours – pushing painfully through this green hell when they could have been making unimpeded progress.

Then he saw the soldiers – Europeans in stained and sweat-soaked khaki and cumbersome leather equipment – wearing white képis. They were resting, sprawled along the edge of the path, about twenty of them, and the bugler was sounding off again, and was being answered as before by other calls further back in the jungle.

'Cor fuggin 'ell,' breathed Somari. 'This sort called Légion Etrangère. Bad buggers – the worst. Always get drunk – make choot with women – fight in bazaar.'

The Foreign Legion, mused Wyndham. Funny that that had never occurred to him when mulling over his future. You served five years with them, and then you could apply for French papers. Fresh start – another name – he wondered if one could enlist locally – but then he remembered hearing somewhere that although they never asked questions, and would accept the sweepings of every prison in Europe, one thing remained outside the pale. Murder. If he was a wanted man throughout British India, it was highly unlikely that they wouldn't know about it in this tiny enclave. If he presented himself at a recruiting office the chances were that he'd find himself in the hands of the police the other side of the border – toute suite, as Somari would say. No, he couldn't risk it. Perhaps, if he managed to get to Europe it might be different –

Other troops were emerging from the jungle – one small group almost underneath them – and whistles were blowing and they were straggling into column of route along the path. Wyndham's first fear was now dispelled. These soldiers were not on their track. His military instinct told him that they had been on a jungle exercise – and, from their appearance, a tough one. 'An advance in echelon through wooded terrain,' as the manuals would no doubt euphemize it, although British Tommies and French Légionnaires would probably have a terser term for it.

They were now marching off, to the thudding of drums and the shrill of fifes, at a deceptively slow pace that nevertheless seemed to be covering the ground at an astonishing rate, and Wyndham felt a sense of loss for the first time. It wasn't such a bad life. These chaps were going back to barracks with not a care in the world, beyond sore feet. Back to such simple but exquisite comforts as a bath, carbolic soap, a rough towel, clean clothes, a full belly, maybe a drink – and then a bed that was raised clear of the ground. But, above all, they were going back to comradeship. He would have given his soul to have changed places with the lowliest private amongst them at that moment.

Somari, watching his face, said softly, 'The sahib was a soldier – no? Officer soldier?'

'How did you know that?' Wyndham asked gruffly, and Somari laughed.

'I bloody barrack rat,' he said. 'Knowing all things about soldier. Sahib look like soldier, walk like soldier, swear like soldier. Have to be careful about that. Madras-side, MPs sometime go into café to see if Tommies there in civvy clothes – that no allowed. They yell, " 'Shun!" and all silly buggers jump up and stand straight – Get pinched.'

Yes, he was right, Wyndham mused. He *would* have to be careful.

They climbed down and pushed through to open ground thankfully. The path was to their right, and Wyndham saw a white stone pylon that had hitherto been out of their sight, gleaming palely in the twilight. They went up to it and he saw the words 'Liberté, Egalité, Fraternité' surmounted by the French Chanticleer, and below it an arrow pointing to the east, and 'Ville de Pondicherri 21 Km.' Thirteen miles, Wyndham calculated. They'd done better than he had estimated. Another two miles due west, plus a further couple for safety, and they could turn north. Some yards away he saw another pylon, in grey concrete. He went over to it and read 'District of Arcot' and another arrow pointed in the opposite direction: 'Villapuram – 4 miles.'

He understood now. They had, in fact, swung towards the

border – or the border had swung towards them – and they'd been marching along it. The French troops had been just inside their own territory, and he and Somari were actually standing in the neutral strip between both borders.

'Do you know Villapuram?' he asked.

'Yes, sahib,' Somari said. 'That big railway junction on British side – just outside Frenchman country.'

'How big?'

'Oh, very big. Train come down from Arcot, Madras – lot of trains. Some go off to Pondicherry – other ones go on down south.'

'What's the country like the other side of it? The country we have to go through?'

Somari grimaced. 'Bloody not nice, sahib. Why?'

'Worse than we've come through today?'

'Little bit.'

'What's the *town* of Villapuram like?'

'All right. Big place. Lot of railway people live there. Why you ask all these things, sahib?'

'Shut up,' said Wyndham. 'Just answer. Plenty police there?'

'Same like other places. But why – ?' The little man was hopping from one foot to another in a frenzy of curiosity.

'Trains run north through there – to Madras?' Wyndham went on inexorably.

'Yes – but – ' Then it dawned on him, and his face broke into a grin of delighted incredulity. 'We go by *train*?'

'Only if it's absolutely safe.'

'Safe? Oh yes – Cor fuggin 'ell – it very nice and safe – Oh, lovely – ' He was dancing with excitement.

'Hold your horses – '

'Oh, bugger horses, sahib – train very good – '

'You'll have to get some clothes first. You look like a rag and bone man in those – '

'Lovely bazaar. Pinch them in ten minutes – '

'You will *not*,' Wyndham said firmly. 'If you take stupid risks here I'll leave you to manage on your own. You will buy the sort of clothes a sahib's servant wears – '

'Madrassi servant – white pants, white jakkut and pukkha shoes? Not bloody pagri and shirwani like damn Hindu bearer?'

'That's right.'

196

'Oh, lovely.'

'Then I'll get dressed properly and come into town – and if things look really safe, we'll take tickets to Madras – but *only* if they look safe. You understand?'

'I understand, sahib,' Somari said ecstatically. They were walking down the path now in almost total darkness, and the sound of trickling water came to them from under a culvert. They plunged down the bank and drank like thirsty animals, then went back some yards into the jungle on the British side and ate the last of their food.

The sun was high above when Wyndham awoke. He lay for some time collecting his thoughts, then rose and looked around for Somari, but he was not in sight, so he pushed his way through the undergrowth to the stream, expecting to find him there, but he wasn't. He drank and then went back and got his few simple toilet things and bathed and shaved, then he beguiled the time away by getting out his other clothes and shaking out the wrinkles. His wardrobe was sparse enough in all conscience, he thought, but it would be quite in character during the day, when most Europeans wore no more than a white shirt and either shorts or slacks and, of course, the ubiquitous topee. Night was different. He would normally be expected to wear a lightweight suit and a tie then. He would just have to keep out of the public eye after sunset, because suits cost money, and he would have to husband his. He hoped he wouldn't have too much trouble in sending Somari on his way, much as he'd miss the little devil. He'd insist on his taking half the money they had left, of course. But what the hell was he going to do afterwards? The actual mechanics of escaping, with the attendant problems to be met and overcome each day had occupied his thoughts up to now to the exclusion of all else, and he had pushed the bigger problems into the background. But now they were crowding in on him, and bringing clouds of black depression with them. How much money had they left – and how long would it last him? He hadn't been keeping a close check because he had come to trust Somari implicitly. They would only have spent a rupee or so on food coming up the beach. He searched through the suitcase for the little oiled silk roll.

But it wasn't there.

He sat back on his heels – the shock, horror and sheer disappointment of it hitting him in the midriff like a physical blow. But why? Why should Somari have done this now? Why had he waited, when he had ample opportunity of robbing him earlier?

Obvious, of course, Wyndham reflected bitterly. He wanted to get to Madras, and he was frightened of traversing the Pondicherry area alone. He was safe now. He only had to go into Villapuram and buy a railway ticket. But he had promised the little swine half his money. Well, he'd got the lot now, hadn't he? Why hadn't he taken everything else, in addition to the money? Too much to carry, and too big a risk of being picked up and questioned by the police. No, the answers were there, all too plainly. Would he never learn? You can trust nobody – *nobody* – black, white or brindle.

So what did he do now? What *could* he do? Walk on to Villapuram? And if so, what then? No money – no food. Steal some? How? He had neither the experience nor the skill of his late companion – though he would probably have to have a shot at it in the future. Go back to the Dravidians – after all, they were 'Brothers', weren't they? Or was that bullshit too, as he had thought in the past? Would the little bastard sell him out to the police now? No. Somehow he didn't think so. If he had wanted to do that he'd have done so when he went into Nagapattinam the first time. It wouldn't be any scruple that would stay his hand – it was just that he more than probably had so much on his plate that he couldn't risk going near the police. Still – one never knew. The bastard could always do it through an intermediary. He'd better shift from this place, just in case.

Then his eye fell upon the bottle of Solan rum, still unopened in the suitcase. Well, that was *something*. Bit early for drinking, particularly on an empty stomach, but what the hell – ? He took it up and looked at it, then felt for his knife to prise the cork out – then, although his whole system was shrieking for a drink, he forced himself to put it back. No, he was going to need all his wits now, and he knew that one small drink would be enough to start the old craving again in all its intensity. Besides, he might conceivably be able to sell it – though the spectacle of a white man trying to flog a bottle of rum in an Indian bazaar would be a little unusual to say the least.

What in the name of God was he going to do? What *could* he do? He balled his fist, screwed up his eyes and beat himself on the forehead.

Then slowly sanity returned. Madras. He still had to go on to Madras. Get up there and stow away on a foreign ship. One that was going to a foreign port where, even if the captain was rancorous enough to hand him over to the police, they might accept his story of being a British or an American sailor who had been attacked and robbed of money and papers while ashore – and had no memory of coming aboard this particular ship. It was all pretty feeble, but it was the best he could think of at the moment, and it was a relief just to have an immediate objective once more. Yes, get to Madras. He started to repack the suitcase. Then he heard Somari calling from the path.

Chapter 20

Somari pushed through the undergrowth and beamed down at him, then placed a canvas valise carefully on the ground.

'Bedding roll,' he said proudly. 'All sahibs have bedding roll when they go on train at night. Not got bedding roll, everybody say, "That funny," and look too much.' And he was absolutely right. In India, the most custom-bound land in the world, a travelling European without his cumbersome but vastly capacious 'Wolseley' valise would have been as noticeable as a bishop minus his trousers in Cheltenham. Wyndham nodded profoundly, but his relief and the inner shame he felt over his previous doubt were so overwhelming that he couldn't speak. Somari, chattering excitedly, was unpacking other things.

'Very nice jakkut. I think it fit all right. Try on sahib – and what sahib call flannel bags – not new, but very good – Oooh! and lovely tie. And for me – very good trouser, shirt, jakkut – '

'It must have cost a packet,' Wyndham said when he was able. 'I hope you've kept enough for the tickets.'

'Got tickets here,' Somari fished them from the waistband of his disreputable trousers. 'One first class for sahib, servant ticket for me. Train go through at eleven o'clock tonight. Slow Express, take six bloody hour to Madras – but that all right. Get good sleep. And here change – hundred and ten rupees, eleven annas – '

'But, for God's sake, we only had about a hundred and fifty to start with!' Wyndham shouted. 'You're trying to tell me that you got all this lot *and* the tickets for forty? You've been pinching, you little bugger – and I told you not to.'

'Not pinching, sahib,' Somari said indignantly. 'We got hundred and sixty-eight rupees, nine annas to start – because I got seventeen rupees I had for long time. Sahib ticket cost thirty-three rupees, mine six. All this lot cost twenty-one rupees, five annas – '

'I don't believe you!'

'Sahib calling me liar? Cor fuggin 'ell – that not nice – '

'Where did you get it?'

'Chor ki bazaar – that's the Thieves' Market. Oh, bloody lovely one here. Got to be early in morning, though. Loose-walas – the burglars – knock it off on French side at night, bring it back this side and flog it quick. Next night knock it off on British side and flog it on French. Very nice business.' He sighed regretfully. 'That's how I get caught. Get drunk – pinch on French side – *sell* on French side. Gendarme don't like.'

And as before, Wyndham started to laugh – and couldn't stop.

They set out after nightfall, both strangely uncomfortable in civilized clothes, with Somari balancing both the valise and the suitcase on his head. Once again Wyndham tried to share the burden, and Somari showed a flash of temper for the first time.

'Yes, sahib very kind – very nice – but I not bloody fool. Somebody see, they say "What the hell?" *No* sahib carry bundle in this country – not even missionary. "Lord appointeth thee to thy station – me to mine. 'Oly, 'oly, bloody 'oly." Shut up, sahib, for Christ sake.'

They hailed a horse-drawn tonga on the outskirts of the town. The cantonment and the bazaar were brightly lighted, and both were different from any other he had seen in India, and it increased his unease, until he realized that it was purely the French influence that made it unfamiliar, because although it was half a mile in on the British side, it still remained very strong in this pleasant little town that had originally been planned and built by Dupleix two hundred years before, when the province of Pondicherry extended nearly to Madras, as an exercise in sheer nostalgia for his birth-place in the Midi. There were pavement cafés with coloured umbrellas still open over small marble tables, although it was long after dark, and shops with signs like 'Le Bon Ton' and 'Magasin du Bébé' and advertisements for Pernod and Dubonnet. Only the red Victorian pillar-boxes were solidly British – and the police. There were lots of the latter. European sergeants and native constables.

Somari seemed to sense Wyndham's nervousness, and he was murmuring soothingly and reassuringly.

'All right, sahib. You don't worry. Everything all right. No copper going to come up to you. You look very nice and pukkha – "Who are you, my man? *I* Lord High General Jesus Christ.

You fug off." That what you look like – and they salute and *fug off*. You see.'

'Yes, yes,' Wyndham agreed tensely. 'But I must have a name and a story ready in case somebody asks me.'

'You got name. You Mister T. S. Walker. I have to give one when I reserve first-class compartment.'

'What made you think of that?'

'Johnnie Walker whisky, and T. S. from another sahib I work for once.'

'Very clever of you – but you shouldn't have wasted money on a first-class ticket. Second would have done just as well.'

Somari smiled. 'Yes – just like sahib say – very clever. Can't reserve whole second-class compartment. Only bed-seat. You get in with other sahib, they want to talk.'

Wyndham looked at him in frank admiration. 'You think of everything, don't you?' he said.

'Bloody near,' said Somari modestly.

They arrived at the station and were immediately surrounded by the usual swarm of baggage coolies that haunt the environs of the entire Indian railway system. They wear red smocks with a notice in English on the chest 'One Anna Per Load Per Trip' – but they call loudly upon the whole pantheon of Hindu gods if given less than eight annas by a European, and Wyndham watched a complete reversal of form as Somari dealt with a flanking movement that tried to make two loads of the valise and suitcase.

'*One* load and *one* trip, my brothers,' he hissed in Hindi. 'And *one* anna if the task is performed with care and zeal – or *one* kick in the hinder parts and *no* anna, if it is not. Right – you at the end there, the big and lazy one making noises like a water-buffalo in labour – to you falls the honour and the profit of bearing the Great One's effects to Platform Three. No, I will *not* help you to raise the load to your thick skull. I am a Klistian gentleman, not a lousy coolie.' And he watched and forestalled Wyndham's attempt to increase the douceur when they arrived at the platform.

'Yes, sahib,' he said. 'I am as sorry for the poor bastard as you are. One anna is probably as much as he might make for a whole day's waiting out there. But I am a mean little jackal of a Madrassi lickspittle – and as such he will write me down and then forget me. If I had helped him and then allowed you to give him more, he might have remembered me. The sahib must learn these simple rules.' Then he lapsed back to the broken barrack English he preferred. 'Piss off to European Refreshment Room and have nice cold beer, sahib.'

'You come too. You could do with one, couldn't you?' Wyndham asked.

'I have *two* – in proper place – at back door. Go on, sahib – don't play silly buggers. You ever see sahib taking bloody servant in for a beer?'

Wyndham crossed the bridge back to the entrance, trying not to shrink as he passed an Indian constable at the foot of the steps. The man saluted automatically, and Wyndham, as automatically, acknowledged it with a languid fingertip to the brow – and with that simple gesture confidence started to return. It wanted half an hour to train time, but the Refreshment Room was fairly full, because they are supplementary clubs in India, where the bar is always open, the drinks are cold, and the punkahs keep the stifling air in some semblance of motion. He found an empty table and ordered iced Carlsberg lager – more expensive and certainly no better than the local Spencers or Murree, he remembered – but there was an advertisement for the former on a mirror over the bar and it set his dry mouth slavering.

He sat savouring it – the second time he had tasted beer in two years. The other time had been with Paul on that Andaman beach a century ago. Where was Paul now, he wondered again? He was conscious of a slight stir at the other tables, and, looking up, he saw two European police sergeants moving round them – and they were asking for papers.

He sat, transfixed, for some moments, then he rose on legs that were threatening to crumble under him and started to move to a door marked 'Gentlemen' and 'Messieurs' – but he was too late. One of the sergeants finished at a table nearby and turned and intercepted him.

'Are you British or French, sir?' he asked. He was a thickset man, red-faced and gingerish, and he reminded Wyndham vaguely of Mr Meakin.

Wyndham gulped and swallowed, and said 'British' in a mumbled undertone.

'I beg your pardon, sir?' There was suspicion in every line of the other's face, and his hard little blue eyes were fixing Wyndham's.

'British,' said Wyndham, more distinctly. 'I'm awfully sorry – cold beer on a hot bladder always makes me want to pee.'

The policeman's face cleared and broke into a grin. 'Sorry, sir,' he said. 'Carload of these bloody Frogs crashed the Douane again. Always doing it.' He saluted and moved on to the next table, and Wyndham went to the Gents, and was nearly sick. But Somari, when he returned to the platform, was ecstatic.

'Oh, bloody fine, sahib – very nice. "What you want, my man? – Fug off" to that copper. I watch through back door.'

'I certainly didn't say that,' Wyndham told him. 'I was too scared.'

'But you *look* like you are saying that,' Somari said. 'That all that matter. And copper fug off all right. Légion Etrangère soldier come over with brandy and very nice scent – flog it and don't pay Customs. Coppers get very angry if they don't get proper baksheesh.' Somari's opinion of police integrity was of the lowest.

The train came in an hour late, and Somari fussed up and down its length with the guard and the stationmaster in search of Wyndham's two-berth coupé. They found it locked on the inside, and a blast of profanity in the ripest Cockney met the guard's efforts to get in.

'Soldier, sahib,' whispered Somari. 'You give pukkha order to come out. Tommies only travel second class.'

'It doesn't *matter*,' Wyndham hissed.

'It bloody does,' Somari insisted. 'You pukkha bara sahib don't forget. You walk away and get into second class, it look funny. Come on, sahib – same like with copper,' he pleaded.

So Wyndham, his every instinct against it, rattled the handle of the door, and rasped. 'Open this door immediately, and come out – or consider yourself under arrest,' and a sheepish private of the Middlesex Regiment emerged, dragging a kitbag behind him.

'Sorry, sir,' he mumbled. 'I thought it was just these bleedin' wogs. No room in the seconds when I got on at Madura,' and he drifted off down the platform forlornly.

'Hang up clothes pukkha, so they don't get crease,' Somari

instructed him as he stowed the luggage. 'Sheet and pillow in bedding roll. I bring shaving water with chhota hazri in morning. Goodnight sahib. I go now. Servant compartment crowded like hell – got to fight to get in.'

'You can have the other berth here, for God's sake,' Wyndham said irritably, and Somari sighed and said, 'Shit! I try to teach you – but you never learn,' and went off.

But he was grinning cheerfully when he thumped at the door next morning, with a Spencer's bearer from the refreshment coach standing beside him carrying a breakfast tray.

'Very lovely, sahib,' he said. 'Bloody train two hours late, same like always, so sahib don't have to get up at sparrow fart. Madras one hour. Here shaving water. Now give shoes, so I can clean in servants' compartment, proper fashion. All right, sahib. Don't do anything at station until I come. Have good breakfast.'

There was porridge, bacon and eggs, hot rolls and coffee on the tray, together with a slice of iced papaya and fresh limes – the sort of breakfast he had so often dreamed of in the last two years – but now he was too nervous to enjoy it.

The train rolled slowly into Central Station, and even before it stopped, his compartment, together with the other first-class ones each side of it, was under siege by a swarm of baggage coolies and hotel touts, wrenching at the door handles and yelling. He was used to it, of course, as is everybody who has ever travelled in India, but now it seemed to be drawing the attention of railway police, officials, other travellers, both European and Indian – making him a focal point – and once again he felt a wave of panic engulfing him. But Somari arrived, pushing, thumping and swearing in a pot-pourri of Hindi, Tamil and barrack English – the efficient and officious sahib's servant to the life – 'Hut jao! Baghao! Haramzada log – black bastards! Sirf ek quli – Only one coolie mangta! No – not wanting hotel – Fuggoff!' He was behaving, in short, perfectly normally, as were the servants of a dozen other Europeans and well-to-do Indians, and Wyndham immediately felt calmer.

There was a European police sergeant outside the barrier, and Wyndham forced himself to walk past him instead of turning abruptly to one side as his every instinct was dictating. Behind him he heard Somari clucking approvingly. They came out into the blinding early morning sunlight, and Somari hailed a horse gharry.

'All right, sahib,' he said. 'We go along seafront, and sahib get out – sit on seat – walk about little bit. Lot of sahibs and memsahibs do that in morning when it nice and cool. I go off with baggage, and come back for sahib later.'

'Where do we go then?' Wyndham asked nervously.

'Very good place – but I got to see if everything all right first.' He grinned wickedly. 'Don't worry, sahib – like yesterday. I don't pinch baggage and bugger off.' Wyndham started to protest, too heatedly, then gave it up. What was the use? This little devil was reading him like a book.

They came out of the station forecourt and turned left into Poonamallee Road, with Somari perched high on the front seat beside the driver, and Wyndham, feeling hideously exposed, sitting behind in regal state. They passed the Central Penitentiary, and Somari turned and winked, then they bore right, round the General Hospital, and Fort St George loomed before them, with the open sea the other side. They stopped on the Esplanade, and Somari said, 'All right, sahib – I come back half an hour, maybe one hour,' and winked again.

Wyndham stood on the pavement and watched the gharry clopping away into the morning traffic, and once again felt the sense of utter aloneness that always came to him when the little man left him. He shrugged impatiently. He'd have to rid himself of this wretched dependence on others. The parting of the ways was coming soon – probably today – and once more he'd be on his own – and this time he'd remain so.

A fresh breeze was blowing in from the sea, and English children were playing on the sands, their white-saried ayahs squatting in a watchful row uttering shrill warning cries from time to time: 'Tommy baba – no, naughty boy – not too near wat-tah!' – 'Come back, Lucy baba – I tell Mam-mah!' – with the kids, as usual, taking not the slightest notice. A ball bounced on the pavement in front of him and he automatically blocked it with his foot and kicked it back on to the beach and a small boy called, 'Thanks, uncle.' It took him back to his own childhood in Risalpur, when all Europeans were honorary uncles and aunts. An officer in starched khaki drill and Sam Browne belt coming briskly towards him from the sallyport of the fort, grinned and said, 'Little devils,' and Wyndham checked himself from salaaming just in time, and grinned back. A short mile ahead of him he could see the long arm of South Pier which, with its twin to the north, formed the huge artificial harbour of Madras, and the other side of it were the crowded masts and funnels of deep-sea ships. Surely he could get aboard one of them? That really was his best chance – his only chance. There was nothing for him in India except eventual apprehension and arrest and return to the Andamans, and then that ghastly platform with Mr Pereira standing at the top of the steps. He shivered and looked out towards the horizon. There they were, those damned islands, over there – waiting. No, by God, anything but that. A ship, but if that failed, then a swim out from this beach – out – out – until he could swim no more.

He stopped and looked towards the harbour. Why not start exploring possibilities now? What was he waiting for? He was fed and rested, with his energy at its peak. He was decently dressed – unlikely to be stopped at the gangway if he boarded a ship with sufficient authority – 'What you want, my man? You fug off' – Then, once aboard, look for a hiding place and slip into it. He'd need food and water for a few days, until they were well at sea – get hold of an official-looking briefcase, or something a bit bigger. The thing to do, though, was to see just exactly what was in port at the moment – and where they were going from here. The shipping columns in the papers would tell him that, surely. But now was the time – *now*. Why go back at all? He wouldn't be letting Somari down. He was in his home town – safe. He'd be better on his own –

Then he remembered the money. He was carrying it all. Somari had insisted on his taking it when they got on the train, in case he got his pocket picked while he was sleeping in the servants' compartment. He'd promised him half. He'd have to stand by that. He sighed and turned back along the Esplanade.

The little man darted through the traffic from under the shadow of the fort and came up to him, grinning delightedly.

'All fix,' he said. 'All fix – bloody lovely. Follow me, sahib.'

'Where to?' Wyndham asked.

'Very good place – not far. Walk little bit behind me.' Somari started to cross the road again, but Wyndham caught him by the arm.

'You walk *with* me,' he said. 'And tell me all about this place as we go along.'

Somari turned his eyes skywards, as one praying for strength and forbearance.

'How many more times I got to tell you?' he demanded. 'You pukkha number one sahib, dressed up like half-pay bloody colonel. I *servant*. We don't walk together. Now follow me, for Christ sake, and don't bloody argue any more.' And Wyndham followed.

Somari rounded the fort, crossed China Bazaar Street and plunged into the maze of alleys on the edge of George Town. They walked for ten minutes, crossing and re-crossing narrow streets, dodging bullock carts, cars and gharries, and then the little man stopped in front of a small shop sandwiched between a café and a native hotel. The café obviously catered for sailors, because the sign above the window read 'Sam's Falmouth Packet' and on the window itself was a garishly painted full-rigged ship. The hotel was 'The Pearl of Asia Palace Good Clean Cheap' – all in one line, while the shop was called, improbably, 'Madame Duval's Haute Couteure, Ladies & Gents Wardrobe – High Class'. All the signs looked as if they had been painted by the same artist a very long time ago, and the three establishments had a uniform air of decay. Somari turned and beckoned and went into Madame Duval's, and Wyndham, now past all wonder, followed.

A woman said, from the dimness at the back of the shop, 'Come in, honey boy. There's nothing to be frightened of.'

Chapter 21

She came forward into the light – an enormous bulk of a woman with rolls of fat starting with quadruple chins that ran down into a bust like loosely filled twin flour sacks which in turn overhung a huge protuberant belly. She had a tiny button of a nose in the centre of a red moonlike face, and small twinkling black eyes behind thick pebble glasses. Her scanty dark hair was pulled back into an untidy bun that held a big Spanish tortoiseshell comb behind her head like a black halo. She wore a damp and dingy peignoir that enveloped her like a collapsed marquee from shoulder to ankle and gave off an odour of stale phul-nana and sweat in a powerful compound.

She took his hand in a clammy paw that felt to him like a dead octopus, and peered up into his face.

'This little soor ka bacha tells me you've been having a hard time, honey boy,' she said. 'Well, there now – you're safe here.' Her voice was deep and gravelly, and although her English was fluent there was a touch of French accent behind it. Pondicherry again, he guessed.

'That's very kind of you, madame,' he began, 'but I – '

'Don't say anything about yourself, honey boy,' she interrupted quickly. 'Not a word. Keep your own counsel. As far as I'm concerned, you're a sahib that needs a place to lay his head for a bit, without someone breathing down his neck, in a manner of speaking. We never refused that to nobody, Gawd knows.'

'Yes, but I must tell you,' he insisted. 'I have very little money – '

'Zut! What's money? It's only important when you don't have none.' She waved it off airily.

'Then, in that case it's *very* important to me at the moment,' he said. 'And I should also mention that if I'm found here I could bring trouble to you, madame.'

'Not "madame", just "Aunty",' she told him. 'Money? Fine. When you move on I'll give you a little bill – and you can send it to me when you're holding a bit stronger. Trouble? Man's born to that, as the spark flies upward, as they say in the Bible. I'd be lonely without it. But nobody's *going* to find you here, honey boy. I don't pay what *I* pay to the coppers' fresh air fund without expecting a little bit of consideration in return.' She turned and called, 'Somari – where are you, you little bleeder? Ah, there you are. Take Walker sahib up to – let me see now – yes, Number Five on the second floor, and tell Neena to get some clean sheets and towels and what-not. You go and get your head down and your breath back, honey boy, until we call you for tiffin – and don't worry about nothing.'

'Yes, Aunty-memsahib,' Somari said, and jerked at Wyndham's sleeve as he hesitated. 'This way, sahib.'

He went out through a door at the back of the shop, and Wyndham followed in a dream. They climbed two flights of dark and dusty stairs to a room that opened off a long corridor. It was large and airy and surprisingly clean, furnished with a big old-fashioned brass bed, an enormous teakwood wardrobe, table, and a couple of roorkhee chairs. French windows opened on to a deep balcony which, being higher than the buildings opposite, gave an unobstructed view of the harbour.

Somari said, 'Very lovely, sahib. What I tell you, eh?'

'Yes, very lovely,' Wyndham agreed. 'But what the devil is going on, Somari? I mean, who is this woman – ?'

'Aunty? Oh, everybody know Aunty – '

'*I* don't.'

'She very rich. Own this place and other one that side, this side, every bloody side – '

'But why the hell should she be offering me free board and lodging?'

'She very kind, too.'

'Not *that* kind. Nobody is. Now come on. What's behind all this?'

'Just like I say. She very kind lady – like nice young man – '

'What?' Wyndham yelled. 'You mean to say – ? *Not bloody likely!* I'd go back to jail first!'

'Not *that* way, for Christ sake.' Somari grinned. 'Anyhow, she got husband.'

'Thank God for that. Where's *he*?'

'Next door. He Sam.'

'A sailor?'

'No – soldier. He quartermaster-sergeant one time. Fiddle the ration account – get pinched – court-martial – go to jail three years.'

'Why does he call his pub the Falmouth Packet and have a ship on the window?'

'Oh, first time call it the Edinburgh Castle and have Scotch soldier on window – but Army put it out of bounds to all troops, so he say "Fug you, General O'Reilly" and make it sailor place. Soldiers still come here though – but he drop little bit baksheesh to Military Police, so it all right – except when there is officer in charge of Town Picquet – then they close for couple of nights.'

'How do you come to know so much about them?' Wyndham asked, and Somari laughed.

'Oh, me?' he said. 'Know him for years. He can't do jail in Madras – get too much prickly heat – so they send him to Ootacamund European Jail. I his barrack servant one time, so Aunty see me and say, "You know bloody ropes, Somari. I got to get whisky, cigarettes, pukkha food, little bit money, up to Sam sahib. Can fix?" So I go up and straighten a bent screw – fix up good. Make one trip a week all time – and everything she send, Sam gets. I don't fiddle nothing for myself – and they know it. She say after Sam get out, "Somari, you bloody good boy. *Honest* boy. We owe you good turn. Call any time." But then soon after, I get pinched down in Pondicherry. Never call before.'

'But it's you they owe the good turn to, not me,' Wyndham said.

'We friends,' Somari said simply. 'You get me off beach when I don't have guts to go through jungle myself – so I owe *you* turn.'

'All right then,' Wyndham said, standing by the window and looking out across the harbour. 'You've paid it. We call it quits now. You're back in your home town, and you've got your own way to make. This is where we split up, Somari.'

'Oh, sure,' said Somari cheerfully. 'But we got to get you away somewhere first.'

'No, I've got to do that myself.'

'You can't – not by self. Only Sam can fix that.'

'How the hell can Sam fix it?' Wyndham snapped impatiently.

'Sam quartermaster-sergeant – second best fixer in India.'

'But he came unstuck, didn't he?'

'Sure, but only because Aunty catch him. She *first* best fixer in India.'

'But you said she was his wife – ?'

'You bet. That why she catch him. Old Sam randy bugger – having it off with Drum-major's memsahib. Aunty say, "You lay off – or by God, I fix you good." He don't lay off – so she fix.'

'How?' Wyndham asked, interested in spite of himself.

'Sam got a hundred and fifty cases of bully beef and half a ton of best white flour in a godown near the docks. Aunty gave military police the tip-off – and Sam get lumbered one night when he's there doing a deal with Parsee contractor.'

Wyndham gaped. 'But you said she sent him stuff in prison?'

'Sure. Why not? She his wife.'

'After shopping him?'

'Oh, that all right. Sam bloody angry at first, but then he laugh like hell and say, "Serve me right. I shouldn't have told old bitch where I got it. Know better next time." Then they good friends again.'

Wyndham shook his head slowly. 'I just don't understand it,' he said.

'That's because you don't know Sam and Aunty,' Somari grinned. 'I hear British Tommy say once, "Sam could walk on water, like Jesus – and Aunty would put screen round and sell Jews tickets to come and see." Very lovely people.'

Wyndham turned and looked at the other. 'Somari,' he said quietly. 'You know where I come from?'

'Sure. Kala Pani,' Somari answered.

'You know what they pay if you turn somebody in from there?'

'Five thousand rupees.'

'Well – if *you* guessed it, won't these people?'

'They know,' Somari said. 'Don't have to guess.'

Wyndham felt again the cold, sickening wave of terror at the pit of his stomach, but his voice remained steady. 'You've just told me that she turned her own husband in.'

'Yes – but not for money. Only because he randy bugger. They don't turn you in, sahib – not for ten lakhs of rupees. No

212

more than I turn you in.' He said it with complete certainty.

'How can you be sure of that?' Wyndham asked angrily. 'Money does funny things to people.'

'Maybe, sahib – but Brothers do plenty things *more* bloody funny to them if they do that. Sam and Aunty both baharis – same like you and me.'

Wyndham stared at him. 'Are you sure of that?' he demanded.

'You don't think I bring you here unless I *am* sure, do you? You give Sam the sign, and see – or maybe he give you the sign first – and be bloody sure you give proper one back – same like.' He made a quick pass across his brow.

'All right then,' Wyndham said, overwhelmingly relieved. 'But how can Aunty be one? I heard that you can only be a bahari if you've been in prison.'

'Oh, *she* been in prison. She madam of jig-a-jig joint in Pondicherry – very nice place for French NCOs, but she don't give proper baksheesh to proper copper, so she get lumbered. Aunty not a bahari? By God, she number one for whole coast.'

'Don't the police here know that?'

'Sure they know it. How you think she runs this business if they don't know it?'

'What *is* this business?'

'Every bloody thing – clothes business – café business – piggery business for pork to the Army – business for making soft drink – lemonade – soda – jig-a-jig business – but biggest business *fence* business.' He waved his hand around. 'And everything here in this block – except pig business. They used to be here, but they stink too much, so she shift them out to Pudupet. Bloody nice money in pigs. Only Klistian and Untouchables can handle 'em.'

'Good God,' said Wyndham faintly.

'Don't you worry, sahib,' Somari assured him. 'You going to be all right here. Now get rest. I call for tiffin.' He winked, clicked his tongue, gave a thumbs-up sign and went.

He woke with a start and sat up. A wizened little white man with a drooping moustache and the face of a sorrowing cocker spaniel was standing at the foot of the bed gently shaking Wyndham's big toe. He relinquished the toe and brushed sweat from his brow in one movement, and Wyndham automatically raised his hand to his nose and pressed each nostril in turn as if blowing it.

'That's all right,' said the little man. 'Somari spoke for you, but it's always best to make certain, as the bishop said to the barmaid.' He put his hand out. 'Name of Horslake. Welcome to the vicarage, Mr Walker.'

'How do you do,' said Wyndham shaking hands. 'You're Madame Duval's husband, I take it?'

'Madame Duval me bloody arse,' said the little man. 'Her name's Horslake, same as mine. We was married pukkha at the Catholic Mission in Veperi. The Duval came off a carton of fancy soap. Feel like a chhota peg before tiffin?'

'Bit early for me, thanks, Mr Horslake,' Wyndham said, swinging his feet to the floor.

'Sam, for Gawd's sake,' said the little man. 'All right – follow me. I hope you like curry. All you ever get in this damn place. You know, I haven't seen the Old Country since before the war, but I still dream of Lancashire hotpot, Yorkshire pudden and Irish stew – and the taste of a pint of mild-an'-bitter straight from the wood, without being gassed in a bottle and screwed up with ice, would bring tears to me bloody mince-pies.'

They went down a flight of stairs and through a labyrinth of narrow dusty passages into a sepulchral room that put Wyndham in mind of the salle-à-manger of a petit-bourgeois family in Lille to whom he had been sent to cram French for his Army Entrance exam. Jalousied windows were hung with dusty velvet drapes, there was a profusion of potted palms and wax fruit under glass domes, the furniture was mahogany and massive and only the feebly swaying punkah hanging limply from the high shadowy ceiling struck a different note. A huge table was set with tarnished silver dishes, tureens, épergnes and ice-buckets. Wyndham blinked, and Sam grunted, 'Don't let it blind you. All swiped from railway dining cars. Can't flog it because it's stamped – can't melt it down because it's only plated – so we're stuck with it.' He raised his voice and yelled, 'Ko'i hai!' and Somari, in fresh, splendidly starched white clothes, with a serviette draped over his left forearm, came through a door and bowed.

'Luncheon served shortly, gentlemen,' he murmured.

'Jesus!' exclaimed Sam. 'Going all Officers' Mess, are we? You been at my whisky again?'

Somari grinned sheepishly. 'Cut it out, Sam sahib,' he said. 'Memsahib saying she want all this done nice because we got pukkha sahib here.'

'Like hell,' said Sam. 'She's just getting you back into training.' He winked at the acutely uncomfortable Wyndham. 'We used to hire him out for Anglo-Indian weddings, dressed up as a Goanese butler. Twenty chips an afternoon. Money for old rope it was.'

Then Aunty arrived, like a Dutch eel-barge under full sail. 'Sleep well, honey boy?' she asked, and added to Somari, 'Serve luncheon, bearer.'

'By Christ, I won't,' snarled Somari. 'Not if you call me bearer. I Klistian gentleman servant, not a bloody Hindu parlourmaid with bollocks,' and he stalked from the room.

'Don't you get temperamental with *me*, you little black bastard, or I'll take a stick to you,' Aunty yelled after him. She turned to Wyndham, quite unperturbed. 'Best little bloke in India that, but he acts up like a Russian ballet dancer if you pull his leg.'

Somari came back marshalling three inestimably humbler minions bearing steaming dishes of prawns, chicken vindaloo, dal, saffron rice and a round dozen side dishes, and Wyndham ate the best curry he had ever encountered in the length and breadth of India before. They ate native fashion as curry should be eaten, in silence except for an occasional rumbling belch of appreciation, with long draughts of iced lager when the going got too torrid for their chili-tortured tongues. They finished with iced melon and magnificent Turkish coffee, then, with a final rumble, Aunty pushed her chair back and rose.

'No, don't get up, honey boy,' she said. 'You'll embarrass that ignorant old bleeder. Have a little talk to him. He'll give you the form – but don't make any hasty decisions. There's plenty of time,' and she waddled out.

'She's right,' said Sam. 'You don't want to rush nothing, but as a matter of common sense we'll have to be thinking of getting you out of it eventually.'

'I must make it clear. I've got no money, Sam,' Wyndham told him earnestly.

'Oh, balls to that.' Sam waved it away. 'Money don't come into it. Not yet, anyway. If it worries you, you can always earn your keep here while you're waiting.'

'How?' asked Wyndham eagerly.

'Books. She's got 'em in a hell of a state – and she won't trust 'em to me.' He chuckled. 'Can't blame her for that, mind you. All the same, this is a big business – and a lot of it's legit. We've got to have *some* sort of accounts – if only to blind the tax bastards with.'

'I'd certainly be delighted to try,' Wyndham said gratefully, 'although I must admit I'm not terribly good at figures.'

'Never met an officer as was,' said Sam. 'Most of the young Percies in our mob had to take their boots off to count up to twenty. But don't worry about that. Aunty'll give you the figures. She's got 'em all in her head, like a bleedin' adding machine. It's her handwriting and spelling that gets everybody down. It's so soddin' awful she can't read it herself five minutes after.'

'Couldn't she get a babu?' Wyndham asked, and Sam looked at him in astonishment.

'You must be barmy,' he said. 'Let a Bachelor of Economics, Calcutta (failed), get his snout into *our* books? We'd be paying blackmail for the rest of our lives.'

'All right, Sam, I'll start any time you wish,' Wyndham said. 'But there's one thing I'd like to straighten out with you first.'

'What's that?'

'*I am not an officer.*'

'Don't try so hard to cover it up,' Sam said quietly. 'You'll only draw attention to yourself that way. We know what you are – we know *who* you are. It's safe with us. Now that's the last time I want to hear it mentioned, Mr Walker. Is it all right to call you Johnnie, by the way?'

'By all means.'

'Good. So let's get on with the next thing. Getting you out, when the time comes. You got any ideas about where you want to go?'

'Anywhere, as long as it's away from here – and isn't England.'

'Australia,' said Sam firmly. 'The *only* place. And not a bad dump either, from what I hear. They breed the best con men and blaggers in the business there.'

'It would suit me down to the ground,' said Wyndham. 'There's only the little matter of getting there.'

'We want a boat – first stop one of the Australian ports. We might have to wait a bit for that.'

'A foreigner?'

'No bloody fear. British.'

'And stow away?'

Sam shook his head. 'Not a chance. Stowaways from India are poison. Other countries are always scared of cholera, smallpox, leprosy and God knows what – so there's a five hundred pound fine put on skippers who arrive in any home or overseas British port with one aboard. That means that gangways are guarded as tight as a bull's arse in fly time and a hundred per cent rummage, *with police dogs*, is carried out before clearing from any Indian port. No, Johnnie, you can forget stowing away.'

'No money or passport, so that rules out going as a passenger,' said Wyndham, 'and no skipper would sign me on as a member of the crew without papers. What's the alternative?'

'A "Private Turnbull",' Sam said, and beamed smugly.

'What on earth's that?' Wyndham asked, and Sam looked hurt and incredulous.

'You mean to say that you never heard of a "Turnbull"?' he squeaked. 'Christ! The whole of India was talking about it for months a couple of years ago.'

'I was a bit preoccupied about then,' Wyndham said, and Sam nodded understandingly.

'Of course. I was forgetting,' he said. 'Sam's greatest tickle. I had five hundred rupees on with old Homusjee, the Parsee bookie, at five hundred to one. Two hundred and fifty thousand smackers. Cried like a little child he did. Pitiful to see. But he had to pay up, the old son of a bitch.' He closed his eyes and made ecstatic mewing noises.

'Very interesting,' Wyndham said. 'But what's that got to do with my getting a ship?'

'Everything,' said Sam, and stabbed a finger downwards. 'All started down there, it did, in the old Falmouth Packet. Two Tommies – Private Turnbull and Lance-Corporal Morphew of the Westmorelands. Saturday night – full of troops – all of 'em with a bit of a skinful aboard. Morphew is due out, time-expired, in two or three months. Bumming his load about it, he is, and taking the mickey out of Turnbull. "Just picture it, eh? Me in a few more months – nice check suit – fourpenny cigar – bit of stuff on me arm – Hampstead Heath on Bank Holiday – and poor old Turneyboy here with another three years' curry and prickly heat ahead of him." And Turnbull goes mad and yells, "You big-mouthed bastard. I bet you fifty chips I'll be in Blighty before you."

' "Wouldn't rob you," says Morphew.

' "Haven't got the guts to take me up," yells Turnbull.

' "You're on," says Morphew, "if you *want* to chuck your money away." So the bet is taken – and there's witnesses there – and while the hubbub is going on, an idea is coming to me, and I remember a Cockney fireman who got left on the beach here – no money, no papers – and the way some Liverpool stokers get him Home with no trouble at all. So I pull young Turnbull to one side, and I says, "You talk too big, laddie – with nothing to back it up."

' "Don't rub it in, Sam," he says, almost crying.

'I said, "If you've got the guts, you can collect that fifty chips – and a few more as well, on a side bet. What about it?"

'He said, "I'd do anything – *anything* – to stick it across that sod."

' "You're under orders from now on," I tell him. "You do just exactly what I say – and you keep your mouth buttoned up. Right?"

' "Right," he says. So I go back and say to the lot of them, "You know – I think that's a pretty sporting gesture of young Turnbull's. I think he might just about do it."

' "Balls," they all say. "You can't beat the system. A poor bloody Tommy's out here for six years, and six he does – on his feet or on his bloody back – please himself – but he *does* it."

' "Well, I'm a sporting man meself," [I says. "And seeing as it's my wife's birthday and the anniversary of the Battle of Waterloo – both major French catastrophes – I'm offering ten to one that Turnbull does it," and then I've got to hold 'em off with the thick end of a billiard cue. They rake up their half-rupees and annas and slam it at me – and they're in next payday with more – then the sergeants get to hear of it, and even some of the younger officers – and within a week I've got over a thousand rupees in bets. I go and see Homusjee – who'll make a book on which of two flies on a wall will fly off first. He say, "Soldier go home before his time? Never been known. Write your own ticket."

' "Five hundred to one?" I ask, and laugh as if I was joking.

' "Sure, why not?" he says, because I'd taken damn good care to see him in front of witnesses, and he's never been known to refuse a bet in his life.

' "You're on," I says. "Five hundred rupees. Here, count it."

'He blinks and gulps a bit, but he's got to take it, or lose face – and ten days later Turnbull is posted "missing, believed deserted" – and every cop in India is on the watch for him, and there's a tighter than ever clamp put on all ships – because I don't have to tell you that a British Tommy only gets two bob a day, poor bastard – but if he goes on the loose they're after him as if he was gold-plated and diamond-studded. Still and all – eight weeks later he walks into a police station in the East End of London and says, "I'm 3297748, Private Turnbull H. of 'A' Company, Second Battalion, The Royal Westmorelands, stationed in Fort St George, Madras, from which place I deserted." They don't believe him at first – but then there's some cabling back and forward – and it's him all right – so back he comes in close arrest on the next troop-ship – court-martial – and a very light hundred-and-twelve days in the moosh – most of which is remitted anyway because of the time he's been in custody – and he's back soldiering merrily on with a thousand rupees I give him for himself – having beaten Morphew home by three weeks.'

'But in God's name how?' asked Wyndham.

'Fireman,' said Sam profoundly. 'Four stokers, two trimmers and two greasers per watch. Three watches – total of twenty-four of them – either covered in coaldust in the stokehold, or going to and from the fo'c'sle – or sleeping in their bunks – and not even the Captain will go and wake a sleeping fireman if he's got any sense. Wild lot of buggers – Liverpool Irish mostly – but the best-hearted boys in the world. A lot of 'em use the old Falmouth – so I fixed it up with them and dropped 'em five hundred chips for beer – and Turnbull went on board with 'em the night before they sailed – dressed like 'em – singing like 'em – and seemingly drunk like 'em. And walked off in Liverpool the same way.'

Wyndham took a deep breath. 'And you think – ?' he began.

'I don't think,' Sam said. 'I know. Come the right ship going to the right place at the right time – with the right crowd of boys aboard – and you're off, Johnnie me lad – and you can give the lot of 'em here the old two finger salute.'

Wyndham sat with his eyes closed, almost as if he were praying.

Chapter 22

The Horslake empire was a triangular city block with the apex cut off, making a fourth, much shorter, side which was taken up by the native hotel, the clothes shop, and the Falmouth Packet. Sam took Wyndham round on a tour of inspection the next day.

'Nicest bit of property in town,' he said proudly. 'Got to hand it to the old cow. She started just with that shop of hers – second-hand clothes bought off the officers' ladies and flogged to the soldiers' wives and the Anglo-Bangloes – then she bought my little place – that was long before we was married, of course. After that she lent a bit on mortgage to a drunken Marwari who owned the hotel the other side of her, and she'd foreclosed on him and had him out on his ear before he knew what had hit him. And so on – buying a little shop here, a house there – a couple of godowns a bit further along, until she had the whole block. She rents the ground floors out, but all the middle and topsides belongs to the old firm. Come the day when they go in for proper slum clearance we'll be sitting on a goldmine.'

'Quite a businesswoman,' said Wyndham.

'Um – yes, I suppose you could call her that.' Sam pinched his lower lip dubiously. 'But I must admit she scares the pants off me at times. She talks like an honest to God Britisher, but she's still French underneath. French with a drop of coffee in the milk. Pure Marseilles, she says, but I think her ma must have had an Algerian carpet salesman calling round occasionally. She married a French Colonial NCO and came out to Pondicherry when she was a bit of a kid, but he used to belt the hell out of her, so she busted a bottle of vin ordinaire over his head one day, and did a face-lifting job on him with the broken bit – and – er – well, went into business down there, in a manner of speaking.'

'A lady of enterprise.'

'Not 'arf. The trouble is that she still *thinks* French. In her day you could buy the whole police force and half the Town Council in Pondicherry for a couple of thousand francs, and she won't realize that things are a bit different on this side of the border. Sure, some of the little men will take a backhander, but not the higher-ups – and I can't get rid of a nasty feeling that they're just giving her enough rope to hang herself. If they ever made a real raid on this block – Jee–suss!'

'You feel that's likely to happen, do you?' Wyndham said uneasily.

'It *could*. Oh, you don't have to worry about waking up one morning to find a cop feeling your collar. We've got a feller straightened in the Department who could give us a bit of warning – but he couldn't *stop* anything. We certainly wouldn't have time to move any hot merchandise out of it. There's about fifty bloody tons of loot stashed away in here.'

'Then why the devil don't you start getting rid of it while you're still safe?' Wyndham asked. 'From what you tell me, you're doing very nicely on the purely legitimate side of things.'

'Johnnie me boy,' Sam said fervently. 'I reckon I'm going to bless the day you came along. That's just my idea, but I'm fighting a lone battle with her. With two of us having a go at her she might listen to reason.'

'I could hardly start giving her unasked for advice,' Wyndham said. 'She'd probably tell me to go and jump off the breakwater, and I wouldn't blame her.'

'You'd be surprised. I wouldn't mind betting that she'd take it like a lamb from you. It's only me she fights with.' He opened a door at the end of a long corridor. 'Look at this bloody lot,' he said.

Wyndham saw an enormous room, or rather a series of rooms that had been roughly knocked into one. Windows that had once opened on to the street had been bricked up or covered with corrugated metal sheeting, and the only light came in from those which faced on to an inner courtyard. It was stacked from floor to ceiling with trunks, suitcases, valises and other travelling impedimenta.

'Knocked off by the Kandh train thieves all over South India,' Sam explained. 'She sends bullock carts round all the chor ki bazaars in the district, and buys it up in job lots. That pile over there I'd rather not touch.' He pointed to some cabin trunks standing by themselves. 'They came off the *Mirimbula* – small cargo-passenger boat that docked here from Shanghai, with bubonic plague on board. Twenty-two buried at sea – another fifteen here. She was in quarantine for months, and all bedding and personal luggage was supposed to be incinerated, but that silly old cow squared the Untouchable sanitary squad to slip it round here at night. It happened while I was in jail, or I'd have stopped her.'

'Good God!' said Wyndham, and stepped back hastily.

'Oh, I suppose it's all right now – it's been here for years – but it still gives me the creeps.' Sam grinned sourly. 'She reckoned it was quite safe, because she got old Father Rubeiro round to sprinkle it with holy water.'

'Did he know what it was?'

'Not bloody likely – or he'd have wanted more than the ten rupees she gave him.' He pulled the door to and sighed gloomily. 'So now you see what I'm up against. That's just part of it. We're sitting on a load of dynamite here.'

'You most certainly are,' said Wyndham with feeling. 'You'll have to do something about it – even if you have to give it away.'

'*Give* it away?' said Sam. 'You try giving a wog something for nothing. He'd know there was something screwy about it, and he'd run a bloody mile. No – we're right up the creek with this lot, like the bloke with the albatross round his neck. Can't dump it or burn it without *some* nosey bugger coming round to see what it's all about. And that's not the worst of it, either. There's the girls.'

'What girls?' Wyndham asked.

'You'll see,' said Sam darkly. 'We got two places. One at four rupees for the troops and sailors, and one at fifty for the bara sahibs. And we've been mentioned in Parliament.'

'Parliament?'

'Yers – House of Commons, back Home. Lady Astor, the woman MP. She's got the dead needle against banging and boozing among the lower classes. A bloody journalist come into the Packet one night dressed like a bosun's mate, and he wrote an article for a London paper about vice in the Far East. According to him we've poxed-up all the Army and half the Navy. Bloody lies. I'll say that for Aunty – she runs the girls proper – doctor on Friday, Mass on Sunday, regular as clockwork. Still, her bloody ladyship has been squawking and the cops have been getting nervous, even the ones we've been paying. They'll be forced to do do something about it before long.'

'Well, I'd certainly get that side of the business closed down right away,' advised Wyndham.

'Isn't that what I've been telling her? But it's like talking to the dhobi's donkey. "My poor little ones! Where will they go if I turn them out?" Poor little ones? Blimey! Cut your throat for fourpence, some of 'em.'

'You certainly seem to have a problem, Sam,' said Wyndham thoughtfully.

'Problem? My Gawd!' said Sam dolefully. 'Still, you don't know what a relief it is just talking to another bloke – a man with a college education and all that.'

'Well, I hope I can be of some help – '

'Damn certain you can be,' grunted Sam. 'Come on – I'll show you the rest.'

They completed the tour, a full quarter-mile of it, and all without once coming out into the open, because the block, although originally comprised of separate houses, had been now knocked into one. The far end – the longest side of the triangle – was formed by a terrace of nine houses, each with its own high-walled courtyard in front, in which grew a few dusty palm trees. There was a narrow lane the other side of the courtyards, each end of which opened on to a wider, busier thoroughfare. Sam brought him to a window on the upper floor of the end house.

'Poojimalla Lane, that out there,' he explained. 'Known to the local jokers as Coconut Alley on account of a missionary getting clobbered by one, off one of them palm trees one night. Right outside Number Seven, it was. That's the bara sahibs' knocking shop. Bloody nigh corpsed him.'

'What was he doing there?' Wyndham asked.

'*He* reckoned he was taking the girls the Word – but the uncharitable pointed out that he was wearing a false moustache and no dog-collar.' Sam went on like a real estate agent's clerk. 'We're now in Number One. Four nice rooms below – four topsides here – kitchen and servants' quarters to the rear. At present unoccupied because Aunty says the bara sahibs don't like to be overlooked when arriving or leaving. Number Two, next door here, is occupied by some brand new Army tentage and some very nice officers' camp furniture.'

'What the hell is that doing there?'

Sam sighed. 'Aunty and her bloody magpie tricks again. A railway truckload came in from the Government Factory at Cawnpore to the Ordnance Depot and got shunted on to a siding just across the next road there, and nobody seemed to know anything about it, so a conductor flogged the lot to her for five hundred chips and a season ticket to the knocking shop. Gawd knows what we're ever going to do with it. It's got broad arrows and "War Department Property" stencilled all over it. Silly old bitch.'

They went down a flight of stairs to the ground floor. 'Odds and ends of hot gear in the next two,' Sam went on. 'Then we come to Numbers Five and Six – bedroom accommodation, but not for sleeping. And here's Number Seven – the salon, as Aunty calls it.' He opened a door and Wyndham looked through into a large room furnished in sombre mahogany and faded velvet, which garishly coloured pouffés and cushions did little to lighten. There was a grand piano draped with a Spanish shawl, a profusion of potted palms, paper flowers and Benares coffee tables, and, gazing down upon it all in slightly disapproving solemnity, a huge oleograph of Queen Victoria, with the Union Jack and the tricolour crossed above it. It smelt of long extinguished joss-sticks and stale phul-nana, and looked as wicked as a Methodist chapel in a South Wales valley on a wet February evening.

'Good God,' said Wyndham, awed. 'Where are the girls?'

'They all live in Number Eight, next door. They don't come on duty until ten at night. Want to have a look at them?'

'No thanks,' said Wyndham hastily.

'Please yourself. You don't have to worry about them seeing you around though. Only English and Irish whores gossip off-duty. Bad initial training, Aunty says.' He shrugged. 'Well, that concludes the look-see round this end. Number Nine, the last house is kept empty for the same reason as Number One.'

'What about the troops' place?' Wyndham asked.

'Oh, the Bullring? That's topsides over the Packet. Handier for them, like. Come and have a look at it.'

Wyndham thought it was considerably more cheerful than

Number Seven, in that it had no mahogany or velvet – an upright pianola instead of a grand piano, and a dart-board surrounded by the cap badges of many famous regiments replaced Queen Victoria. A half-obliterated, crudely executed sign on the white-washed wall stated that sailors and sergeant-majors paid half-price, with lewd anatomical reasons for the reduction beneath it. It smelt of stale beer.

'We're always painting that damn sign out,' Sam said. 'But then some joker smuggles in a pot of paint and slaps it up again. The lads love this place. Real home from home it is for 'em. And that bloody woman back in Blighty wants to close it down. That means they'll be going to the sand rats in the back alleys, and taking Home more than they came out with.'

'What sort of women do you have here?'

'Oh, same ones. Aunty shuttles 'em down from the other end when they're wanted. They're tarted up with a few more frills and furbelows when they're working in Number Seven, of course.' He grinned. 'Well, I hope I ain't told you nothing that shocks you.'

'Shock *me*?' said Wyndham. 'You know where I come from.'

'Yes,' said Sam, 'and I told you not to refer to it again. Forget it, lad. Come and have a drink.' He walked to a small bar in the corner and unlocked it. 'Whisky or gin?'

'Beer, please.'

'Don't you like spirits?'

'Too much. We were talking about problems earlier on,' Wyndham said. 'That happens to be mine. If I don't have any, it doesn't worry me. If I do, it starts the whole thing off again.'

'I see what you mean,' Sam said understandingly. 'Very sensible. Right, I'll have beer too.'

'Don't let me stop you.'

'Nobody ever stopped me doing anything that I really wanted to – not even Aunty.' He poured two glasses of lager. 'Mud in your eye.'

Wyndham caught his breath sharply, and said, 'Cheers.'

He took a sheet of plain writing paper and an envelope from a side table in the dining-room and went back upstairs after dinner.

Aunty, in an extremely décolleté electric-blue satin evening gown and an ostrich feather in place of the Spanish comb, had waddled her way up to Number Seven, and Sam was at the seat of custom down below in the Falmouth Packet.

He wrote painstakingly in a backhand scrawl that he hoped did not resemble his normal hand too closely, 'Poste Restante, GPO, Madras,' and underlined it, together with the date, then,

Dear Mr Richards,

I understand that you deal in morchi shells, in which I am interested. I am in Madras at present, although I do not intend staying here long. Perhaps you might care to drop me a line, but please don't put yourself to any trouble if you happen to be busy.

Yours sincerely,
John Moody.

He addressed the envelope to Paul at 72 Palighat, Frazer Town, Bangalore, and sat back and looked at it, with rising doubt assailing him. Was he being fair to Paul in dragging him back into this? Wouldn't it be better to let the past bury itself? Perhaps, yes – but then again he had promised to let the other know. It *was* Paul's idea. But to allow him to get in touch here? Suppose things did go wrong ... and this contact was traced ... He weighed pros and cons for nearly half an hour before finally making up his mind. Yes, he'd send it. Paul had a right to know how things had worked out, and what he, Wyndham, was going to do in the future – and only by making contact could he get that information to him. He put the letter in his pocket and went downstairs again, and then stopped nonplussed. He had not been out since he arrived, and the only exit that he knew was through 'Madame Duval's' – but the door to that was now closed and locked. He walked along the passage towards the Falmouth Packet, only to find that the connecting door also was locked, but there was a bellpush beside it. He hesitated a moment, then pressed it, and it opened almost immediately and he was relieved to see Somari the other side.

'Hello, sahib,' the little man greeted him. 'How you?'

'Fine, thanks,' Wyndham said. 'Is Sam sahib there?'

'Sure – come in.'

'I'd better not, Somari.'

'Oh, nobody here. Things don't get busy for a couple of hours yet.'

Wyndham went through, feeling as naked as a snail without its shell. Sam, practising complicated shots on the battered billiard table, looked up and said, 'Hello, Johnnie. Come to see how the other half lives, eh? Care for a quick game of snooker?'

'Not at the moment, thanks, Sam,' Wyndham said.

'Don't blame you. Bloody table's never been the same since some Charlie out of the Third Dragoons slept on it one night without having the manners to take his spurs off. How about a cold beer?'

'No thanks. As a matter of fact I was wondering if it would be all right to go out for a breath of fresh air?'

'Why not?' Sam said. 'I know how you feel. Same meself for months after I came out. The bleeding walls seem to close in on you, don't they? Like Somari to go with you?'

'I don't think so. I just feel like a stroll along the sea front on my own.' He was hating this mendacity, but he wanted to post his letter and he was not prepared to debate the wisdom of his communicating with anybody outside, even with this understanding soul.

'Sure. I wouldn't go waltzing into the Officers' Club or anything like that, if I was you,' Sam said. 'You'll be safe enough on the Esplanade, though. Act natural. If a sahib says "Good evening" you say "Evening" back. Cop salutes, you give him one finger up to the old eyebrow and grunt, "Salaam, bhai". Christ – you know the form without me having to tell you.'

'I think so. I've got to face it sometime – and the longer I stay under cover the harder it will be.'

'You couldn't have put it better, lad,' Sam said approvingly. 'That's psycho-ology, that is. Come back through Aunty's bug-trap next door. Two shorts and a long on the door bell.' He bent over the table again in an agony of concentration, and Wyndham went out into the warm night air.

It was the dead hour between dinner and the time when Europeans come out to enjoy the scant respectable night life available to them in any Indian city – the Club, the cinema and the infrequent Italian or Parsee owned sahibs' cafés. Indian shops were still open – small, cramped and lighted with naphtha flares – their proprietors sitting cross-legged on the floor in the glassless windows – and the ubiquitous beggars were limbering up for their nightly foray, but he didn't see a single white face for half a dozen blocks and it worried him because it made him feel conspicuous. But there were a few on the Esplanade – husbands and wives enjoying the soft sea breeze for the most part, white dinner-jacketed and silk-gowned, safe, secure and as sure of themselves as they were of the sun that was never going to set on the British Empire.

He remembered seeing the post office on South Beach Road, facing the harbour, the morning he arrived, and he made his way there, but found it shut. It was a small setback but for a moment it seemed to him cataclysmic, because he wanted a postage stamp – but then he saw the letter-writers, who sit all day and all night outside every post office in India, cross-legged before their foot-high desks or sleeping beside them, waiting for the patronage of the illiterate at two annas a page, and he took the precaution of buying half a dozen two-anna stamps from one of them. He posted his letter and went back to the Esplanade feeling relieved and lighter of heart, as if that simple act had lifted a burden from him. He was enjoying his walk now. An elderly Englishman coming towards him with an unlighted Burma cheroot in his mouth said, 'Haven't got a match, have you, old boy?' and Wyndham, delighted, said, 'Yes – certainly. Do please keep the box. Beautiful evening, isn't it?' and, once started, found he had difficulty in curbing his tongue from running on.

'Thanks,' said the other, puffing at the cheroot, the flame of the match rising and falling behind his cupped hands. 'No, wouldn't dream of it – might need 'em yourself. Much obliged – 'Night to you,' and moved on.

'Good night, sir,' Wyndham called after him, too heartily, and then recognized this dangerous euphoria for what it was, and merely grunted a reply when a young couple said good-night a little later.

This was all to the good, he felt – but he'd have to avoid over-confidence. Another couple of night outings like this, and he'd feel up to risking a walk by day. He'd have to, if he wanted to collect an answer from the poste restante, because he remembered now that main post offices closed at six – just before dusk. He wondered how long a reply would take. Only a matter of days if Paul was still in Bangalore – weeks if he had returned to the Andamans – probably long after he himself had left this place. Oh, God – was the 'Private Turnbull' going to come off? The complete answer to everything if it did. Australia – a new start – a job – any damned job at all – maybe one with horses – something he *did* know about.

He walked past Fort St George, right to the end of South Beach Road, reluctant to start retracing his steps to the Falmouth Packet. The overhead arc lights were coming to an end. He'd allow himself another hundred yards before turning –

A European police sergeant stepped out of the shadows and said, 'Just a moment, please, sir.'

Chapter 23

Had Wyndham's legs obeyed him he'd have run – straight ahead into the darkness. But they didn't. The strength just went out of them, and he stood drooping miserably at the shoulders, looking at the ground. He didn't raise his eyes even when the sergeant came right up to him, and said, 'Stranger to Madras?'

He nodded wearily, and the man looked at him curiously, 'Are you all right, sir?' he asked.

'Touch of fever,' Wyndham managed to mutter.

'Ah, I thought so,' the other said. 'From the Officers' Convalescent Sanatorium, eh? Well, I wouldn't go any further down there, sir. They've got the manhole covers off the sewers. Another blockage. If the wind was the other way you'd have been getting it before this.'

'I – I see,' said Wyndham. 'Er – thank you.' He turned and started to walk back along the Esplanade. The sergeant fell into step beside him.

'You don't want to overdo things, you know,' he said conversationally. 'These cool evenings are deceptive. Bring on the old shakes something awful. What's your station, sir?'

'Er – Calcutta,' Wyndham said.

'That so? *I* was at Fort William for a couple of years when I was in the Army. Lancashire Fusiliers. Who've they got there now?'

'I'm afraid I couldn't tell you.' The cogs in Wyndham's brain were beginning slowly to mesh again. 'I wasn't at the Fort. I wasn't anywhere, actually. I was coming down to take up a Staff appointment at Headquarters, but I got laid low with malaria on the train and went straight into hospital.'

'Bad luck – but you didn't miss much. Lousy stinking hole it is. What's your permanent station?'

He was ready for that one. 'Meerut – that's up in the United Provinces, you know. Very pleasant at this time of the year. I'm with the Punjabis.' He was safe there. British troops are seldom familiar with regiments of the Indian Army, all of whom, with the sole exception of the Gurkhas, they tend to lump together as 'bloody wogs'.

'Big buggers with bobbed hair.' The sergeant nodded. 'Yes, I've met some of 'em up north. Have you walked all the way from the Sanatorium, sir?'

'Er – oh – yes,' Wyndham answered. 'I quite enjoyed it.'

'Tidy step, though, for somebody just getting over fever. You looked a bit wobbly back there, if I might say so.'

Wyndham laughed. 'Did I? I'm better now. Nothing that dinner and a drink won't put right. But I must get back.'

'Hadn't I better call you a gharry, sir?' the sergeant suggested, and in that Wyndham saw a way out.

'Thank you,' he said. 'Perhaps it would be wiser.'

'Hang on then.' The sergeant halted under a light. 'Ah, here's an empty one.' He raised his arm and whistled, and a passing gharry wheeled into the kerb. 'Officer sahib ke hospital ko lejao,' he ordered the driver, and saluted. Then he added, 'I suppose I couldn't scrounge a lift, could I, sir? I'm just coming off duty.'

'By all means,' said Wyndham, his heart sinking.

'Thank Gawd for that,' the sergeant said gratefully, climbing in after him. 'My feet are giving me hell.'

'I'll drop you wherever you want to go first,' Wyndham said hopefully.

'No need,' said the sergeant. 'We pass the Sanatorium on the way to my place. I'm at the Mount Road Station. I'll take him on. I won't let him charge any more.' He added confidentially, 'I'm supposed to do the full patrol on foot. Taking a gharry back on my own could get me a winger off the Inspector, but taking an officer who's a bit wobbly on his pins back to hospital is quite all right. I couldn't have your name, could I, sir – just in case some nosey bugger happens to see me?'

'Walker,' said Wyndham hollowly.

'Captain?'

'Yes.'

'Lovely,' said the sergeant, settling back comfortably against the upholstery. 'You didn't happen to know a Captain Galvin, did you, sir? He left us to go to one of the Indian regiments – I think it *was* the Punjabis – '

'Afraid not,' said Wyndham shortly, and batted the ball into the other's court. 'How do you like this job?'

'Bloody awful. I wish I was back in the Army.'

'But the pay must be better?'

'Ah, yes – but you've got to buy everything. No free rations and quarters and other baksheesh. You know, when I was a corporal in the old Lancashire Boozy-beers I could count on eighty chips a month clear and – ' He kept up his plaint on the hardness of a policeman's lot for the next ten minutes, until the gharry turned into a dark driveway.

' – and that's not all. This bloody Inspector had the nerve to say to me – ' the sergeant was droning on.

'Look,' Wyndham said. 'I think I'd better get out here. If the duty sister sees me arriving back in a gharry – with a policeman – '

'Ah, yes – see what you mean,' the sergeant said understandingly, and halted the driver with a poke in the back with his loaded cane, 'Bas! Roko, tum.'

Wyndham climbed out, his heart pounding, and thrust a five-rupee note at the driver. 'Thank you, Sergeant – thank you very much indeed. Good night,' he gabbled.

'Christ!' yelped the other. 'You're not giving him *five chips*, are you? Some of you gentlemen ruin the buggers. Twelve annas is the proper fare.' He poked again with the cane. 'Give the sahib his change,' and Wyndham had to wait a further agonising aeon as the complaining driver fumbled through his rags – and a medical officer in mess kit strolled slowly past and glanced at them curiously in the light of the gharry's oil-lamps.

'Piss off, for Christ's sake,' Wyndham hissed at the sergeant – which was probably his most natural speech during the whole encounter, and it got an instant reaction.

'Yes, sir – sorry, sir – Good night, sir,' said the sergeant, and applied the cane once more. 'Jaldi! – ek dum! – Get a bloody move on when you're told.'

Wyndham leaned against the trunk of a palm tree and mopped his streaming face as the clopping of the horse's hooves died away in the darkness, and then he started to creep back to the gate.

A soft voice behind him said, 'Jesus, Mary, Joseph – that scare the shit out of me.'

It was breaking-point for Wyndham. He turned and struck out blindly, making strangled animal noises in the back of his throat.

'Go easy, sahib,' said Somari reproachfully. 'Not *my* fault.'

'What the *hell* are you doing here?' Wyndham demanded, almost sobbing with rage.

'Follow sahib just to make sure he all right,' Somari explained.

'Spying on me,' Wyndham accused.

'Sure, why not? First time out you go and make bugger up of things.'

'It wasn't my fault. The bloody cop came up on me out of the dark.'

'I know. I hear him talk.'

'Where were you?'

'Under sea wall right by you.'

'How did you get here?'

'Run like hell after gharry. Nearly bust guts. Come on, sahib – we got long walk back. I go in front.'

'All right,' said Wyndham. 'But there's something I want to clear up first.'

'What's that, sahib?'

'Have you been following me the whole time?'

'Sure – ever since you leave Packet.'

'So you saw what I did?'

'That's right. Post letter.'

'That's what I want to tell you about – '

'You don't have to, sahib,' Somari said quietly.

'I want to. That letter was to someone in my family. The only man who knows for sure that I got away from Kala Pani. I had to tell him that I was all right. Only that – no more. Sahib's word – officer's word – bahari Brother's word – '

'Sahib,' Somari pleaded. 'You say it's all right – it's all right. Don't worry.'

'Yes, but it would *look* bad – to Sam, I mean – if he thought I was sending letters to people.'

'So we don't tell Sam.'

'That's what I want to clear up. If you think you *ought* to tell Sam, you tell him – then I'll explain afterwards.'

'I sahib's man – not Sam's man,' said Somari simply. Wyndham reached forward and gripped his hand.

'Thank you, Somari,' he said. 'God knows why you should want to help *me* – but I won't forget that. And I won't ever drop you in the cart – or Sam.'

'I know that. Come on –'

'Just one more thing. There may be an answer to that letter. I sent it in the name of "John Moody" and said I wanted to buy some sea shells. We fixed that up when I got out. I haven't told him where I am, except Madras.'

'Poste restante?'

'That's right. But I can't take the risk of going out again in case I run into this cop –'

'Sure. Just give me a chit: "Please hand all letter for Mister John Moody to bearer." That mean bearer of chit – not bloody Hindu servant,' he added hastily. 'I do it for Sam when Drum-major memsahib write to him. He call himself "Colonel Winstanley" – randy old bugger.' He giggled. 'I wonder what he do with her when he got her? Aunty say he been no good for last twenty-two years.'

He followed the white blur of Somari's back through a maze of dark alleys – starting at shadows and cringing as they passed other people – with all his fear and nervousness once more upon him. Would he ever really rid himself of this again he wondered? Even if he succeeded in getting away and reached Australia or some other country the far side of the earth, would he still shy at the sight of a policeman, and sweat every time a knock came at the door? Had it turned him permanently into a slinker through the shadows, furtive, frightened and feral? If that were so, was it any good going on? It would almost be better to give himself up and put an end to it. But that, in truth, *would* be the end. He'd hang – and, ironically, not for the man he had killed but for the woman he hadn't. No, anything was better than that. Even suicide.

Ahead of them was a brightly lighted stretch of Poonamallee Road. Somari crossed it unhesitatingly and halted the other side like a casual stroller. A native policeman stood on the kerb, idly swinging his club, and Wyndham slipped back into the dark doorway of a closed shop, and froze in a cold agoraphobic sweat.

Somari waited for some minutes, then lighted a cigarette and came back. Wyndham whistled softly through his teeth and the little man joined him.

'What's the matter, sahib?' he asked gently.

'There's a cop over there.'

'Sure – plenty cops. Another one along further a bit – two more at corner. Cinema come out soon – silly young bugger sometime start fight. They don't look for *you*.'

'I wonder –'

'I *know*, sahib. Our cop just come off duty – right? Good – then now he sitting in his quarters with boots off and smelly feet up in the air, with bloody big pint of beer in fist. He don't come out again tonight – not for JC he don't. Come on, sahib – pull self together. You officer sahib.'

'Shut up about that, will you,' Wyndham raged. 'I'm a convict on the run, and if I'm caught I'm due to be hanged.'

Somari shuddered. 'Don't say that word, sahib,' he begged. 'Don't say it – ever – *ever*. It bad luck. *Please*. Listen: I hear you talk to that cop. Bloody lovely – pukkha bara sahib talk. "What you want, my man? You fuggoff." No – "you *piss*off" – pukkha gentleman don't say "fuggoff" – only Tommy and low-down bugger like me. You do that all right. You don't frighten then. Why you frighten by yourself when there no cop here?'

'I "frighten" then, too, Somari,' Wyndham said grimly. 'Don't make any mistake about that.'

'But you don't *show* it. That all that matter.'

The words of that lecture came back to him again: 'you'll be deathly frightened – you'll cope when the men are there to watch you – worse on your own –'

He grinned pallidly. 'You're right, you little bugger. Somebody lost a damned fine officer when you decided to go pinching for a living. Give me that cigarette of yours and push off. I'll be right behind you.'

But he panicked again when they reached the Falmouth Packet. The short street was crowded and there was a military truck outside into which men, dressed for the most part in white shirts and blue dungaree trousers were being loaded by military police. He turned to run back into the darkness but Somari grabbed him by the arm and said calmly, 'That's all right, sahib. Only MPs. Often happen. Follow me.'

He dodged across the street and went up the side of the native hotel and pressed a bellpush beside a door. It opened just as Wyndham arrived and they slipped inside. A woman's voice whispered sibilantly in Tamil, and Somari laughed.

'Old Sam sahib going to be bloody angry about this,' he said. 'Come on, sahib – up to your room. I bring you a drink.'

'I don't want a drink,' Wyndham told him.

'You do,' Somari said, and went to get it.

He sat on the side of the bed and felt the shivers subsiding as the whisky coursed down his throat.

'That's better,' he said, and held the glass out. 'All right, I'll have the other half.'

'You won't,' Somari said firmly. 'One drink, medicine – more drinks just damn silly buggers. Don't worry. Sam tell me all about it.'

They heard the truck drive away amid a ragged burst of rather forlorn cheering, and then Sam came up, surprisingly cheerful.

'Bloody officer's patrol tonight, and they didn't warn me,' he said.

'Will there be trouble?' Wyndham asked.

'No more than usual. Nobody here in uniform,' Sam chuckled. 'We keep a stock of shirts and pants in the wog hotel next door, and they change in there. If the MPs come in under a sergeant, the boys wink and say they're off a ship. But tonight there's a young Percy in charge and two of the silly buggers jump up and click their heels. They might still have got away with it, but the Percy says to one of them, "What's your unit, my man?" and the bloke says, "I'm not a soldier, you stupid bastard. I'm a fuggin missionary," and Percy pinches the lot.'

'Six months in moosh for that one,' said Somari knowledgeably.

'Nah, not for *him*,' Sam said. 'Plays rugby for the Gunners – wing-three-quarter – and it's the McIlwaine Cup next week. He'll get a ticking off from the Old Man and seven days jankers – no, *five* days jankers. And I don't have to pay the MPs their fifty chips dropsy – for not warning me – so everybody's happy.' He smiled beatifically. 'Everybody, that is, except young Percy tomorrow morning. There happened to be three *real* sailors amongst that lot, but he wouldn't believe 'em. The Brigadier'll have his guts for garters when their skipper puts in an official complaint.'

Wyndham started work on the books the following morning. It was a simpler task than he had expected, because Sam, with his trained quartermaster's acumen, had in fact already made a start on them.

'Just bring the property on at book value to start with,' he said. 'In other words, just what the old bag paid for each lot. You'll find all the receipts in this file. After that you can link up in the next three columns what she's paid in rates and taxes – that's all in this file. Do it in pencil and we'll check it over together; then if it's all right you can ink it in. Meantime I'm going to have a proper go at getting rid of the hot loot once and for all.'

'How?' Wyndham asked.

'What I should have done years ago. Get a contractor to book half a dozen big railway trucks – load the stuff into bullock carts and have it shifted up to the goods yard quite openly – and then consign it all to Ram Dass, in Jubbulpore.'

'Who's Ram Dass?'

'Buggered if *I* know. Ram Dass out here is like John Smith in Blighty. If I know the Indian Railways it'll just stand on the sidings in Jub for the next six months – during which time the train thieves'll be knocking it off right, left and centre.'

'Um, sounds all right,' Wyndham agreed. 'Providing of course, the contractor doesn't talk.'

'The one I have in mind won't,' Sam said smugly. 'I've got him by the short and curlies. I got enough on him to put him where the crows won't crap on him for the next five years. He ain't a bahari, you see.'

Wyndham gave Somari the chit the following day, and then put it out of his mind and became thoroughly immersed in his book-keeping. Ten days at the minimum, he calculated, before he could possibly expect an answer – or as many weeks – or never. But in fact Somari brought him a letter within a week.

Dear Mr Moody (he read)

Thank you for your letter which I have just received. I have left the place where I used to collect morchi shells, and will not be returning there, but I have a few with me which I will be delighted to show you if we can arrange a mutually convenient meeting. I can run down to Madras at any time, as I am now employed on the railway. Please feel at complete liberty to write to me as I can safely assure you that the shells I have will be of great interest to you.

Yours faithfully,
Paul Richards

He read and re-read the letter, noting that the words 'liberty', 'safely' and 'assure' were written somewhat heavier than the others. Could he risk it, he wondered? He would dearly love to see Paul again and to know just what happened after that night, but not if there was to be the slightest chance of involving him if anything went wrong.

But where *could* he meet him? Certainly not on the Esplanade, where his friend the sergeant could easily happen upon him again, and a café or restaurant would be even more dangerous.

He mulled over it for the rest of the day before it came to him, then he took another sheet of paper and an envelope and wrote,

Dear Mr Richards,

Thank you for your letter. My movements are a little uncertain at the moment, but I could pick you up in a taxi any evening outside the Central Station if you would let me know by which train you will be arriving.

Yours faithfully,
John Moody

And he sent Somari to post it.

Chapter 24

Paul came down the station steps with a straggling crowd of other passengers, and stood for a moment under a street lamp, and Wyndham, watching from the back seat of the taxi told his driver to go forward. He waved briefly from the window as they passed, and Paul overtook them and climbed in. Wyndham said heartily, 'Nice to see you, old boy,' and added in an undertone, 'This fellow probably understands English.' They exchanged banalities after that until Wyndham halted the driver just short of the South Beach yacht club and paid him off, then they went down on to the deserted sands.

'How in the name of God have you managed this?' Paul asked as he gripped Wyndham's hand. 'It's good to see you, Charles.'

'And you. In the fewest words possible: I got swamped the first night, clung to the canoe and was picked up by a Japanese trawler – '

'Had you got rid of your collar?'

'No, hadn't time. They took it off me, and threw it into the sea.'

'So they knew what you were?'

'They did. They took up a collection for me, gave me a shirt and a pair of pants and landed me on the beach two hundred miles south of here, three or four weeks later.'

'Couldn't have known about the reward – '

'Perhaps. Personally I preferred to think they were just good blokes. They could easily have turned me in had they wanted to.'

'How did you get up here?'

'Walked a lot of it. Did the last bit by train.'

'But the clothes? You look like a prosperous business sahib.'

'Bought for me in the chor ke bazaar by a little Madrassi jailbird on the run from the Pondicherry prison.'

'So that's somebody else who knows about you?'

'Yes, but he's quite safe.'

'How can you be certain of that?' Paul paused. 'Sorry. I'm

240

putting you through a catechism. Go on in your own words.'

'He's safe because he's a bahari,' Wyndham said. 'That means a – '

'You don't have to explain to *me*,' said Paul. 'But how did that affect *you*? Christ! You're not telling me that you're – ?'

'A member of the great and unholy Brotherhood? Yes – in good standing,' Wyndham laughed.

'When did this happen?'

'Oh, it goes right back to the Cellular Jail days. It wasn't by my seeking. I happened to do one of them a good turn when I was a CO – and I was just told I was in. Then they showed me some of the mumbo-jumbo of it, and made it quite clear what would happen to me if I ever blew the gaff on them, and I'd almost forgotten it – until I ran into this type.'

'And you just made yourself known on spec?'

'The other way round. He spotted the mark on my neck where the collar had been and made a couple of mystic signs which I was able to respond to correctly. And that was it.'

Paul took a deep breath. 'And the mark? Is it still – ?'

'Not a trace of it left. It was only where it had been shielded from the sun. It's all tanned over evenly now.'

'Thank God for that,' Paul said fervently. 'But how have you been managing here?'

'Quite well. I'm a book-keeper in a brothel.'

'You're a *what*?'

'Well, not quite *that*. Actually I'm doing some clerical work for an old rascal called Sam – '

'Horslake? And Aunty?'

'Oh, you know about them, do you?'

'Who doesn't? How did you come into contact with them?'

'The Madrassi took me there.'

'Do *they* know about you?'

'Sure. But they're both baharis too.'

Paul sat down on the sand. 'Excuse me,' he said. 'But I'm finding all this just a bit – er – surprising – '

Wyndham chuckled and sat down beside him. 'And shocking? Sorry, but what choice had I? And to be quite honest I'm extremely grateful to them.'

'Maybe – but what's going to happen eventually?'

'They're going to help me out of the country. We're thinking of Australia – '

'How? Without papers – passport – ?'

'It's a trade secret of Sam's.'

'Not a "Turnbull"?'

'So you know about that too?' Wyndham was a little chagrined.

'Smuggled out in the fireman's fo'c'sle? Yes, I know about it. It's all down in a police pamphlet that is handed to every ship's captain on arrival in an Indian port. First place they search before departure nowadays.'

'Shit!' said Wyndham explosively.

'Sorry to disillusion you, old boy. But we'll have to think of something a bit better than that,' Paul said.

'Not "we",' Wyndham told him firmly. 'This is our last meeting, Paul. I only called it because I feel I owe it to you to let you know what happened. I'm not risking your being dragged into it if everything comes unstuck. That must be clearly understood.'

'We'll discuss that later.'

'Understood *now*,' Wyndham said. 'Otherwise I'm getting up and walking away.'

'Sure, sure, sure,' Paul said impatiently. 'But I'd better tell you what happened on my side – unless you've seen the papers?'

'What papers?'

'The Press – here in Madras – all over India, and even the Home ones – '

'I haven't seen a damned thing.'

'Actually it was a nine days' wonder, although they certainly blazoned it under huge headlines at the time,' Paul said. 'There was an inquest – open verdict of "murder by person unknown". Then it was adjourned. The search for you went on – extra police drafted in from Calcutta – trackers – dogs – everything – but they entirely missed the fact that my canoe had gone, until the survey vessel picked it up, waterlogged and upside down fifty miles out, with a prison shirt jammed under a thwart – with your number on it – and traces of blood still visible. The inquest was reopened then, and the verdict amended to "murder by a person not in custody" – and your name was mentioned for the first time. They'd been keeping the escape dark until then. Of course the balloon went up. Reporters flocking in from the mainland – your original case revived – photos of you – not very good ones – in uniform and without a moustache and all that. *I'd* certainly never have recognized you as you are now. You were labelled "The White Dacoit" – and all sorts of liars up on the Frontier had stories about you.

'There was a Court of Inquiry after the Inquest, on the escape as distinct from the murder, and an official finding of "Absconded, believed drowned" was brought in. That is the generally held belief. It's certainly what *I* believed until I got your letter.'

'Were you in trouble over the canoe?'

'No. It had been checked with all the others by the police in charge of that sector. It was their fault for not noticing that it had gone. I was up in the bush in charge of a search party, so I wasn't involved in any way at all. Philimore got it in the neck, though.'

'What happened to him?' Wyndham asked.

'He went before a Departmental Disciplinary Board for lack of supervision, gross dereliction of duty, negligence, irregularities – everything.'

'Any suspicion of the murder fall on him?'

'Absolutely none. There was no doubt in anybody's mind about that. *You* did it – and you were dead. Philimore was fired and bundled on to the first boat for Calcutta.'

'I wonder where the bastard is now?' Wyndham mused.

'I heard somewhere that he'd gone to England,' Paul said.

'Poor old England,' said Wyndham. 'What's she done to deserve that? How about his girl in Cornwallis?'

'God, *she* wasn't a girl. She dropped him like a hot potato when the bubble burst.'

'Lucky escape,' said Wyndham. 'So I'm officially dead then? That's good news, anyhow.'

'No, not *officially* dead,' Paul said. ' "Believed drowned." '

'Same thing, surely?'

'Not quite. The file will be kept open for seven years. Then, if nothing is heard of you in the meantime, it will be destroyed and you *will* be dead.'

'Roll on seven years,' Wyndham said fervently. 'But go on. You haven't told me about yourself.'

'Nothing much to tell,' Paul shrugged. 'I was held back until after the inquest, then I came on leave. I reported to the Railway Interview Board when I arrived in Bangalore, and I got the job. So I sent my resignation in to the Prisons Department.'

'Good. Married yet?'

'Next month. Seventeenth.'

'Congratulations. She's a lucky girl. You're a good bloke, Paul.' He stood up. 'Every happiness for the future, old chap.'

'Sit down,' said Paul. 'We haven't discussed *your* future yet.'

'And we're not going to, because, ungracious though it may sound, you don't in any way figure in it,' Wyndham said. 'I'll get out of the country all right, and some time in the future I'll send you another John Moody letter telling you all about it.'

'Yes, I think you'll do it,' Paul said quietly. 'You've glossed over things, but you've overcome some pretty stiff obstacles along the route. It would be a hell of a pity to come a cropper now, wouldn't it?'

'I'm not going to come a cropper.'

'You will if you go on as you are now,' Paul said. 'Sit down, Charles. There are one or two things you ought to know.'

'Stop worrying,' Wyndham said irritably. 'I know what I'm doing.'

'I don't doubt that at all, but at least listen to me. Sit down, Charles,' he begged, and reluctantly Wyndham sat again. 'Seven years,' Paul went on. 'After that you'll be reasonably safe anywhere in the world – but until then your fingerprints are on record in this country, and if they are ever checked you're positively identified. If you're pulled in for anything, however trivial, they *will* be checked.'

'There's an awful lot of balls talked about fingerprints,' Wyndham said. 'They're not as positive as all that. This place isn't Scotland Yard.'

'They didn't teach you much at that expensive English school of yours, did they?' Paul said drily. 'This is where the whole system originated – in Bengal. Sir Edward Henry started it when he was Inspector-General of Police. It was so successful that he was invited to lecture on it in London – and then asked to take over as Commissioner of Scotland Yard – and the whole world has taken it up since. Oh, don't make any mistakes about fingerprinting out here, Charles. They're mustard.'

'Well, it's just a matter of keeping my nose clean, as old Meakin used to say,' Wyndham said.

'Exactly, and you won't do that by trying to slip through any of the ports. The police wouldn't be looking for you specifically, no doubt – but stowing away is a serious thing in India, and they really search ships before leaving.'

'Damn you,' said Wyndham angrily. 'This is the only chance I can see ahead of me – and you cut the ground from under my feet.'

'I'm sorry,' said Paul miserably. 'But I wouldn't be much of a friend if I let you stick your head in a noose like that – '

'Don't rub it in.'

'That wasn't very tactful – but unfortunately it happens to be the literal truth in your case.'

Wyndham balled his fist and punched it into the sand beside him. 'What the hell *am* I going to do then?' he demanded.

'There *are* ways. There's a solution to everything if one looks long enough.'

'Such as?'

'I haven't anything at my fingertips – but I still think our original idea of an Arab dhow to one of the foreign ports is best.'

'Don't they search those?' Wyndham asked.

'Not to the same extent – particularly on the west coast. They ghost in and out of a hundred tiny ports and nobody bothers about them much. A couple of hundred rupees would get you across to East Africa – Portuguese Beira – Dar-es-Salaam – one of those places. Then you could work your way down into South Africa – '

'But that's British.'

'So's Australia for that matter – but both are pretty remote from here,' Paul said. 'You certainly wouldn't be noticeable as an Englishman in either place. You could get yourself established.'

'So you're advising me to cross over to the west coast?'

'It's an idea. You could go by train, quite openly. I'd send you some money – '

'Like hell you will,' Wyndham said. 'I've still got most of what you gave me. If you're getting married next month you're going to need every sou you've got.'

'You'll require more than that. You've got to live. And you'll have to pay your passage.'

'I'll have enough. Old Sam is going to pay me for cooking his books for him,' Wyndham grinned.

'That's another thing. You'll have to leave Sam's – and damned quick,' Paul said.

'Why? I'm as safe as houses there – *whore* houses.'

'I'll tell you why. I was Prisons, not Police – but one used to hear things. Sam and Aunty have been paying protection money to a pretty unsavoury crowd of cops here for a long time – British, Indian and Anglo-Indian – and they've got away with a hell of a lot. But now there's a new Inspector-General out and he's leaning on them – the cops, I mean. He apparently doesn't want a first-class scandal in his early months, so he's doing it very khabardari – giving them the option of resigning and going to premature retirement, or going before a Court of Inquiry. Nobody's chosen a Court yet. They say that he just wants the bad boys off the Force – then he's going to clamp down hard on the rackets, starting with Sam and Aunty. They're the two biggest fences in India.'

'I see,' said Wyndham slowly. 'Actually old Sam hinted as much to me. I just said something about cooking his books. That's not true. I'm helping him to open an honest set. He's in process of getting rid of all stolen property on the premises – and not by selling it, either. He's seen the light, in other words.'

'The red light,' snorted Paul.

'All right, the red light if you prefer. But they're definitely moving over on to the side of the angels, and, villains or not, they've been damned good to me, and I can't very well play the rat on a sinking ship.'

'What's the alternative? Just stay there until the place is raided one night – and get pulled in with the rest – and fingerprinted?' Paul asked. 'Listen, Charles: be sensible. Sam and Aunty will undoubtedly go down for a long stretch – but they'll come out to a nice little nest-egg which you can bet your life they've got salted safely away. You *wouldn't* be coming out.'

Wyndham sighed. 'Bloody awful, isn't it? They're like a pair of monkeys with their hands in glass jars, holding a fistful of nuts – and they can't get their hands out until they drop the nuts.'

'Which they can't bring themselves to do. Exactly.'

'How long do you think they've got?'

'I've no idea, but I should say it would be sooner rather than later,' Paul said. 'I've got a cousin on the Force down here – father's side of the family, not yours – an honest cop, if there is such a thing. He was up home a couple of weeks ago. He said that the whisper was the new IG was really setting it up for them. He's got about another three he wants to winkle out first.'

Wyndham rose. 'I see,' he said. 'All right, Paul. I'll do everything you say. I'll go to the west coast. Where would you advise in the first place?'

'Train from here down to Salem, then across to Calicut – that's smack in the middle of the Malabar coast. There must be a hundred small ports north and south of there. The dhows come in and out after scratch cargoes – rice – coconuts – sisal – all sorts of things. I'll send you a map tomorrow to the post office, and some money.'

'No money,' said Wyndham firmly.

'Don't be a chump. They refunded my Provident Fund contributions and I got a gratuity. I've got over six thousand rupees in the bank at the moment. You can always return it in the future.'

'But *why the hell* should you?' Wyndham demanded.

'Charles, if our positions were reversed and I was being framed for a murder I hadn't committed – and you knew as much about me as you know now: would you help?'

'I don't know.'

'Be honest,' Paul urged. 'Come on – a straight answer. Would you?'

'Oh, I suppose so,' Wyndham mumbled. 'But you're overlooking something, aren't you?'

'What?'

'I was framed on that one, certainly. But don't forget I was already a convicted killer. And a thief.'

'Did you mean to kill that man?'

'No, of course not. But I had been taking graft and helping to rob – I let the family, the regiment, the – ' He broke off.

Paul was silent for a moment, then he said quietly, 'You were being blackmailed. I read the defence at the time, don't forget, in the papers.'

247

'I shouldn't have allowed myself to be blackmailed,' Wyndham said passionately. 'I should have put that bastard in close arrest the first time he brought me that bribe – but I didn't. I took it like a greasy-palmed bazaar pimp.'

'And you paid for it – and you'll go on paying for it all your life,' Paul said. 'But I don't see that you should pay for things you *didn't* do.'

They walked slowly back across the beach to the deserted road.

Wyndham said dully, 'You'd better walk on ahead, just in case we're stopped by a policeman.'

'That's not likely to happen,' Paul answered. 'Let's keep going until we spot a taxi.'

'You bet it's likely to happen,' Wyndham told him. 'It happened to me the very first time I came out on my own, not far from here. Go on, there's a good chap, or it will worry me.'

'All right then. I can just about make the Mail back at midnight,' Paul said. 'I'll post the map to you tomorrow. You should get it the next day. Then, Charles, don't waste any more time. Get out of it – fast. Old Sam will probably thank you for it, anyway. He wouldn't want a harbouring charge stuck on him as well as everything else they've got stacked up.'

'Yes, you're no doubt right there.'

'Take this,' Paul said, and pushed a roll of notes into his hand. 'There's only a hundred there because I couldn't get to the bank before leaving, but tomorrow – '

'For Christ's sake, will you stop!' Wyndham shouted. 'If you push any more money at me I won't go, I tell you.'

'You're behaving like a fool,' Paul told him curtly. 'Cut it out, and pull yourself together, Charles. Call at the post office the day after tomorrow – and again the day after if there's nothing there. Now remember: if you keep your head you're not in any great danger. You're supposed to be dead. You're only likely to be in trouble if you're picked up for something – so don't do anything you *could* be picked up for. It's as simple as that.'

'I'm sorry,' Wyndham said contritely. 'I must sound an ungrateful swine – '

'You sound like a man under a hell of a strain, and I'm amazed that you're in as good a shape as you are,' Paul said, as they shook hands. 'Good luck, old boy. Let's have a letter from John Moody from time to time – with an address if you think it's safe.' He turned abruptly and walked off into the darkness, and Wyndham, with the familiar lost, lonely feeling once more upon him, waited ten minutes or so before wending his way back to the Falmouth Packet.

Somari was looking worried when he brought Wyndham's chota hazri next morning. He put the tray down on the bedside table then went back and carefully closed the door.

'I think we better move from here, sahib,' he said quietly.

'I've been thinking that for a long time,' Wyndham answered. '*I* certainly ought to be moving – but you're not wanted for anything in particular, are you?'

'*Everybody* picked up in this place get chubbidustered if cops come,' Somari said glumly. 'Maybe they send me back to Pondicherry. By God, I don't want that.'

Wyndham sat up straight. 'You think they *are* coming, do you?'

'Don't know what to think, sahib. Something bloody funny go on.'

'In what way?'

'Last night – after you go out, everything going fine – plenty soldier, sailor here – Sam making jokes – Aunty doing plenty business along at Number Seven. Then Sam called to telephone. He come back and say, "Get all people out and close up." I ask him why and he bite my bloody head off. Tell me to shut up – asks where you are. Oh, he got hell of a liver on.'

Wyndham felt strangely relieved. If things were indeed happening it would make his departure that much easier. He climbed from under the mosquito net. 'All right, Somari,' he said. 'I'll see Sam at breakfast and try and find out what's wrong.' He reached under his pillow. 'I've got a couple of hundred chips now. Here's a hundred in case you have to move quickly.'

'No fear.' Somari shook his head. 'I got more than you. Pick up plenty baksheesh in Packet. All right, sahib – I hear anything, let you know right away.' And he went out.

So Paul was right, Wyndham reflected as he dressed quickly.

Chapter 25

'Sahib! Sahib! Sahib!' The voice was coming from a great distance, and something was holding him down and choking him. He struggled and lashed out, and the voice was nearer, 'Sahib! God's sake sahib! Wake up! Wake up!' and only then did he realize that Somari was shaking him. His eyes were streaming and smarting and his lungs felt as if they were stuffed with cotton-wool.

'Come on, sahib!' Somari was yelling. 'Bloody fire – whole place – ' But Wyndham couldn't see him because of the smoke. He fought his way from under the mosquito net and felt himself being dragged towards the door, but as they reached it the flames came whipping along the passage outside and he could see the whole stairwell at the end was ablaze.

'No bloody good!' Somari gasped. 'Other way, sahib – balcony.' They stumbled across the room through the french windows, and as he took his first breath of clear air, his wits started to return.

'What the hell – ?' he began.

'No good, sahib – don't know,' Somari was sobbing and wheezing. 'I sleep down below – wake up hearing crackle – look out – fire everywhere – come up to wake sahib. By Christ – you nearly goner. Fire worse below – smoke worse up here – '

'Money – clothes – ' snapped Wyndham and darted back inside the room. His clothes were on one of the roorkhee chairs and his money under his pillow, but he had no sense of direction and he was blundering round blindly. He tripped over something and fell flat, and found that the smoke was less dense at floor level, and that he could make out the white blur of the bed. He crawled across to it and felt under the pillow and grabbed the handkerchief in which the money was rolled, then he turned and started to grope his way to the chair, but now the rush matting by the door was alight and the flames were sweeping across the floor towards him. He jumped to his feet and ran to where he thought the french window was, but cannoned up against the wall. He felt his way along it and realized he was moving in the wrong direction, and the smoke was choking and stupefying him again – then Somari grabbed him by the arm and pulled him out on to the balcony.

'Bloody fool thing, that, sahib,' he said. 'What good clothes, money, if hide burnt off?'

'Couldn't get far without them,' gasped Wyndham.

'Can't get far with them, either,' said Somari gloomily. 'Look over into street.'

Wyndham moved to the balustrade and peered over cautiously, then stepped back appalled. The whole scene was bathed in light and a cordon of police was forcing the crowd back and trying to make way for a couple of red fire-engines. They seemed to be strangely silent, then he realized that it was his own hearing that was at fault, because the crackling of the fire was drowning all other sounds from below.

'Climb down into that lot and we going to be held for questions,' Somari went on. 'All coppers in Madras down there.'

'Is everybody else out?' Wyndham asked.

'Dunno. I yell down into servants' compound before coming upstairs, but I think they go already.'

'Sam and Aunty?'

'They'll be all right – you bet. I *kill* that old bastard, when I see him.'

'Why?'

'He start it.'

'How do you know that?'

'See him taking big can of kerosene along passage yesterday. He say it for white ants in floor – I don't think any more about it – not then I don't.' He spat. 'White ants my arse. He getting rid of loot before cops come and catch him. Bloody smart – but why don't he tell us first?'

Wyndham shook his head. 'I can't believe that,' he said.

'You don't know old sunnervabitch like I know him.'

'But he's a Brother.'

Somari laughed drily. 'Don't get funny idea about Brothers, sahib,' he said. 'Only thing Brothers don't do is tell *cops* about other Brothers – because they know they get bloody throat cut

jaldi-jaldi if they do. Oh, one Brother help another Brother if it
don't cost him anything – but he'll still pinch from him – drop
him in the shit – do anything if it mean some good for himself.'

There was a crash from the room behind them as the blazing
door fell inwards, and an oven-gust of super-heated air, smoke
and sparks enveloped them. Simultaneously the top of an escape
ladder rose above the balustrade and a helmeted fireman gestured
to them urgently.

'Better go, sahib,' said Somari. 'Either that or get cooked up
here like bloody chicken. Maybe it'll be all right – with that
smoke and dirt you blacker than I am. Say you Ram Dass, Hindu
bearer – '

The fireman was yelling soundlessly against the roar of the
flames and beckoning to them angrily.

'Me first,' said Somari, climbing down the balustrade. 'I conk
out when I get down – you try and sneak one side and bugger
off in crowd – See you other end – Coconut Alley – '

The fireman climbed down a few rungs and Somari took his
place – then Wyndham followed. The whole façade of Madame
Duval's, The Falmouth Packet and the Indian hotel were glowing
incandescently and there was a crash as a portion of the balcony
to one side of them collapsed, and the resultant blast of heat
nearly made him lose his grasp on the ladder. He reached the
platform of the turntable wagon scorched and singed, with the
loincloth he wore in lieu of pyjamas smouldering. Hands caught
him and guided him down on to the ground, and a European
policeman grabbed his arm.

'*Ko'i aur admion uncha hain?* – Any more men up there?' he
yelled.

'*Nahin, sahib,*' Wyndham croaked. He saw it was the sergeant
he had encountered before, but there was no recognition in the
other's face.

'Good. Go over there and wait with the others.' He shoved
Wyndham to one side and started to lay about him with his
loaded cane as the crowd, which had dropped back as the mass of
masonry fell, now started to surge forward again. Somari, staging
a realistic collapse on the ground, rose and got him by the wrist
and pulled him back behind the wagon.

'Right, sahib,' he muttered. 'Up side lane – run like bloody hell.'

They circled round behind the crowd and kept going until they reached the street of the nine houses, all of which were well alight – the palms in front of them blazing like a line of torches. Wyndham could see the pattern of things now. The fire had obviously started in the middle of the dingy complex and spread outwards until now only the perimeter walls were still standing, with the entire centre a white-hot inferno which the fire brigade was not attempting to subdue, playing their hoses on to buildings the other side of the triangle in an effort to keep it from spreading. The crowd had been driven out of Coconut Alley itself by the threat of the blazing palm trees and the reflected heat off the walls on the other side, and was now concentrated at each end. An attempt had apparently been made to salvage some of the contents of Number Seven, because Wyndham could see the grand piano wedged sideways in the front door, with Queen Victoria burning on the steps. Then he saw Aunty in the forefront of the crowd, screaming and gesticulating, with the Union Jack and the Tricolour round her massive shoulders inadequately supplementing the deficiencies of a tentlike nightgown which had suffered some damage. She was being pushed back by a flying wedge of police and firemen, and as they got nearer Wyndham could her screeching in a bastard mélange of barrack English and brothel French.

'Les poumpiers! Fuggin useless bastards! Ou est mes filles? Ou est mon mari? Get the poor old bugger out! Damn and blast your bloody eyes! Fils du putain! Useless lotta sods!'

Somari chuckled. 'I bet old Sam not inside,' he said. '*He'd* get out all right.'

Then they saw him. He pushed through the crowd in front of them and came up behind his wife.

'Thank Gawd you're all right, luv,' he bellowed. 'Been looking for you everywhere.' And she turned on him in sheer berserk fury, clawing at his face.

'Looking for *me*, were you, you lying old soor ka bacha!' she shrieked. 'I bet you found the cash box easy enough. If anything has happened to them girls of mine I'll kill you – kill you with me own hands, I will! And if you think you've got a fiddle on with the insurance, by God you'd better think again! I'll turn you in first, you bastard!'

The wall of the nearest house collapsed and the crowd surged back in blind panic as the flames shot out laterally, singeing the front ranks. Sam turned and wriggled his way out, and Somari left Wyndham and went after him. Wyndham lost sight of them for a few moments, then he heard Somari behind him again.

'Come on, sahib,' he said. 'We push off.'

'Where to?' asked Wyndham.

'Oh, got good place,' Somari told him. 'Well, not *good* place – bloody stinking place – but *safe* place.'

He led the way down an alley, across some waste ground, into another alley, then along the sea wall, and finally, after half an hour or so, into an area that stank to high heaven. It was a long open ditch with crumbling masonry each side of it, and tumble-down huts built back into the earthern banks above it. Even the soft dawn light could do nothing to soften it. It was a scene of complete and utter desolation.

'The chawls,' said Somari. 'Only Untouchables live here. Cops don't come here – nobody don't come here. Hope sahib don't mind stink – but like I say – very safe.'

'Who the devil am *I* to mind?' Wyndham said wearily. 'When are you going to stop pulling my chestnuts out of the fire, Somari – and start looking after yourself alone?'

'What "chestnuts", sahib?' Somari asked, puzzled.

'Only something we say in England. What I mean is, you shouldn't waste your time looking after me – '

'Balls,' said Somari. 'Tomorrow everything going to be all right – you see. No, by Christ – everything going to be all right *today* – It's tomorrow now. Come on, sahib.' He slid down the bank, kicked at the tin wall of a hut and gabbled in Tamil, then pushed aside a sacking curtain hanging over a low doorway and went in. Wyndham hesitated, then followed.

It was pitch dark inside and Wyndham banged his head on the roof as he straightened, then somebody struck a match and lighted a wick in a clay lamp, and in its dim light he saw a small half-naked man crawling from a bed on the floor, and a woman was stirring the other side and gathering up a tiny wizened baby from a rough wooden cradle. They went out through the curtain without a word.

'You mean we're turning these people out?' Wyndham said and moved to the door. 'No, by God, we're not. Call them back.'

'It's all right, sahib,' Somari assured him. 'They got to get up with sun for work – and they very happy. I tell them I give twenty-five chips tomorrow – no, *today*. They don't earn that in three months.'

'What work?' Wyndham demanded suspiciously.

'Pig work. That's what stink is – not these people. They very clean.' He grinned. 'I tell you before – only Klistian and Untouchables work with pigs.'

'We live and learn,' Wyndham said. 'Well, I hope you've got the money to give them. I must have dropped our two hundred rupees coming down that ladder.'

Somari grinned wider. 'You didn't,' he said, and held up a roll of notes. 'You stick it in waistband of dhoti, and I whip it back off you quick. I bloody fool. *My* money get burnt.'

'Well, you keep that then,' Wyndham told him.

'No fear. This for clothes for sahib and new servant's clothes for me when chor ke bazaar open.'

'I've got some more coming either today or tomorrow,' Wyndham said, 'if you'll go to the post office for me again. I'll need a sheet of paper and a pen to write a chit for you first, though.'

'Sure. But I got money coming today too – pukkha today. Lot of money. Lie down on bed, sahib, and get rest.'

'I – er – I'd rather not,' said Wyndham. 'I'm a bit dirty.'

'It quite clean. These people work with pig – then come home, scrub like hell in tank down there – put on clean clothes – *every day*.'

'Then why do they call them Untouchables?'

'Because Hindu bloody silly bugger, that why. They only *religion* dirty – not *dirt* dirty. Nice people. I work with them long time.'

'Are they Brothers?'

'No – honest.'

'Will they talk?'

'No fear. Who they talk to? Go near copper, he say, "Fuggoff you, or I lose caste." No – they all right.'

Wyndham sat on the dirt floor with his back against the wall. He said, 'I want to talk to you, Somari. I'm moving on.'

'Where to?'

'Over to the other side – West Coast.'

'Bombay?'

'Not as far north as that – Calicut – Malabar – maybe even Goa.'

'That good,' said Somari approvingly. 'Old Sam try to do another Turnbull this side, you get caught for damn certain.'

'So you know about the Turnbull?'

'*Everybody* know about the Turnbull. He do it once, sure – but then he go flapping big mouth about how clever he is. He never do it again.'

'Then why was he pulling my leg?'

'Like I say – show how clever he is.' He blew a resounding raspberry. 'Clever like my arse. So we go to West Coast. That very nice place.'

'Not you.'

'Why not?'

'Because you've got to settle down here in Madras, where you've never been in trouble. Get a job – '

'I tell you something, sahib?'

'What?'

'I never been in trouble in Madras because I don't stay here long enough. If I *do* stay here, then I *do* get in trouble – then I don't have nice place to come to die – 'oly, 'oly, 'oly – when I'm old man.' He grinned again. 'So I come to West Coast. Now you rest while I go to get you some breakfast.'

'Where from?' asked Wyndham a little nervously.

'Oh, Christ – don't be like bloody Hindu, sahib.' He reached up and took two shining brass plates and a pot down from a shelf. 'You ever see cleaner pot and pan than that?'

'No,' Wyndham agreed. 'But – '

'But nothing, sahib. Every time they use they wash, scrub with clean sand and ashes from fire, polish up like hell. Same like with clothes – same like with selves. Decent people – if only Hindus *and sahibs* give them bit of a chance.' He went out with the plates and pot, and Wyndham sat on, feeling humbled. Then he slept

He woke when Somari returned, with fried eggs, several rashers of bacon, a small loaf and a pot of tea.

'Here you are, sahib,' he said cheerfully. 'Cooked better than in Officers' Mess.'

'Have you been taking these people's food?' demanded Wyndham.

'Oh, Christ,' sighed Somari. 'We start again. Eggs, milk, tea, bread I buy – bacon I pinch from curing shed.'

'Where's yours?'

'Had bread and eggs while I cook this. Can't eat bacon – it's bloody Friday.' He genuflected, and Wyndham spluttered into his tea.

'You cheeky bugger,' he said. '*You* talk about the Hindus!'

Somari looked sheepish and changed the subject. 'Old Sam coming down in a minute,' he said.

'*Sam?*' Wyndham started. 'What's *he* doing here?'

'He here because I tell him last night. This their piggery. I say "you get out there tomorrow or I tell Aunty about that kerosene and she'll cut you Goddam throat." Scare the shit out of him.'

'But what the devil do you want to see him about?' Wyndham asked.

'You wait,' Somari said succinctly. 'He won't know whether he's on head or arse when I've finished with him.' He held up his hand and listened. 'Here he is now.' He got up and raised the curtain, and Sam stooped in through the doorway.

'Hello, Johnnie,' he said heartily. 'Good to see you, lad. I was worried about you.'

'Cut out bullshit,' growled Somari. 'Sit down.'

'Where?' asked Sam looking round.

'On floor,' said Somari. 'If it good enough for officer sahib it good enough for bloody quartermaster-sergeant. Sit, you old bastard.'

'No need to be nasty,' Sam said plaintively as he lowered himself to the floor. 'I didn't mean the whole shebang to go up like that.'

'I understand you laid it on,' said Wyndham.

'Sure – but I meant it for tonight.'

'Don't you think a word of warning might have been in order?'

'I was going to tell you the whole thing last night but you were out gallivanting.'

'Why didn't you tell Somari?'

'Because he was on your tracks. He always is when you go out. Surely you know that?'

Wyndham looked at Somari quickly. Somari dropped his eyes.

'I set it up because I'd had the buzz that the Law was going to drop in tomorrow,' Sam went on. 'Only one thing for it. Burn the bloody lot – or we'd both have been inside for the next ten years. I'd have done it long ago if she hadn't stopped me. I fixed a little bonfire in the baggage room and another between Number Two and Number Four, ready to drop a match into it tonight, but some careless bugger must have done it for me.'

'Balls,' said Somari calmly. 'How much you bring with you?'

'Two thousand. All I could lay me 'ands on at the moment.'

'Not enough,' said Somari, and tears came to Sam's eyes.

'I swear as a Brother – ' he began, raising his hand reverently.

'More balls. Five, Sam sahib – or Aunty going to get bloody big earful – '

'I don't know what this is all about,' said Wyndham.

'This little bastard is putting the black on me, that's what it's all about,' snuffled Sam. 'Looked after him like a father, I have – and this is me thanks.'

'Hand it over to the sahib,' ordered Somari, and Sam took a roll of notes from his pocket and held them out to Wyndham. 'I never thought you'd do this to me, Johnnie,' he said sadly.

'I haven't done anything to you,' Wyndham said. 'And I certainly don't want your wretched money.'

'*I* do,' said Somari, reaching across and intercepting it. He looked at the money carefully, note by note. It was all in hundreds – twenty of them. 'Don't like big money,' he sniffed. 'Too many bloody questions when you spend it.'

'If you'll wait a bit I can change it into smaller stuff,' Sam suggested helpfully.

'Like hell,' said Somari, tucking it into his waistband. 'All right – you can fuggoff now – but just watch it.'

Sam rose to his feet. 'How long are you staying here?' he asked.

'What that got to do with you?' Somari demanded belligerently. 'You going to get cops to move us on?'

'That's a bloody insult!' Sam said hotly.

'Fuggoff,' said Somari again. He drew his right thumb across his throat, then sharply downwards over his chest and belly and made a peculiar clicking sound with his tongue.

'No need for that. I never done you no harm,' Sam mumbled, and went out hastily.

'You shouldn't have made him angry,' Wyndham said.

'I don't make him angry.' Somari grinned happily. 'I just make him frightened. Very nice sign that. It just tell him what happen if he open Goddam mouth too much. Right – now I go to buy clothes.'

Chapter 26

He was as nervous as a cat as he went through the barrier on to the platform. It was just before midnight, but the station was crowded and there seemed to be more police about than usual. A beggar clutched at his jacket, and a European inspector standing by the gate brought his cane down round his skinny rump and said, '*Hut jao, teri ma ka choot!*' and grinned sourly at Wyndham. 'Sooner you were travelling with this lot than me,' he said.

'What lot?' Wyndham asked.

'Pilgrims going back from the Velagunj Mela. Same every year. All the stiffs and bums in India come down to chuck coconuts into the bloody sea. Supposed to wash away their sins. Pity the bastards let go of the coconuts when they throw 'em – *Hut jao! Hut jao! Hut jao!*'

'Silly bugger Hindoo doing 'oly, 'oly, 'oly,' Somari supplemented as they followed their baggage coolie through the crowd. 'Cor! Stink worse than bloody pigs. Why you pick this damn train, sahib?'

'You know perfectly well why,' Wyndham said. 'There will be fewer British people travelling on a "Slow Mixed" than on the Mail.'

'Damn right,' grunted Somari. 'But you worry too much. Everything all fixed now.'

'Maybe – but I still can't afford to take risks.' They had argued long and acrimoniously over this during the preceding three days – Somari, in a wealth-engendered euphoria, wanting to book a first-class coupé, with Wyndham insisting on an economical second-class 'open'.

'Full of bloody rich Hindus and damn Tommies,' Somari had grumbled.

'I can deal with those,' Wyndham told him. 'In a first-class compartment I might find an officer shoved in with me – and that could be awkward.'

'Not if we book whole compartment.'

'I'm not throwing money away. I'm going to need every anna later.'

'We got plenty.'

'And I'm not touching any of Sam's.'

'Not Sam's – ours.'

'Yours if you like. Not mine.'

'That bloody silly.'

'Do as you're told – or I'll go off on my own. That would be the sensible thing to do anyway.'

And so it had gone on, but Wyndham had his way in the end.

They found their coach without difficulty. There were only four second- and two first-class compartments in the entire length of the long train – the rest being cattle-truck-type thirds, already filled to bursting point. The seconds and one first were half full, with luggage strewn over the vacant seats to discourage late-comers, but the other first-class compartment was locked and empty, with a railway babu standing outside with the expression of one whose sole concern was his passengers' comfort. He produced a huge T-shaped key and unlocked the door.

'In here, sahib,' Somari said.

'This is first class,' Wyndham said angrily.

'But I only pay *second* class, for Christ's sake,' Somari said over his shoulder as he followed the coolie into the carriage. 'Look at bloody ticket if you don't believe me.'

'And how much baksheesh to this fellow?'

'Couple of chips, no more.'

'I don't like it.'

'But everybody do it.'

'If a ticket inspector gets on I'm going to look damned silly.'

'No, sahib. Ticket inspector get on, this babu gives him eight anna and he fuggoff. All sahibs do it. Quite honest.'

More pilgrims were crowding on to the platform and trying to fight their way aboard the already grossly overcrowded coaches, so, fuming, Wyndham bowed to the inevitable and climbed into the compartment. Somari beamed beatifically when he swore at him, and set about unpacking the opulent bedding roll he insisted he had only given five rupees for in the thieves' bazaar – 'Quite honest, sahib.'

Outside the makings of a riot were building up as a party of Muslim Moplahs swaggered on to the platform, elbowing the more docile Hindus aside and pushing baggage through carriage windows before charging in themselves. Some of the more agile pilgrims had climbed on to the roofs of the coaches and were being unceremoniously kicked off by pursuing police. A European railway official was fighting his way through the crowd waving a green flag and blowing a whistle, and there was an answering screech from the engine and a tentative jerk and rattling of couplings as it started.

Somari said, 'I go and get into servants' compartment, sahib,' and Wyndham snarled, 'Stay here, you idiot. You'll never make it now.'

Somari winked and opened the door and jumped down on to the platform, and as he did so, a European bundled a bedding roll and a suitcase into the compartment. Somari yelled, 'Reserved compartment for my sahib! Can't go – ' But it was too late, and Wyndham saw him disappearing in the crowd as the train gathered speed.

'Sorry about this,' said the newcomer apologetically. 'I've only got a second-class ticket – '

'Don't let that worry you,' Wyndham grunted. 'So have I.'

'That's all right then,' the other answered. 'Going far?'

'Salem,' said Wyndham shortly. He had his story ready, but he was not volunteering anything until it became absolutely necessary.

'Kolar Gold Fields me. Got to change at Tiruppattur. You don't know when we get there, I suppose?'

'No idea, I'm afraid.' Wyndham yawned cavernously and leaned back in his berth with his eyes half-closed, but the other man didn't take the hint.

'Some damned awful hour like four in the morning, I think,' he went on. 'Can't get any sense out of these Indian railway babus. Hardly worthwhile unpacking my bedding roll. Cigarette?' He held a packet under Wyndham's nose.

'No, thanks, if you don't mind,' Wyndham said, and yawned again. 'I'm pretty tired. Had a hard day.'

'Me too,' said the other. 'Been travelling for ten days. Boat from Rangoon to Calcutta, then the train down to Madras.' He was a young man, probably about Wyndham's own age – unmistakably European, but with the slightly sing-song accent of the country-born and educated. Not unlike Paul's, Wyndham thought. And he was obviously a compulsive talker. He sighed inwardly.

'Know the Kolar Gold Fields?' asked the other.

'Heard of them. Never been there.' He closed his eyes tightly and even essayed a gentle snore, but there was no stopping the young man.

'Wonderful concern. Nearly seventy millions' worth of gold taken out since 1882 – pounds sterling, not rupees. Six companies working the reef now. My crowd is South African. When I say *my* crowd, I mean the company I'm going to, of course. Very progressive – better even than the Home companies. You from Home?'

'Yes.'

'Me too. What part?'

'Cornwall.'

'Oh – Leicestershire me. Came out as a small kid. My old man was in the Burma Police – Armed Constabulary – in the Leicestershire Regiment before that. Sergeant-major. You Army?'

'No.'

'Know Burma?'

'No.'

'You've missed nothing. Lousy place – I hate it. My people died when I was six – the big cholera epidemic. I missed it because I was sent up with the other European and Anglo-Burmese kids to Maymyo – that's the hill station for Mandalay, you know. I had no other people, so they kept me there – military orphanage. Most of the boys get enlisted in the British regiments when they're old enough, but I had flat feet; otherwise I'd have been in Blighty years ago. They kept me there until I got my Senior Cambridge – that's like matric, you know. Seventeen then, so they gave me a teacher's course and I've been knocking the three Rs into the snotty-nosed little bastards ever since. Seven years of it. And do you know what they paid me?'

Wyndham didn't answer, but it did him no good.

'Thirty bloody rupees a month to start with – and my keep, of course. Nigger's pay. You got a raise of two rupees each year if you kept your nose clean. I was only getting forty-four chips when I left. Not keeping you awake, am I?'

Wyndham snored loudly.

'I was always applying for jobs advertised in the *Teachers' World*,' the young man went on inexorably. 'Same answer every time – when the buggers did answer at all: "Indian and Burmese qualifications not recognised at Home". Had to do an extra year in an English training college. What a hope. Nearly seven hundred rupees for the fare, then keep yourself for a year – plus the fees, of course. Then I saw this advertisement for the Kolar Gold Fields. Are you sure you won't have a cigarette?'

The packet was under his nose again, and in sheer desperation Wyndham took one – which was fatal. The young man lit it for him and beamed. 'That's better,' he said. 'Hope you don't mind me going on like this, but I haven't spoken to anybody for days, and it's been getting on my nerves.' Wyndham understood.

'Go ahead,' he said. 'I'm listening.'

'Thanks,' said the other gratefully. 'You don't know what a relief it is to talk to somebody.'

'I think I do,' said Wyndham.

'My name's Martin, by the way,' said the young man, and put his hand out. 'Timothy Martin. Most people call me Tim.'

'Mine's John Phillips,' said Wyndham, shaking hands. 'Most people call me Jack.'

'Pleased to meet you, Jack,' said Tim.

'And you, Tim,' said Wyndham solemnly. 'Go ahead with your story. I find it very interesting.' He bit back a genuine yawn.

'Well, I applied, you see,' Tim went on. 'Never thought I had a chance. I ask you – five hundred rupees a month! Right out of my class. But by God I got it!'

'Good for you,' said Wyndham. 'What's the job?'

'Storekeeper – but there's a chance you may get selected for trainee-foreman.' His voice dropped to an awed whisper. 'A thousand a month starting grade, boy.'

'Jesus,' said Wyndham. 'That's *real* money.'

'Of course I'm not saying I'll *get* selected – but there's no harm in trying, is there?'

'Not a bit. You go right to it – and the best of luck to you.'

'I mean, there's nothing wrong with my education, is there? Senior Cambridge is not to be sneezed at.'

'I should say not.'

'I'll show you,' said Tim. He delved into his suitcase and produced a flat leather folder. 'Here we are.' He handed Wyndham a pamphlet. 'See? "Suitable candidates may be selected from time to time for the trainee-foreman's grade." In black and white.'

'You've got a great opportunity ahead of you,' Wyndham assured him.

'You bet. Five hundred chips a month – *and* a rent-free bungalow – well, I mean a man could save out of that, couldn't he?'

'He certainly could.'

'Another cigarette?'

'I don't think so, Tim – and if you don't mind I'm going to be a bit rude, and go to sleep. I've had a hell of a day.'

'And I've been talking your head off,' Tim said penitently.

'Not at all, I've enjoyed hearing about it.' He fanned cigarette smoke from in front of him. 'Would you mind if I opened the window?'

'No, go ahead.'

Wyndham wrestled with the clumsy wooden frame that held the allegedly mosquito-proof screen over the glass and let down the window itself, and a wall of spray blew across the compartment.

'Good God!' said Tim, and dived for his scattered papers. 'Rain? You don't get the monsoon as early as this over here, do you? Not due until June in Burma.'

'Chhota barsat,' Wyndham told him. ' "The little rains". Not every year – but it certainly does come down when it decides to. A dry river bed on the Frontier can be a raging torrent within an hour.'

'You've been on the Frontier?' Tim asked, interested.

'Me? No, just what I've heard – '

'What *is* your line, by the way?'

'Bugger this window,' Wyndham said, wrestling with it again. 'The wood's warped. Have to shut it or we'll be flooded out.' He managed to get it closed. 'Well, Tim, I really think I'll get some sleep now. Good night – and once again, good luck.'

'Thanks. And if you're ever around Kolar, look me up – the Redesdale Company. Good night. It's been great talking to you.'

Wyndham switched the light off over his berth. Tim kept his on, once more reading through his pamphlets.

There was a white sky above him and a smooth snow slope running down towards him with the tiny black figures of two skiers on it. One skier took off and circled in the air, and then landed again. And his jaw was hurting. Both skiers were circling in the air now. His jaw wasn't hurting any more, but somebody was bending over him and pushing something up his nose. He tried to hit him, but couldn't raise his arm – so he cried.

He was travelling now – down a long white passage with lights at the end of it. His jaw was hurting again – and his leg – and his shoulder. He tried to shrug into a more comfortable position, and then he was hurting all over – agonizingly, in a red sea of pain. Mr Meakin was counting – one – two – three – four – and he knew that the final count had to be thirty – and he was hanging on a triangle by his wrists – and Mr Pereira was standing waiting patiently with a noose for them to finish.

He wanted desperately to pee, and there was nowhere to go, because the Adjutant was saying sternly, 'Gentlemen only' – so he giggled and let it go just the same – and somebody said, 'That's better.'

Somebody else said, 'For God's sake send that Madrassi bearer away, will you.'

'He won't go,' a woman answered.

'Get the police to him then, Sister,' the first voice said impatiently.

'Sahib, sahib – you all right, sahib. You Mister Timothy Martin sahib,' Somari was saying in an urgent whisper. 'You all right – you *Mister Timothy Martin sahib*. You give me job in Madras – and if this bastard call me "bearer" I cut his bloody throat.'

'Look, if I catch you hanging around here again, you black bastard, I'll have you arrested. Footsackl'

'Mister Timothy Martin sahib – remember, sahib – *Mister Timothy Martin*,' Somari was whispering. Then he drifted off again, down a white river – and the red sea was paling.

'Can you remember your name?' somebody was asking gently.

'Timothy Martin,' he said, but not distinctly, because his jaw was hurting abominably again.

'Well, that's something,' the voice said with satisfaction, 'and at least he didn't try to hit me this time. Another five grains, Sister.'

It went on for a century or more until the morning he was able to croak 'Where am I?' to somebody who was doing something to a tube in his wrist.

A pretty Anglo-Indian nurse bent over him and said, 'So you're back with us, are you, Mr Martin? That's better – but you mustn't try to talk. You've got wires and things in your jaw.'

'What happened?' he managed to get out.

'Train accident – but please – no talking, or Doctor Rienitz will be very angry,' she said.

Things moved a little faster after that.

'This sudden flood had weakened the centre span of the bridge. The engine and the first three coaches went into the river – all pilgrims – third class, poor devils. Yours – the first- and second-class portion – was left hanging by the couplings, with the side ripped out,' the doctor told him. 'You were jammed into the wreckage of one of the compartments – and they got two other Kolar people out of the next one. The rest weren't so lucky, I'm afraid. They must have been thrown out into the river.'

'Where am I?' Wyndham asked again.

'You're in the Company hospital, and you're going to be all right, Mr Martin – but no more talking now, there's a good chap.'

'I had a servant – '

'You certainly had – Little Bantu fellow. Damn nuisance. Keeps on creeping in here to worry you. He's all right. Now go to sleep again.'

They seemed to give up the unequal struggle against Somari after that, and let him make himself useful as an unpaid orderly. He used to squat beside the bed with a wary eye cocked at the door against the coming of Authority.

'You got broken leg, broken arm, broken jaw, bang on head, busted nose,' he explained. 'Christ, sahib, when I see you first I say – "That it. Sahib chubbidustered. Finish." Blood all over.'

'You weren't hurt?'

'Me? No, I all right. First part of train go arse over tip into river. Your part left hanging. My part still on rails. It pissing down with rain. I run like hell along track. Everybody yelling, screaming. I think your part gone into river with rest, but then a sahib climb up over broken bridge. He hurt bad, but by Christ he got good guts. He say, "More people in that part. Want help to get out," but guard say, "No, for God's sake leave alone or whole bloody lot drop into river. Leave alone till we got proper lights. Coming soon – I send back down track." I say, "I only little bugger – not heavy. Somebody got flashlight, I go," but they say, "No – you fuggoff – only make things worse," and guard give thump on ear'ole. Then it get light and rain is stopping and rescue train come up with railway people, doctors, police, whole bloody lot. I can see somebody through smashed side of first class, all crushed under broken wood, but I don't know if it is you or that other sahib. They get you out, with two other people from other compartment – one alive, one dead – and there's a suitcase near you so they bring that too. Then I see one of live people is you, and I pretty glad, sahib. I sit with you while you on stretcher, and police inspector come along and say, "Who are you?" I say, "I this sahib's servant." He say, "What's his name?" and I say, "Walker sahib." Inspector open suitcase and I see some clothes inside – not ours – but quite good. Inspector say, "Your sahib's clothes?" I say, "Yes." Then another policeman come and they find small leather case with some papers and I can hear them talking. They say, "Timothy Martin – come from Rangoon – going to job in Kolar Gold Field." I listening with ears stretched out like bloody dhobi's donkey. Inspector turn round and I pretend to be asleep. He kick me with foot and say, "What this sahib's name?" – I say, "Martin sahib." He say, "You said, Walker sahib." I say, "I get bang on head – make silly. Walker sahib *last* sahib I work for. He go back to Blighty. This Martin sahib – he just come from Burma side. Tell me he go to Kolar – want servant. I get job." He say, "You get kick up the arse – make wise." Then he write in book and give me little leather case and say, "All right. You stay with sahib until he get to hospital – see that nobody pinch kit." So I stay. I scared you going to say something in sleep so I keep on sneaking in and telling you your name Timothy Martin, but your busted jaw make that all right.'

'I can remember that,' Wyndham mumbled. 'When did all this happen?'

'My God – long time ago. Twenty days – more.'

'How have you been managing?'

'Me? Fine. Plenty money. Got mine and yours. Pinch yours while you are on stretcher – just leave fifty chips in pocket – so coppers' fresh air fund don't get the rest.'

'What are you going to do now, Somari?'

'What the hell you think? Stay here till you get better – then we move on. I got good place to sleep, under verandah – free grub – few messages for nurse miss-sahibs. Lovely.'

'You'd better move on *now*. When they find out I'm not Martin sahib you might get into trouble.'

'Balls,' said Somari. 'You go to sleep, sahib – so you get better quicker.' He winked, gave a thumbs-up sign, and slipped out of the door.

His shoulder healed first, and ten days later they lowered his plaster-encased leg from the trapeze in which it had been suspended – but his fractured jaw took considerably longer to mend. But eventually that, too, came about, and they removed the underpinning, and a giggling nurse let him look in a mirror for the first time. He giggled himself then. It had left him with a deep scar running from the lobe of his left ear to the corner of his mouth, and the loss of his teeth on that side had altered the configuration of his face. His nose had suffered too, and it had a slight list to starboard.

'No more pukkha sahib,' Somari said. 'Look like bloody bazaar boxer now.'

'That's fine,' Wyndham said.

'Of course we can take a few kinks out of it yet,' Rienitz, the South African doctor told him. 'This new plastic surgery is pretty good. And, naturally, we'll fix you up with some bridge-work in place of the missing teeth.'

'I don't think I'll bother,' Wyndham told him.

'Nonsense, man,' Rienitz said. 'All on the house. This company is very open-handed. Your job is being kept open for you, you know. In fact you're on full salary now.'

He mulled long over this. Could he risk it? The nagging fear was there that somebody from Rangoon might come across to India to see him – but as the weeks went by, even this faded. They sent him up to the company convalescent home in Ootacamund and while there he went through the papers in the briefcase thoroughly. Poor Timothy Martin, he thought. Here was the reason for his loquaciousness. He didn't appear to have a friend in the world. There wasn't a single personal letter or photo among the papers – just the correspondence with the company – his prized Senior Cambridge certificates – a birth certificate showing him to have been born on the twenty-seventh of March, nineteen-hundred-and-three, in the Military Families Hospital, Mingladon, of Janet Mary Martin, née Fuller, wife of Company-sergeant-major Arthur George Martin, The Leicestershire Regiment (seconded Burma Armed Constabulary), and a cold little testimonial to the effect that Mr Timothy Martin had carried out the duties of junior teacher (primary – locally qualified) at the Lawrence School for Army Orphans 'with satisfaction' and was relinquishing his post at his own request after seven years.

No, it didn't appear likely that anybody over there was going to the trouble of looking Timothy up.

He had a birth certificate now. That was all he needed to apply for a passport – that and somebody who had known him for a reasonable time to endorse the application form. It wouldn't do to start things rolling immediately, of course. Wait a year – saving money the whole time – he'd need to do that, anyhow, because he had returned the thousand rupees Paul had sent him to Madras.

So he came down from Ootacamund, still a little wobbly, and walking with a limp, but otherwise quite fit, and reported to Mr Walderstein, the fat and jolly Johannesburg Area Manager of the Redesdale Mining Pty, (S.A.) Kolar, Mysore, who welcomed him heartily and put him to work.

PART TWO

Chapter 27

Wyndham felt the line go slack and thought it had snapped, so he started regretfully to wind in, but the big fish was only sulking at the bottom of the pool, and when it felt the hook again it was off on another run towards the sunken tree at the bottom of the falls. The line was screaming through the rings and he knew he didn't dare apply the drag as he would for a salmon, because a mahseer doesn't pull steadily. It can check in the middle of a wild run, allowing the line to slacken for just an instant, then punch forward again immediately, often snapping the strongest tackle, in much the same manner as an old-fashioned shopkeeper used to snap the string after tying a parcel.

He yelled to Paul the other side of the river to cross by the stepping-stones with the gaff.

'You won't need it yet,' Paul answered, but came just the same. 'There's plenty of fight left in that one.'

'He's about twenty-five pounds, and he's been fighting for forty minutes,' Wyndham said. 'Fifteen minutes of borrowed time there.'

'A minute a pound, you mean?' Paul said. 'I don't know anything about salmon – but mahseer don't seem to have heard of that rule.'

The fish jumped and appeared to hang in mid-air, a glittering silver crescent, for a long moment before smacking the water with a crack like a pistol shot.

'Oh, you beauty,' Wyndham said regretfully. 'Why the hell can't we leave you alone?'

'The trout wouldn't agree with you, Charles,' Paul said. 'He and his pals have cleared this stretch of water.'

'Don't call me Charles,' Wyndham told him.

'Sorry. I don't slip often nowadays.'

'He's shot his bolt now,' said Wyndham, winding in steadily. Paul went forward into the river and got the fish behind the gills with the gaff, and together they hauled it on to the bank, and

clubbed it with the 'priest', and Wyndham felt the pang again
that comes to all fishermen at the moment of victory. He weighed
it with his eye.

'Not quite twenty-five. A good twenty, though,' he said. 'Nice
eating. Anything above this tends to be coarse. We'll shove it on
ice and you can take a chunk back to Bangalore with you tomorrow. At least Tina will know you *have* been fishing then.'

'I'm *supposed* to be inspecting the permanent way,' Paul said.
'I'm a humble railway employee, not an overpaid, underworked
goldfields foreman.'

'*Probationary* foreman.'

'You still get a thousand a month, you lucky devil. Why the
hell didn't I have a go at this instead of the railway?'

'You still could. They're recruiting again. Two more companies opening up this year.'

'Too late to change now. I shouldn't moan. The railway has
been very decent to me in the two years I've been with them.'
He sighed. 'I wish to God I'd had the money – and the gumption
– to have gone Home years ago and got a degree.'

'Oh, stop bellyaching about "Home",' Wyndham said. 'This
is your home – and mine.'

'You've finally given up all ideas of – of – ' Paul broke off
awkwardly,

'Say it. Of moving on? Yes. I like my job. I love the country.
After all, it's mine as well as yours, you know. The shadow has
been lessening all the time. And – '

'And Julia?' asked Paul. 'What's the latest?'

'Still the same,' growled Wyndham. 'It's "no".'

'You're not firm enough with her.'

'What the hell do you expect me to do? Belt her over the head
with a club and drag her in front of the priest?' Wyndham was
ramming the tackle into a basket angrily. 'She says there's nobody
else – and I know there isn't.'

'Well, what reason does she give?'

'None. None that makes any sense, I mean. She just says she
likes her job and her independence. Ah, shit – come on. It'll be
dark soon.' They climbed the bank to the path above the river,
carrying the fish between them slung from a bamboo.

'She could still keep her job after you were married,' Paul said.

'You don't think I haven't told her that, do you? I wouldn't like it – I'd prefer to support my wife – but I'd agree to it. I'd agree to anything.' He shrugged. 'Still, I've only got myself to blame, I suppose. I've got no right to ask any girl to marry me – not when I couldn't tell her the truth about myself.'

'Don't start that again, Charles,' Paul said. 'That's all dead. It died two years ago.'

'Exactly – and you just called me Charles again. It will never die. Not inside me. I still wake up sometimes in the early hours in a cold sweat, expecting a knock at the door – '

'Stop it,' said Paul sharply. 'That's not going to happen, and you know it. You're a different man now. Damn it, you don't even *look* the same. Tim, listen to me. I saw as much of you as anybody back there, but if I had run into you now, without having seen you in the meantime, I wouldn't have known you. How old are you?'

'Same as you. Twenty-five.'

'You look a good thirty-five to start with. Greying round the temples moustache your nose is a different shape – '

'You should have seen the bloody thing before they straightened it,' Wyndham said ruefully.

'But it's your expression that really changes everything. You looked like the rest of the poor devils then. Dead. Then in Madras you looked hunted – '

'And felt it.' Wyndham chuckled. 'God, I'll never forget the first time I went out there – and a cop got into conversation with me and scrounged a ride in my gharry. I died a thousand deaths.'

'Well, let's drop it. You certainly don't look like that now.'

'Oh, talking about it to *you* doesn't worry me,' Wyndham said. 'I honestly don't think I'm ever likely to be recognized and picked up again – touch wood. It's having to sail under false colours with Julia that sticks in my gizzard. She was asking me about my childhood a few days ago – and there I was cooking up a yarn from what that poor little sod on the train told me in the space of fifteen minutes. Lying like a Guardsman. I tailed it off by saying that it was all very unhappy, and that I preferred not to dwell on it – and she started to cry. Can you imagine how I felt?'

'She didn't have such a hell of a lively time of it herself,' Paul said. 'That would explain her interest.'

'You knew her as a kid, did you?'

'Yes, in so far as everybody in Bangalore knows everybody else – the old Anglo-Indian families, I mean. She had much the same life as you – Tim Martin – had. Parents died when she was very young, and she went into a Catholic orphanage.'

'Treated badly?'

'Good God no. The nuns don't treat people badly – but it's not the same as having your own parents, home and family is it?'

'What made her decide to go to England?' Wyndham asked. 'That is something she never seems to want to talk about.'

'It's what made her decide to come back here that puzzles me,' Paul said. 'Most of us spend a lifetime dreaming of getting away to the Old Country, and the few who do usually put down roots there, and wild horses wouldn't drag them back. But here she was, with a local teaching certificate and a couple of thousand rupees that came to her when she was twenty-one – so she was off like a shot to England to do the extra year there to get full Blighty qualifications. She passed her exams all right and got a good teaching job – but after six months she chucked it in and came back. Silly little devil.'

'She was lonely and homesick,' Wyndham said defensively. 'She told me that.'

'She didn't give herself much time to get over it, did she? My God, if I'd had her chance this place wouldn't have seen me again.' He sighed wistfully. 'Fancy living in London. Theatres – concerts – '

'I'm quite content with Kolar, a bit of fishing and the Redesdale Amateur Dramatic Society's Christmas pantomime,' Wyndham grunted.

'Yes, but you *have* seen the other side of things. You *have* lived in London – '

'For three months, during which time I certainly never heard a concert, and my only contact with the theatre was having it off with a chorus girl – and that was mostly in Brighton anyway.'

'You're a cynic,' said Paul sadly.

'I'm a realist.' They arrived at the road, where they had chained and padlocked their bicycles to a tree. 'Thank the Lord for that,' he said, dumping the fish and the heavy tackle basket on the grass. 'At the present moment you could have the whole of

274

London for one long cold beer. Now how the hell are we going to carry this thing without getting it mixed up with the wheel?'

'Sling the bamboo between the two crossbars.'

'Then the tail will be dragging on the ground.'

'Across the carrier?'

'Damned thing is bound to slip. I really ought to buy a good second-hand car – '

'Just for carrying mahseer home? Bloody plutocrat.'

'I could also take Julia away out into the jungle and then say, "Right – say yes or walk home, you silly bitch." '

'Worth trying.'

'She'd undoubtedly walk. She may look sweet, gentle and Madonnalike, but she's as stubborn as an Army mule. What that gal wants is a good swishy rattan cane round her ass – '

'A pity you haven't got one with you,' Paul said drily. 'Here she is.'

A tonga was jingling along the road towards them, and a girl was kneeling on the back seat, looking over the driver's head. It stopped, and she jumped down.

'Somari told me you'd come this way, so I thought I'd risk it,' she said, and Wyndham caught his breath sharply, as he always did when he came upon her unexpectedly. She was no more than middle height, but her slenderness made her appear taller. Her luxuriant hair was black – Indian black – gathered in a heavy knot at the nape of her neck when she set out, no doubt, but the breeze had freed it, which delighted Wyndham because her usual impeccable neatness used to fret him. But it was her eyes that one saw first. They were not Indian, nor Mediterranean nor West of Ireland, but rather something of all three – deep brown, but not unfathomable because there seemed to be a light lurking in their depths. Her flawless skin would have been starkly white against the hair and eyes had she constantly shielded it against the sun with topee and sunshade, as did most Anglo-Indian girls. She didn't, so she had a soft olive tan and even a few freckles over the bridge of her short straight nose. Her mouth would have been rather sad in repose, but now she was smiling. She was more than smiling – she was grinning impishly.

'Why the hell didn't you come with us when you were asked?' said Wyndham gruffly.

275

'I told you. I had a pile of marking to do,' she said. 'So you did catch one? You or Paul?'

'Him,' said Paul.

'He,' she corrected.

'Oh, Christ – cut that out,' Wyndham snarled. 'You're not in your bloody schoolroom now.'

'What's the matter with him?' she asked Paul.

'You. He's just been bellyaching because you won't marry him,' Paul told her.

'Can you blame me? He's got the manners of a pig. Ask him if he wants me to take it in the tonga?'

'Tell her yes,' Wyndham said. 'But see that that thieving damned cook of hers keeps his filthy paws off it until *we* get there.'

'Would you like to come to supper, Paul?' she asked.

'You bet – but I've got to catch the midnight train back to Bangalore,' Paul said as he dumped the fish into the tonga.

'You'll be off the premises well before then,' she promised. 'You can bring your uncouth pal, if he's stopped behaving like a five-year-old – oh, and some beer. He's guzzled all mine.' She jumped into the tonga. 'All right, my brother – go back.'

They watched the tonga jingling up the road in its own cloud of dust.

'Silly little cow,' said Wyndham softly. 'Did you ever see anything more heart-breakingly beautiful in all your life?'

'Christ, you *have* got it bad,' said Paul. 'But you did rather ask for that lot, didn't you?'

'I always do. She makes me feel like a pimply-faced yobbo – then I act like one.' He unlocked the chain and freed the two bicycles. 'Why does she do it, Paul? If she really disliked me, or I got on her nerves or something – or if there was somebody else – I'd accept it. She'd only have to tell me.'

'There's nobody else, and she doesn't dislike you,' Paul said quietly. 'I can tell you that with absolute certainty.'

'How?'

'I'm relying on you to keep this to yourself,' Paul said as they pushed their bicycles on to the road.

'Naturally.'

'Last time she was in Bangalore, Tina, who's as inquisitive as a monkey, was kidding her about you. Now you know Julia. She's good-natured and doesn't mind a bit of leg-pulling usually, but this time she blew up – really blew up – and turned on poor old Tina like a wildcat, then finished up in floods of tears.'

'Well, what the hell does that prove?' Wyndham said impatiently.

'Nothing maybe,' Paul shrugged. 'But in the shindig she did say among other things that there was nobody else but you – and never would be – but that she couldn't marry you.'

'But why, for God's sake? – Why? Why? *Why?*' Wyndham demanded.

'If I knew, I'd tell you. But I don't know – neither does Tina, or I'd get it out of her,' Paul said. 'But there's something I *can* tell you – although I don't think you're going to like it.'

'What?'

'She said if people didn't leave her alone – and that included you – she'd just chuck her job here and go away.'

'Oh, Jesus,' said Wyndham hollowly.

'Actually Tina's got a theory.'

'What?'

'A vocation – '

'A what?' Wyndham stared at him open-mouthed. 'You mean she wants to be a *nun*? How absolutely damned ridiculous!'

'Why?' Paul asked. 'She's a Catholic – brought up in a convent – '

'Bloody nonsense!' said Wyndham explosively. 'Not Julia. She's just not the type.'

'How the hell do you know what the type is?' Paul said angrily. 'They don't *all* go round telling their beads and looking holy beforehand. I've known some pretty sporting wenches in Bangalore who've suddenly upped sticks and gone over the wall without a word of warning.'

'But surely, if that were the case she'd have told me, if she didn't want me to pester her.'

'That would be the last thing she'd do,' Paul explained. 'It's a pretty difficult thing for you Protestants to understand. If a girl thinks she might have a vocation, she usually does a lot of heart-searching on her own first – then sees her priest. Invariably the old priest is pretty khabardari about it. Tells her to go and do some more heart-searching and a hell of a lot of praying and all that, and come back in six months if she still feels the same – but to keep it to herself in the meantime. I understand that the majority don't go back – but if they do, they get a further period of deep thinking. The Church has to be completely certain before they admit them.'

'Oh my God,' said Wyndham in deep dismay.

'Don't take that as certain,' Paul told him. 'As a matter of fact I reacted the same way when Tina sprung it on me. Personally *I* don't think she is the type either – but it *could* be the reason. Anyhow, you can rest assured that there isn't some other fellow lurking in the shadows – and she doesn't hate your guts. I saw the way she was looking at you just now – when you were being bloody rude to her.'

They rode on in silence to the Redesdale Compound. It was a huge area, resembling a military Cantonment, accommodating the whole of the European and Anglo-Indian staff. An attempt had been made, quite successfully, to soften the starkness of the place by avoiding a geometrical layout, so the interior roads wound pleasantly round the hillside, and where trees and clumps of bamboo had not hampered building, they had been left standing, and even supplemented by a central park on a plain which had been artificially levelled on the edge of the jungle, where there were playing fields and tennis courts. There was a clean, well-ordered bazaar to one side, and on the hill dominating the whole area, two churches, the small but magnificently equipped hospital where Wyndham had spent his first days here, and the children's school.

Wyndham's bungalow was rather isolated. It was a wooden structure of only three rooms, which had originally housed the site office when the more solid bungalows further down the hill were being built. It had been the only one available then, and they had promised to move him to a more palatial quarter later, but he had grown attached to it and liked its remoteness – and now, two years later, he had a garden in front of it, and a belt of rhododendrons and azaleas all round.

Somari came through on to the verandah and grinned as they pushed their bicycles up the path.

'Hello, sahib,' he said. 'Wet arse, no fish, eh? What we give Paul sahib for supper now? He Catholic, like me, and it Friday.'

'Don't talk so much,' Wyndham said shortly. 'And get a couple of baths ready.'

'Oho!' scoffed Somari. 'Got sore head too, eh?'

'We got a lovely fish,' Paul smiled. 'Julia miss-sahib has it. We're going there for supper.'

'My God!' yelled Somari. 'Get own baths then. I go over there before that bloody Hindu cook bugger it up!' and he dashed down the path.

Wyndham grinned in spite of himself. 'I'll never train him,' he said apologetically.

'I wouldn't try,' Paul said. 'You don't find blokes like Somari very often.'

'Thank God,' said Wyndham, going to the icebox for beer. 'Joke, of course. I don't know what the hell I'd do without him.'

They sat on the verandah watching the sun going down into the jungle behind the main town, three miles away across the valley. Its dying rays were striking the white buildings of the school on the slightly higher hill in front of them, and on Julia's bungalow behind it. Somari, antlike in the distance, was running frantically along the winding path that led up to it from the intervening gulley.

'Peaceful,' said Paul softly. 'I love this place.'

'So do I,' said Wyndham glumly, sipping his beer. 'I hate the very thought of leaving it, but I'll have to be thinking of moving on.'

'Talk to her first,' Paul begged. 'Talk sensibly – coolly – without fighting, just for once. Don't do anything hastily before doing that, Charles.'

'*Tim*, blast you,' Wyndham said, then leaned across and gripped Paul's shoulder. 'All right, old lad, I promise you I won't.'

Chapter 28

They walked back through the warm darkness after putting Paul on the train. Wyndham's earlier ill-humour had passed, but he was still withdrawn and depressed, and Julia matched his silence. They turned into the compound and climbed the hill towards the school, but when they reached the path that forked off towards his bungalow, she said, 'Can I come up to your place, Tim? I want to talk.'

'Good God, yes,' he said. 'But there's no chaperon. Somari sleeps down in the servants' lines.'

'Do you feel you need one?' she asked.

'Don't be silly. It was you I was thinking of. You know what these gossiping old biddies are like. If you were seen there as late as this it would be all round the compound tomorrow.'

'There's less chance of being seen at your place than mine. All right then – if you'd rather not.'

He turned and grasped her roughly by the shoulders. 'What the hell is this?' he demanded.

'Don't make it too difficult for me, my dear,' she said, and her voice was steadier than his. 'I want to talk. I *must* talk. This is something that concerns us both.'

'I've been trying to talk sensibly to you for the last six months,' he said. 'But you've been behaving like a stupid little pigtailed flapper.'

'I know. So don't wave me off when I've finally screwed up my courage to tell you all about it.'

'All about what?'

'Please,' she begged. 'I've got to tell this my own way. Right from the beginning. Without questions.'

They turned on to the path and he took her by the elbow and neither spoke again until they reached the bungalow, then she felt her way to a chair on the verandah and dropped into it. 'Don't put the light on,' she said. 'Just sit there.'

'Shall I get you a drink?' he asked.

'No, just listen. Tim, you've asked me to marry you – and I've put you off – '

'Put me off be damned,' he said angrily. 'You've said you *couldn't*. All right, you're entitled to do that. You're entitled to tell me to go to hell if you want to. My grouse is that I caught you off guard once, and you told me you loved me – '

'I do,' she said, in a voice scarcely above a whisper. 'Tim, I *do*. Whatever happens, you must believe that.'

'Then damn it all, woman, tell me why you won't marry me.' He reached out to take her hand, but she drew further away.

'I've never said I won't. I said I can't.'

'That's a quibble.'

'It's not a quibble. I *can't* – ' She broke off.

'Then have the honesty to say why you *"can't"*. That's all I'm asking.'

'I'm trying to.' There was a long pause, then she added, 'Tim – I'm married already.'

He felt for his cigarettes, then had difficulty in finding his matches.

'I see,' he said in a flat voice. 'It would have saved a certain embarrassment on both sides if you'd told me that before, don't you think?'

'If you only knew how many times I've been on the point of doing so,' she said.

'What stopped you?'

Her voice rose. '*You* stopped me. You and your beastly temper and wretched schoolboy tantrums. I wanted advice – help – I thought I might get it from you, but all you ever did was to bellow – call me a silly bitch or a stupid flapper. Well, now you know, so leave me alone in future.' She was sobbing quietly. 'I've only told you because Paul said you were going to throw your job up and go away, and there's no need to – because *I'm* going away.'

'I suppose it's no use my saying at this stage that I'm sorry?' he said slowly.

'It's not your fault.'

'You just said it was – and I have been damned rude.' He paused. 'You also said something about help and advice.'

'It's too late now.' She was drying her eyes.

'Where is he?'

'Who?'

'Your – husband.'

'I don't know. I don't want to know.'

'I take it that things haven't worked out?'

'That's an understatement.'

'Any possibility of a divorce?'

'I'm afraid not. You know the reason, of course?'

'You're a Catholic, I know – but surely that's winked at these days?'

'I'm not a very good Catholic – not any more,' she said, 'but somehow – no, I couldn't face that. He's a Catholic too, which makes it even more difficult.'

'And you say you don't know where he is?'

'I left him in England – '

He stared at her through the darkness. 'In England?'

'Yes, but he found out where I was working and – ' She broke off again. He reached out and took her hand, and this time she didn't draw away.

'Would you like to tell me about it?' he asked gently. 'Don't if you'd rather not.'

'I think I would, now that I've gone so far. Could I have one of your cigarettes?' He lit one and passed it to her. 'I don't know if you know anything about my background?' she went on.

'Only the little I've heard from Paul. He hasn't been gossiping or anything like that,' Wyndham said.

'It wouldn't matter if he had. Like you, I was an orphan – and also like you I took the local certificate, and I carried on teaching at the convent in Bangalore. I was quite happy – you know what it's like, so I don't have to explain anything.' She drew on her cigarette. 'I suppose *you* used to beat on the bars a bit too.'

'I certainly did,' Wyndham said with feeling.

'I'd never been anywhere outside the convent in my life. We used to be taken up to Ooti for a holiday in the hot weather – but only to another convent. Even my teaching course was taken in the convent. I knew I had between three and four thousand rupees to come to me when I was twenty-one – under my grandmother's will – so I just counted the days. The Mother Superior was a little sad and disappointed when I told her what I wanted to do, but she put no obstacles in my way – and even helped – so I had no difficulty in getting into the Portsmouth Teachers' Training College. I met Jim on the ship going Home. He's rather older than I – Anglo-Indian – and like me he was leaving India for the first time. He was kind, considerate and full of self-confidence. I, on the other hand, was awkward, scared and desperately lonely.' She laughed softly. 'I certainly must have looked it, too. My clothes were just what the nuns, bless them, thought were suitable for a modest girl venturing out into the wicked world for the first time – and I felt that all the other passengers were laughing at me. Looking back, I don't suppose for one moment they were, but it certainly drove me into my shell still further – and I was very grateful to him. He was a link with the only world I knew – and I felt pretty lost when we parted in Southampton. He had no particular plans. He was just fed up with the lack of opportunity for local boys out here, and he had the courage and initiative to leave and try his luck at Home when he had saved enough money.

'I settled in quite happily at the College. Everybody, both staff and students, were very kind, and I was working hard and had no time to feel sorry for myself. But the weekends were lonely, because most of the girls lived locally and they used to go home. I was often invited to their houses, but I was such a shy little fool that I seldom accepted – so when Jim showed up again he was something in the nature of a godsend. He'd got a job in a garage in Southampton. He had no formal training, but he had a natural mechanical aptitude, and lots and lots of ambition. His idea was to gain experience and save money and eventually start up in business himself.'

She was silent for a long time, and Wyndham thought she wasn't going to continue, but then she started again.

'We used to go out every Sunday. He was able to borrow a motor-cycle and sometimes even a car most weekends, and we used to go to the New Forest and along the coast. You've no idea what England is like in the spring and summer, Tim – '

'I've heard of it,' said Wyndham gruffly. 'Go on.'

'Then he proposed – and I shied off quickly. It would have meant the end of my career before I'd even started. A married woman can teach in this country, but not in England, although they're trying to alter the rule – and I did so desperately want to get established there and see something of the world. But he had an idea. It frightened me at first – but then I started to see the sense of it. We could get married quietly and I'd go on teaching under my maiden name when I had qualified. He said that he knew of a man in the garage whose wife was actually doing that – and in fact I'd heard whispers of it among the students. And it would solve a more immediate problem, sordid though it might sound. The Long Vacation was coming up, when the College would be closed for three months – June, July and August – and I hadn't an idea of what I was going to do, because my money was running out fast. I'd paid for a year's board and residence there, but that only covered term-time. Yes, it seemed such a sound idea. And two salaries later on would bring the business that much closer. So that's what we did. A friend of his at the garage rented us a room in their house in Southsea, just outside Portsmouth, and we were married very quietly in the Catholic church by special licence, with only his friend and his wife as witnesses.'

Again she was silent. Wyndham took her hand. 'Don't go on if you'd rather not,' he said quietly.

'I want to,' she said in a flat voice. 'Our wedding feast was in a pub on a Saturday night – and Jim and both our witnesses got drunk – and there was a fight with some sailors. Then we went back to the house with some other people who had tagged on – carrying two bottles of whisky and a crate of beer – and Jim was sick – and the others serenaded us under the bedroom window until the police moved them on – '

'No more – no more, Julia,' Wyndham begged, because now she was sobbing again. He took her in his arms and rocked her gently, patting her and making silly, soothing noises as one would with a baby.

'Let me finish now,' she said after a time. 'Somehow or other we got through our – our – *honeymoon*. He was doing some rather mysterious night work with his friend at the time, and drinking a lot – and that helped. I went back when the College reopened, and in spite of everything I managed to pass. They help you to get your first job. Mine was a temporary one – "Supply", they call it – relieving while somebody is on sick leave. It was in

Reading. I went off without telling him where I was going, and wrote him saying I wanted time to think things over. But he traced me through the College, by the simple expedient of going there and saying he was a relative from India and he'd brought me some parcels from the family, so they gave him the address of the school without question – and he waited for me outside the playground and threatened to make a scene. He was in some sort of trouble at the garage and needed money. I gave him what I had and promised to send him some more when I drew my first salary. I know I'm making myself sound like one of the martyrs from the Book of Saints – but it wasn't entirely like that. I *did* fight him, but I was so terribly frightened that my marriage might come to light and that I'd lose my job and even have my certificate revoked. So I just kept him quiet with money for the three months I was in Reading. Then, when I was transferred to another post, in Slough, I slipped away without telling him – but once more he traced me, and the whole ghastly business started again. I was paying him to keep away and leave me alone – but I was always frightened that he would turn up when he was drunk and make more scenes. Can I have another cigarette?'

He lit her one and passed it to her. 'How did you make the break eventually?' he asked.

'I didn't have to,' she said. 'He did. He just stopped turning up. Then I got a letter from him, from Lewes prison, full of remorse and asking me to go and see him on visiting day. He and his friend had been caught dealing in stolen cars, apparently. I didn't answer it because by then I had been accepted for a job I'd seen advertised in *Teacher's World* – this one. I knew I'd never have any peace of mind there because he would always find me. So I abandoned the idea of a career in England.'

'Does he know that you've come back to India?' Wyndham asked her.

'No. I think I covered my tracks this time. I was becoming more experienced. I didn't leave a forwarding address in Slough, and took lodgings in London for the last couple of weeks while the negotiations were going on at the Redesdale London office – and I certainly told nobody else I was returning.'

'Do you think he would follow you if he knew?'

'Actually I don't. I have a feeling, from something he once let slip, that he'd been in some sort of trouble here too – and he always said he loathed India anyway.' They sat hand in hand for a long time in silence.

'You said you were leaving here,' Wyndham said at last. 'Why?'

'Purely on your account. I realized I was upsetting you – and I thought it so unfair for you to have to give *your* job up.' She turned to him. 'You won't, will you?'

'I won't,' he said softly. 'Not if you'll stay.'

'But there can be nothing ahead for us, my dear,' she said. 'And you'll be angry and frustrated – and – and I couldn't bear that. I've joked and teased you – but it's been tearing me apart.'

'I won't be angry again, my love,' Wyndham promised. 'Not now that I know.'

'I'd live with you,' she went on. 'And I wouldn't even think of it as a sin – if only we weren't in this goldfish bowl where everybody knows everybody else.'

'There *are* other places,' he said slowly.

'Not in India. It's funny, isn't it? A country bigger than the whole of Europe, but for the handful of Europeans – and to a lesser extent the Anglo-Indians – we might all be living in one parish in England.'

'I wasn't thinking of India – or England.'

'Where then?'

'A place I'd once thought of going to in the past. Australia.'

'Do you know anything about it?'

'No, except that it's said to be a land of opportunity – and it's certainly not parochial from what I've heard.'

'But how would we get there?'

He caught his breath sharply. 'Listen,' he said. 'It's coming to me even as we're talking. You have a passport?'

'Of course. I had to get one to go to England.'

'So have I. I got it over a year ago, when I was feeling a bit unsettled – before you came.' The excitement in his voice was rising. 'What's to stop us going there separately – and joining up? Mr and Mrs Tim Martin – who's to know? I've got some money – not a fortune, but enough for our fares and to keep us going until I find a job.' He pulled her to her feet and took her in his arms. 'Julia – Julia darling. That's the answer. It's there – plainly ahead of us. A fresh start, the whole slate wiped clean – because there are things in my life that I want to forget too, things that I must tell you about first – before you make a decision.'

'You really think – ' she began.

'I don't think – I *know*. We *can* – we haven't a soul in the world between us to be answerable to.' He pushed her back into her chair roughly. 'Sit down, blast you,' he said, and laughed. 'I can't talk to you like this – not sensibly, anyhow. Now listen: what notice would you have to give before leaving this job?'

'A full term – that's a little over three months.'

'Well, there you are again,' he said joyously. 'It clicks! It's made for us. My first contract ends in *exactly* three months. They've offered me a renewal but I haven't accepted yet. All I've got to say is that I want to enlarge my horizons – that I'm going to try my luck in South America or somewhere. In your case you can say you want to go back to England, to teach there for a bit. Neither of us mentions Australia – '

'I wouldn't know how to go about things – ' she said uncertainly, but his excitement was now communicating itself to her.

'You don't *have* to know.' He jumped to his feet and paced up and down the verandah. 'It's all coming to me. There are ships on the regular run to Australia – P & O and Orient – they call at Bombay and Colombo every month. Each of us goes to one place or the other – separately. We could even book on the same ship, and make it one of these beautiful shipboard romances we hear about – '

'I could tell you quite a lot about that,' she said ruefully.

'Shut up!' he said in mock anger, and pretended to hit her.

She said 'Don't!' sharply and drew back, then laughed shakily. 'Sorry,' she said. 'I could tell you quite a lot about the more violent side of married life too.'

'The *bastard*,' he swore.

She put her hand over his mouth. 'It's finished,' she whispered. 'Let's forget it – completely. It's dead, Tim darling – *dead*. Yes, whatever you say – I'll do it. I promise.'

He was kneeling by her chair. He took her hands in his and rubbed his face gently against her palms.

'And I promise too,' he murmured. 'I promise that you'll never regret this – not even in the deepest recesses of your explosive

Catholic conscience. Never, never, never. But I've got to clear something with you first. I told you – there's something in *my* past – '

'I don't want to hear it.' She shook her head firmly.

'I'm afraid you must, my darling.'

She laughed, and there was an edge of hysteria to it.

'Don't tell me you're married too?' she said.

'No.'

'Not that it would matter now. Please don't tell me, Tim. Your own words: "a fresh start – the whole slate wiped clean." I've done enough soul-baring for us both tonight.'

'What you have told me was not your own fault,' he said. 'Mine *was* – at least, some of it.'

'I still don't want to hear.'

'Julia, don't make it hard for me,' he pleaded. 'I've *got* to tell you this.'

'Tim – no – *please*.' She was crying again. 'Don't you realize? I feel as though I have been wading through slime – but just telling you has made me clean. Almost like coming out of the confessional. Please, *please* don't spoil it.'

'All right, my darling,' he said gently. 'As you wish. It's dead.' He drew her to her feet. 'I had better take you home now. It will be light soon.'

'Yes, there's my reputation to consider.' She smiled through her tears. 'The whole night together – without a chaperon. Make certain I haven't left anything in the bedroom.'

'You're like a chameleon, aren't you?' he said, amazed. 'One minute you've got all the sorrows of Satan on your shoulders – the next you're cracking jokes in extremely questionable taste.'

'Badly brought up,' she said.

'What – in a convent?'

'Yes – you ought to have been at some of our wild parties. Saints' Days mostly. We used to get as much as half an orange each sometimes.'

'Who from? The monks?'

'You'll roast in hell for that, you filthy-minded heretic.' Then she was serious again. 'I suppose we will have to be careful in future – if we don't want them to put two and two together when we both leave at the same time.'

'It would be better,' he said. 'But I'm damned if we're going to avoid each other for three whole months. We'll just have to be a little discreet about being at each other's bungalows at night – sans chaperons.'

'You've got them on your mind, haven't you?' They were walking down the path to the nullah before commencing the climb to the school bungalow. 'Where on earth can we go when we want to be together?'

'Picnics,' he said. 'Sundays are our own. That fishing pool of mine. It's only three miles away, but once there you might be in the middle of the Gobi desert.'

'Picnics it is,' she said happily, holding his arm with both her hands and laying her head on his shoulder. 'Do I get half an orange?'

'You'll get a clout under the ear, my girl,' he warned, then added, 'Just one thing, my darling, before we finally bury it. Does anybody at all over here know about this marriage?'

'Not as far as I know,' she answered. 'His family used to live in Bangalore, but I don't think there are any of them left – and in any case, he told me that he had been out of touch with them for years.'

'What was their name?' he asked.

'Philimore,' she told him.

Chapter 29

Paul said drily, 'Well, at least you know where he is now.'

'Where he was,' Wyndham corrected. 'She didn't say how long he'd got. He may be out by now.'

'But Julia of all people – to marry a swine like that.' Paul shook his head in bewilderment. 'I just can't understand it.'

'You'd have found it easier to if you'd heard it as she told it to me,' Wyndham said. 'Loneliness – the feeling of being completely cut off from all you have ever known. Don't forget, she had no experience whatsoever of the outside world. And he'd have been a totally different Philimore from the one we knew. At first, anyhow. Before reverting to type.'

'And even then you didn't tell her about yourself?'

'I tried to – believe me, I tried to. She just wouldn't listen – '

'Are you going to? Before you go away together, I mean?'

Wyndham stared into the distance. 'I wish I could make up my mind. Sometimes I think I must – that I'm absolutely bound to. Then I feel that it might undermine her present sense of security. She's been taken in once by a rogue – now she's met another.'

'You're surely not putting yourself into the same category as Philimore?'

'No, of course I'm not. But I realize that it would be a hell of a shock to her to find out that everything I've told her about myself is a tissue of lies, that I've been in jug too – and for something a bloody sight more serious than pinching cars.' He turned to Paul pleadingly. 'Paul, for God's sake advise me. Be perfectly honest. Should I tell her now – and risk her chance of happiness?'

'And your own,' said Paul.

'Never mind about mine. Just try to look at it from her point of view – or better still, completely impartially. You know me – you know her – you know the circumstances. Paul, *what do I do?*'

'I don't think there's any question about that,' Paul said. 'You keep your mouth closed – tight – certainly until you're

290

clear of this country and safely established somewhere else.'

'You really think that?'

'I'm positive of it. As you've just said yourself, it would completely cut the ground from under her feet to spring it on her now.'

'And later?'

'I'm not God, Charles. You'll just have to be guided by circumstances. If you feel at some time in the future that you've just got to tell her – then go ahead. Pick that time, of course – and remind her that you did try to tell her at this stage, but that she wouldn't let you. Also tell her that you asked my advice – and what my advice was – and I'll write and confirm it.'

Wyndham gave a deep sigh of relief and sat back in his chair and closed his eyes. 'Thanks,' he said. 'How easy it is to take advice – when it coincides with one's own views. But I promise you, Paul, that I'd have told her now if you'd thought that I should.'

'I'll be very sorry to see you both go,' Paul said. 'But it's by far the wisest thing to do. If that son of a bitch ever turned up – ' He shuddered.

'She doesn't think there's much danger of that,' said Wyndham. 'No, England's got him for keeps now.'

'Maybe,' said Paul thoughtfully, 'but – ' He trailed off.

'But what?'

'I was thinking of deportation. It's sometimes done, you know.'

'Oh my God,' said Wyndham, appalled. 'You don't think – ?'

'Don't let it worry you at this stage,' Paul went on, 'but it's best to face the possibility. I wish we knew how long he'd got. It's not always done, of course, particularly with first offenders – but if they've checked on his background and think he might be a nuisance in future, they *could* put him on a ship back to India when he came out.'

'At least he doesn't know she's come back,' Wyndham said hopefully.

'I don't want to be a Job's comforter,' Paul told him, 'but it didn't take him long to trace her each time in England. Here, he'd only have to go to Bangalore and make a few inquiries. How much longer have you both got?'

'Term finishes for her on the twenty-seventh of next month. She's going down to Bombay to try and book on the *Otranto*, which calls there on the way to Fremantle two weeks later.'

'And you?'

'My notice expires on the thirtieth of *this* month.'

'How did they take it?'

'Walderstein was very disappointed. He said that if I'd re-engaged they were going to send me to South Africa – to their training school on the Rand.'

'What a pity,' Paul said regretfully. 'The chance of a lifetime.'

'Not really. If I went to South Africa I'd eventually be sent back here. When we go it's got to be a complete break.'

'Of course, you're right. What are you doing about your booking?'

'I'm going down to Colombo to fix that up,' Wyndham said.

'Yes, that's wise,' Paul said.

'We're being very khabardari in the meantime. Quite polite if we run into each other, but nothing more.'

'It must be pretty trying.'

'It is – but we do meet occasionally.'

'Where?'

'At the mahseer pool – the Lunda Falls – places like that – on Sundays – but not too regularly.' He took a deep breath. 'God, will I be happy when the need for all this subterfuge is over!'

'It won't be long now,' said Paul. He looked at his watch and rose. 'Time I got back to the station.'

'I'll walk down with you. As a matter of fact – ' Wyndham hesitated.

'What?'

'I've been thinking – ever since Philimore swung back into the firmament. It might be wiser if you weren't seen around here between now and the time I leave.'

'Oh, nonsense,' Paul laughed. 'Let's keep a sense of proportion about things. He's not going to drop out of the blue after two years. I was only mentioning possibilities – '

'That's all I'm doing. Just suppose he did turn up – and recognized me – and turned me in, as he undoubtedly would, for spleen as well as the reward – questions would be asked. If *he* recognized me, why hadn't *you*?'

'I'd tell 'em I was a railway official, not any longer an Andaman screw. Come on. If we hurry we can have a cold beer at the station before my train arrives.'

Walderstein called him from the club verandah as he cycled past on his way home from the mine, and Wyndham repressed a start of annoyance and went across.

'Come and have a drink,' said the manager.

'I'm a bit damp and dusty,' Wyndham equivocated.

'So am I. That's when a drink is best, man. Come on. I want to talk to you.'

They walked round the deep verandah to the raw cement patio surrounding the newly finished swimming pool, and found a table at the far end.

'Well, what about it?' Walderstein asked.

'Beer, please,' said Wyndham.

'I know that, for God's sake.' Walderstein snapped, flicking a finger to a bearer. 'I'm talking about the job.'

'I'm sorry, sir, but my mind is made up,' Wyndham said. 'Anyhow, my notice is in.'

'It can be rescinded.'

Wyndham sighed. 'I must seem an ungrateful swab,' he said.

'No, just a blind one. Blind to your own interests.' He waved his hand towards the mine. 'There's not a fellow in your grade there, or the one above it, who wouldn't give his ears for the chance.'

'I know,' said Wyndham regretfully. 'That's what makes it so hard for me to turn it down.'

'You haven't got a job, not a definite job, to go to in – where was it again?'

'Rio de Janeiro.'

'Jesus! There's no gold there.'

'No, diamonds,' said Wyndham, who had been reading the subject up. 'It's not Rio itself – it's upcountry from there.'

'That's changing horses in midstream – just when you were getting your nose into the gold business. Why, man, why?'

'It would be very hard to explain, Mr Walderstein. You'd have had to be born in this country and never had the chance to get out, fully to understand.'

'But I'm giving you the chance.'

'A year in South Africa.'

'A wonderful country.'

'Yes, I know – which would make it all the harder to come back here.'

'You needn't come back here of necessity. You could stay on over there – go to West Africa – even Australia. We've got places all over the world where there's gold – or some prophet thinks there's going to be gold.'

Wyndham sipped his beer. 'Sorry, but I've burnt my boats now,' he said.

'It's that schoolmistress, isn't it?' said Walderstein, and Wyndham went hot and then cold.

'I don't see how Miss Ramsden comes into it,' he said stiffly.

'Christ! Don't get porcupiney about it, boy,' Walderstein said. 'I mean to say, you were pretty friendly once, and now it seems to be all off. The women have been talking about nothing else for weeks.'

'That's one of the reasons why I want to get away,' Wyndham said angrily. 'People can't mind their own business in a place like this.'

'Oh, come off it. Nobody meant any harm. They were all hoping for a romance.' He clicked his tongue appreciatively. 'Bloody pretty girl that. She's quitting too, you know – more's the pity.'

'I had heard,' Wyndham said noncommittally. 'But her going has nothing whatsoever to do with mine. I understand she's going to England.'

'That's right. She's only been out a few months. Some of you youngsters don't know which side your bread's buttered.' He shook his head sadly. 'What's the real trouble? Colour?'

'What the hell do you mean by that?' Wyndham demanded.

'Hey! Hey! Hey! Don't jump down my throat. I know there's a touch in her, and none in you,' Walderstein said. 'I'm afraid we're a bit preoccupied with that sort of thing in South Africa. What I mean to say is, if that *is* the reason you're both leaving, you don't *have* to go to Jo'burg. You can stay on here – '

'What *I* mean to say, Mr Walderstein, is that you can mind your own bloody business,' said Wyndham, getting up from the table.

'Fine,' said Walderstein. 'I'm minding it. The offer's withdrawn. You can take yourself off to Rio de Whatsis or Timbuctoo for all I care. Good day to you, Mister Bloody Martin.'

Wyndham walked away shaking with rage, aware of eyes on him from other tables. The rage was with himself. He had drawn the attention of the whole compound now. Why the hell hadn't he just laughed it off? Schoolmistress from the Kolar Gold Fields? You don't take a sandwich to a banquet! He'd heard there was some pretty potent goods in Rio. That's why he was going there – and a broad wink. The dirty-minded old bastard would have understood that. But he knew he couldn't make that sort of joke, even to himself. Not about Julia.

He stood on the verandah later that evening and looked across the dark nullah at Julia's bungalow. The light was on in her bedroom. She would be packing, he thought, because she was catching the early morning train to Bangalore in order to connect with the Bombay Mail. A two-day journey there, the same back, and two days to do some shopping. Six days away – then, when she returned, he would go off to Colombo. That would take a little longer. Three days each way, and, because of awkward train and ferry connections, four days there. Sixteen days before they were both back here again – and then, thank God, only a month left before she was free. The school was closed for the summer holidays, but her relief, to whom she had to hand over formally, would not be arriving until just before the new term started. He himself would be finishing at the end of this present week, but there had been a gentlemen's agreement that he would see his successor comfortably settled in before leaving the station. He wondered if the row with Walderstein altered that. Would he be expected now to take his departure on the last day of the month? He hoped so. It would make things easier in so far as Somari was concerned. He hadn't told him yet. It was going to be difficult. Paul was going to give him a job – but the little man would undoubtedly take it badly. He wished they could take him with them, but it was just not possible. Asiatic immigration was forbidden by the Australian government.

Julia moved across a lighted window, and he was conscious of an irresistible desire to see her once more before she left. This artificial separation of the last two months had been an unbearable strain upon them both – relieved only by a few magical hours together in the jungle on Sundays. He wondered if it had all been necessary. Was he being too cautious? Julia sometimes thought he was – but then she was unaware of the coincidence that made Philimore an even more deadly threat to him than to herself. No, he had, for once, been right. This elaborate covering of their trails was now doubly necessary, if they were to have real peace of mind in the future.

But he still had to see her, if only for a few moments.

He climbed down into the nullah and jumped the narrow stream at the bottom, and then walked up the path the other side. He could hear her singing softly to herself as he slipped into the dark garden. She stopped suddenly as he whistled to her, and it was some little time before she came to the open window and looked out. She was as jumpy as a cat, poor kid, he realized, and he was angry with himself for startling her.

'Only me, you chump,' he said, and she laughed happily.

'No chaperon?' she said. 'Aren't you risking your reputation?'

'Come on out of the light,' he told her. 'I can always feel those damned nurses straining their eyes from their quarters across there.'

'They and their boy-friends have got far too much on their minds dodging the matron to bother about us.' She crossed the verandah and jumped down into his arms and clung to him for a long minute in silence.

'Oh, I'm glad you came,' she said at last. 'I was *willing* you to come. The thought of going to the station in the morning without seeing you was horrible.'

'Frightened?' he asked.

'Good Lord no. There's nothing to be frightened of. It was just that this would be the first time we were apart since we met.'

His arms tightened about her. 'It won't be long now,' he promised. 'Be careful.'

'Of what?'

'Everything – train thieves – evil buggers in Bombay who'll try and whip you off to Grant Road.'

'Why Grant Road?'

'That's where they put young women in cages.'

'Why?'

'To attract young men – and old men.'

'Attract them to what?'

'To the knocking shops, you silly little twit.'

'What are knocking shops?'

'Oh God,' he groaned. 'Forget it.'

'Stop worrying about me and I will. You don't realize that I'm an experienced traveller. I've been to Bombay twice – once going, once coming back – and to Portsmouth and London and Reading and Slough. *You're* the country boy who'll have to be careful.'

'Cheeky little bitch,' he growled. 'All right, darling – I'll go now. I only wanted to see you, and to touch you – and to know it wasn't all a dream. Look after yourself. Break the journey in Bangalore on the way back next Thursday. I'll be waiting at Paul's place.'

'Oh, lovely!' she said. 'I didn't think you'd be able to get away.'

'Things have altered a bit. I might be finishing at the end of this week now,' he told her, and broke away before she could question him further. 'Au revoir, my sweet.' He kissed her, spun her round and pushed her gently. 'Go and finish your packing.'

He turned and looked back at her as he climbed the fence on to the path. She was standing outlined darkly against the lighted window. She waved.

He stood on the verandah again next morning and watched the tonga that was taking her to the station jingle down the road and out through the compound gate, and knew again the old feeling of utter aloneness that had been absent for the last two years. He would be sorry to leave this place that had given him the only security he had ever known. Even sorrier now, after the row with old Walderstein. Should he go and apologize? – make his peace? Or were things best left as they were? He'd think about it later.

Somari arrived up from the servants' lines. 'I see Julie miss-sahib going to station, sahib,' he said. 'Why you not go to see her off?'

'I didn't wake up in time,' Wyndham said.

'You and Julie miss-sahib have fight?' Somari asked. 'You don't go there for long time.'

'Get me some breakfast,' Wyndham said shortly. 'I'm going to the office early.'

'Sure. What you fight about?'

'Breakfast!' Wyndham shouted. 'And don't ask so many questions.'

'Cor fuggin 'ell,' said Somari, unabashed. 'Got bloody liver on this morning, eh?'

'Sorry, Somari,' Wyndham grinned. 'Yes, just little bit of a fight. When she comes back maybe we'll fix it all up again.'

Chapter 30

Walderstein shook hands and said, 'Oh, hell, man – forget it. Everybody gets a bit strung up before the monsoon breaks.' There was a long rumble of thunder far to the south. 'Looks like we haven't got long to wait for it now, though,' he went on. 'When will you be off?'

'Not for a few days,' Wyndham told him. 'Unless, of course, somebody wants my bungalow right away.'

'Take your time,' the manager said. 'I think they're planning a farewell party for you at the club, anyhow.'

'So I heard. That being the case, I'll run down to Madras and say a few goodbyes and do some shopping and then come back and collect my stuff.' They walked out on to the verandah of the office block as the first tentative drops pattered on the tin roof. It was barely five o'clock but the black, rain-swollen clouds that had been banking up all afternoon were hiding the setting sun and it was already dark. The sweet, heavy scent of rain on baked earth came to them, and Wyndham took a deep breath, 'Beautiful, isn't it?' he said.

'Just so as it doesn't flood the lower workings again, and wash away any more bridges,' said the practical Walderstein. 'You're not riding that bike of yours home, are you? You'll get soaked.'

'I don't mind that in the least,' Wyndham said. 'It's good for prickly heat, they say. Good night, sir. I won't say goodbye yet, then.'

The rain came down in earnest as he pedalled along the road to the compound, cascading down the hillside and flooding the gutters and culverts, but he was enjoying it. Full circle, he thought. It was in weather like this that he had arrived here. He took his sodden topee off and turned his face up into the downpour, then suddenly sobered. Yes, weather like this – and a bridge had carried away – as the damned things did so often in the early floods. And Julia was coming in on the midnight train from Bangalore. He had had a letter from her that morning: '. . . a stupid box-up. We should have made certain before I left. Next month's boat misses Bombay and goes straight to Colombo, and they couldn't give me a reservation until they had checked – and that, believe it or not, will take over a week. I'm not going to wait – Bombay is horrible just before the rains break. Everybody and everything waiting with bated breath. I'll come back on tomorrow's train, so I'll be hard on the heels of this letter. Don't be angry with me, darling, because I'm missing you terribly. Even just seeing you across the nullah is better than nothing . . .'

She'd be arriving on the midnight train from Bangalore, he reflected uneasily. He wished he could get in touch with Paul to tell him to meet her there and to break her journey with them overnight – and he would risk going over in the morning. But Paul would have left the office by now – and few people had private telephones in their bungalows in this benighted country. But he was being stupid. The forty-five-mile stretch of railway between here and Bangalore crossed no major rivers. He shrugged his fears off and turned into the compound gate. The chowkidar was cowering in his shelter and didn't come out to give his customary quasi-military salute. Wyndham smiled. It was funny how they gasped for rain for nearly nine months each year, yet ran for cover when it arrived.

The thunder was crashing immediately overhead now. It was that that scared the locals more than the rain itself.

He saw the car parked at the fork of the path, momentarily in a blindingly brilliant flash of lightning. Some visitor who had strayed off the drive up to the main residential area, he thought, and wondered if they were still inside. He dismounted and waded across to it, intending, hospitably, to invite whoever it was up to the bungalow until the worst of the storm had passed He opened the door and received an additional deluge from the sagging canvas hood as he bent forward to look inside. But it was empty, so he went on up the path.

The lights were on in the bungalow but Somari didn't answer his shout as he stumped up on to the verandah, shaking himself like a dog coming out of a pond, then, as he looked across the nullah and saw the lights of Julia's bungalow dimly through the curtain of rain, he remembered that he had told him to go over in the evening and open up and get in groceries, milk and bread, because she had given her servant a few days' holiday while she was away.

He dragged off his soaked shirt and shorts and towelled himself vigorously. The soft rainwater felt so good on his skin in contrast to the heavily chlorinated domestic supply that he decided to skip a shower. He put on a bathrobe and helped himself to a rare whisky, then sat on the verandah and watched the lightning. The thunder was now keeping up a continuous drumfire, and he did not hear Somari's approach until he came up the verandah steps, his white clothes plastered to him. 'Bloody bastard!' he shrieked over the noise.

'Don't be silly,' Wyndham shouted back. 'Lovely rain.'

'Not rain,' Somari said, his mouth close to Wyndham's ear. 'Bloody sahib over Julie-miss-sahib's bungalow – think I bloody Hindu – call me bearer – tell me get him beer. I say no beer – he call me bloody fool and say get whisky – '

Wyndham felt himself go cold all over.

'What sahib?' he yelled.

'Sahib come in motor from Madras side – ask for Julie miss-sahib. I say she not come till midnight train – he say he wait – '

'Have you see him before?'

'No – don't want to see him again – '

'What does he look like?'

'Bloody awful – not pukkha sahib – got coffee in the milk – sunnervabitch – '

There was a brief lull in the thunder. Somari went through the bungalow picking up discarded clothes, still fulminating, but Wyndham no longer heard him.

He knew. He knew with a certainty that allowed no room for the most tenuous shred of doubt. The dread that had never really left him, waking or sleeping, over the years had now crystallized into stark reality. There had been times when he had forced himself to face this possibility. What would he do if he came face to face with Philimore? He had answered the question positively. He just knew that he would never surrender quietly and allow himself to be taken back to face a trial that could only end one morning in the prison yard at Port Blair. He would take matters into his own hands before that happened, he told himself. He could, of course, slip away now and avoid a confrontation – but that would solve nothing. It would only be delaying the inevitable. This evil thing could not be shaken off. Even if he ran again, the danger to Julia remained – and that was now more important than anything they could do to him. No, it had to be finished. Here and now. Tonight.

But Julia had to be kept away. This must not touch her – or Paul – or Somari. This was for him alone.

He got up and went through to Somari as the obvious solution came to him – and he felt strangely calm.

He said, 'I don't want Julie miss-sahib to come on the train from Bangalore tonight, Somari.'

'All right. You go over and stop her. Go to Paul sahib's place. Maybe bloody rain stop in morning.' He looked at the clock. 'You got plenty of time. Seven o'clock train from here get into Bangalore half-past eight. Bombay Mail get in one hour later.'

'No, I've got work to do here. I want you to go,' Wyndham said.

'All right, sahib,' Somari said cheerfully. 'But what about that feller in miss-sahib's bungalow? He might go pinch something. Proper bad-looking bugger.'

'Don't worry about him. I'll go and get rid of him.'

'What do you think he want with Julie miss-sahib?'

'Oh, maybe he wants to sell her something for school – books, paper, pens – '

'Kabariwala – damn travelling salesman?' Somari said contemptuously. 'Yes, sod look like that. "*Bearer* – get me beer – get me whisky – bloody fool." ' He spat.

Wyndham laughed. It was strained and cracked in his own ears, but Somari appeared not to notice it. 'Don't worry about him,' he said. 'Oh, and Somari – don't say anything to the miss-sahib about him. She wouldn't like to think there was some stranger in her bungalow. Tell Paul sahib I'll telephone him in the office in the morning.'

'All right, sahib. What train you want us to come back on tomorrow?'

'I'll tell Paul sahib when I call. Maybe I might come over myself – then we'll all come back together. You better hurry now. Take my bicycle to the station.'

'No fear – go quicker on feet in this bloody rain.'

'Take some money from the desk,' Wyndham said, and went through to his bedroom.

'Cold meat in icebox, sahib, and salad and cheese,' Somari called, and then the thunder started again.

Through the window he watched the white figure going down the path, intermittently illuminated by the lightning, then he turned away and rescued his wet clothes from the laundry basket. He pulled them on again and unlocked a drawer in the dresser and took out his revolver. It was a Webley .38 he had bought on impulse a year ago from somebody who was going back to England, together with a dozen or so rounds, and he had fired it only once or twice at tin cans down by the mahseer pool, but his army training had impelled him to keep it cleaned and oiled. He 'broke' it, and loaded all six chambers, then put it in the front of his shirt and went out slowly.

The thunder was in full blast again, and the rain was coming down in a solid vertical sheet. He slid down the streaming wall of the nullah, and waded waistdeep across the normally dry stream-bed at the bottom, and commenced the climb the other side. He wondered how he would react if he found a total stranger in the bungalow – and then pushed the thought away from him. It was too late now for wishful thinking.

He stopped at the top of the path. He could see a single light in her living-room, and knew from its position that it was the reading lamp by her big comfortable sofa, and the thought of this man probably stretched out at his ease on it coldly enraged him. He turned back and looked across towards his own bungalow, but the rain was blotting out the light he could normally have seen from here. He crossed the garden, squelching through liquid mud and went up on to the verandah. The french windows of the living-room were open, and he could see the top of a man's head making an indentation in a cushion. The thunder had ceased again, but the rain was drumming on the roof, and the man didn't hear him when he said, 'Good evening,' so Wyndham moved round into his view. He sat up then, and all doubt, and the microcosm of hope that had persisted, now vanished.

Philimore said, 'Oh, hello. I'm afraid Miss Ramsden's not here. I'm waiting for her.'

'My servant told me that you were here,' Wyndham said. 'She won't be back until tomorrow.'

'Damn,' said Philimore. 'I've come up specially to see her.'

'I'll tell her you called. What name shall I say?' Wyndham said.

'No need,' Philimore grunted. 'I'm not driving back in this weather tonight.' He was peering closely at Wyndham. 'I think we've met somewhere, haven't we?'

'Have we?' said Wyndham.

'I don't know . . .' He screwed up his face in puzzlement. 'Your face is kind of familiar – voice too. You're from Home, aren't you?'

'Yes.'

'Could have been back there. I've just returned to this bloody place myself. When did you come out?'

'Fairly recently.'

'Portsmouth? Southampton?'

'I've never been to either,' said Wyndham. 'If you're staying then, I can offer you a bed over in my bungalow.'

Philimore grinned. 'Thanks, but not if it means getting as wet as you are now – ' He peered closer. 'I *have* seen you – *and* heard you. I never forget a face or a voice.'

'I can give you some dry clothes – ' Wyndham began.

'Don't worry. Miss Ramsden and I are by way of being relatives. She won't mind my bunking down here,' Philimore said, and shook his head in exasperation. 'Damn it, I *have* seen you. Now where – ?'

'Yes, you've seen me, Philimore,' said Wyndham wearily. 'Just get up on your feet and walk ahead of me through that window.' He had the revolver in his hand.

'Oh, my Christ – Sirdar,' whispered Philimore. 'Look, just forget it. I've never seen you in my life before – '

'Forget it for how long? Until you can reach the nearest police station?' Wyndham asked.

Philimore swallowed hard and moistened his dry lips. 'You don't need to worry about that,' he said. 'Those days are past. I've had a bit of trouble myself since then.' His face cracked into a wobbling smile. 'Can you imagine that? The biter bit, eh? I've been inside – in Blighty. No, old cock – I'm not hollering copper on anybody.' He was on his feet now, and his eyes were darting round the room like those of a cornered animal searching for a bolt-hole. 'Put that gun away, for Christ's sake. There's no need for that. Look, Sirdar, I've got a car here. Just let me get into it and you'll never see or hear from me again – '

Wyndham nodded slowly. 'I'd want some pretty strong guarantees on that,' he said. 'Come over to my bungalow and we'll talk about it.'

'Yes, but that gun – put it down – leave it here somewhere – it's giving me the bloody willies – '

Wyndham pushed it back into the front of his shirt. 'It needn't,' he said. 'Walk ahead of me – through the gate and down the path into the nullah.' He leaned across and switched the lamp out, then pushed Philimore in the small of his back. 'Come on – move.' The thunder was rumbling again and the room was an alternating kaleidoscope of pitch darkness and blinding whiteness as the lightning flashed.

Philimore was babbling. 'Sirdar – listen to me – Sirdar – people know I'm here – they know I've come across to see my wife – I mean – if anything happened to me – if I didn't turn up tomorrow – there'd be questions and – '

'*Move!*' snarled Wyndham, and pushed harder. Philimore ran forward blunderingly, through the window and over the edge of the verandah. He continued on until the garden fence brought him up sharply, then he struggled over it. Wyndham was a short two paces behind him when they reached the top of the path. He strained forward until the muzzle of the revolver was hard up against the spine of the other. He fired, and Philimore stopped running and appeared to stiffen, then, as his knees slowly gave way beneath him, Wyndham pressed the trigger twice again, and Philimore jerked forward and fell flat on his face in the liquid mud of the path.

He felt no emotion other than a slight easing of the previous tension as he hoisted the body across his shoulder. It was almost as if he were watching somebody else – somebody who was executing a complicated manœuvre step by step. The first had been negotiated without a hitch. That he was going to kill Philimore had never been for one moment in doubt – but he had to do it outside – away from her house and garden – somewhere where the blood would not show. Step two: he had to get him away from the compound altogether. The means were there ahead of him – the car. He slid down the path. The stream was higher now – well above his waist – and he almost dropped the body as he lost his footing in the middle. But now he was across. He wondered if he was leaving a blood trail. It didn't matter really – there'd be no sign of it in the morning after a night of this rain.

He blundered up against the car before he saw it. It was an old and battered Morris Cowley, and he had difficulty in getting Philimore through the narrow door into the cramped rear. He got into the driver's seat, praying that the plugs and leads were not soaked, then he saw that the prudent Philimore had carefully draped a waterproof sheet over the bonnet. Then he had to search the other's pockets for the ignition key, which necessitated dragging him out of the car again. But finally, he managed it, and he listened with satisfaction to the asthmatic roar of the ancient engine. He didn't risk headlights at this stage. He backed and filled three or four times and finally got the car pointing down the path again. He drove slowly on to the compound road using his parking lights only. The chowkidar was still sheltering in his shed, and he didn't acknowledge Wyndham's wave through the misty talc side curtains as he drove out on to the main road.

He turned left and switched on his headlights. This was the way he would be going if he were driving down to Madras.

The surface of the tarmac road was covered with a thick layer of mud washed down from the hillside round which it wound, and the car slipped and slid, and sometimes the wheels failed to make traction, but he reached his objective in about fifteen minutes. Lunda Falls – just five miles from the compound. The rain was bucketing down even heavier now and he almost missed the white rails of the bridge that crossed the deep gorge the river ran through as it emerged from the hills on his left. He switched the lights off and got out, and the roar of the river deafened him. He peered down at it, and as the lightning flashed he could see that the surface was almost up to the decking of the bridge, where normally it was a good thirty feet below it.

He went back to the car and opened the rear door and hauled the body out and carried it in a fireman's lift back to the railing – heaved, balanced, then heaved again – and a lightning flash

306

coincided with it hitting the raging white surface and disappearing. Step three completed successfully.

He returned to the car and drove it off the road on to the shoulder, and there met his first real difficulty when he bogged down in the mud, but eventually by dint of reversing and driving forward in violent jerks, and finally laying down the waterproof sheet that had covered the bonnet, he got it up to the guard rail of the bridge. He manœuvred it diagonally across the roadway, put it into first gear, declutched and revved the engine to its maximum then drove straight at the edge, holding the course until the last split inch before jumping clear. Like the body before it, the ancient car just vanished. He threw the waterproof sheet after it, and stood for a moment taking deep draughts of air down into his heaving lungs. Step four accomplished.

The first fury of the storm abated somewhat as he trudged back, and the rain settled into a steady rather than a violent downpour. He left the road short of the compound and circled round the perimeter fence to a point near his own bungalow, then he climbed through the wire. Dawn was breaking as he retraced his steps to where the car had been parked, and then across the nullah and up to Julia's bungalow. There were no traces left of the events of the night – not outside. He went into the bungalow. Here there were some muddy footprints and a scattering of cigarette ends in the living-room. He spent some time meticulously tidying the place and then came away. Last step completed.

He showered and then washed the clothes he had been wearing and made himself some coffee, and stood on the verandah drinking it. The sky above was clear and cloudless, but the surrounding jungle was steaming in the rising heat of the morning. The monsoon was following its invariable pattern. The clouds would start to gather again towards noon, and the daily storm would break in the evening, but with decreasing violence over the next month. Then there would be a lull for some days until it swung completely round and came back on its gentler reciprocal course for a further three or four weeks and finally petered out, to leave the sub-continent to parch for another nine months.

Up to this point he had been concentrating on each step as he essayed it, and not speculating further, but now he found himself reviewing the probable course of events. The body would undoubtedly be carried downriver for miles, to emerge, if it ever did, a battered, unrecognizable piece of the tragic flotsam that the monsoon threw up each year all over India, picked clean by vultures and mugger on some sandbank between here and the coast. In his own case the death-roll of the accident had been estimated at nearly two hundred – but less than fifty bodies had been recovered, of which no more than a dozen had been positively identified. The car? That, of course, would not be carried as far, and it would pretty certainly be found when the river dried up eventually, but that would not be before three months or so, and its value as a clue would then be negligible. In fact it would point to a logical conclusion – that of a motorist blinded by the storm and missing the approach to the bridge. Would there be a search for Philimore in the meantime? That was a moot point. He had said that people knew where he had gone last night and that he was expected back – but that had sounded like the desperate invention of a badly frightened man. By the very nature of things, Philimore would not have advertised his return too widely. He had left under a cloud and had been in prison since. Why had he come back at all? Possibly deported as an undesirable, as Paul had suggested. Tracing Julia would have presented little difficulty. He no doubt knew her whereabouts even before leaving England – and if he hadn't it wouldn't have taken him long to find out in Bangalore, which Julia visited frequently. But had he been to Bangalore? If he had, surely Paul would have known about it? It would have been common knowledge in that tight community within a matter of hours – and he'd certainly have warned Wyndham by telephone immediately. He said that he'd come by car from Madras. That seemed more likely. Was the car bought or hired? Probably the latter – in which case the hirers would start making inquiries before along, although it would avail them little at the moment.

Well, the first thing was to talk to Paul. He packed a change of clothes, pyjamas and toilet things in a case and walked down to the station and called Paul's office from the telephone booth in the refreshment room.

'Hello, old boy,' Paul said brightly. 'Not washed out? God! Didn't it come down? No damage on the line, thank the Lord –

but I think it was a good idea to keep Julia here. She and Tina were up till all hours talking like mynahs.'

'How is everything?' Wyndham asked.

'Fine. She's very guilty about the booking – but it wasn't her fault.'

'No other news?' Wyndham asked casually.

'About what?'

'Oh, anything at all – like the papers say – "Arrivals and Departures – " '

' "Births, Marriages and Deaths",' laughed Paul. 'Who the hell do you think *I* am? The social editress of the *Bangalore Times*? Why the sudden interest in tea-table chit-chat?' There was a pause. 'Oh, I get you now. Yes, she says she'll either go back to Bombay or down to Colombo after you've fixed yours – if that's what you mean.'

'That's what I did mean,' said Wyndham. 'Good. Then I'll get the next train over and we'll talk about it.'

'Splendid. We'll expect you for tiffin, then. So long.'

Wyndham felt a wave of relief. So obviously they didn't know of Philimore's return. Then they'll never know, he swore to himself. This was one burden he expected nobody to share. This was his responsibility alone.

Now the slate was, in truth, wiped clean – and the way ahead would be safe.

Chapter 31

His business was completed quickly on the first morning in Colombo. A perfunctory glance at his passport, and the pleasant young man at the passenger counter was extolling the merits of a single-berth cabin on B Deck.

'Any other cabins vacant?' Wyndham asked casually.

'Oh yes, plenty at this time of the year. But I can assure you that this one is very pleasant, Mr Martin,' the young man said.

'A friend of mine might be booking in Bombay,' Wyndham told him. 'No chance of his being crowded out, I hope?'

'Not the slightest. But you could pencil one in for him if you wish – ' and for a moment Wyndham was tempted to do so, but he decided against it. No, he'd stick to their elaborate plan to the very end. He changed some Indian rupees into Ceylonese money and collected his ticket. It had all been so very easy.

He spent the rest of the day seeing the usual tourist sights without particular interest: the Cinnamon Gardens, the Buddhist Temple and the museum, and he bought Julia a moonstone ring, which the Singhalese jeweller swore was a star sapphire, then the afternoon monsoon rain, as heavy here as across the narrow strait in India, drove him back to the discomfort of the modest hotel he had booked into.

Bored and restless at the prospect of three further heel-kicking days here before he could catch the twice-weekly train the other side, back to Bangalore, he took the advice of a garishly-coloured tourist poster and went out to Mount Lavinia next morning. This was better, although the white, palm-fringed beach put him strongly in mind of the long trek to Madras. He stayed at a small hotel run by a Dutch Eurasian, and swam and basked in the sun during breaks in the weather, and on the fourth day he went thankfully back to Adam's Bridge and crossed on the ferry.

Three days of it now, he thought wryly – and four changes along the winding metre-gauge jungle railway. He wished now that he had taken Paul's advice and returned on the more direct east coast line, but that would have entailed a further day's delay waiting in Madras for a connection to Bangalore. This way meant that he would go straight there, albeit more slowly and less comfortably. But Julia would be there – and they would have two days together with Paul before she went off again to Bombay. There must be no slip-up this time.

The train was twelve hours late arriving in Pelaghat, the last change before the final fifty-mile stretch to Bangalore. The rain, which had kept off for most of the two previous days, was now slashing down again and the miserable little wayside station was dark and deserted, and there was no connecting train waiting at the opposite platform. A figure came running from the shadows as he hauled his suitcase and bedding-roll from the compartment and grabbed them from him, and Wyndham swore irritably, because he could feel the familiar shivers of an attack of malaria coming on.

'Quick, sahib,' Somari said urgently. 'Along to end of platform and down on to line.'

'What the hell are you doing here?' Wyndham asked, amazed.

'Never mind now, sahib,' Somari gabbled, setting off into the darkness. 'Paul sahib here – '

'But what's going on?' Wyndham demanded angrily, but Somari had already vanished. He walked down the ramp at the end and somebody took him by the arm.

Paul said, 'Sorry about this. It may be all right, but I had to warn you.'

'About what?'

'Come on – out of this damned rain.' They stumbled over the tracks and Wyndham felt himself being pushed into a small shed beside the line.

'The police want to see you,' Paul said without preamble.

'What for?' Wyndham asked, completely without expression.

'Better let me tell it in sequence,' Paul said, and went on. 'They fished somebody out of the river a few miles below Lunda Falls four days ago. An Englishman called Mayhew.'

'Called *what*?'

'Mayhew. He'd hired a car in Madras and shown an English driving licence. They've recovered the car, but the chap himself was pretty well unrecognizable – smashed up on the rocks, and the mud turtles had had a go at him, but his wallet was still on him. Just the licence and some money – nothing else.'

'But how do I come into it?'

'Let me finish. He'd been to the compound. The chowkidar saw him arrive the night the rains broke, and leave again some hours later.'

'But why do they want to see *me*?' Wyndham demanded again.

'I'm trying to *tell* you,' Paul said urgently. 'Shut up, for Christ's sake and let me. They want to know who he'd been to see. They've interviewed everybody who was known to be there that night and have drawn a blank. That just leaves you unaccounted for.'

Wyndham felt the faintest glimmer of hope. 'Well, he certainly didn't come to see me,' he said flatly. 'I don't know anybody by that name.'

'That feller who come to Julie miss-sahib – ' Somari broke in.

'Have you told anybody about that?' Wyndham spun round and caught him by the arm.

'Only Paul sahib,' Somari said. 'I not bloody fool.'

'Well, *don't*.' He turned back to Paul. 'Have they been questioning Julia?'

'Only a routine check. They know she wasn't there, and they appear to be quite satisfied.'

Wyndham heaved a sigh of relief. 'That's all that matters,' he said. 'What the hell's the fuss about? People have been known to drive into rivers before.'

'Yes, but this chap had three bullets in him,' Paul said quietly. 'There was enough of him left for them to be able to find that out.'

Wyndham was silent for a long time, then he said, more to himself than to the others, 'Why was he calling himself Mayhew, I wonder?'

'It was – ?' Paul began, then broke off and answered himself. 'I guessed as much.'

'So did I,' Wyndham said wearily. 'I knew as soon as Somari told me he was waiting there.'

'He recognized you?'

'Yes. Not immediately, but it was inevitable.'

'Where did it happen?'

'Not in her bungalow. I went back in the morning and made

312

certain that I hadn't left any signs.' He laughed drily. 'Me and Eugene Aram. We don't seem to have much luck, do we? I'll tell them that he had heard a whisper somewhere that I was still alive and working in Kolar, and he came to check.'

'You'll tell them nothing,' Paul said. 'You're going away with Somari – tonight.' He reached through the darkness and took Wyndham's arm. 'You've done it before. You can do it again.'

Wyndham shook his head. 'I'm not running again,' he said. 'I've had enough of that. There's nowhere to run to – not any more.'

Somari said, 'Good place, sahib – good people – not far from here. All Brothers, same like before. No bugger ever going to find you if you don't want them.'

'You keep out of it, Somari,' Wyndham said firmly. 'Right out of it – and you, Paul. Go back. I'll come in later.'

'How the hell I keep out of it now?' Somari asked him. 'Already they ask me questions: "Where the sahib? Where he go? *When* he go? Bloody black bastard liar." Kick up the arse, smack over ear'ole. Oh, no, I don't go back for more of that.'

'There won't be any more, Somari,' Wyndham said gently. 'Not once they've got me.'

'They don't get you, sahib.' Somari was weeping. 'They don't – they *don't* – not if you come with me.'

'Listen to me,' Paul broke in sharply. 'You'll have to make your own decision, but for God's sake don't make it blindly. Don't you realize that they haven't connected Mayhew and Philimore yet?'

'What difference does that make?' Wyndham asked. 'They damned soon will.'

'But *will* they? Don't you see? Philimore was obviously on the run himself from something – and covering his tracks.' He shuddered. 'I saw him when they brought him to the mortuary. Just a battered lump of flesh with half a jacket still clinging to it – you could hardly recognize it as a man.'

'Then how did they know he'd been shot?'

'You can't tell these police pathologists much about gunshot wounds. They spotted that immediately.'

'It won't take them long,' Wyndham said obstinately. 'They'll trace him back to the port of entry. It doesn't matter what name he was using.'

'Balls.' Paul shook him. 'Think, man, think. Slipping *into* this country is easy enough – you know that yourself. It's getting out that's difficult. Now listen to me – please, Charles – listen to me. The railway police office is next to mine. They've been talking about nothing else for the last four days. If there had been the slightest hint that Mayhew and Philimore were the same man I'd have heard it. But there hasn't been. But if you give yourself up and your fingerprints are checked, as they will be as a matter of routine, and you're identified as Wyndham, then they're going to put two and two together damn quick. Then they *will* trace back – trace right back to England – and Julia's marriage will come out – '

'Oh, Christ,' Wyndham groaned. 'I hadn't thought of that.'

'I know you hadn't,' Paul said. 'And there's something else you hadn't thought of. If they find out that you are Wyndham they're going to start asking *me* a few questions also. Why hadn't *I* recognized you and reported it? You mentioned that possibility yourself once, didn't you?'

Wyndham broke another long silence. 'Where's Julia now?' he asked.

'With Tina.'

'How is she taking it?'

'Very well, all things considered. She gave me a message for you.'

'What?'

'A typical bit of feminine logic. She knows you didn't do it – but if you did, she knows why – and that whatever happens she'll always be waiting.'

'For what?' Wyndham asked bitterly. 'What the hell can there possibly be ahead of us now?'

'There's always hope, Charles,' Paul said. 'Just as long as you don't walk in like a lamb to the slaughter.'

'I won't do that,' Wyndham promised, and Somari chattered with relief. 'But she said that if I did it, she knew why? You mean she guessed that it was Philimore?'

'Not guessed – but the possibility came to us both, immediately.'

'I see.' Wyndham nodded slowly. 'All right then, I'll do as you want – go with Somari.'

'Bloody good place, sahib – nice people – coppers never find it in ten thousand bloody years,' Somari said eagerly.

'But tell her that she must leave this place,' Wyndham went on. 'Just wait for the dust to settle and then go to England – as she has told people she intended to do. Not Australia. They're going to find out before long, if they haven't already, that I booked a passage in Colombo. Thank God she wasn't able to. That would have roused suspicion immediately if they'd found we were both going out on the same ship.'

'She said she was going to stay here,' Paul said uncertainly.

'She mustn't,' said Wyndham quickly. 'You've got to persuade her, Paul. Tell her we can always keep in touch through you.'

'You can,' said Paul. 'I've shown Somari a place just up the line from here where you can pick up a letter and leave one – '

'No,' said Wyndham firmly. 'There must be no more contact. You've taken a hell of a risk coming down tonight.'

'No risk,' Paul assured him. 'This is part of my area. I inspect the permanent way at least twice a month – oftener in the monsoon.'

Somari was looking out of the door. 'Going to be light soon, sahib,' he said. 'We better be going.'

'Yes, on your way, old boy,' Paul said gently. 'I'll be down in a couple of weeks again, with any news that crops up. Send her a letter then. Any messages now?'

'Tell her – ' began Wyndham, but couldn't go on. He took the moonstone from his pocket and thrust it into Paul's hand. 'Give her that,' he mumbled, and followed Somari out into the darkness.

Paul called after them softly, 'There's always hope – *always*.'

The rain had eased to a soft drizzle and the sky was lightening to the east. Somari, after the familiar brief tussle, seized the suitcase and bedding roll and balanced them on his head, and then set off at a brisk half-trot down the narrow footway beside the tracks.

'Two miles along railway first, sahib,' he said cheerfully, 'then we slide down and go into jungle. *Plenty* jungle, sahib. Bloody miles and miles and miles. Nobody ever come here – nobody except Mundavers.'

'What are Mundavers?' Wyndham forced himself to ask. Somari hated silence.

'Oh, nice people – funny buggers. All Brothers,' Somari chattered happily. 'Go rob trains all time. Take off clothes, rub on cheetah fat. Get up on roof then climb down through windows when train going like hell – just like monkey. Pinch everything inside carriage when sahibs and memsahibs asleep – jump off train.' He kept it up hour after hour, satisfied when Wyndham responded with an occasional brief question.

'How do you know these parts?' Wyndham asked him once.

'Oh, this where Sam sahib in jail – up in Nilgiris.' Somari grinned. 'He meet plenty Mundavers inside. When he come out he come back and see them – buy plenty pinched stuff. I come with him. I talk Mundaver monkey bhat very good. I got wife up here somewhere.'

'She'll be glad to see you.'

'Maybe. Funny buggers. Don't want too many kids. Eat too much, so one woman have three-four husbands. I number three – twice.'

'If they're train robbers why do they live so far from the railway?' Wyndham asked.

'So railway police don't catch,' Somari explained. 'Rob one train – two trains – then run like hell back into jungle. Police don't like jungle – don't chase far. Very good.'

They walked for miles along a faintly defined trail, under tall rain-forest that met densely overhead, then the path ended abruptly on the bank of a swollen creek. Somari waded into it up to his waist. 'Come on, sahib,' he called, and breasted the stream, walking a good two hundred yards against the current before emerging again on the same bank. He plunged into the undergrowth and cast around for some minutes before finding another path which seemed to Wyndham to be leading back the way they had been coming, parallel to the original one.

'Remember that, sahib,' Somari said. 'Mundaver path always do that. Come up to river – finish – start again other side – but finish again in middle of bloody nowhere. Proper way – get into river – walk little bit against water – look for first lot of rocks on same side, where you don't leave footmarks – climb out – find next path – follow till it turn round and take you back to river. Cross there. Mundaver clever bugger.'

It happened again and again until Wyndham lost count and was walking mechanically behind Somari, who had been strangely silent for the last hour, stopping from time to time as if to listen. Then they came to the village – or rather the village came to them. Wyndham heard a soft piping whistle high above them that differed in pitch from the evening chorus of small green parrots that flitted among the branches. It was repeated on either side and behind them, and Somari stopped him with upraised hand and chattered softly in a tongue that Wyndham didn't understand. Then small near-naked men were all around them and Somari was making signs, only some of which Wyndham understood. They nodded and grunted and set off up the path ahead of them, then turned abruptly and pressed through a screen of undergrowth that appeared to be impenetrable but was only a camouflaged fence of bamboo.

There was a ring of huts clustered about a circular area of hard-beaten earth, and half-a-dozen cooking fires that gave off no smoke, and along one side of the clearing ran a small brook, while all around rose the solid, claustrophobic wall of the jungle, making the place a small oasis in a vast green desert.

'Now you see, sahib,' Somari murmured. 'Nobody ever find this place. Every year they move – little bit this way – little bit that way. Jungle grow over old place in couple of weeks – finish.'

'How did you know your way here, then?' Wyndham asked, and found that he was speaking instinctively in an undertone like the other. 'You haven't been here for years.'

'Send word last night from railway,' Somari told him. 'All day they been showing us proper way. Sahib don't see them – *I* don't see them – but they there whole time. Very clever – very chahlaki. Soon I show you how they do it.'

They followed one of the little men to a hut and crawled through a low entrance. Wyndham was only dimly aware of Somari unbuckling the bedding-roll and telling him to rest while he got some food. Then he slept.

It was daylight when he woke. He was conscious of the aromatic smell of the khus-khus thatching of the hut, of the sound of rain outside and of the fact that he was thirsty – but of nothing else.

317

There were periods of complete blackness after that, punctuated by other periods of frenetic awareness, when he fought and screamed and Somari and some of the little men had to hold him down. There were faces around him – Jawan – the Japanese – Paul – Walderstein – and always they were forming a barrier between him and Julia. He could see her in the distance, infinitely sad and drawing further away from him – and he could hear her crying softly. And once he came face to face with Philimore and they were fighting on a broken bridge – and he killed him with a gun, with a club, with his bare hands – killed him over and over again, but always he came back, emerging from a raging river and reaching out for him with dead hands – and the face changed to that of Tim Martin, of Somari, of himself. Then, mercifully, the blackness would loom before him again and he would sink into it – to the sound of his own weeping.

Somari was supporting his head and giving him something to drink, something that was bitterer than raw quinine and was making him gag and retch. He was saying softly, 'By Christ, sahib, you were sick when we come to Kolar first time – but not like this. Oh by God, no – not like this. Nobody ever been sick like this before. But you going to get better – you going to get better – you going to get better – '

It was nearly a month before the fever finally broke in a welter of sweating that left him a trembling yellow dehydrated skeleton, but with his head strangely clear. He had had malaria before. It was endemic in India and the Andamans, but hitherto it had troubled him no more than influenza might have done in a more temperate climate – something that quinine and a few days off duty had always coped with. But this, he realized, had been something more. This had been a complete nervous collapse.

'By Jesus, you fight,' Somari told him in tones bordering on admiration. 'You fight me, you fight these little buggers – you get away twice and run like hell through jungle before we catch you.'

'I've given all of you a lot of trouble,' Wyndham said apologetically. 'Too much trouble. Tell them I'm sorry, Somari.'

'Oh, they don't mind,' Somari said cheerfully. 'They got funny 'oly, 'oly, 'oly. Say God love mad buggers. They make some medicine that fix you up.'

'That was very good of them.'

'Yes – bloody awful medicine, though. Monkey piss, goat shit, chewed-up leaves – oh, everything. Make you sick as hell for two days – then you start to get better.'

He put down the bowl from which he had been spoonfeeding Wyndham with some sort of broth. 'When you bit more better,' he said, 'I go in and see if Paul sahib leave a letter in that place.'

'You mustn't take any risks, Somari,' Wyndham said, although his soul was aching for news – any news – even bad news.

'Don't worry, sahib,' Somari said. 'Safe place. Tin can under a rock half mile from resthouse. You want to send a letter? You got notebook and pencil in suitcase.'

He managed to scrawl a few lines to the effect that he was well and safe, and Somari set off with two of the 'little buggers' that afternoon.

Chapter 32

Somari brought back two letters. The first was merely a short reassuring note intended more to establish communication than to give news. It was dated the tenth of July which, as closely as Wyndham could reckon, because he had lost track of time, was shortly after he had met Paul. The other was fourteen days later, and was more anxious in tone. He gathered that 'someone' was worried at the absence of a reply to the first note.

The monsoon was in its final stages now. The rainfall was easing off and breaks of fine weather were longer and more frequent. It paralleled his own condition. He would lie sunk in a vacuum of misery for hours, conscious of the everyday life of the Mundavers around him, and even responding intelligibly to Somari's ceaseless chatter, but with his active thought processes halted. There was nothing ahead of him, so why plan – or even think? Then he would drift into periods of almost manic euphoria, and he would get up, bathe in the stream, shave and then pace endlessly round the village to get the strength back into his legs. He made plans, wild and completely impracticable for the most part, but, as the physical exercise served to get his atrophied muscles back into use, so did these flights of fancy help his mental cogs to mesh again.

Lack of orientation worried him. He knew that the wayside station at which he had left the train was about fifty miles to the south-west of Bangalore, and as far as he could gather from Somari this place was some twenty miles to the south-east of that again. That placed him, he believed, in the foothills of the Nilgiris. Portuguese Goa, therefore, would be between two and three hundred miles to the north-west. He would have to get Paul to send him a map again, and a compass. Goa was to India as Gibraltar was to Spain – a constant irritant, like a grain of sand in an oyster. There was an extradition treaty between them but no love lost. He remembered a case in Kolar of a supervisor who had got away with twenty ounces of gold and had made it across the border. That was more than a year ago, but he was still at liberty over there, thumbing his nose at the Indian police. Murder, of course, was in a different and far more serious category than theft – but then there was no definite charge against Timothy Martin as yet. Or was there? A set of false papers bought from some venal official – pass himself off as a sailor stranded there – even work a 'Private Turnbull'? Things were that much easier in the big port of Marmagoa. Or was it all wishful thinking?

Julia? Had she gone to England yet? If she hadn't, could they risk a meeting there? God! If things turned out well – if he had just one more stroke of luck – they might still get away together –

Goa – yes, that was it. The Promised Land. His thoughts kept swinging back to it like a compass needle – continuously and obsessively. He had money. He had drawn his entire savings from the bank before leaving Kolar – nearly eight thousand rupees. Fifteen hundred of that had gone for his ticket, and some more for the expenses of his visit to Colombo, but it still left him with over five thousand. It was just a map and a compass he needed now. And news. He had to have news. Where was Julia? How was she? Had he been definitely named as a suspect yet? Was there, perhaps, a warrant out for him? Had 'Mayhew's' real identity been established? And finally, had Timothy Martin and Charles Wyndham now been linked?

He had made up his mind to sever all connections with Paul after sending his note in with Somari, but he knew he would have to abandon this. Only Paul could give him the answers, without which he would be moving blindly. He made out the points in the form of a questionnaire on two pages from his notebook, and on another he wrote:

Going to Goa. Will write from there. Need map and compass together with answers to attached if possible. In good spirits. Love to all concerned.

And he pinned a hundred-rupee note to it.

Somari was pleased, as the lack of communication until now had obviously been worrying him. 'Oh, bloody good, sahib,' he said as Wyndham gave him the message, rolled and pushed into a short section of plugged bamboo. 'I get in and get back fast. Little bugger show me quick way last time.'

'I'll come with you,' Wyndham said on an impulse, and Somari protested.

'You not strong enough yet,' he said.

'Nonsense,' said Wyndham. 'It will do me good. I'll get weaker sitting round on my backside.'

They set off at dawn next morning, with two Mundavers moving like black shadows ahead of them, sometimes squatting down at the side of the almost invisible path and letting Wyndham and Somari pass – to reappear some miles further on, once more in front of them.

'I must give these people some money,' Wyndham said.

'Why?' asked Somari.

'We can't expect them to keep us for nothing.' It had been worrying him for some time.

'They don't understand if you do that. We both Brothers,' Somari explained. 'Plenty food here – catch chital deer – fish in river – rice in paddi – milk goats and water buffalo – '

'But tea, sugar, canned fruit?' said Wyndham. 'There's always been plenty of that. They must buy it somewhere; it's costing someone some money.'

'Oh no. *I* buy that,' Somari told him.

'Where?'

'From Sam.'

Wyndham stared at him, his jaw dropping. 'Sam?' he said. 'You mean to say he's been here?'

'No fear,' Somari chuckled. 'Too far to walk through jungle for that old bugger. He come in motor-car from Mysore to road ten miles away from village. Come every month. Been twice while we been here.'

'Do you mean to say that he knows *I'm* here?' Wyndham demanded furiously.

'No, don't know that,' Somari said calmly. 'Little bugger buy stuff from him – I only give money.'

'But damn it all,' Wyndham said. 'He's bound to guess that there's *somebody* here using European stuff.'

'No, little bugger use that stuff sometime too. Don't worry, sahib.'

'But why does he come here?'

'Like I said – buy stuff from Mundavers. He finish in Madras

322

after fire, because new top copper get after him and Aunty. Open shop in Mysore – sell stuff front side – buy stuff backside.' He looked severe. 'Bloody thief. He don't give little buggers proper price. Good stuff – suitcase – sahib's clothes – field glass – whisky flask – silver – gold – giving one, two rupees, bar of soap, tin of jam – then sell them more stuff – sugar – salt – take rupees back again.'

'I don't like it, Somari,' Wyndham said, troubled.

'Oh, don't worry, sahib,' Somari assured him. 'He don't know we're here. If he find out and tell somebody – ' he drew his finger quickly across his throat – 'he finish damn quick. He know *that* all right.'

'Now listen, Somari – ' Wyndham began, but then the Mundavers dropped from the branches overhead and tapped themselves on the lips.

'We keep quiet now, sahib,' Somari whispered. 'Getting near place.'

They came to the railway with dramatic suddenness. One moment they were in the green half-light of the deep jungle – the next they were on the edge of a wide cutting and Wyndham was looking down through the undergrowth at the metre-gauge line below. There was a small bungalow directly opposite them the other side of the line, with a couple of outbuildings behind it. Indian children were playing in the compound and two cows were grazing on the lush monsoon grass outside.

'Railway resthouse, sahib,' Somari explained. 'That where Paul sahib stay when he come down to look at line.'

'Who else lives there?' Wyndham asked.

'Only chowkidar, wife and kids. Look after place and do cooking when sahib come.'

'Where does Paul sahib leave the messages?'

Somari pointed to the left. 'Right down there. See pile of rocks?'

Wyndham saw the outcrop on the bare sloping side of the cutting and realized that it would be in plain view of the resthouse. 'Damn,' he said. 'We'll have to wait at least another two hours for darkness.'

'Why?' Somari asked.

'Because if you go down there in broad daylight you might

be seen from the bungalow,' Wyndham said impatiently.

'You worry too much,' Somari said, and slid like an eel into the undergrowth. Wyndham watched anxiously for half an hour but saw no movement near the rocks, then he jumped as Somari came silently up behind him.

'I hate bloody jungle,' the little man said, 'but know what to *do* in jungle. Here you are, sahib.' And he handed Wyndham a bamboo message cylinder.

There was one slip of paper in it, dated the fifth of August.

'All well this end,' Wyndham read. 'Relieved to hear from you, but necessary I see you. Next visit seventeenth this month. Try and wait this spot after dark.'

He sat back in a sweat of frustration. What the hell was today's date? Before or after the seventeenth? And what was it that Paul deemed sufficiently urgent for them both to risk a meeting?

He pondered for a long time before deciding that the seventeenth had not passed, or Paul would have left a further message. That placed today, therefore, somewhere in the twelve-day span between the fifth and the seventeenth. There were two trains a week over this section, he recalled: Tuesday and Friday – with two going north to Bangalore on Wednesdays and Saturdays. So there was nothing for it but to wait for each south-bound train for possibly the next twelve days. Three trains, if he was unlucky – two or, hopefully, only one if he was not. He made a mental note to keep a rough calendar as soon as he was certain of the date.

He explained his predicament to Somari, who looked thoughtful and then held a twittering conversation with the two Mundavers.

'All right, sahib,' he said. 'No good for you to walk this way that way too many times. Knock hell out of yourself. Little buggers say they make small hut – go back – get some food – stay here.'

He watched them as they worked with the economy of effort that marked all their activities, and within an incredibly short time they had cut nim branches and plaited them into a rainproof shelter half a mile further back in the jungle. Then they just vanished soundlessly into the darkness, leaving Wyndham and Somari the cold rice and dhal they had brought with them. They were back before first light with a cooking pot and a bundle of dried palm pith, which burned with a fierce white heat but gave off no smoke, and when Wyndham tried to thank them in the few halting words of their language that he had managed to master, they looked politely puzzled and vanished again.

'No good, sahib,' Somari chuckled as he cooked breakfast. 'They do things own way. You say thank you, they think you bloody mad. Go away, laugh like hell.'

They heard the train whistle far in the distance late that afternoon, and saw the chowkidar and his family waiting beside the line, but although it slowed down and something was dropped, it did not stop, and Wyndham watched it, fuming, as it rattled on round the bend in the cutting, out of sight.

But the next one halted briefly three days later, and they saw Paul get off, with two Indians in the blue dungaree uniform of the railways, and they carried a light trolley from a shed near the line and set it on the rails and slowly trundled up and down inspecting ties and track ballast for two dragging hours until it was too dark for them to work any longer. He followed Somari along the edge of the cutting then, and down to the outcropping, and waited a further hour until they heard someone climbing up the loose sloping side.

He called softly and Paul came round the rocks, a dark bulk against the night sky, and gripped his hand. Somari said, 'All right – you and Paul sahib talk now. I go up topside and wait,' and climbed back up the slope.

Wyndham said, 'You shouldn't be taking this risk and I've no right to let you – but Christ, I'm glad to see you. How is she?'

'All right,' Paul said. 'I have a letter here – and a torch, if you want to read it first.'

'Later. Where is she now?'

'Back in the convent in Bangalore.'

Wyndham was silent for a moment, then he said, 'I had been hoping that she'd have gone away by this.'

'The letter explains that,' Paul said. 'But hadn't I better bring you up to date first?'

'Of course. I'm sorry.'

'They're still looking for Timothy Martin. They know you tried to book a passage in Colombo although that hasn't been made public. They were hoping that you'd turn up to claim it, I think.'

'Philimore?' Wyndham asked.

'No mention of him at all, but they *have* traced the real Mayhew. He was a ship's engineer originally, with a prison record in England: theft and smuggling. He was wanted again for something, but he signed on a ship – the *Orlando* – as a stoker, and deserted in Calcutta. The police theory is that he had gone to Kolar to look for a job. Personally I think that Philimore either bought or stole his papers and used them.'

'So that would mean that Mayhew is still about somewhere,' Wyndham mused.

'Yes. Probably in England lying low – and thanking his lucky stars if he's heard about this case.'

'So Wyndham is still dead?'

'As far as I know the possibility of his being alive just hasn't crossed anybody's mind. Why should it?' Paul said.

'I hope to God it doesn't,' Wyndham said fervently. 'The bastard has caused enough trouble. But about Julia? Has she made plans for moving on?'

'She'll do whatever you say,' Paul said quietly. 'But in the circumstances it would be advisable to wait for a bit. The letter explains it.'

'I'm sorry, Paul,' Wyndham said, 'but I'd rather read it on my own.'

'Then I'd better tell you. She's going to have a baby.'

'When?' Wyndham asked quickly.

'In about another four months.'

Wyndham tried to fight down his rising anger without success.

'Why the hell didn't you get her out before?' he asked harshly.

'Because we didn't know,' Paul explained. 'She kept it to herself at first, then when she was certain she went back to the convent.'

'But why the bloody convent?' Wyndham demanded.

'Because the "bloody convent" happens to be her home,' Paul said coldly.

'Sorry,' Wyndham mumbled. He sat hunched on the ground with closed eyes and clenched fists. 'Paul – tell me the truth, for Christ's sake. How is she? How is she really?'

'She's anxious about you, naturally. But as far as the baby is concerned, Tina says she's radiantly happy.'

'But the nuns? I mean to say – '

'Are they dressing her in sackcloth and ashes and praying at her? Is that what you mean?' Paul asked. 'If it is, the answer's no.'

'Do they know who – who – ?' Wyndham couldn't go on.

'Who the father is? No. Nor would they dream of asking. Whatever your ideas on the subject may be, Charles, the nuns are decent, kindly women, with a wide knowledge of human nature, and all the compassion in the world. They've known her since she was a tiny kid – brought her up. I told you, it's her *home*. She's safe there, man – safer than she could be anywhere else.'

'But what will she *do*?' Wyndham whispered. 'What's going to happen to her – and – the baby? I keep making plans and scrapping them, kidding myself that somewhere – sometime – we're going to find safety – make a new life – but I know, and you know, that we haven't a chance. Not a chance.'

'She doesn't think that,' Paul said deliberately. 'Maybe it's because she's got more guts than you.'

'You're right there,' Wyndham agreed. 'I haven't *any*. They've been kicked out of me.'

'Oh, for God's sake stop being sorry for yourself,' Paul said angrily. 'I've told you what her attitude is. She's worried about you – but *only* about you. As far as the baby is concerned, she's looking forward to it. "The Wyndham line is going on," she said to Tina.'

Wyndham stared at him through the darkness. 'You mean you've *told* her – ?'

'Yes. I thought it better to – in case the whole thing came out without warning,' Paul said. 'She knows everything now – knows and understands.'

Wyndham took a deep breath. 'Thanks,' he said slowly. 'Thanks, Paul. I'm glad. Yes, I'm glad. That has been the only thing that I've really regretted – having to keep up this lie to *her*. I don't give a damn about lying to anybody else.'

Paul rose to his feet. 'I'll have to get back, old lad,' he said, 'or my two gangers will be wondering what's happened to me. I'll leave you the torch. Read your letter. Have you got anything to write an answer on?'

'Yes.'

'All right. I'll come back up here just before daylight.' He gripped Wyndham's hand tightly. 'You know,' he said, 'you might find this hard to believe – but I envy you. Poor old Tina has been told finally that she can't have any kids. Some damned thing wrong inside. You don't know what a feeling of desolation that can bring to a couple like us. Kids are a second chance – a chance to put all sorts of things right.'

'Not Wyndham kids,' Wyndham said bitterly. 'The bastards make a balls of everything. Well, at least this one won't be burdened with the name.'

'Don't say that,' Paul begged. 'That's the one thing she's sad about. Women are funny creatures. Good night, Charles. I'll see you in the morning.' He turned and went off, and Wyndham stood in the darkness listening to him sliding down the bank, then he crouched behind the rocks and read his letter – but the torch was trembling and the writing was blurred.

He was still there when Paul came back. He said without preamble, 'Priests and nuns can be trusted to keep their mouths closed about anything they're told, can't they? Even by Protestants?'

'They're experts,' Paul said. 'Why?'

'Fix up a date,' Wyndham told him tensely. 'I'm coming in at night – to be married.'

Chapter 33

He dropped from the empty freight car and crossed the tracks quietly to the dark area behind the floodlights of the marshalling yard. He memorized Paul's instructions – a gate in a high stone wall. If it was open there would be a chowkidar stationed there, in which case he would walk through boldly, returning the man's salaam with a casual wave. If it was closed he would have to climb, and that could be tricky, because the chowkidar would be patrolling the other side and it wouldn't do for a sahib suddenly to drop on him out of the darkness. But it was open, and he said, 'Salaam, bhai,' and went through – a European in neat and anonymous khaki shirt and slacks. Left here – walk round the wall to the square in front of the station. It would probably be busy. Indian long-distance trains always seem to start and finish at night. He would be all right if he kept out of the light, even if he ran into somebody from Kolar. Shaving off his moustache had certainly made a difference.

A horse-gharry had just dropped a passenger at the entrance to the station. He hailed it and said, 'Lal Bagh,' and sat back against the worn cushions. So far, so good. He felt he was not nearly as jumpy as he had been in Madras – but he must be careful to avoid the traps that yawn before the over-confident.

The Convent of the Sacred Heart stood behind walls in a grove of peepul trees that overlooked the Government Gardens of Lal Bagh, and the heavy scent of cinnamon and cinchona came to him as the gharry came out of the crowded naphtha-lit bazaar and started to clop round the circular perimeter road. He stopped it and paid the driver off short of the convent and walked the last quarter-mile.

A grille opened in the heavy teakwood door in answer to his ring and an old, wrinkled face appeared, as white as the coif that surrounded it.

He said awkwardly, 'I believe I'm expected, Sister.' She smiled and nodded and slid back bolts and let him in. The room was

small and clinically clean – bare except for two chairs and a statue
of the Virgin – and it smelt of soap and beeswax. She pointed to
a chair and went through a door into a long passage, but before
Wyndham could sit she came back, followed by a priest. He was a
middle-aged man with cropped hair and a white beard which
spread over the front of his soutane. He smiled and held out his
hand, and Wyndham was put in mind of a kinder and rather more
portly George Bernard Shaw. He said, 'Come with me, my son,'
and led him through to a booklined room. He motioned Wyndham to a chair and sat down the other side of a table and looked
at him directly with piercingly blue eyes.

'I know that which I need to know from Julia,' he said. There
was a slight lilt of the Scottish Highlands in his voice. 'From you
I want the answer to one question – and one only. He paused,
then added slowly and distinctly, 'Do you, Charles Wyndham,
know of any reason why you should not marry?'

Wyndham stared at him helplessly. 'Since you know my own
name, Father,' he said, 'you must know the answer to that. I
have no right to marry.'

The priest shook his head. 'I think you misunderstand my
question,' he said. 'Let me put it another way. Are you at present
married?'

'No.'

'Have you ever been married – and if so, is the woman still
living?'

'I have never been married, Father.'

'Do you *want* to marry this girl – or is this purely to give the
child a name?'

Wyndham smiled faintly. 'There's little enough in the name of
Wyndham to give any child,' he said. 'Yes, I want to marry her,
Father.'

'Then that's the question answered. There's of course the
technical one – referring to the child's upbringing and religion.'
He smiled puckishly. 'I always feel like a salesman securing an
advance option when I ask this in a mixed marriage – '

'The child will be brought up in Julia's religion,' Wyndham
promised.

The priest rose and came round the table and took both
Wyndham's hands in his.

'No sermons, and no advice, my son,' he said quietly. 'And no earthly comfort, I'm afraid. I can tell you, however, with absolute certitude, that you are both within the orbit of God's love – and always will be. The sister will take you up to her now. I'll be ready for you in half an hour.'

Wyndham followed the old nun along the passage and up a flight of stairs. She tapped on a door, opened and looked in, then stood aside and motioned him to go through.

Julia stood in the middle of the room.

He stumbled forward blindly and took her in his arms and for a long time they were both silent, then she said softly in exaggerated stage Irish, 'And about toime, too, Timmy you spalpeen. The neighbours would have been talking soon.' And that served to break the tension. He held her off at arm's length and looked at her. She wore, strangely enough, a white silk sari and there were flowers in her dark hair – and she was smaller and more fragile than when he had seen her last – like a porcelain Hindu goddess.

He said, 'You little devil. I thought I was coming to a respectable Christian wedding, not a Brahmin ramsami. What's the meaning of this?'

'Hardly respectable, darling,' she laughed, 'although the nuns, bless them, have been doing their best. They've tried every dress in the place on me – but I still looked like Bridget O'Flaherty betrayed. Then Reverend Mother had a brainwave. You'd be surprised what this sari is hiding.'

'They – I mean – they haven't made it hard for you?' he asked anxiously.

'*Hard* for me?' she said. 'Never once by so much as a look. Any irregularity in things is being put right tonight, and they're delighted – but even if it hadn't been there wouldn't be a single word of reproach.' She looked up at him. 'You're not angry because I came here?'

'No, I'm not angry, darling,' he said. 'I'm just grateful – '

'Timmy,' she said. 'Can I still call you Timmy? The baby will be Charles – '

'How do you know it won't be Charlotte?' he asked, keeping his voice steady with difficulty.

'Somehow I know it will be a boy – and he's going to make up for such a lot.' She clung to him tightly, her eyes closed. 'The

331

three of us. It's going to be all right. You know it's going to be all right, don't you?'

'Yes,' he mumbled.

'We're going to get away from here. What was it you said? "A fresh start. The whole bloody slate wiped clean." ' She smiled up at him again. 'You swear too much, you know. You'll have to be careful in front of young Charles.' She held up her hand. 'I never thanked you properly for my lovely moonstone.'

'I hope that bloody fool Paul – sorry – I hope Paul hasn't forgotten the wedding ring,' Wyndham said.

'He won't. They've been wonderful, Tim – both of them.'

'So they ought to be. They're family, you know. Has he told you that?'

'Oh yes – and shown me. His mother had a family bible with the whole tree in it. I felt very proud.'

'That's the last thing to be. The Wyndhams have been a pretty scrawny lot.'

'I'm not going to let you say that – and even if they had been, they won't be from now on. Mistakes don't matter – they're not held against us, as long as we learn from them – and put them right. You believe that, darling, don't you? You *do* believe that?'

'Of course.'

He sat on a chair, with her on the floor beside him, her head on his knee. There were long periods of silence, broken occasionally by inanities and giggling when the strain became too great. Then there was a soft tap on the door. They both rose. Julia turned to him and whispered, 'I will never be happier – I *can* never be happier – than I am tonight, my darling. It's going to be all right – *It's going to be all right.*'

The old nun was beckoning from the doorway. They followed her downstairs and along more passages and finally into the chapel, and Paul came forward from somewhere along the route and took Julia from him, and pushed him forward. Wyndham was conscious only of the priest before him at the altar, and of the heavy scent of massed tropical flowers, and of an organ playing softly. There was only the old nun, the tall distinguished Mother Superior, Paul and stout little Tina crying happily in the background. Then Julia was beside him again.

They were back in the booklined study and Father Lauder had produced a bottle of champagne, and the Mother Superior a small wedding cake – and then on a hidden signal from somebody, the others put down their glasses and disappeared, leaving them together, and the moment they had both been dreading had arrived.

Wyndham said, 'I won't be far away – just out there in the jungle – and there'll be letters every time Paul comes down – and then, when Junior is big enough to travel, I have plans – safe plans. I haven't had time to tell you about them, but they *are* safe – I promise you. Goa – a foreign country not two hundred miles from here. We can get away together from there – *together*, my darling – and we'll be together always after that.'

'Take care, my love,' she whispered. 'Oh, take care. Look after yourself – no risks – '

'I promise,' he said. 'I must go now. Paul will be waiting.'

'I'll come to the sister-porter's lodge,' she said.

'No,' Wyndham said sharply. He held her tightly, his lips moving over her cheek as he spoke. 'Just stand here. I shall look back once at the door. You won't be crying, will you? You're not going to cry?'

'I won't cry,' she promised.

'I'll be back the night he arrives.'

'No risks – no risks – ' she pleaded.

He broke away and reached the door in long strides. He turned but saw her only as a blurred white figure with arms reaching towards him. Then Paul had him by the arm and was leading him out through the porter's door. Father Lauder said, 'We'll look after her, my son. God be with you.'

They drove back through the bazaar. Wyndham said, 'You shouldn't be doing this. I can get a gharry back to the marshalling yard.'

'There's no train out tonight,' Paul told him.

'But you said there was,' Wyndham protested.

'That was only to save an argument. I fixed all this up with Somari last time I was down. I've hired this car and I'm taking you down the Mysore road to the forty-seventh milestone. He's meeting us there.'

'But damn it all, you've no right to take chances like this,' Wyndham raged. 'If we were stopped – '

'Cool off,' Paul told him. 'This is a darned sight safer than you blundering round the marshalling yard and probably getting on the wrong train.' He changed the subject. 'How do you think she was looking?'

'Beautiful. How else could she look?' Wyndham said. 'But – what's the word? – fragile.'

'Yes. I suppose I should have warned you,' Paul said, 'but I didn't want to worry you. She's had a rough time – a lot of malaria, and she'd heard somewhere that quinine could be harmful to an unborn baby, so she wouldn't take it. Then, naturally, she was worried about you. But you needn't be anxious any more. The doctor says she's doing fine now – and they're looking after her very well in there.'

'I'll never be able to thank them adequately.'

'They wouldn't expect you to.'

'That still doesn't let me off anything. I'll have to find some means of paying them in the future.'

'You just concentrate on getting out,' Paul said. 'Are you still thinking of Goa?'

'Very much so. I'm going to make my way over there as soon as she's safely through this.'

'The convent has a sister house in Panjim,' Paul told him. 'That should make things easier when the time comes.'

The road was dark and deserted when they came to the forty-seventh milestone, but Somari pushed his way out of the undergrowth as Paul pulled up and blipped his headlights.

'I'll go on a couple of miles before turning and coming back,' he said. 'Cheerio, old lad. There'll be a letter in the other place each time I come down. You've got the dates. Chin up.'

Wyndham stood watching the tail-light until it was out of sight, then he turned and followed Somari into the darkness. They had a ten-mile walk ahead of them across two steep ridges, with intervening valleys and one major river to cross, and not even the tireless Somari could negotiate that sort of country and talk at the same time, for which he was thankful.

His lethargy and depression had left him now, and it was not replaced, as formerly, by what he had come to realize was wholly unjustified euphoria. He was thinking clearly and constructively again. If a moron like Philimore could move around the world without let or hindrance and successfully cover his tracks, surely *he* could. Just let him get through the bottleneck of a port. Papers – that's all he needed. He'd got them before – admittedly by sheer chance – but surely he could do so again by the exercise of a little intelligence. Buy, or steal if necessary, a seaman's discharge book. He'd seen one or two while staying with Sam. The British ones looked vaguely like a passport – same size – blue-cloth covered – with the sailor's particulars and description on the first page, together with a photo, and on the succeeding pages a record of voyages made on various ships, with a terse testimonial as to character, conduct and ability summed up by the captain in the last column as 'Very Good', 'Good' or a damning 'Decline to Report'. It was common knowledge that in various parts of India – Calcutta in particular – the forging of documents was an industry. For sums ranging from a thousand rupees up, one could buy anything from a matriculation certificate to a medical degree – so good that they had been known to deceive the official bodies in England. A seaman's discharge book had only to pass the perfunctory scrutiny of a ship's captain when signing on, and again when being paid off – just a glance and an initial and a rubber stamp. For God's sake, hadn't prisoners of war in Germany made complete sets of papers for themselves that had completely taken in police and eagle-eyed frontier guards? Made with odds and ends picked up around the camps.

That was it. A simple seaman's discharge book. And where better to pick one up than a big port like Goa? To hell with this nonsense of buying a passage on a dhow to the East African coast. He'd probably get his throat cut for what he was carrying long before he got there, anyway. This way he could take his time, pick his ship and his destination, bribe a sailor to desert if necessary and present himself at the ship just before sailing – or, if that failed, slug one and leave him up a dark alley. He couldn't afford the luxury of scruples any longer. He wasn't running just to save his own neck now. There were two others dependent upon him. Yes, a discharge book, with the particulars convincingly altered to suit himself, and a genuine photo inserted in place of the original.

He was in a ferment to get started. He wanted to set off on the trek to Goa immediately, but he kept a tight rein on himself. He had told her that he would be near. He couldn't go back on that. There was only a little over two months left now before the baby arrived. Five fortnightly trips by Paul; five letters each way. She would be waiting for those – and for the visit he had promised he'd make. No, he'd stay until then and make good use of the intervening time. He would get Paul to buy him some good boots – his present ones were dropping to pieces – more clothes, both to stand up to the journey through the jungle and others to present a decent, sailorly appearance round the docks. There'd be nothing hit-and-miss about this. This would be a carefully planned operation, with every move examined minutely in advance – tested, analysed, step by step – with an alternative ready to be adopted at each stage should anything go wrong. And time was on his side because by the very nature of things the search for Timothy Martin would be bound to slacken in intensity as the weeks went by.

He wrote long letters to her – and read and re-read hers until the paper became shredded through constant handling. Paul had taken a photo of her in the convent garden, close up, in a simple smock, her left hand raised to show the moonstone and the wedding ring, and that was never far from him.

He sat on the edge of the cutting as the sun went down. He had a carefully marked calendar and a timetable now and he could time his visits accurately. This was the fourth since that night, and it might possibly be the last if the doctor's reckoning was correct. 'The little devil is making his presence felt,' she had written in her last letter. 'I think we shall have to make a footballer out of him.'

She was well, Paul had told him. A little anaemia after all that malaria, but they were treating her for that.

The train whistle came to him through the twilight and he braced himself against the unbearable impatience he knew would bedevil him from the time he saw Paul alight until it was dark enough to move to the rocks to meet him. Fortunately the days were shortening and the wait had become appreciably less each time.

Paul got down with his two gangers and raised his hand casually, studiously not looking towards the top of the cutting. Then he walked up to the resthouse and Wyndham moved along the top towards the outcropping. He had not brought Somari this time in spite of his protests, because he had had a short but very sharp bout of fever recently, and Wyndham had insisted on his resting. The Mundavers had provided a silent and inter-mittently invisible escort, of course, although he had tried to leave them behind also. He knew his way about now, and could move almost as silently as they.

He slid down to the rocks. Darkness had fallen completely, and he heard Paul's soft whistle almost at once. He answered, and called, 'Come on, you clumsy old bugger. You ought to learn some junglecraft. I could hear you a mile off.'

Paul said very quietly, 'You have a son, Charles. A fine little chap. He arrived three days ago. I wish we could have got word to you earlier, but there was no way – '

'I'm going in!' said Wyndham. 'I'm going in even if I have to walk. I'm going tonight! How is she?'

'Sit down,' Paul said.

'Sit down be damned! How is she?' Wyndham shouted.

'She – she died yesterday morning,' Paul told him.

They sat in the darkness for a long time without speaking, then Wyndham said flatly, tonelessly, 'What was it?'

'It was a long and difficult confinement, and her heart gave out. She'd had rheumatic fever as a child. They knew it, of course, and they did everything that was humanly possible. Please believe that, Charles.' He reached out and put his arm around Wyndham's shoulders. 'There's no letter this time. Things happened suddenly, and prematurely. But she gave me a message for you. Do you want to hear it now, or would you rather wait? I've made an excuse to stay down over tomorrow.'

'Now,' Wyndham said.

'First of all, Tina and I have offered to take the boy as our own. From a purely selfish standpoint we'd love that, naturally – but she said the final choice had to be yours. She said, "Tell Tim he must not give up. This must not change anything. He must get out of this country which has brought him so much unhappiness – and if possible take the boy out later. All the things we discussed in our last few letters – a wonderful new start – a clean slate – they must be his now." Then she said, "Tell him I love him." '

Wyndham sat in silence, staring into the darkness, then he said, 'I've got to sweat this out on my own, Paul. You understand that, don't you?'

'Not on your own, Charles,' Paul begged. 'I can stay here with you as long as you wish. You needn't talk if you don't want to.'

'I'll be better on my own,' Wyndham said, and got to his feet. 'I'll come back here tomorrow – or there'll be a letter.'

'Is Somari with you?' Paul asked anxiously.

'Yes, waiting at the top,' Wyndham lied. 'Good night, old lad – and – and thank you – for everything.'

'Charles – ' Paul called. But the other had already gone.

'Take the boy,' Paul read. 'I promise I will never interfere in his upbringing – but her wishes must be fulfilled. He must have his chance – the chance you never had, and which I threw away. She wanted him to have an English education – possibly a degree – a happy and a useful life. It will take money – *but the money will be provided – without stint*. That will be my responsibility. Never tell him about me – and forget the name Wyndham – but she wanted him christened Charles. Goodbye – and the love and gratitude of both of us to the three of you – always.'

Chapter 34

Sam pulled his ancient Model T into the verge and peered up and down the road. It ran arrow-straight like a knife-thrust through the tall surrounding jungle, and he could see a mile either way. It was clear now, as it always was at this hour of mad dogs and Englishmen, but he liked to be absolutely certain. He shifted into reverse and backed through the undergrowth until, after a bare three or four yards, the road was out of his view, then he got out and took an empty gunny sack from the back and brushed over his wheeltracks in the dust. There was no real need for this last nicety. Only bullock carts used this byway and most of those halted during the heat of the day. But a man couldn't be too careful – no, by Christ he couldn't – not in this business.

He took a 12-bore shotgun and a cartridge bag from the back. This was another precaution – not against a possible assault on his person – the Mundavers didn't go in for that sort of thing, certainly not in broad daylight – but as a raison d'être. If he did run into some nosey bleeder he was just after a few jungle fowl. No harm in that, was there?

He pushed his way through the dense scrub for about half a mile, swearing irritably to himself as he felt his shirt becoming sweat-soaked. Then he came to a stream. This was the part he hated most, taking his damn boots off and wading. He'd got a leech between his toes last time. He walked knee deep upstream until he came to a pile of boulders, climbed out and pulled his boots on again, and continued along the path. Yes, you had to be careful, but he'd have to talk to these little devils, and get 'em to pick a spot nearer to the road. He wasn't getting any younger, and this monthly trip was knocking the hell out of him.

He arrived at a little clearing on top of the hill and sat on a fallen tree in the middle. He knew they were here already – as he had known that they had been shadowing him on the way up – but they would keep him waiting for a time now. It was all part of the bundobas. The little bastards would suddenly drop in like shadows. One minute the place would be as bare as a bandicoot's arse, the next they'd be squatting in a silent row in front of him. He was used to it now, but it gave him the creeps at first. They'd go through the whole Brotherhood mumbo-jumbo then – signs and grunts and squeaks, like a monkeys' Masonic Lodge on parade. After that would come the real business. They'd start producing all the bloody rubbish in the world, the harvest of their previous month's thieving: tins of talcum powder, sponge-bags, tatty old dressing-gowns, and he'd sit there like Buddha on a rock-cake shaking his head, until they brought out the real stuff – and the bidding would start 'way, 'way up – but in the end they would get just what they knew they'd be getting all along. Twenty-five silver rupees – take it or bloody well leave it. They'd take it.

A voice behind him said, 'Hello, Sam,' and simultaneously the shotgun which had been resting against the trunk beside him was whisked away. He let out a yell of sheer terror and spun round.

A tall, lean, bearded man stood behind him. He was naked except for a brief loincloth and a small green turban, and he was bronzed to the colour of old, weathered mahogany. He had a long knife in the waistband of the loincloth and he was toying with the shotgun.

'Who are you?' Sam quavered, then added in tones of flabbergasted amazement. 'You spoke English, didn't you?'

'Yes. I'll switch to Mundaveri if it suits you better,' the lean man said.

'Keep it in English,' Sam told him. 'Christ, you scared the crap out of me. Who are you, if it's not a rude question?'

'The locals call me Daku.'

'You don't let 'em, do you?'

'Why not? Nice easy word for them to get their tongues round.'

'But it means "cut-throat" – like "dacoit", only worse.'

'That's right.'

'But, hell – you're a white man, aren't you?' He peered uncertainly at the other. 'Or are you? You sound like one, but – '

'Who and what I am, Sam, is not important,' said the lean man. 'What I have to say to you *is*.'

'Look,' Sam said nervously. 'I'm only out after jungle fowl. I don't want any trouble. As a matter of fact I was just going.

There doesn't seem to be anything in this part of the jungle.'

'You're right,' the other agreed gravely. 'Not a damned thing this time. I suggest you come back next month – carrying more than the twenty-five chips you usually bring.'

'What do you mean by that?' Sam blustered.

'I mean that the jig's up, you thieving old bastard. You'll be paying fair prices for loot in future – like any other honest fence.'

'Now look here – ' Sam began, but the other man cut him short.

'Twenty-five chips last month for a swag that included, among other things, a crocodile dressing-case by Finnegan's of Bond Street – cut-glass bottles and gold fittings which would have cost at least five hundred pounds originally, this gun I'm holding now – one of a pair of beautiful Purdeys, a Colonel's dress sword, two pairs of Zeiss binoculars and a Leica camera. Kee-rist! You *did* have a killing, didn't you?'

Sam took a deep breath and said, 'Mister – I don't know who or what you are exactly, but I'm happy to talk to you – 'specially if you've got any control over these little sods of Mundavers. That's the trouble, you see. The stuff they've been bringing along for the last few months has been *too* good. Crocodile dressing-case? You bet. Lovely. But every bloody thing in it in the way of fittings with a goddam coat of arms on it – the Earl of Albiondale's crest – and since that young bleeder happens to be the Governor's ADC it completely buggers it for re-sale, if you see what I mean. Same with the guns – custom-built *and* numbered and inscribed for General Sir John Laxton. Have a look at the one you're holding. You can see where the engraving's been filed off – and ruined – in among all that beautiful chasing. Bloody shame.'

'All right then,' said the lean man. 'I take your point. That type of merchandise would be a bit difficult to dispose of at a reasonable price. But it doesn't alter the fact that you've been robbing these people – '

'Robbing them hell!' wailed Sam. 'Look, I'm hardly making my overhead costs. I tell you, the bottom has fallen right out of the train knocking-off racket – '

'Exactly,' agreed the other. 'That's what I've come to talk to you about. I've been studying things for the last six months. These people are artists at boarding a fast train and making a quick foray through the compartments in the dark and chucking the loot out and collecting it up later – but by the very nature of things they can't be too discriminating – ' He broke off as Sam jumped to his feet and peered closely into his face.

'Johnnie!' yelled Sam. 'Johnnie Walker! That's who you are! What the hell – ? What in the name of God are *you* doing here, dressed up like a bloody hubshi? Where have you been? What is it? Two years? No, more than three now since you and that little tyke Somari clipped me of a couple of thousand chips. No hard feelings,' he added hastily.

'I'm glad of that,' Wyndham said drily. 'That's generous of you – considering that you nearly roasted us alive.'

Sam sighed gustily. 'That wasn't my fault,' he said. 'I told you so at the time. The damn thing went up too soon. Ruined us, it did. The bloody insurance robbers refused payment – the municipal council wouldn't recognize our title to the property – and that new son-of-a-bitch of a police commissioner was breathing down our necks. The hard work of a lifetime swept away overnight. We got out of Madras in just what we stood up in. Nearly killed poor old Aunty, it did.' He brushed away a tear with the back of his hand.

'You're breaking my heart,' said Wyndham. 'All right then, you're broke. But you have got a business in Mysore – '

'A bloody little junk shop that hardly pays the rent.'

' – and you're still fencing.'

'You don't call flogging the few bits and pieces the Mundavers bring in *fencing*, do you? I tell you, we're just living from hand to mouth – '

'I see,' said Wyndham understandingly. 'I only wanted to know the form. The thing I have in mind *would* be a bit big for you.' He put out his hand. 'It's been nice meeting you again Sam. Give my love to Aunty.'

'Sure, sure,' said Sam ignoring the hand. 'But what was it you had in mind?'

'Don't worry about that. I'll be seeing Mordecai of Madras, or Bansi Lal of Belgaum,' Wyndham said. 'It's more their kind of proposition, but I thought I'd sound you out first – for old time's sake.'

'*Them* bloody thieves?' Sam said, aghast. 'They'd rob you rotten – l'

'I don't think so, Sam,' Wyndham said gently. 'If they, or anybody else for that matter, were ill-advised enough to do that, I'd – ' He made a swift pass across his throat with his forefinger. 'But I'm sure they wouldn't.' He handed the gun back politely. 'I won't keep you any longer. Good hunting.' He turned and started to walk away.

'Hey! Wait a minute,' Sam said. 'No need for any of us to go off at half-cock. We can *talk* about it, can't we?' He went after Wyndham and took his arm.

'What would be the point, since you're out of business now?' Wyndham asked.

'I didn't say that. I meant – ' He peered up into the other's face in an agony of avarice. 'Come on – what is it?'

'Gold,' said Wyndham.

'How much gold?'

'Approximately half a ton.'

There was silence for a moment, then Sam laughed shakily. 'You're pulling my leg, of course.'

'I'm not.'

'There isn't that much gold in the whole of Kolar,' Sam said shrilly.

'Don't talk like a fool,' Wyndham snapped. 'They've taken thirty-six million pounds' worth out of the field in the last ten years. Pounds sterling, not wretched rupees.'

'You mean – ? You're not thinking of knocking Kolar off, are you?' Sam asked incredulously.

'Of course not. Any more than I'd think of making a frontal attack on the Bank of England.'

'Then what – ?'

'The monthly gold *train.*'

'But damn it all,' Sam protested. 'They must have half the coppers in Madras Province guarding it, surely?'

'On the contrary, they have four rather elderly gents from the so-called Security Staff travelling in the alleged strongroom with it. They sleep and play cards most of the trip.'

'How do you know that?'

'Because I've done the duty myself – twice – when one of them has either been sick or on leave.'

Sam stared at him. 'You mean you've worked at *Kolar*?' he breathed.

'I have,' Wyndham said.

'There!' said Sam. 'Beat that for woman's intuition. Aunty said at the time – when it was in all the papers a year ago – "This Timothy Martin," she said, "you know I wouldn't be surprised if that wasn't our Johnnie," she said. "The description just fits him – six foot – blue eyes – about thirty." Well, I'll be damned – '

Wyndham reached out slowly and took Sam's arm and squeezed – and the other yelped in pain. 'Sam,' he said very softly. '*Please*, Sam – never mention that name in connection with me – or the other name you know about – or *think* you know about. Because if you do, Sam – even absent-mindedly – and I hear you – then I'm afraid I'll have to kill you. And that, of course, goes for Aunty too. Understand me, Sam?'

Sam moistened his dry lips. 'Yes – yes – sure – sure. I understand, Johnnie – er – I mean – is "Johnnie" all right?'

'There's no need to use *any* name – but if you find it absolutely necessary, then I'd prefer "Daku".' He released Sam's arm and smiled. 'There – let's have no more mistakes in future, eh?'

'Sure – no – no mistakes, Johnnie – er – I mean Daku,' Sam mumbled hoarsely.

'Good. Well, to continue,' went on Wyndham. 'The system for shipping gold out of Kolar never varies. It is collected from each of the six independent companies by the Central Registry, where it's cast into ingots and marked with three stamps – that of the company concerned – the Kolar Consortium – and the Indian Treasury Department. This is always done on or about the first of each month – unless the first falls on a Sunday or in a holiday period. It is sent by rail to Bombay then, where it is lodged in the Imperial Bank of India until the next mail steamer leaves for England. It is never kept at the Central Registry in Kolar for more than a day or so. With me so far?'

'With you, J – er – Daku.'

'The ingots weigh fifty-six pounds – exactly – and each is packed in its own teakwood box – steel-banded and sealed. There are usually twenty of them – sometimes one or two less, sometimes one or two more. They travel over the forty-five-mile spur line to Bangalore, and from there through Dharmaparam to Wadi, on the main Hyderabad line – then on through Sholapur and Poona to Bombay. The whole journey takes two days and one night. They are never trans-shipped at the various railway changing points. The gold coach is coupled on to each train in turn. It is always the last coach for this reason. It is a specially-constructed steel-built job which is kept in its own siding at Kolar. It consists of a passenger compartment for the guards, the strongroom itself, a lavatory and shower, and a small caboose where they prepare their own meals. It has four heavily-barred windows and two reinforced doors. The doors are locked and sealed on the outside once the gold and the guards are aboard, and they are not opened again until arrival at the Treasury siding in Bombay – but, of course, the guards can open them from the inside in case of accident. It so happens that there never has been an accident.'

'Jesus!' said Sam. 'You've certainly been doing your home-work.'

'I have,' said Wyndham. 'I've been studying this for quite some time.'

'But knowing the drill and knocking it off are two different things,' Sam said doubtfully. 'That coach sounds a pretty tough nut to crack, from what you say.'

'But it can be cracked,' Wyndham told him confidently. 'And comparatively easily.'

'Are these blokes armed?'

'Oh yes – they've each got a revolver, but I don't think any of them has ever fired one,' Wyndham said. 'You see, in the fifty-three years that the Kolar Gold Fields have been operating, they've never been robbed. There have been small pilferages – the odd ounce or two from the mines themselves – but never an attempt on the train. It would be unthinkable.'

'But the Mundavers – ?' began Sam, but Wyndham cut him short.

'The Mundavers, as we both know, can jump a fast train, swing from coach to coach and climb through windows – ordinary windows – like monkeys. But these bars are a different proposi-tion. And then again, they are inoffensive people under normal circumstances. Oh, they'd turn on you with a knife if you cornered them at night – but only as a last resort. They'd much prefer to take a flying header out of the window. They'd certainly never tackle an armed man.'

'So you're not going to use Mundavers?'

'I am – but not for a frontal attack.'

'I don't see how you're going to do it,' Sam said doubtfully.

'You don't have to,' Wyndham told him. 'All I require is a little absolutely foolproof co-operation beforehand, then somebody to handle the gold intelligently afterwards.'

Sam whistled. 'Half a ton? That's going to *take* some handling too.'

'It will be hidden in the depths of the jungle,' Wyndham said. 'Then it will be melted down and recast into small bars – eight ounces or a pound each. Could you see any difficulty in handling those?'

Sam's face lit up. 'Christ, no! That would be easy enough,' he said enthusiastically. 'Hell of a lot of eight-ounce bars in half a ton. What would the total value be?'

'Twenty lakhs – that's two million rupees,' Wyndham said quietly. 'Or one hundred and fifty thousand pounds approximately.'

Sam whistled again. 'I don't want to be rude – ' he looked coy – 'but what handling charges would you be allowing me?'

Wyndham said, 'Your cut would be exactly one quarter of it.'

'Five lakhs?' Sam squeaked ecstatically, then sobered suddenly. 'But this co-operation beforehand? I mean, I'm an old man now – and I'd be no good slinging a gun on anybody – or hopping on and off trains – '

'You wouldn't be required to,' Wyndham assured him. 'All I want is somebody to watch the Central Registry siding in Kolar for a few days – and to make a telephone call when he sees the gold coach hooked up to the engine for the first part of its run to Bangalore.'

'That should be easy enough.'

'Yes, but as I said, the operative word is "intelligent". Do you know Kolar?'

'Never been there in my life.'

'The Central Registry is on the outskirts of the town,' Wyndham explained. 'There's no bazaar or anything like that there, and a European hanging about for two or three days would arouse somebody's curiosity, if not their suspicions. You'd have to go back to your soldiering days.'

'In what way?'

Wyndham drew a rough map in the sand with a twig. 'This is the CR,' he said. 'In front of it runs the main road, with the railway siding lying parallel a few yards away. This side of the road is rough scrubland – then there's the river – here – and on the bank this side, a range of low wooded hills, about a quarter of a mile from the road. You'd have to get in there with a couple of days' rations, and just watch. When you see the coach move out, you'd have to go in to the railway station and make a call to a number in Bangalore – and just say, "George's sore throat is better" or something like that. We'd fix all the details later, of course.'

'Dead easy,' said Sam.

'Yes, but it's usually the dead easy things, in my experience, that get fouled up. There would have to be no mistakes about this.'

'There wouldn't be. Where would the job itself be taking place?'

'That doesn't concern you, Sam,' Wyndham said. 'But for your peace of mind, it will be a long way from Kolar – which means a long way from you.'

'Oh, I wasn't thinking about anything like that,' Sam said hurriedly. 'It was just interest.'

'Which does you credit,' Wyndham said solemnly. 'Right – I take it you want to come in?'

'You bet your sweet life I do,' said Sam fervently.

'Very well. I shall meet you here a month from today,' Wyndham told him. 'That will be the fifteenth. I shall give you dates, timings and the final briefing then. There'll be no loot from the Mundavers in the meantime, because I'll be training the best of them for this thing.'

'Who'd want to be frigging around with dressing-cases and electro-plated hairbrushes with this on his mind?' Sam breathed. 'Migawd! This would put the old woman and me back where we was before the bleeding catastrophe. If it comes off I think we'd sling our hooks out here and go to England – or France or somewhere. What about you? You're not settling in the jungle for keeps, are you?'

'That remains to be seen,' Wyndham said smoothly. 'Goodbye, Sam. Until the fifteenth. Oh, just one thing.' He touched his own throat, and then ran his extended thumb down his bronzed belly. 'You don't discuss this with anybody – '

'Christ, no!' Sam yelled. 'You don't have to worry about that, John – Daku. Not a blind word.'

'To *anybody*,' Wyndham repeated softly. 'You understand me – don't you, Sam?'

'Yes – yes – sure,' babbled Sam. 'We're both in the same club. I don't want any visitors at night – oh, Jesus, no. Don't worry about that, Daku. I'm as silent as the grave.'

'*Exactly*.' Wyndham laughed mirthlessly. 'I couldn't have put it better myself.'

He turned and slipped into the bush behind him, without a rustle, and Sam shivered, although the day was very hot.

Chapter 35

Wyndham said, 'I shall speak in Hindi, Somari, which you will translate into their tongue. You will give them my words as I utter them – *exactly* – adding nothing, omitting nothing and changing nothing. Do you understand me?'

'I understand, sahib,' Somari answered solemnly.

'When I have finished, they may talk among themselves and then put to me any questions they may wish, and I will answer them,' Wyndham went on. 'After that I shall ask each man if he is satisfied with the plan. If he is not, and has a better one, he may speak freely and we will discuss his plan and then put it to the vote – for in this we are Brothers in Council. Tell them that much now.'

He listened as Somari twittered at length in the birdlike language of the Mundavers, watching the expressionless faces of the little men who sat on the ground in front of them. He was fluent enough in the language himself to have been able to dispense with an interpreter, but this way he was free to study them as they listened to Somari, while mentally preparing the next part of the detailed briefing.

Somari finished, but there was no acknowledgement from the little men. They just sat and watched him.

'In this we are Brothers in Council,' Wyndham repeated. 'And we shall remain so until the plan goes into operation. Then I cease to be a Brother, and become a Father, expecting instant obedience from each man. I know that Mundavers never work under the orders of an outsider, and that some of the Brothers now listening to me may not wish to do so. I ask therefore at this point that any man who is not prepared to accept me as leader, should declare it – and leave the Council without ill-will on either side.'

Somari translated, and Wyndham waited for a movement. One man leaving now would mean a trickle of others – and the trickle would grow to a spate – and the whole thing would be stillborn.

But no man stirred. It could, of course, be curiosity at this stage, and the run-out would come later when they had heard the plan in detail – but he felt a little heartened, and some of his nervousness left him.

'I thank my Brothers,' Wyndham said gravely. 'I shall continue then without further pause. You all know the Great Train – the Mail – which runs through your jungle each night from Bangalore on its way to the north where it meets another greater and faster train which runs to the west. Some of the younger men have tried to board this train, and have been injured – and some, in the past, have been killed – so the Elders have said that no man must attempt it again. That is wise, because here the land is flat and the train goes at great speed. But a day's march to the north the hills begin – at Lona, where the train halts and takes on water for the long climb – ' There was a slight stir among his audience. He nodded slowly. 'Yes, I know,' he said. 'Just the other side of Lona your territory ends and that of the Khands begins – and you may not rob a train there. But hear me. From Lona to the White Rock, which is your boundary, there is a stretch of twenty miles – *uphill*. My plan is that two men – the two ablest, strongest and most agile, who shall be chosen by *you*, in Council, shall board the train as it leaves Lona and shall uncouple the last coach on a certain night – just before it reaches White Rock. This coach will slow down gradually and stop, and will then start to run back. Ten miles down the gradient – that is two miles the other side of Lona, a party of you, who will be waiting in the jungle, will drop a heavy tree-trunk across the line after the train has passed. The coach that is running backwards will be halted by this. We will take from the coach that which we shall be seeking, and bring it through the jungle to this place.' He waited while Somari translated, and this time there were questions.

'Will there not be people in this coach – and will they not fight when we rob it?' asked old Bundoo, one of the Elders.

'There will be four men only,' Wyndham told him, 'and they will be dealt with by me.'

'So the white man will be with us?' one of the youngsters said, and Wyndham thought he detected a sneer. 'Can *he* board a train travelling fast?'

'No, only a Mundaver can do that with the skill and bravery

350

that is required,' Wyndham said gently, 'I shall already be on the train – on the roof of the last coach when it leaves Lona.'

'How does the white man know that there will be only four in the coach?' somebody else asked. 'And how will he deal with them?'

'I *know*,' Wyndham said simply. 'How I shall deal with them is my affair – but no Mundaver will be asked to kill.'

'And what is in this coach that we should take such risks for?'

'Gold,' Wyndham told them. 'So much gold that every man, woman and child of the tribe may take one thousand silver rupees – when the gold has been disposed of.' He heard a sharp intake of breath, and then there was a long silence.

'Can Daku promise that?' old Bundoo asked at last. The use of his name instead of the impersonal 'gora' was a good sign.

'Daku can promise that,' Wyndham said. 'Provided that each man carries out his orders – and the sun does not rise in the west on that particular morning.' There was a slight snuffle, which passed among the little men as a laugh. This was their own idiom for the impossible.

'Does Daku think it an easy matter to uncouple a coach when the train is travelling at speed?' the youngster asked, and Wyndham, prepared for this, smiled at him paternally.

'None but a fool – or a very brave young man – would attempt to,' he said. '*If* the coupling was secured properly. But it is Daku's intention to loosen the coupling-screw at Lona and then insert a greased pin in its place. A sharp tap with a heavy hammer will release this. Daku will, of course, have both the pin and the hammer with him.' The snuffle was louder and more full-bodied this time.

'How does Daku know the timings and the speeds of the train?' Bundoo asked. 'And where the gradients are – and what the country is like near Lona?'

Wyndham did not commit the cardinal error of being either flippant or patronizing with the old man. He inclined his head towards him gravely and said, 'I have spent much time on this, my father. I have travelled the route three times between Bangalore and Dharmaparam – once as a Marwari, once as a Madrassi – and once on the roof of the last coach. I have a picture of the ground.' He held up a map. 'I have walked over it – and I know the escape route we will take. Tomorrow, if the Council approves, I shall take some of the young men with me through the jungle so that they, also, will see these things and will be able to instruct the rest.'

'And when would this take place?' Bundoo asked.

'Within four nights of the third quarter of the next moon. Our men must lie in the jungle near Lona at this time, and wait until they see a signal – thus – ' he flashed an electric torch – 'from the roof of the last coach.'

He could feel their mounting excitement. This was the moment to stop and let them argue together – and so avoid further questions, the answers to which he had not yet worked out. He held up his hand in a gesture of benediction and said, 'I go to my hut now, my father – and await the decision of the Council.' He turned and walked away, but before he had left the circle of firelight old Bundoo called after him, 'It is well, my son Daku. We agree.'

Wyndham pointed to the railway track through the screen of undergrowth. 'There,' he said softly. 'That is the last bend before the run in to the station two miles ahead. It is there that the engine whistles and starts to reduce speed, and it is there that I shall give my signal – and Tapa and Sindal, waiting by the embankment will prepare to spring for the last coach. Is it clear, my Brothers?' The two men with him grunted. 'The station, as you will see when we go forward, is but a short platform, with the water-tower beyond it. The engine stops there, leaving more than half the length of the train in the darkness, short of the platform. Sometimes one of the three railwaymen who live in a hut on the platform walks along the train with a lamp. His duty is to inspect the couplings and the brake-boxes, but he does it quickly and without care. Sometimes he does not do it at all – but we must be prepared for one who does – therefore you, Tapa, will remain on the roof and watch for the approach of a man carrying a lamp, while Sindal and I unscrew the coupling, and you will give us warning so we can hide in time.'

'What if he comes after we have unscrewed it, and sees?' asked Sindal.

'He would notice it only if he inspected the coupling closely,'

Wyndham said. 'That, I tell you, he does not do – but should bad luck befall us that night, and send us a conscientious man, then I shall have to use the hammer for more than knocking out the pin later. But *I* shall do it – not either of you. Right. While this is happening, Gunga and Sabha, whom I have already instructed, will climb those posts beside the line – one here and one two miles the other side of the station – and will cut the telephone wires. Have you any questions so far, my Brothers?' They shook their heads, and Wyndham clucked approvingly. 'Then follow me,' he said.

They pushed through the thick scrub beside the line, moving swiftly and silently, until they came level with the station. It was merely a single wooden platform some ten yards long, with the water-tower standing stark and black against the green of the jungle about fifty yards further on. There was a siding here, where the single track of the permanent way split into two to provide a passing point. It was mid-afternoon, and they could see the three gangers who formed the staff of the place taking their siesta in the shade of a hut beside the track. A lean, yellow pi-dog came out from under the platform and sniffed the air, then started to bark, and it was joined by others, a dozen or so of them, in a canine chorus of yelping, snarling and howling. One of the gangers sat up and groped for a rock and hurled it at the nearest of them angrily. Wyndham quickened his pace and they hurried on until the barking had died away in the distance.

'It is because of the dogs that you must take the risk of boarding the train at speed down the line,' he explained to the others. 'If you waited near the station they would give the alarm.'

'It is no risk,' Tapa answered shortly. 'We are Mundavers.'

They went on for a further two miles, then Wyndham stopped and whistled softly, and a group of little men appeared like shadows in front of them, coming from the undergrowth and dropping from the overhead branches.

'Yes, you are Mundavers,' Wyndham said approvingly. 'Here, my Brothers, is where the thing will happen. The train will start from the station, and will be gathering speed at this point, before commencing its climb up the long gradient. You will watch for my light to flash from the roof of the last coach, and when it has passed you will deal with the tree – ' he slapped the trunk of a tall nim – '*this* tree. Today we shall cut through the trunk, to this mark, so that the tree remains standing – but a few blows of an axe later will cause it to fall – that way – across the line. It must be done quickly, my Brothers, but it must be done accurately and it must fall truly, because on the tree rests the success of the whole thing. Ten minutes later – maybe a little longer or even a little less – the last coach will come back down the line, detached from the train and running free. The tree must stop it – and hold it. Tapa and Sindal and I, Daku, will have jumped clear before this, in case the sudden stop should throw us off the roof. You others will lie here in the jungle, silent and unseen, until the doors are opened and I have dealt with the men inside. Then you will come forward, two and two and two together, as I call you – and each two will take a box between them. The boxes are not big, but they are heavy, although not beyond the strength of young, stout men. They have a rope handle at each end, which makes their carrying easier. We will set out then along the path by which we came here last night – back to the river – and the canoes. Twelve canoes, as you know – two boxes and four men to each. We paddle upstream for two hours, then land at the place you have already seen, and we take the canoes out of the water, and carry them deep into the jungle and hide them. Then we set off with the boxes – moving as only Mundavers can in the dark, and leaving not a sign or a mark behind us. A night and a day and we will be back in the village. It will be a hard journey – and for food we will have only the handful of cooked rice each man will carry – to be eaten as we march.' He paused and ran his eye round the circle of faces. 'And now I ask again if any man wishes to withdraw? – and I promise that none shall think the worse of him.' They looked back at him steadily, and this time there was the occasional shy grin.

'Thank you, my Brothers,' he concluded softly. 'Let us work together – and in fifteen days all shall be rich men.'

Sam said, 'Here's the gun – a Webley .45 one of the cheeky little sods knocked off a sergeant when he was asleep on the Madras Express. Only five rounds with it – '

'That will be sufficient,' Wyndham said.

'You're not going to use it on nobody, are you?' Sam asked anxiously.

'I hope not. All right. Now how do you intend to get to Kolar?'

'That's been worrying me rather. I don't want to go right in on the train in case I run into a cop I might have met before. At the same time I can't risk driving my old tin lizzie – '

'Good God no,' Wyndham said. 'The thing to do is to go to Tirrupattur by train on the thirtieth, then take a taxi from there in the evening. There's a government dak bungalow about a mile short of the Kolar Compound. Stop him there and pay him off, as if you were going in. Wait until he's out of sight, then cross the road. Have a look at the map again – this is the dak bungalow. Keep that dead behind you – there's a light over the gate. You'll come to the river in a matter of minutes. You'll have to wade it. It's not deep at this time of the year. Turn right on the opposite bank – here – and walk for half a mile as near as you can judge – and go to ground in the scrub on the hillside. About here. Got that?'

'Got it,' Sam said rather glumly.

'You should be bang opposite the Central Registry now. You won't be able to pick it out at night, but you can't miss it by day. It's a big square white building with a railway spur running up to it. Have you got a good pair of binoculars?'

'I could sell you twelve of the bastards,' Sam said sourly.

'I'd take hard rations for four days if I were you – bully beef and army biscuits – '

'I got false teeth – and the bloody things don't fit,' Sam grumbled.

'Too bad. You needn't carry water, because the river is right in front of you. You must have a clean change of clothes with you, though – for the return journey. A scruffy European is noticeable. You'll want a razor, comb, towel, and soap also, of course. Carry the lot in a small suitcase. Now, what have you got to watch for?'

'Christ! We've gone over that half a dozen times already,' Sam wailed.

'Again,' said Wyndham sharply.

Sam sighed. 'A single grey-painted railway coach which will be pushed along the spur line up to the Central Registry,' he said.

'It will be loaded there with wooden boxes – twenty or more, we hope. The same engine will come back for it later, and pull it on to the main line, and then off towards Bangalore.'

'And what do you do?'

'Get over to the railway station at the double and phone Bangalore three-nine-five-two – '

'Which is?'

'A crummy pub called the Star of the East Hotel.'

'And you ask for?'

'An Indian Christian gent by the name of Mister Daniel. I speak English – with a chee-chee accent – '

'What do you say?'

'I say, "Is that you, Dan? Have you heard about Uncle George?" – and he says, "Not lately. How is he?" – and I say, "He was all right when I saw him – quarter of an hour – half-an-hour – an hour – ago" – according to how long it's been between the coach moving out and me getting through to him.'

'Good. Now, unless you're very unlucky – or very stupid – you shouldn't run into anybody who knows you, police or otherwise, but if you do, have your story ready. Don't try to disguise your identity – just say things are a little tough with your business in Mysore and you've come over to Kolar to see if there's a chance of a job. You can travel back on the next train quite openly. Any questions?'

'Yes,' said Sam. 'When do I hear from you again – after the whole thing is over?'

'Come back to this same spot on the fifteenth of next month. If I don't turn up, make it the fifteenth of the following month,' Wyndham told him.

'Jesus,' said Sam, and looked disappointed. 'Is it going to take as long as all that?'

'To melt the whole lot down and recast it into small bars is going to take the better part of six months,' Wyndham said. 'For you to filter the stuff out is going to take another year. I'm not going to risk anything by flooding the market all at once. Just try to use your head, Sam.'

'Oh, don't worry about my part of it,' said Sam, tapping the side of his nose. 'I wasn't born yesterday, you know. How will you be wanting your cut?'

'I'll tell you that later. Probably half in silver rupees for the little men, half in used ten-rupee notes,' Wyndham said.

'That's going to be pretty bulky.'

'It has to be. The Mundavers won't touch paper money, and I'm not in a position to handle notes of a big denomination – yet.' He rose. 'All right, Sam. Best of luck.'

'Suppose I wanted to get in touch with you sooner,' Sam said. 'Any way I can? I mean, if something really urgent cropped up that you ought to know about?'

Wyndham considered for some moments, then he said slowly, 'The forty-seventh milestone on the Bangalore-Mysore road. Drive past it in daylight, going north. Wear a white handkerchief knotted round your throat, like a sweat-rag. Continue on into Bangalore and then come back after dark and stop at the same spot. Pull in off the road out of sight – like you do here.'

Sam gave a thumbs-up sign. 'I'd feel more comfortable if we weren't cut off altogether,' he said.

'And *I'd* feel more comfortable if you didn't use it,' Wyndham told him. 'It must only be in a case of dire necessity. You understand that?'

'Oh, sure, sure,' Sam said. 'Well, the best of British bloody luck to the both of us, Johnnie – sorry – Daku.'

'Be careful, Sam,' Wyndham said softly. 'Do please be very careful.' He made the sign again with forefinger and thumb and went off into the undergrowth silently – and once more Sam found himself shivering.

Chapter 36

'Have you heard about Uncle George?' said the voice the other end of the line.

'Not lately,' said Somari. 'How is he?'

'He was all right when I saw him – exactly forty minutes ago,' said the voice, and Somari hung up.

'It is customary for a guest to give a small gratuity when called from a bedroom down to the telephone,' said the room-bearer in Tamil, hopefully.

'Fuggoff,' answered Somari in English, tersely, and walked out of the dingy lobby into the late evening twilight. He breathed deeply and appreciatively. Twelve months in the jungle had made his three-day incarceration in the smelly little hotel bedroom sheer hell. He crossed the crowded Station Square to the bazaar the other side, and went through it to the Peshwa Gardens. He sat on a bench overlooking the lotus pond, and a tall Marwari wearing dark sunglasses strolled slowly past and leaned over the stone balustrade a little further along. Somari rose and joined him.

'Forty minutes, sahib,' he murmured, 'and five more to reach here.'

'Good,' said Wyndham, without looking at him. 'Now get my suitcase from the Left Luggage office and buy me a second-class ticket to Guntakul. Use the suitcase to reserve me a seat as near to the end of the train as possible, and wait in the crowd on the platform. I shall come at the last moment.'

'Let me go with you, sahib,' Somari begged.

'We have argued enough about this,' Wyndham told him. 'Don't give trouble now. You will return to the village and wait my arrival. If all goes well I shall come after two days, then there will be much for us both to do.' He chuckled and switched from Hindi to the type of English Somari knew and appreciated. 'Beat it, you little bastard, or I'll kick your arse. You want to be a rich man, don't you?'

'Sure,' said Somari gloomily. 'But I worry like hell over this one. All right for little buggers to jump fast train – but not for you. You'll break bloody neck.'

'I'm not going to jump any fast trains, you stupid little clot,' Wyndham said. 'That's why I'm starting from here – dressed up like a damned boxwalla. Go on – hop it.'

'All right. Good luck, sahib,' Somari said and started to move off disconsolately.

'Don't worry any more, old lad,' Wyndham called after him softly. 'Everything's going to be fine – you see.'

He collected his ticket from Somari on the platform, nodded curtly and got aboard. His compartment was in the last coach but one, with only the combined mail and guard's van behind it. A fat Brahmin was already installed, sitting cross-legged on one of the seats with his luggage spread ostentatiously about him to discourage crowding. He glared at Wyndham as he got in. So far, so good. A Brahmin was not likely to get into conversation with a mere Marwari, who was three rungs lower on the ladder of caste. He opened one of the windows and leaned out, idly looking at the crowd on the platform. Things had changed in the last three years, he reflected. Travelling had been a purgatory in the early days, when his scalp used to prickle at the sight of a police-man's uniform and he'd jump if anybody spoke to him.

Whistles were shrilling and the guard was holding a green lantern aloft. The train started to jerk forward, then ran slowly out of the station into the darkness. This was the moment he had been dreading. If the Kolar coach was not hitched on now, the whole thing fell to the ground. He craned forward out of the window and looked up towards the engine. Yes, someone beside the track was waving a red lantern. The train stopped and the buffers bumped along its whole length, then it ran back a few feet. Behind him he heard another engine whistle sharply, and turning, he saw through the darkness the bulk of a coach being shunted slowly from a siding. It passed under a light and with a surge of relief that almost overwhelmed him for a moment, he recognized the two heavily barred windows at one end. It was directly behind now, and out of sight, then there was another sharp toot from the shunting engine, followed by a bump as the coach came forward and hit the buffers of the mail van. He closed the window and sat down. The Brahmin, in the manner of his kind, was contemplating his navel and infinity, looking down his nose as superciliously as a camel. Well, he could have the whole damned compartment to himself in an hour and a half. The train moved forward again and bumped over the points, then it was running smoothly and picking up speed, and the lights of Bangalore were sliding past.

He closed his eyes. They'd be passing through Frazer Town shortly. He wondered what Paul and fat, comfortable little Tina were doing at this moment. It was over twelve months since he had had any communication with them. A clean break. They'd be hurt and anxious, he knew – but it was better so. He'd brought enough trouble to them. To all his friends. The money was going to worry Paul when he received it. Five thousand rupees a month he intended sending him – for the next year. Ten-rupee notes in a parcel through the mail, posted in different places, with no accompanying letter. That would be roughly five thousand pounds – enough to cover the first five or six years of the boy's education at Home. Then later there would be more. He hoped to be out of the country himself by then, and he would be able to communicate with them openly. Yes, five thousand pounds. That would take him right through prep school – from the age of nine to thirteen, then another five to see him through whatever public school they chose for him – from thirteen to eighteen, and a further five for university, and a final lump sum to launch him on his career. He wondered what that would be – and hoped it wouldn't be the army. But that would be the boy's affair – and Paul's. He wasn't going to interfere. He had no right to. His was only the self-imposed task of providing the means – and, by God, they'd be adequate means. There'd be no penny-pinching here. The world would be the lad's oyster. Yes, Julia my darling, in this, if in nothing else, your wishes will be fulfilled, he promised inwardly. In this he would keep faith. It was the only thing he lived for now – this, and providing that silly little loyal bastard Somari with enough to live on comfortably and keep him out of mischief for the rest of his life – if that were possible. For himself he wanted nothing, even if he got out of the country eventually. He'd earn his own living honestly.

He felt drowsy. The last three days had been a strain: waiting for Somari to contact him with the news, wondering whether

Sam would make a mess of things at the last minute, uncertain, in fact, of the gold shipment still keeping to its tight schedule. He grinned drily. They'd certainly change things after this. He hoped there would be no trouble with the four guards. Those he had known were amiable and inoffensive people: McDermott, Griffiths, d'Mello and Hawkesley – Anglo-Indians who normally formed the searching team at the mines. They had a whole day on the loose in Bombay each month, and they'd come back grinning covertly and winking – implying that they had set the town alight. On the occasions he had been down with them they had done nothing more desperate than some shopping for their wives, after which they had sat in the YMCA drinking innumerable cups of tea. He yawned and looked at his watch. An hour to go. He yawned again.

He woke with a start as the train stopped. He got up and looked out of the window. Yes, they were at Dondabagh, the point where they had to wait for the down Mail to pass them. Like Lona, it was merely a siding branching off from the single track. He felt himself go cold. He could have missed it so easily. The Brahmin was now sleeping, cocooned in a white sheet. Wyndham picked up his suitcase and dropped down from the train on the blind side and slid under the coach out of sight of anybody who might pass along the platform. He opened the suitcase and took out a suit of blue dungaree rail-worker's clothes, then dragged off his Marwari garments and dressed in the others. He stowed his revolver and flashlight in the pockets, together with a mask he had fashioned from a piece of black muslin, pulled a tight woollen cap over his head, repacked the suitcase and came out again. He had thought of everything – even to the long piece of cord to pull the suitcase up to the roof after he had climbed on to it. He could hear the down Mail whistling in the distance. The wait here varied from five minutes to anything up to an hour, according to the punctuality of the other train. Tonight it seemed to be almost dead on time.

The climb was easy. Just a quick heave on to the couplings, then there were iron plates welded on to the end of the coach to form footholds. He shinned up and lay flat on the roof, facing forward. He could see the full length of the long train now. The fire-doors of the engine were open and the red glare was lighting the trees at the side of the track. He pulled the suitcase up and wormed his way backwards to a round ventilator which stood some six inches 'proud' to the gently convex roof. This, he knew from his previous experience, would be a friend in need later when the train was moving at speed. It was something solid to hang on to and it broke the slipstream. He looped the cord round it to secure the suitcase and to provide a convenient handhold for himself.

He could hear indistinct male voices through the ventilator, and an appetizing smell of curry came up to him. That would be d'Mello cooking in the caboose. He was a dab hand with a curry.

The down Mail thundered through, its whistle screaming, the lighted windows forming one unbroken yellow line, and then the signal light at the end of the siding turned from red to green and they started to run slowly back on to the main track. He fumbled in the suitcase for the pair of motor-cyclist's goggles he had told Sam to get him, and put them on. He had been half-blinded with flying ash particles last time.

They were picking up speed now, and he settled himself down for two hours of acute discomfort. Lona next stop. He was thankful for the long bridge over the Ghanda River five miles short of it. They would slow down considerably to cross it and would not get back to full speed before the point where they had to decrease again for the stop – the point where Tapa and Sindal would be boarding. The night was warm but the wind of their own making was chilling him, and he found himself envying the driver and fireman on their comfortable footplate up forward. Still, it was a good thing, as it stopped him from feeling drowsy. He shuddered to think what would happen if he went to sleep.

The whistle wailed and he felt the brakes being applied, and far ahead of them he saw the two pinpoints of light that marked the approach to the bridge. He eased his cramped muscles and sat up as the slipstream slackened. They rumbled across the bridge, the lights from the carriage windows flickering over the basketwork girders each side. Now they were clear, and picking up speed again. He started to count. Three hundred at something slightly quicker than boxing count-out time, he reckoned. He could have timed it more accurately by his watch, but he couldn't see the luminous dial clearly through his goggles – and if he took them off his eyes watered. He pulled the flashlight from his pocket and shielded it with his body against a chance backward glance from the engine. '. . . two nine-seven, two nine-eight, two nine-nine, three hundred.' He flashed two longs and a short, and exhaled shudderingly in a long sigh of relief as he felt the brakes going on again. Dead on time. His reckoning had been accurate. 'Time spent on reconnaissance is never wasted,' as they used to teach at Sandhurst. But they'd have to lose a lot more speed before even Mundavers could possibly hope to board . . . Then he gasped as a dark head emerged above the line made by the edge of the roof – at the front, in between the two coaches – and was followed by another.

The two little men slid along towards him and he reached out and slapped each in turn on the bare, greased shoulder approvingly, and saw the flash of white teeth in the darkness as they grinned. They were a taciturn people, but like all true artists they relished appreciation.

The single red signal light of Lona was now in sight and the train was sliding to a standstill with locked wheels screeching and throwing sparks. He felt in the suitcase for the hammer and the six-inch-long, one-and-a-half-inch-diameter steel pin Sam had had made for him by a Mysore blacksmith. They stopped, and Wyndham and Sindal climbed down quickly in the pitch dark between the coaches. He groped for the 'You-and-I' couplings. The term was a facetious but apt description of the U-shaped shackle on one coach into which the straight, or I-shaped, bar of the one in front of it fitted. A pin ran through holes in the top of each arm of the 'U' and the 'I' between them – screw-threaded at one end and secured with another, shorter, pin which fitted into a keyway. The shorter one slid out easily, but the screw on the main pin gave trouble, because dust had become caked in the grease in the threads, and the thing jammed. Wyndham sweated and strained without success, then as a last resort he had to use the hammer, and to his ears the clinking sounded thunderous. Then somewhere nearby but unseen the dogs gathered and started to snarl and bark, and Tapa hissed from the roof of the coach that somebody was coming along the line with a lamp. Wyndham gave one last desperate thump with the hammer and felt the screw give. He fumbled it out somehow and inserted the pin and then took shelter under the coach. The whistle sounded from the engine and he panicked for a moment and lay flat between the rails, expecting the train to jerk forward, but it was only a warning blast, and he had time to crawl out shakily before the signal light changed from red to green. Sindal was sitting on the buffers unconcernedly, and Wyndham risked a quick flash of his torch in order to show him the pin and to demonstrate in dumbshow how it was to be knocked out, then, as the engine whistled again and the train moved forward, they climbed back to the roof.

They picked up speed quickly and the glare from the open firedoors was fierce and prolonged as the fireman stoked up for the climb. Wyndham counted sixty and then started to flash a series of longs and shorts to his right, keeping it up for a further three minutes to make certain that the signal would be showing clearly as they passed the two-mile point. This was dangerous, as he knew that the driver and fireman could not fail to see it if they looked back, but it was a risk he had to accept.

He felt the clacking rhythm of the wheels changing gradually to a slower beat, and the speed was dropping, and he knew that they were now on the gradient. It commenced with a long narrow cutting, and the lights from the windows were reflecting back off solid walls. There was a banked turn to the right at the upper end, followed by one to the left – a prolonged S-bend. He started to count again. From zero to a possible sixty miles an hour, average thirty miles an hour for four minutes – total distance run, two miles. Then the cutting, and the speed decreasing in a steeply descending curve to a calculated fifteen miles an hour by the time they came to the end of the S. That would be a further two miles. He took his goggles off and chanced another flash of the torch as he consulted his watch. Dead on – he hoped. He nudged Sindal and handed him the hammer, and the little man slid over the fore end of the coach and disappeared into the darkness. He reappeared again almost immediately, and Wyndham felt a sickening sense of let-down, because the coach was still running steadily, but then, as he was about to react angrily, there was a slight jerk and a check, and he realized that the air-hose of the pneumatic braking system had been holding them for some moments before snapping under the strain. The gap between themselves and the lights of the coach in front was perceptibly

364

widening – and he wanted to yell in sheer exultation.

It had worked!

They slowed and stopped and he strained his ears at the ventilator to hear if there was any reaction from the men below, but there was no sound other than some loud concerted snoring. They were running back gently now, and the sound of the labouring engine was dying in the distance. He inched forward to the two Mundavers and patted each on the shoulder again. They chuckled happily and their teeth flashed in the darkness.

But now his worries were commencing once more. The only thing he had not been able to calculate in advance had been their speed backwards downhill. At first it was less than a snail's pace, but now it was quickening and he had no means of judging it, and the motion was vastly different from that of their forward progress. It was jumpy and uncontrolled, and the rhythmic 'clacketty-clack . . . clacketty-clack . . . clacketty-clack' had become a wild 'clack-clack-clack-clack' and they lurched sickeningly, first left, then right, on the S-bend. They were back in the cutting now. He could tell that from the noise echoing from the walls, but there was no light reflecting back because the electric cable had snapped with the air-hose.

Now they were out of the cutting, and Wyndham was really frightened, because their speed seemed to be at least equal to that of the fastest they had travelled forward, and he knew that he faced the probability of serious injury if not death if he tried to jump – a probability which would become almost a stone-cold certainty if he remained on the roof until they hit the tree.

But he reckoned without the Mundavers. They were completely unconcerned and they seemed to know instinctively exactly where they were from one flying minute to the next. Grinning and chuckling with sheer enjoyment, they placed themselves each side of Wyndham and guided him feet-first and flat on his belly to the new rear end of the coach, then, with Tapa below on the buffers, placing his feet on the climbing plates, and Sindal with the trebled cord belayed around him, they got him down on to the relatively firm platform of the couplings. They rested here for a minute or so, then Sindal craned round the corner of the coach and gave Wyndham a warning nudge, and together, with a strength that amazed him, familiar as he thought himself with their capabilities, they each took him by an arm and lowered him until his feet were just clear of the flying road-bed – then released him. Then his own instincts took over. He had been thrown from horses often enough to know how to fall at speed. He folded up into a ball and let himself roll – and almost before the shock hit him, the Mundavers had him in their iron grip again and had hauled him to his feet. It was just another of the little men's workaday miracles. He stood stock-still while his heart descended slowly from the back of his throat. He hadn't sustained a scratch.

Down the line, a bare hundred yards in front of them, there was a terrific crash.

He ran forward. The coach was on its side, slewed at a drunken angle across the track, the uppermost wheels still spinning – and the shattered tree trunk had been flung like a matchstick into the ditch a good dozen yards in front of it. Black shadows were already flitting noiselessly out of the jungle towards them.

He took out his torch and made a quick examination. The heavy steel sides had withstood the impact and there appeared to be no exterior damage, but he was well aware that the shock to those inside would have been cataclysmic. He climbed up the couplings on to the side and felt his way to the door, hoping that it might have burst open – but it was still tightly closed. He moved to the nearest window. It was shattered, and he could hear groans. He rapped on the wall with the butt of his revolver and shouted, 'Quickly, sahib! There has been a bad accident! Open the door!'

Somebody said dazedly in English, 'Oh, Jesus! What's happened?' and followed with the same question in Hindi.

'Quickly, sahib,' Wyndham repeated urgently. 'There's fire coming!'

There were other voices now, mixing in lurid profanity and frightened questions. Wyndham moved away and tapped on the door to guide them to it. There was a long pause and he fretted and fumed until he heard a metallic rattle the other side, and then the heavy door lifted an inch or so.

Somebody said, 'But we're not supposed to open it,' and somebody else growled, 'Bollocks, man! You please yourself. I'm not getting roasted for any bugger!'

Wyndham muttered to Tapa and Sindal, and they grabbed the

door-handle and heaved it open like a trap. He shone his torch down on the men inside. They were standing on the wall of the strong-room, which now formed a floor – four badly shaken people, one of whom was bleeding copiously from a cut in his head. He could see the key they had used still in the lock – on a ring with a second key hanging from it. He sighed with relief. That, he knew, was the one to the strong-room itself. He hadn't been relishing the prospect of having to be tough with them, although he was quite prepared to be had it been necessary. He jumped down behind them, letting them see his revolver in the beam of the torch, and patted them over, taking a gun from each, then ignoring their frightened and bewildered questions, he prodded them into the caboose and lowered the door down on to them. He unlocked the strong-room and looked down into it and saw a tumble of boxes. He whispered his instructions to Tapa, who relayed them back to the waiting Mundavers, and the unloading began – swiftly and dexterously and in complete silence. There were twenty-two boxes. One thousand, two hundred and thirty-two pounds of raw, unalloyed gold.

Wyndham stood and watched the last pair of little men slip away into the jungle with a box between them, then he and Tapa lowered the outside door down again and locked it, leaving the key in position. He shone his torch on to his watch. It had taken them just under the hour. The Mail would not reach the next stop, Dharmaparam, for another two. Allow an hour for the inevitable flap that would occur when they realized that the gold coach was missing, plus at least another three for the search engine to get back here. A six-hour start.

Perfect. He followed Tapa down the path to the river.

Chapter 37

Sir Jeremy Cardwell, KCIE, hurried up the steps of Police Headquarters, Madras, and along the verandah to his office, without, for once, returning the sentry's salute at the main entrance. Superintendent Westcott, his PA, came in through the connecting door before being summoned – another departure from the norm.

Sir Jeremy said, 'If you've called me down from Ooti on a wild goose chase, Bill, I, personally, will order your castration.'

'I shudder to think what you'd have ordered if I *hadn't* let you know, sir.'

'Tell me again – right from the beginning,' the inspector-general said.

'The hammer was picked up between the rails – right smack in the middle of the track,' Westcott said. 'If it had been accidentally dropped from a passing train it would have been at the side. Thank God the DSP – Selwyn – was there at the time, and he used his head. There seemed to him to be a logical connection between the hammer and the coupling-screw found at Lona, and a steel pin picked up near the top of the gradient. They'd all been handled pretty extensively by the search parties, but he wrapped them up and sent them down for fingerprinting, just on the forlorn off-chance that they might find something.' He spread a series of photographic blow-ups on the desk. 'Our chaps couldn't find anything useful on them, but Forsythe thought it worthwhile to forward them to Calcutta.' He pointed to one of the photos. 'By God, *they* found something. Half a thumbprint – right – and a perfect middle and third on the haft of the hammer – *there* – and another rather more indistinct thumb – *there* – but still unmistakable – and a damned good *left* thumb on the coupling-screw – there. Nothing of any value on the pin. Now, these are the only reasonable-sized prints – the rest are small and are obviously Mundaver.'

'Wyndham,' breathed Sir Jeremy. 'I just can't believe it. The wretched feller's dead as far as we're concerned.'

'Not officially,' Westcott said. 'He's got three years before he goes through the full obsequies and his dabs come off the record.'

'What was the report at the time?'

'That he made a break from the Andamans after a warder's wife had been murdered, and got clean away in a canoe, which was subsequently picked up fifty miles offshore after a hell of a storm – with his blood-stained prison jacket in it.'

'How the *hell* did he arrange that?'

'God knows. It never occurred to anybody that it *had* been arranged. It told its own story, and as you've just said yourself, sir, as far as we were concerned he was dead.'

Sir Jeremy pinched his lower lip. 'I suppose there's no chance of this being a mistake?'

'*They* say they'll stake their reputations on it. Look for yourself, sir.' Westcott pointed to another photo. 'That's a copy of the CRO dabs. I'm not an expert in this field, thank the Lord, but I know enough about it to say that that and *that* are identical.'

'Um.' Sir Jeremy nodded slowly. 'Yes – I agree.'

'And it checks,' Westcott went on. 'The guards say that the fellow in charge was a tall man. Wyndham was six feet one inch. Secondly, Hawkesley said that he thought the chap's Hindi was a bit too good for an Indian. He meant too grammatical – not idiomatic enough – a language that had been learnt and not naturally acquired. "Officer's bhat" he called it. And it *was* Hindi – not Madrassi or Tamil or Telegu or Malayalim as one would expect a local Indian to be speaking in those parts.'

'Where on earth has he been for the last four years? Sir Jeremy fumed. 'A European can't stay underground that long in *this* country – not if every policeman is doing his job and keeping his damned eyes and ears open.'

'Quite obviously with the Mundavers. The guards all agree that he spoke the language. None of them speaks it himself but they recognized his fluency in it. Have you ever had a go at it, sir?'

'Good heavens no. It takes me all my time to rub along in Hindi and Urdu.'

'It's a horror – all clicks and grunts. I tried to pick up a few words when I was after an old devil . . .' He broke off and said '*Jesus!*' and Sir Jeremy, who disapproved of intemperate language, looked at him coldly. 'Sorry, sir,' went on Westcott, 'but something just occurred to me. Horslake? Remember him?'

'Very well indeed,' Sir Jeremy said. 'Far too old to be in this sort of racket. Besides, he was only a little runt like a superannuated jockey.'

'I know. But at the time of the fire there was a whisper of a sahib who had been living in that rabbit-warren of theirs. A tall man they called Johnnie Walker. I tried to follow it up but got nowhere, so I put it down to bazaar gossip and just forgot it . . .'

'Yes, I think I remember seeing something about that in the report . . .'

'Well now, when I was DSP up in the mofussil before coming here, an informer told us that Horslake – Sam sahib, as they call him – was heavily involved in fencing stuff stolen by the Mundavers. He and that old besom of a wife of his, Aunty, were running a small general store in Mysore . . .'

'Yes – go on.'

'We turned him over once or twice, but never found anything on the premises, so I gave him a gipsy's warning on general principles . . .'

'So?' said Sir Jeremy, and Westcott shrugged somewhat lamely.

'Well, it strikes me that there might be a connection somewhere there: Sam, a tall European, Mundavers – and all in the Mysore area.'

'A bit nebulous,' said Sir Jeremy doubtfully. 'But we can keep it in mind. I'm going to ask for troops.'

'Troops?' said Westcott, startled.

'I don't see that I have any alternative.' Sir Jeremy left his desk and went to a big wall map. 'Look at this, Bill.' He ran his finger round a wide green area. 'Four hundred square miles of well-nigh impenetrable jungle. We know the gold is in there somewhere, but we haven't enough police in the entire province to comb one corner of that properly, let alone the whole area. It will take at least a brigade of seasoned, experienced, jungle-trained troops . . .'

'With the Mundavers running rings round them, literally,' said Westcott bitterly. 'The little devils will just pick the stuff up and move in front of them, and round their flanks and finish up behind them. I *know* them, sir. Heavy-hoofed soldiers wouldn't stand a chance against them. The Mundavers would just laugh at them.'

'It's all very well for you to stand there theorizing,' said Sir Jeremy acidly. 'But just put yourself in my position for a moment. The robbery took place three months ago, and we haven't come up with a single lead of any value. New Delhi, Simla and Whitehall are screaming their heads off, the Gold Consortium has raised its reward to *fifty thousand pounds* – nearly twenty-five per cent of its value . . .'

'Panic money – in case it happens again,' said Westcott.

'As it very well might, if this fellow Wyndham *is* running things. And can you see the heads rolling in the dust *then*? Mine among them.' Sir Jeremy shuddered. 'Sorry, Bill. I don't like doing it, but I've just got to eat humble pie and tell the governor that the problem is beyond us, and say "Can I have some soldiers, please?" He'll agree with me wholeheartedly. He made some pretty caustic remarks about the police last time I saw him. His damned ADC was robbed of his pretties on a train, and he dragged up that Kolar murder – the European, what was his name? and the suspect who just walked through us and disappeared . . .'

'Oh, my God!' Westcott gasped. 'Timothy Martin – *he* was a tall man too. He worked there! He'd have known the routine . . .'

'More theories? Splendid,' said Sir Jeremy drily. 'I wonder why nobody thought of taking a few random fingerprints round *his* bungalow at the time? Not that it would have done much good. It's taken them three months to come up with this lot.' He flicked the photos on the desk. 'Incidentally, I want the name of Wyndham kept absolutely dark at this stage – and ask Calcutta, of their charity, to do the same, or we'll have the world-wide Press yammering round our ears again and making a Robin Hood out of the murdering swine.'

Westcott was trembling. 'Yes, sir, I'll do that – but, sir – *please* – before you ask for Army co-operation – can I have a few days on it? Can I be relieved of my duties here and given a free hand?'

'A free hand where?'

'A free hand with Sam. If he knows anything about Wyndham, he'll cough.'

'Cough?'

'I'm sorry, sir,' said Westcott. 'I'm not a gentleman copper, like my colleagues from the Imperial Police College – saving your presence. I came up the hard way. "Cough" is low rozzer's cant for "squeal, sing, lisp or grass". Oh, yes – if there's anything in this that he knows about, he'll cough all right – if he's frightened enough.'

'Yes, Bill,' said Sir Jeremy uneasily. 'But there *are* limits, you know . . .'

'And I'll observe 'em, sir – but please, *please* give me this chance. Don't you see what it could mean? Wyndham, Martin *and* this lot cleared off the books – and by *us*.'

'You're letting your imagination run away with you,' Sir Jeremy said, but some of Westcott's excitement was transferring itself to him. 'All right – seven days. No more. If you haven't come back here with something solid then – and I mean *solid* – nature takes its course and the Army moves in – and you and I would be well advised to look for a couple of good commissionaire's jobs in London.' His last words fell on empty air, because Westcott was already on his way along the verandah.

'All right, all right, I'm coming,' said Sam irritably as the knock sounded again on the shop door. He put the lamp down on the counter and slid back the bolts and opened the door a bare couple of inches on its chain. 'Who is it?' he demanded fretfully.

'Don't open whoever it is,' Aunty called from the back room. 'Bloody bastards! Three o'clock in the morning . . .'

'Right, Sam, you know me,' the dark figure the other side muttered. 'Open up.'

'Oh, my Gawd!' Sam quavered. 'Mr Westcott. Look, sir . . .' He fumbled the chain out of its groove. 'I don't know what this is about, but . . .'

'You didn't do it,' said Westcott gently as he slipped inside. 'Yes, I know that. I just happened to be passing and I thought, "My old pal Sam. I haven't seen him for ages. I wonder what he's doing now?" That's what I thought, Sam. Then I thought I'd drop in – just to pass the time of day.'

'Which happens to be three o'clock in the bleeding morning,' said Sam. 'Not that you're any the less welcome for that, sir,' he added hastily. 'Can I get you a drink?'

'Not at the moment, Sam, but thank you for the kindly thought.'
He shivered slightly. 'Gets quite nippy here before dawn, doesn't
it? Of course Mysore is that much higher than Madras. Last time
I was up here it was to see a topping. Damn nearly freezing it
was. Everybody, including the client, shivering like dogs passing
razor-blades.'

'I'm afraid I don't follow, sir,' said Sam innocently. 'A topping?'

'Low English criminal slang, Sam. Of course, they call it
phansi dena here, don't they? A hanging.'

'Aw, shit!' said Sam. 'What a bloody subject! Here – if you
don't mind I'll get a drink for myself. Sure you won't join me?'
He took a bottle of whisky and two glasses from under the
counter.

'No, thank you, Sam.' Westcott watched him as he poured a
stiff peg for himself, then he reached out and took the glass.
'And I think it might be a good idea if *you* waited until later, also.'

'Hey! What the hell do you think you're doing?' Sam demanded
indignantly – but there was a noticeable shake in his voice.

'For your own good, Sam,' Westcott said kindly. 'I don't want
you to be under an unfair disadvantage. Nothing like a liquor-
loosened tongue for getting one into trouble.'

'I'm not in any trouble,' Sam said earnestly.

'I hope not indeed,' Westcott said. 'But . . .' He sighed and
shook his head ponderously.

'You can search the bloody joint here and now,' Sam screamed.
'Go on – search it – whether you've got a warrant or not. You'll
find nothing here. I'm clean, I tell you. Have been for years.
You know that yourself.'

'Sam,' Westcott said quietly. 'Use your head. I'm a superintendent – a bara sahib – a very senior police officer. You don't
honestly think that I'd be coming all the way up from Madras to
drop in on you at three o'clock in the morning just in the hope
of catching you with a couple of hot suitcases, do you? No, Sam,
this is serious – bloody serious.'

'What's serious?' Sam shouted. 'What the hell is this all about?'

'The law of the accessory, Sam,' Westcott told him. 'Personally
I'm not altogether in agreement with it. I think it's a bit unfair –
but then I don't make the laws. I'm only here to see that they're
obeyed.'

'Don't tell the smarmy son-of-a-bitch nothing,' Aunty called from the back room. 'Tell him you want a lawyer.'

'A typically feminine contradiction,' Westcott smiled. 'But actually she's right. You certainly *ought* to have a lawyer. You can phone from the station.'

'*What* station?'

'The police station, naturally.'

'Mr Westcott, for Christ's sake,' Sam pleaded tearfully. 'What the hell's this all about? What am I supposed to have *done*?'

'I don't think you did do it, Sam,' Westcott assured him. 'In fact I'm certain you didn't. But you *were* an accessory, you see? In so far as you associated with him. Two murders, Sam – damn it all – plus one he was already doing life for. You must have known.'

'Known what?' Sam was shaking in every limb, and gasping. 'What the hell are you talking about?'

'The bastard's mad,' Aunty yelled. 'Not a word, Sam – not another bloody word to him.'

'If you interrupt again, madam, I shall send you down to the station first,' Westcott told her, and there was a rumbling silence from the back room thereafter. 'All right, Sam,' he continued. 'This fellow Johnnie Walker . . .' Sam jumped, then tried to cover, too late. 'I see you remember *him* all right,' Westcott interrupted himself softly. 'You must have known when he was staying with you in that dunghill of yours in Madras that he was one Charles Wyndham, an escaped murderer from the Andamans.'

'I didn't – as God's me judge, I didn't,' Sam whispered.

'And you certainly knew him again as Timothy Martin when you were fixing up the Kolar gold train job – wanted for yet another murder by this time.'

'I didn't meet him until long after . . .' Sam began, then Aunty came storming out of the back room like a bedraggled Valkyrie, in a flapping night-gown, scanty hair awry and her face contorted.

'You bloody old fool! Shut up!' she shrieked. 'Can't you see the bastard's leading you on? You're giving your guts away with every word you say!'

'Get your clothes on,' Westcott told her grimly. 'I'm sending you down.'

'On what charge? Go on – tell us – on what charge?' she

demanded. '*I* know the law if that silly old sod don't.'

'Impeding a police officer in the execution of his duty,' Westcott said, wiping his face with his handkerchief. 'Also spitting at that same officer. You've forgotten to put your teeth in, madam.' He moved to the door, opened it slightly and called softly. Two Anglo-Indian sergeants entered. 'Take this lady down to the station and see that she's comfortably accommodated,' he ordered. 'I'll be down later to see her charged.'

'No need for that,' Aunty said, deflating like a punctured balloon. 'All right – I'll keep me mouth closed, Mr Westcott. But Sam lovey – be careful what you say. Oh Jesus! Be careful.' She went back into the room and closed the door, and Westcott dismissed the two policemen with a curt nod.

'Mr Westcott,' Sam said brokenly. 'I've never given you no trouble. I don't want to give none now – but I swear I had nothing to do with any of this. Nothing, Mr Westcott. You've got to believe me.'

'Now listen, Sam,' Westcott said very quietly. 'We know that Wyndham is out there in the jungle, not far from here, with the Mundavers. We're going to winkle him out, even if it takes half the Indian Army to do it – and when we get him he's going to stand trial for two more murders – one in the Andamans and one in Kolar. He's a cert for hanging, Sam – you can see that, surely? Now, consider your own position. Just suppose we, the police, turned really nasty and charged you as an accessory – and turned the heat on full. You could very easily be standing alongside him when he went through the hole in the floor, you know?'

'Oh my Gawd – no – no . . .' Sam moaned.

'And even if we didn't charge you, you'd still be called as a witness for the prosecution, and then word would undoubtedly go round that you'd fingered him.' Westcott made a sign across his throat and belly. Sam winced. 'Yes, we know all about the Brotherhood,' Westcott went on. 'How long do you think you'd last? Your name would be up in every criminal lodge in India. No place to hide, Sam. Not a damned place.'

'You – you – wouldn't do that . . .' Sam whispered brokenly.

'I'm sorry, Sam,' Westcott said gently. 'We'd have no option. But it needn't happen that way at all. Suppose you decided to help us . . .'

'I can't,' Sam wailed. 'I don't know *nothing*.'

'Let me finish, Sam,' Westcott said. 'Suppose you *did* know something – and as a result this man was caught, and a fair proportion of that gold was recovered – then your name needn't come into it at all.'

'But *they'd* know,' Sam said. 'What bloody chance would I stand then?'

'They needn't know – and you would be under police protection the whole time.' He paused. 'The whole time – until you landed in England. There's a reward of fifty thousand pounds – *pounds*, Sam, not rupees – *and* another five thousand rupees from the Government for the apprehension of an absconding convict. You'd be eligible for the lot – paid nice and quietly in Bombay – after you had got on the ship.' Westcott's voice dropped to a whisper. 'And not a soul would know – except us – and we're not likely to talk. You know that.'

Westcott reached across and poured whisky into the second glass. He balanced one in each hand. Sam looked at him, and moistened his dry lips. Westcott waited. He could hear the ticking of his own wrist-watch.

Sam whispered, 'He – he – told me – if – if I ever wanted – to see him – I had to drive past the forty-seventh milestone on the Bangalore-Mysore road – with – a white handkerchief – round me neck. Then come back – after dark.'

Westcott nodded slowly. 'I see,' he said. 'He has that spot watched constantly?'

'I – I – think so. Probably by a Mundaver. He didn't tell me the details. Just that,' Sam said.

'Have you ever done so?'

'No, never. Had no reason to.'

'Good,' said Westcott, and handed him a glass. 'Drink that, Sam – you'll feel much better.' He watched while the other gulped the whisky down, then he set his own glass back on the counter untouched. 'That's fine. Now remember: I've made you no promises. I'm not allowed to – but I think you can safely take it that that's the way it will be. Yes – that's the way it will be. A white handkerchief, eh? That's better than a nasty brown rope, isn't it? *And* fifty thousand as well.'

Sam gagged, retched, and spewed his whisky across the floor. Then he wept.

'There'll be a couple of policemen watching this place front and rear,' Westcott told him, and the gentleness had gone from his voice. 'Don't go out until you hear from me again – and pass that on to that woman.'

He went out into the night.

Chapter 38

The work was taking much longer than Wyndham had anticipated. He had melted down small quantities of lead in the past to make fishing-line sinkers, but half a ton of gold was a vastly different proposition, he reflected ruefully. The wastage was sinful. Dust glittered everywhere from the hacksaws he used to slice the bars like sandwich loaves. The moulds had given him a lot of trouble. He had searched the rivers nearby for clay without success, and had finally to settle for damp sand, which tended to collapse under the weight of the molten metal and spill it into uneven shapes. And he had to guess at the weights of the small ingots, because he had no scales. He'd really have to get in touch with Sam, because this way he would have no check on the old devil whatsoever. But it was the fuel supply that presented the biggest problem. The dried palm tree pith that the Mundavers used for their cooking fires gave off a fierce heat and no smoke, but it didn't burn long enough, and he had to use vast quantities of it for a relatively small amount of melted metal in the huge iron cauldron that in itself posed yet another difficulty, because it took a superhuman effort and too much time to get it off the fire to pour the stuff into the moulds, which meant that it used to cool and set before he had slopped half of it out.

Still, he was making progress, although it was going to take much longer than the six months he had told Sam. But that, in a way, was an advantage. The longer that elapsed between the raid and the first trickle of gold into the illicit markets the better.

He straightened up from the rough saw-bench he had constructed, as Somari pushed through the undergrowth into the small clearing beside the village.

'Little bugger just come in from road, sahib,' he said. 'Sam go past in car this morning – with white handkerchief round neck.'

Wyndham grinned. He had been wondering how long the old devil could possess his acquisitive soul in patience before cooking up some cock-and-bull story as an excuse to get in touch. Well, this was fortunate. It would save him the risk of a night journey into Mysore. But ten miles through difficult country to the road, and the same back again – that would be the better part of two days wasted – and if he wasn't constantly keeping the little men up to their fuel gathering they slacked off and went hunting. And then there was the time factor. It would take a Mundaver two hours to make the one-way trip – Somari possibly three – himself, jungle-toughened and fit though he was, at least four. He looked at his watch. It was nearly four o'clock. It got dark just after seven. That decided it.

'I think you had better go instead of me,' he said.

Somari chuckled maliciously. 'Sure,' he said. 'Scare the piss out of the old sunnavabitch when I come out of the jungle and say Boo! Bring him back here, sahib?'

'Good God, no,' Wyndham said. 'Just hear what he's got to say, and give him a list of things I want: a pair of good scales, more hacksaw blades, some heavy mechanic's gloves, coffee, cigarettes . . .'

'Whisky?'

'No, I'm better without it when I'm working. Tell him to come back with the stuff in three days same time. Now, you know what to do, don't you?'

'Sure. Wait in jungle near forty-seven milestone till he come, then say "Hello Sam, you old bastard. How's Aunty?" '

'Are you taking a Mundaver back with you?'

Somari shook his head. 'No fear. Little bugger don't like staying in jungle all night by self. They go out every morning before sun-up – come back sundown.'

Wyndham was scribbling a list on a page of his notebook. 'Be careful there's nobody on the road – and if Sam wants to know anything else tell him . . .'

'If Sam want to know anything else I tell him fuggoff,' Somari said.

'Right, you little horror,' Wyndham said, handing him the list. 'You'd better be on your way. You haven't much time before dark. Good luck.'

'Chin-chin, sahib,' Somari grinned, and went.

Wyndham wiped sweat from his face and turned back to his task. He regretted his decision about the whisky. He could have done with a couple of good stiff pegs when he finished for the day. Still – it was better this way.

Somari sat with his back against a tree trunk. Across the road he could see the white milestone glimmering faintly in the starlight. Nothing had passed either way, not even a bullock cart, since he arrived two hours previously, just as the sun slid down behind the range of hills to the west. An owl hooted nearby, and far in the distance he heard the shrill yapping of a jackal pack on the trail. He didn't like owls – or jackals. He didn't like the jungle either – not at night – superbly well-versed in its lore though he was. It would take him at least four hours to get back in the dark, but he didn't mind it so much when he was moving.

Far to the north, borne on the soft night breeze, he heard the sound of a car. He sighed with relief and stood up. Of course, it could be any car, one that would just flash by in a cloud of dust. He'd know in a few minutes, but he felt, hopefully, that it would be the old bastard –

He saw the headlights far in the distance, momentarily as the car topped a rise, then they were gone again – to reappear on the next rise before disappearing once more. Now they had come round the last bend and were making a lane through the darkness. The car came up fast – too fast if it was stopping here, and he felt a stab of disappointment, but then, as it passed the milestone, it braked hard and checked, then slid noisily into reverse and backed down a few yards, turned into the shoulder of the road, and stopped. The lights went out, then blipped on again for a second and dowsed finally, and the engine was cut. His night-accustomed eyes made out the stark, awkward lines of the old Model-T, with its tattered canvas hood. He could see one man in it, and, as he lit a cigarette, Somari recognized the shabby, old-fashioned khaki topee Sam habitually wore – and there was a white kerchief round his neck. Somari grinned happily and went forward.

He called softly, 'Hello, Sam sahib – long time no see. Still making bloody big fires?'

There was no answer – and some jungle-acquired instinct made him pause half-way across the road, and in that split second he heard the other, unlighted car screaming up. He turned and darted back into the undergrowth and someone shouted, 'Stand where you are, or we'll fire!' and then guns were blasting, and Westcott was bellowing furiously, 'You bastards!

You bastards! You *bastards*! I told you to hold back two miles! I'll bust every one of you for this!'

Somari felt no pain – just a shock as if he had been hit in the back with a brick. He kept running, his feet finding and following the unseen path by pure instinct. Behind him the confused shouting was getting fainter.

He rested after an hour, which was a mistake, because he stiffened then and his progress became slower. He paused from time to time to listen, and knew a dull satisfaction when he was finally certain that he had lost the pursuit. Everything had dulled, except the pain that was now supplanting the numbness in his back, and the screaming urgency to get to the village to warn the sahib. That was all that mattered now – that and the savage gratification of a few words to the 'little buggers' about Sam sahib. Yes, that last was very important indeed.

He made it in five hours, which, for a fairly small frame almost entirely drained of blood, was a creditable performance.

Wyndham sat in the middle of the village supporting Somari's head. Old Bundoo said gently, 'My men have heard from the tree tops, Daku. They come with dogs – following the blood trail. They will be here soon. It is time to go.'

'He cannot be moved,' Wyndham said. 'Take the gold and go, old one.'

'This one will be dead within the hour – and the gold is cursed. We leave it. Come, Daku. They cannot hurt him further,' Bundoo urged.

'I stay,' said Wyndham. 'Thank you for your hospitality. I am sorry for the trouble I have brought upon you and your people.'

'It is nothing,' Bundoo answered. 'Good robbing, Daku.' He turned and slipped silently into the jungle.

Somari murmured, 'Don't play silly buggers, sahib. You go.'

'Shut up, you little bastard,' Wyndham told him. 'You talk too bloody much,' and Somari chuckled.

'Been a lot of fun some time,' he said. 'You remember bloody pig farm, sahib? Cor – fuggin 'ell – when we clip that old sod for two thousand chips – see his face.'

'Yes, I remember,' Wyndham said. He could hear the hounds baying close in now.

Somari coughed, and vomited blood. 'Goodbye, sahib,' he

said unconcernedly, twitched, and went limp.

'Goodbye, Somari – and thank you,' Wyndham answered. He wiped the little man's face and then spread the handkerchief over it, and stood up. Heavy feet were crashing through the undergrowth, and someone called, 'All right, Wyndham, stand where you are and put your hands up.'

Wyndham shook his head and took his revolver from his hip pocket. There was a single shot from the bush, and he sank slowly to the ground. Westcott came up behind him, his revolver held stiffly in front of him with both hands. He kicked Wyndham's gun from his relaxing fingers.

'Actually I was going to do it myself,' Wyndham said. But 'thanks for saving me the trouble.'

'Not at all,' said Westcott. 'Just so long as you can stand up on the day.'

Father Lauder said, 'He's entitled to see me alone.'

'But he's down on his records as Church of England, Father,' said the worried doctor.

'Mistakes can happen in the best regulated prisons,' Father Lauder said gently. 'Do I have to report to superior authority that you refused the last request of a dying man?'

'But he didn't ask to see you. You asked to see him.'

'Exactly,' said Father Lauder, with Jesuitical ambiguity. 'May I go in, my son?'

The doctor sighed and nodded. 'It won't make much difference now,' he said.

Wyndham's eyes flickered as the priest bent over the bed.

'They wanted to come,' Father Lauder whispered, 'but I felt that you would not wish that. Was I right?'

Wyndham nodded feebly, and the priest hurried on, 'They have been trying to let you know for a long time, but of course they weren't able. In the absence of a male heir, the Wyndham Trust is being wound up and shared among the female descendants, which means that Paul will receive his late mother's portion. You understand?' Again Wyndham nodded. 'He wants you to know that Julia's wishes will be carried out.'

Wyndham stirred slightly and smiled – and the priest murmured something, touched him on the head and went out.

Chapter 39

Aunty said querulously, 'Why the bloody hell can't we go all the way from Mysore by train?'

'Because,' Sam said patiently, 'I've got a buyer for the car – and I'm not leaving the bloody thing here in the street.'

'Who the hell would buy that heap of scrap iron?' Aunty demanded.

'Peter Lobo of Bangalore – that's who,' Sam said. 'And it's a bloody good car for its age.'

'How much?'

'Five hundred rupees.'

'You're robbing him,' said Aunty. 'We don't need that sort of chicken-feed now, anyway.'

'You're getting delusions of grandjer already,' Sam snorted. 'Five hundred chips isn't chicken-feed. Now come on, and stop nattering. Final check up. Tickets?'

'Got 'em.'

'Passports?'

'Got 'em.'

'Letter of authority to the Bombay bank?'

'Got it.'

'Then for Christ's sake pick up them two bags and get into that damn car. We got to get to Bangalore before six.'

He followed her out and turned to lock the door of the shop, then swung the handle of the Model-T and climbed in, pausing to wave a farewell to the Indian constable who lounged on guard the other side of the narrow street.

'Get past that bloody forty-seventh milestone as quick as you can,' Aunty said. 'It gives me the creeps. He wasn't such a bad young feller. Always polite, I'll say that for him.'

'A fool to hisself,' said Sam sententiously. 'He shouldn't of hung around so long after he'd got hold of the boodle. Asking for it, that was. Well, it's an ill wind, I suppose.'

The tree crashed down across the road just as they approached the forty-seventh milestone, and little dark men flitted out of the jungle silently. Aunty screamed once – but Sam didn't have time.